Captivity

Debbie Lee Wesselmann

Captivity

John F. Blair
PUBLISHER
Winston-Salem, North Carolina

The paper in this book meets the guidelines
for permanence and durability of the Committee on
Production Guidelines for Book Longevity
of the Council on Library Resources.

Library of Congress Cataloging-in-Publication Data

Wesselmann, Debbie Lee, 1959–
Captivity / by Debbie Lee Wesselmann.
p.   cm.
ISBN-13: 978-089587-353-8 (alk. paper)
ISBN-10: 0-89587-353-2 (alk. paper)
1. Women primatologists—Fiction. 2. Chimpanzees—Fiction. 3. Animal welfare—
Moral and ethical aspects—Fiction. 4. Human-animal relationships—Fiction. I.
Title.
PS3573.E81495C37 2008
813'.54—DC22
2007037816

For Dan and Courtney

"They are not monkeys."

Captivity

ONE

*D*ana loved dawns like these, when the world was blinded by humidity. The October fog caressed her throat with a lush moisture that made her want to throw her head back and drink up its coolness before the sun burnt it off. From the empty dirt and gravel parking lot, she could barely make out the form of the main building and knew only by memory where the electric fence lay. She could imagine she had emerged from her truck not in South Carolina but somewhere else entirely—another country, another continent.

A hunched figure about four feet tall raced through the half-darkness. Dana cried out and clutched her briefcase strap so fiercely it buckled in her grip. She peered into the mist. Nothing—no movement, no sound to track. She dropped her briefcase to free her hands and began to pant-hoot, softly at first and gradually louder and more urgent—*Hoo, hoo, hoo*—until her voice erupted into a shriek—*WRAAAAA, WRAAAAA*. From inside the electric fence, several chimpanzees called back, but another, closer one hooted behind her.

Dana jerked her head toward the hoot, which she immediately recognized as that of Barafu, a female chimp who had arrived at the sanctuary from a medical laboratory only the month before. Through the fog, a dark shape moved along the branch of a nearby tree before it stopped and settled almost invisibly into the surroundings. Dana could not believe it. Until now, Barafu had sat impassively in her holding cage, chewing her fingers until they bled, staring with the glassy, heartbreaking incomprehension of someone who had endured too much.

Dana removed her lunch from her briefcase, took an apple from the brown bag, and crouched beneath the tree. At first, she could not get her legs comfortable, so she shuffled, finding the right droop to her butt, the right tension in her thighs, a balance to her body that connected her to the earth. As much as she hated to admit it (and would not to anyone other than herself), her body no longer stretched and settled as easily as it once had. She prodded the pine needles with her free hand as though she were foraging for food. From the tree, Barafu watched, but the mist guarded her expression, so if she was curious or fearful, Dana could not tell.

Dana grunted, then took a crackling bite of the apple. With a fluid motion, she stretched the fruit toward Barafu, offering, watching the chimp for the moment when the fog brushed away from her face and Dana could judge what was going to happen next.

Barafu stiffly—in a manner far too elderly for her age—began her descent. The two primates, chimpanzee and human, faced each other in the lifting fog. The chimp brought her hand across her nose, wiping it, and stared at the apple. She lifted her gaze to Dana's with an unspoken question in her eyes: *May I have that apple?* Dana paused, studying the fruit as though reluctant to part with it. Barafu extended her arm, gestured with her fingers. *Come on, please.* Because Dana could not break a small portion of the apple off the way some of the chimps would, she placed the whole fruit in Barafu's upturned palm.

Instead of rushing back up the tree or into the shrubbery with her prize, Barafu began eating the apple at once, crunching loudly, pausing only to remove the woody stem from between her gum and cheek and then push it toward the center of her mouth. Except for a decided sag on the right side of her face, Barafu was a beautiful chimp with large, deep-set eyes and a full, contemplative mouth. Dana reached out tentatively, as if by touching the chimp's arm she could learn Barafu's heart and history. The chimpanzee edged closer, offering her left side and back for a grooming. Dana almost forgot to breathe as she worked her fingers through the ape's wiry hair. She had touched many chimps in her lifetime, but each new encounter was a miracle of intimacy: the warmth rising off the body, the solid, yielding muscle underneath, the individual shape and smell of each chimpanzee. Her fingers found a ridge of hard scar about four inches long on Barafu's back, the hair gone from the skin around it. Barafu, once at the mercy of humans, let *this* human touch her. The trust was almost too great for Dana to bear. *Oh, Annie*, she thought, *Annie*. Touching Barafu's scar felt like a connection to long ago, when Dana was even more helpless than she was now.

Barafu tensed, and Dana stopped grooming. The chimp stared at something in the thinning fog, her mouth stretching into a tight grimace of fear that exposed her gums. A hunter, Dana thought, and she prepared to spring between the intruder and the ape, but instead another chimpanzee, the adolescent male Nyuki (Swahili for "Bee," from the strange buzz he was able to create with his lips) ambled toward them with the leisurely knuckle-walk of a chimp coming into his own.

Nyuki? But he had been in a *separate* holding cage. A small panic whirred inside her. The two cages had different entrances and locks, making it unlikely that both chimps had escaped. Something must have gone wrong inside the building.

From inside the electric fence, the Group A dominant male, Mwenzi, roused his group with a raucous shout and shaking of branches, startling the others into a hooting, screaming crowd. The more distant voice of the dominant male in Group B woke his own group. Nyuki paused, his head cocked to listen to the ruckus. Then, as though he had orchestrated the distraction, he lunged toward Dana's briefcase, snatched it up, and carried it out of her reach. Vibrating his lips with his peculiar buzz, he emptied the briefcase. Papers slid across the dusty ground.

"Here, Nyuki. Do you want a pear?" She took it out of the bag and dug her fingernails into the fruit's flesh until she had a mashed piece of pulp on the end of her fingers. "Come on, Nyuki, Barafu. I'll give you this inside."

As the chimps ambled toward her, Dana walked backward to

the main building, leading them with the pear. Either chimp could overpower her, even break her neck with a well-timed leap, but they remained calm, patient for the food they were sure she would share. Dana reached behind her to feel for the door. Not surprisingly, it swung open easily.

The crackle of sticks and stones beneath car tires punctuated the air: someone arriving for work. Barafu screamed and dashed past Dana into the building, followed closely by Nyuki, who snatched the paper bag from Dana as he rushed past. Without waiting to identify the car, Dana lunged through the front door after the chimps and bolted it from the inside.

The hallway was strewn with papers, books, a smashed coffeepot (worried, Dana inspected the glass for blood but found none), staplers, floppy disks, reams of data reports, scientific journals, and an overturned computer monitor with its cable hanging limply over its screen. Six or seven pens stuck out like seedlings from the grate of an air vent; an elaborate squiggle of pen marks decorated the wall above it. Dana stepped over a pile of framed family pictures assembled in the middle of the floor—one of the chimps must have scavenged them from the offices. On top, fittingly enough, was the image of her brother, his blue eyes squinting against the sun, T-shirt hanging loosely, one arm on the hood of Dana's truck as though he owned it.

From the soft buzzing, Dana could tell that Nyuki was in her office, so she peeked in. He had climbed onto Dana's desk to eat her lunch and was licking the hummus off the pita bread. He raised an arm threateningly when he saw her.

"Relax and eat your lunch," Dana told him. "I'm not going to take it." She closed the door, locking it behind her.

The building had six large holding cages, each with its own outdoor area and with open bars between them to allow physical contact with neighbors. These cages were used solely for new arrivals not yet ready for the outdoor groups and for what the assistant director, Mary Nakagawa, called "the hard-timers"—chimps who were dangers to themselves or others or who, for whatever reason, could not adapt to the social hierarchy of a large primate group. As Dana neared the end of the hall, her stomach lurched: all the cage doors were open.

She rushed toward the first, which belonged to a chimp family confiscated from a small Florida zoo. In one corner, thin Maggie crouched, nursing her infant son, Mbu, but the rest of her family—her ten-year-old son, Sifongo, and her adult daughter, Neema, who was in estrus—had vanished. Dana grunted reassurances before closing and locking the holding cage.

The next cage was Barafu's, to which the female chimp had returned of her own accord. Barafu lowered her chin and hugged herself. She stared at Dana in her frightening, dull, unnatural way, then held out a long arm. Stepping inside, Dana hooted, offering the pear, now bruised and soft, ready to lock the two of them inside if Barafu made a dash for the exit, but Barafu gingerly removed the fruit from Dana's palm. A glimmer of pleasure was in Barafu's face, an enjoyment of the moment, a huge triumph for such an emotionally wounded chimp. As Dana stepped backward into the hall, Barafu knocked the door shut with her free arm like a teenager closing herself in her room.

Across the hall, Kitabu and her beloved rag doll were gone.

Someone was pounding at the front door, but Dana could not answer it now. She hurried to the other cages. Tekua, the sizable and sometimes hysterical male infected with the HIV virus, and, worst of all, Benji, dubbed "Psycho Chimp" by some of the less sympathetic graduate students, were both gone. Dana checked Nyuki's cage to see if any of the escaped chimps had wandered in, but it was empty. Her lungs could barely work from the panic. The nearby population, sparse as it was, had no idea of the danger now lurking in the woods.

"Dana!" a muffled voice—Mary's—yelled through the thick door. "What's going on?"

By the time Dana got back down the hall, Nyuki had figured out how to unlock her office. He burst into the hallway but then, seeing Dana, ducked back inside with a playful shriek. Dana closed and locked the door again, hoping to give herself enough time to unbolt the front entrance.

As Dana opened the door, Mary slipped through in a single side step. Mary Nakagawa was a small-boned woman who stood only as tall as

Dana's chin. Despite the size difference, Mary looked at Dana squarely, and at once the hallway filled with breathable air.

"Who escaped?" Mary asked.

"We're still missing five."

"Jesus! Five? How—"

"It looks like someone let them out. We're still missing Kitabu, Sifongo, Neema—and worst of all, Tekua and Benji."

Mary briefly closed her eyes. "We're screwed."

"Pretty much."

"What about the nursery?"

Dana had not thought about the nursery, but if someone had chosen to sabotage the sanctuary by liberating animals, the pale-faced, large-eyed juveniles would be prime targets.

They ran through the thready fog and down the short path leading to the small outbuilding, Dana a few strides ahead of Mary, her long legs carrying her over the gravel. At the entrance, Dana fumbled with her keys, but Mary had already selected the right one from her ring and now fit the key into the lock, pushing the door open with her shoulder as soon as the bolt slid. They rushed inside. All the doors—to the food and medical supplies, to the examining room, to the infirmary cage— were closed, secured. The groups of orphaned children, already awake and playing with the branches, gourds, fake rocks, and ropes, appeared undisturbed behind the windows.

Dana rested her forehead against the glass. One small victory. She wished she were the kind of person who could hang onto such a triumph, for strength if nothing else. Instead, her imagination—her overanalysis of what could be—had already predicted the closure of the sanctuary, her firing, and, even worse, the grim repercussions of primate worlds colliding. No, she was getting much too far ahead. She pushed away from the glass. "Come on. We need to round up the chimps. I really don't want to have to call the police."

Mary grimaced. "That'll give us permanent status on the dean's shit list."

"Like we don't already have that."

They left the nursery building, Dana first, Mary barely a step behind.

The sun had risen fully, and with it most of the fog, though some mist lingered in primeval strata, woven through the trees and the Spanish moss like transparent scarves. With her free hand, Dana shielded her eyes against the hazy brightness, searching the trees as they strode toward the main building. A woodpecker hammered against a tree in the distance, and a few birds twittered as they chased one another among the branches, but no large, dark forms moved with them. She dried her palms against her shorts. The chimps, especially *these* five chimps, had few survival skills, their innate ones having been stripped from them after years of captivity. And too many people in these parts owned shotguns and hunting rifles.

"I don't see them," Mary said as they neared the top of the path. "I *know* Kitabu can't be far because she'll need a toilet soon."

Several graduate students came across the parking lot in a cluster, trailed by the steam rising off the coffee cups they carried.

"Escapes!" Dana shouted through cupped hands.

The students snapped out of their morning laziness. The more experienced among them, the ones who had been with the sanctuary since its opening, had rounded up escapes before, particularly during the first year, when the kinks in the security of the outdoor enclosures were easily discovered by the innovative animals. These students knew firsthand how the chimpanzees' intelligence and ability to fashion tools out of available resources made perfect containment impossible. Once, the alpha male Mwenzi had used folded palmetto fronds as protective mitts to climb the electric fence. Usually, all it took to lure the chimps back in was a special meal or toy, but today, Dana suspected, would be different.

While two of the graduate students entered the main building to secure it, the rest prepared to scour the woods. Dana left behind the tranquilizer gun; that approach would just have to wait until the sanctuary's veterinarian, Andy Holloway, arrived. Although the university required that she know how to use a tranquilizer gun, she had never leveled a barrel at another primate, human or chimp. She was not going to start now.

The forest group fanned out in different directions, each person armed with a bag of fruit and a compass to navigate among the endless pines, sweet gums, and oaks that cushioned them from human civilization. They carried two-way radios, but Dana did not want to frighten the chimps with the electronic hiss and squawk of radio communication, so they were turned off, available only for an emergency or a sighting. Dana pocketed her compass; she knew these woods as nowhere else on earth. This was home, more so than her small house ten miles away, or her childhood home in Oklahoma, or the one-story ranch she had shared with her then-husband in Arizona. Even before the sanctuary buildings existed, she had walked among the loblolly, shortleaf, and longleaf pines, learned the peculiar arrangement of many of the groves, how a white oak might punctuate them, how the underbrush of ferns and cherry laurels spread out from their bases. She knew where the stream that traversed the property forked, and where she was at any moment in relation to it. She could tell by the sponginess of the ground where the land dipped low enough to nurture live oaks and where it rose just high enough to shift into a different landscape. In the wetter portions of the tract, she navigated by cypress knees, the raised knobs projecting from the roots that allowed the trees to breathe. The large framed map in the main building always struck her as unreal because of its absence of tangible landmarks and modulations of terrain, of sections that were always moist underfoot or difficult to navigate, of the tangle of roots rising from the ground. A graduate student had once asked her why she regularly patrolled the woods, when the chimps were contained within its heart and not in its perimeter, and Dana found herself unable to express why intimately knowing the buffer zone between chimps and humans seemed so crucial.

As she trudged, she listened for cracking twigs and shaking branches, soft grunts of satisfaction. The scent of pine dampened by dew and fog hung acridly about her. This was a relatively new smell, a five-year-old aroma, that reminded Dana of nowhere else. Her early childhood in Oklahoma had been scented with dust and electric skies, the evaporation of rain on pavement. Her teenage home in Rhode Island had a briny city smell: salt, exhaust, the mingling of Portuguese bread and Italian sauces. In Arizona, where she had been a professor, the air had a sweet dryness to it, the pollen of nonindigenous plants and desert and the purity of mountains clinging as one. But in South Carolina, she found a primordial density to the forest—layers of pine, rotting wood, boggy peat, both silky and thick, wet and hot, ancient and neonatal. She liked to believe her nostrils had picked up the pungent trails of both past and future.

Although wild chimps could move in complete silence, Dana had not expected it of these novice climbers. Occasionally, she heard the soft rustle of pine straw, but when she turned, she could see no sign, not even a dark shoulder, of a chimpanzee. Instead, she saw a large pine cone that might not have been there before, or a thrush scratching up a flurry of pine needles in search of grubs, or a squirrel darting across the ground.

After thirty minutes, she stopped in the center of a small clearing. She would have to return to the compound without a single chimp. *Please, please, please,* she prayed as she scanned the trees encircling her. Nothing. She could not afford to wait any longer; she had to notify the university and the local authorities. As soon as she did that, the loose chimps would be hunted down by armed police officers and excited residents spreading out in bands across the area. She wanted to call her father and shout at him that *this* was what happened to captive chimps. She kicked a fat, decaying stick and sent it tumbling and disintegrating across the forest floor. When the stick came to rest, she stared at the soft remnants, blinking as she sometimes did from the bewilderment of finding herself out of control, not desperately so but on the verge, a glass teetering on the edge of a counter.

She started back toward the compound.

She had taken three steps into the woods beyond the clearing when an anomaly of shadow in the underbrush caught her eye. Something looked strange, though she could not tell what. She stepped back, squinting. Then, as amazingly as an optical illusion coming into focus, the motionless form of Sifongo materialized, crouched in a small gap between a bush and a clump of ferns. His eyes met hers with a flicker of amusement, and she realized with a laugh he had been following her. Now that she could visually separate Sifongo from the surroundings, she noticed that Kitabu, wearing her favorite pair of navy-blue athletic shorts, was sitting under the boughs of a pine tree a few feet behind Sifongo. The juvenile female was watching Dana intently, one arm stretched over her head and tugging on the opposite ear.

Dana laughed. Kitabu rushed through the brush, her mouth wide in an eager play face, and leapt onto Dana, the muscular arms grasping her neck and shoulders. Kitabu tried to tickle Dana, but Dana knew the chimp's most sensitive spots and got to Kitabu first. The chimp writhed with panting laughter.

"Sifongo!" Dana called to the other chimp, gesturing with her arm. "Come." Although the primatologists at the sanctuary specialized in teaching the youngest captive chimps how to act like chimps and not humans, Dana allowed the use of spoken language for practical reasons. All the chimps understood, in varying degrees, English, since spoken language enabled easier communication between the species, especially for the newer graduate students, who had yet to learn a gestural vocabulary. Calling the chimpanzees by names had two purposes: to let a chimp know he was being singled out, and to assist the staff in accepting the chimps as individuals with their own personalities and needs. Oddly, many students who wanted to study primates had no concept of chimps' hominid nature. Chimps had individualized facial features, gestures, habits, likes and dislikes, and, most of all, temperaments. They were more like humans than some students had imagined.

Kitabu settled into Dana's arms, straddling her hip like a human child and not the chimp she was, and took the banana Dana offered. Then, mimicking Dana, Kitabu gestured for Sifongo to come out of the underbrush.

Sifongo, at ten years old, was not about to be ordered by the young Kitabu, but he understood Dana's role as dominant human female. Among a staff of mostly women, with male graduate students filling the lower ranks of the human hierarchy, only Andy, the veterinarian, was accorded greater respect by the chimps. That Andy worked under her did not faze Dana, who understood the sexism of chimp society. Dana looked Sifongo in the eye, grunted, and walked a few paces toward the compound. She paused to look over her shoulder at Sifongo. When she began walking again, she heard the crackle of Sifongo emerging from his hiding place and following them through the woods. Every twenty feet or so, Dana stopped to make sure he was still with them, which he was, although he was not always directly behind them. Sometimes, he stopped to strip a few leaves off a sapling twenty feet to the right or left.

When they emerged at the edge of the parking lot, Dana noticed that Andy had arrived; his red SUV was parked at a forty-five-degree angle to the other cars, as though he had leapt in panic from it. Kitabu scrambled down from Dana's arms and scampered, leading with her right hip and shoulder, toward the door. When the door would not open, she pounded on it, shrieking.

One of the graduate students, Barbara, opened the door. "Kitabu!" she cried. "You're home."

Kitabu gave Barbara's knee an affectionate smack as she hurried inside. Dana knew she was headed for the toilet.

"I have Sifongo here in the parking lot," Dana said. "Getting him inside might be a challenge."

Sifongo settled into a dusty depression in the ground.

"Spinach for breakfast!" Barbara called.

Although he started to shift his weight forward as though to move, the chimp settled back down and looked about him, tipping his head back to see to the tops of the trees. He blinked as he took it all in.

Mary came out of the building, a streak of reddish dirt across one cheek. She always had dirt somewhere on her person, and Dana loved her for it. "We found Tekua a hundred yards into the woods," Mary said. "He has a broken leg. We think he tried to leap between trees but missed. Even after he was sedated, we had quite a tussle with him, though he's out now."

Dana pulled a clean tissue from her pocket and handed it to Mary, who knew exactly where the dirt was without being told. Dana returned her attention to the male chimp. "Sifongo, come!"

The male chimp hunched his shoulders slightly, as though pretending he had not heard his name and was just minding his own business. He began studying the bottom of his foot, picking bits of crushed leaves off it.

"Who's still out?" Dana asked.

"Neema and Benji."

Dana waved the remaining banana at Sifongo. "Si-*fon*-go!" When Sifongo continued to ignore her, she slapped the banana into Barbara's hand. "Keep at it. I have to call the dean."

A chimp inside Group A called out. Sifongo jumped to his feet and dashed toward the electric fence, leaping onto it in a flash. As the shock ran through him, he fell to the ground with a shriek. The three women rushed to him. He bared his teeth in fright and flung out his arm, giving Dana only a moment to jerk her head backward before the limb landed across her face with a numbing, dark impact. She squeezed her eyes shut against the pain and covered her nose with her hands to catch the pooling blood.

"Let me see," Mary said.

"I'm okay. I don't think it's broken." She lowered her hands from her face and looked at her palms, half-expecting to see a lost tooth there.

Upon seeing the blood, Sifongo cried out. Inside the enclosure, a chimp responded by screaming and tearing through the bushes—Dana could see the rapid progress by the thrashing of leaves—until it crashed into open ground: Sifongo's sister, Neema. Neema dashed back and forth along the fence line, her red, swollen rump in full view.

"We've found Neema," Mary laughed. "Inside another cage. How the heck did she get in *there*?"

Grinning, Dana wiped her hands on a clump of pine needles. The irony of Neema's choice of destination poked at her like Kitabu's fingers. She tossed the needles aside with a laugh. "So much for gradual introduction. Boy, is she going to get a quick sex-education lesson."

"Why else do you think she went in there?" Barbara asked. "Heck, Mwenzi is a pretty virile guy. And she's at the height of her cycle."

Neema calmed to a slow pace. Sifongo grunted, then took a couple of steps closer to his sister, then stopped, looking the fence up and down. From behind the shrubbery, Mwenzi called out. Neema froze, her expression changing from concern for her brother to interest in the other male. Slowly, she knuckle-walked toward a shaking bush, giving only one long look over her shoulder at her brother before she disappeared into the vegetation. Dana rubbed the old, jagged scar on the back of her hand and found the numbness where the nerves ended.

Sifongo went to Dana and threw a heavy arm over her shoulders, grunting apologetically. Dana hugged him. She knew he had not meant to harm her, that he had been frightened and confused by the harmless but punishing electric shock. After wiping her nose with the back of her scarred hand, she allowed Sifongo to work his fingers through her hair in a conciliatory grooming.

Mary squatted next to them. Her gaze drifted from Sifongo to the forest behind the parking lot. "That leaves Benji," she said. "Our worst nightmare."

Dana let her eyelids flutter shut. She loved Benji the way a parent might love a mentally ill child—desperately, passionately, fearfully, the whole of it as large as it would be for any child. But Benji had no allegiances, no restraint, nothing to keep him from viciously attacking whomever he came upon, whether a staff member or a young child playing in his backyard three miles away. She could not bear the thought of the two worlds colliding.

Two

Crouched on the floor, wearing two layers of latex gloves, Dana turned Tekua's head to one side so the saliva could drain down his lolling tongue. She did not have to hold him, not really, because he was out cold, but she wanted to be able to feel the first stirrings of consciousness, in case they needed to sedate him further. The reversible anesthesia, while safer for Tekua, was not entirely reliable. Dana could barely look at Tekua's broken leg, which had swelled into a grotesque, clublike limb.

Andy wrapped the plaster around the chimp's leg below the knee and over the foot while Darryl, their most medically minded student, imitated Andy's motions with gestures in the air. Mary stood a few feet away, intently monitoring the green blips of Tekua's heartbeat for signs of distress.

"Almost there," Andy said.

"Have the police gotten here yet?" Dana asked, though no one had left the room. The others seemed to understand her question as a voicing of concern, not a real inquiry, and so remained silent.

They all wore surgical gloves, masks, plastic visors, and full body aprons to protect them from HIV. In fifteen minutes, Andy had set the leg in a cast. As they carried Tekua into the infirmary cage—Andy armed with the reversal agent—Kaylee opened the front door and shouted down the hall, "The sheriff is coming!"

They laid Tekua on the new straw bedding. For ease of treatment, the infirmary cage was much smaller than his regular one, but Dana imagined it would seem even tinier to Tekua after his escape into the expanse of what lay beyond. Using a syringe, Andy administered the reversal, and they all scampered out of the room. Although Dana hated to be so afraid of a chimp, Tekua's erratic behavior and his HIV infection demanded caution, even with his own kind. They had tried several times to introduce him to a companion; each time, it had been disastrous, Tekua raking his own face with his fingernails and banging his head incessantly on the wall until he fell unconscious.

"You two go meet the sheriff." Andy nodded to Dana and Mary. "Darryl and I can monitor Tekua until he comes to."

Dana and Mary tossed their surgical garb into the medical waste bin and hurried down the corridor toward the front entrance. As Dana placed one hand on the door, she hesitated. If she did not open it, if she did not step into the parking lot to meet the sheriff, then perhaps things would right themselves. She felt that certain moments in her life were dreams and that someone touching her cheek would wake her from them; however, as much as Dana wanted to believe in that fantasy, she knew it could not be so. She glanced at Mary, who reflected her apprehension with the clarity of a mirror.

"We can do this," Mary whispered. "We can pray for Benji and his safe return."

Dana flung the door open and stepped into the day.

—◠◠◠—

Benji, born in Africa thirty-four years before, had known the taste of fresh figs and berries and the springiness of his mother's nightly nests.

As a child, he arrived in the United States as the property of an animal trainer known in professional circles for his harsh treatment. Benji fought back viciously and relentlessly until the trainer surrendered and sold him to a roadside zoo that billed him as a "Ferocious Ape from

Africa," the scientific name of his species, *Pan troglodytes*, written in small italic letters at the bottom of the sign. Dana had learned of Benji a month after she was chosen to direct the as-yet-unbuilt sanctuary. Bruce Caras, a caretaker at the San Diego Zoo, had been approached by the zoo owner, who wished to retire and sell his remaining animals, but the San Diego Zoo housed bonobos, not chimpanzees like Benji. Over the phone, Bruce talked the owner into keeping Benji until a suitable home could be located; however, when Bruce finally met Benji, he knew at once that the chimp's mental instability would preclude placing him in an accredited zoo. Even though the South Carolina Primate Project's sanctuary had not yet broken ground, he asked Dana to fly out and meet Benji.

The primatology community was a relatively small one, so most primatologists, upon learning of Dana's appointment, knew the underlying philosophy she would bring to the SCPP. Especially with the old films of her continuing to circulate, Dana stood in her field as a naked statue in the park, her pitted imperfections there for all to see. You could look at her and say, *I know what she represents.* Since chimps raised in captivity had no hope of surviving in Africa, Dana believed it her personal responsibility to take those most damaged by human whim and to introduce them to the complexities of social groups, to awaken their instinctual longing for ape companionship, to provide a rich environment of natural puzzles, food sources, and exercise opportunities while gradually decreasing their interaction with humans. She was known to fight for hard-luck cases and for that reason seemed a perfect savior for Benji.

When Dana arrived in San Diego, she made Bruce drive her up the coast to the private zoo even before she checked into her hotel room.

"You don't want to come up and see my bonobos?" he teased. "Now that you're single again?"

"Sorry, but I'm a chimpanzee woman." She wanted to make it seem as though her separation from Charlie was just another minor event in her life, like running over a garbage can as she backed out of the driveway. "You're out of luck today."

The owner had already closed the zoo, having rid himself—how,

Dana did not want to know—of more than half the animals. The biting stink of urine saturated the air. In one cage, an emaciated and listless leopard paced back and forth across a rough concrete floor littered with feces and pieces of paper that had blown in from the highway. Dana tried to block out the horrors—dank cages, protruding ribs, patchy fur, the stench of feces and urine, the sounds of wheezing and growling, the abandonment.

Her breath caught when she saw the full-grown Benji at the back of his cage, seated like a dying Buddha. His stomach was distended from malnutrition, and his arms, usually the strength of a chimpanzee, hung like scrawny ropes at his sides. One side of his head had been worn almost bald.

"Hello, Benji," Dana said gently, crouching.

Benji looked at Dana with something she had seen only once before in a chimpanzee: malevolence. He bared his teeth and charged. Using his arms, he battered the cage with all his energy, rattling the chicken wire woven around the bars. Bruce stepped back, but Dana, despite her racing heart, held her ground, trying to calm him with soft hoots. Benji's weakness quickly felled him, and he collapsed, panting, white spittle gathering in the corners of his mouth.

Bruce laid one hand on Dana's shoulder. "It may be too late."

If any chimp needed a sanctuary, she thought, this one did. His life had been limited to a small, unkempt cage; his memory of freedom must have seemed to him like a dream. In South Carolina, with Dana, he could thrive and be loved. She imagined him climbing, playing, rediscovering the outdoors of his babyhood, mating for the first time in his life. Dana did not believe in hopeless cases; instead, she believed in degrees of happiness. She could give him a life. Standing, she said, "I'm going to take him. As soon as I can."

"Dana—"

"Bruce."

Bruce drove Dana to the owner's home, two miles away, where Dana negotiated a commitment from the owner to appropriately house and feed Benji until the sanctuary could safely take him. Before she left, Dana wrote a personal check out of her retirement account, since she did not yet have access to the sanctuary funds. She did not see the sum as lost money. She was saving a life, and there was no cost to that.

Benji quickly become a symbol of her idealism. Or, if she was being hard on herself, a screaming example of her naiveté.

Benji never made it into the open acres of the outdoor sanctuary. In an enclosure much larger than his last, with a door leading to an outside area, he paced out the size of his old cage—two strides to the left, two strides to the back, two to the left, two to the front—unless someone entered, and then the new, more nourished Benji charged with the force of ten men, arms held high and teeth bared, screeching. The door to the outdoor area was always left open, but Benji showed no inclination to explore. Dana sat for hours on the hallway floor outside his enclosure, trying not to cry. At the end of six months, Benji had shown only physical improvement.

If she could not give Benji a normal life, then she wanted him to know some kindness. It was the least she could do, after Annie.

⌒〜ʌ〜⌒

As Dana walked the short path to the parking lot, where the sheriff was getting out of his car, her stomach was racked by sharp pains. She should have notified the police as soon as she discovered Benji missing. She had placed the community at risk unnecessarily. Had her idealism, her personal need to erase the wounds of his past, clouded her judgment? She considered it might be so. Almost any chimp besides Benji would have been easier. The others were gentle souls, craving love and touch. Squabbles and male displays were temporary, soothed by kisses and embraces, but nothing had ever quieted Benji. In his years housed at the SCPP, he had been touched only under heavy sedation as Andy stitched together his skin after his rampages. Like a severely autistic child, Benji was locked in the separate container of himself. Anything and anyone could be a target of his aggression.

The only person who would unleash a chimp like Benji was either one who did not know him or one who wished to inflict harm.

As Dana explained Benji's erratic behavior to the county sheriff, he touched his holstered weapon with an open palm.

"He's just a chimp, right?" the sheriff asked. "It's not like we're tracking down a gorilla."

Dana hesitated. If she told him the truth, Benji might be shot on sight, but if she hedged, then people could get hurt. "Despite their size, adult chimps have the strength of several men. This particular chimp is incredibly aggressive, unnaturally so. People who live around here should be warned. And the chimp should be captured, unharmed, as soon as possible."

"Benji is a special case," Mary said. "He was our first chimpanzee. Please try to bring him back alive. We're giving you tranquilizers."

"I have to consider the safety of my officers," the sheriff said. The handful of men around him swayed with the words, like a silent chorus. "If there's no time to use your darts, we'll have no choice."

Andy had joined them and now stood with his fists balled in his armpits, spreading his shoulders so they looked wide and square, defiant in a way Dana never could be. "*We'll* find him first. I'm taking a tranquilizer gun myself." He liked to dress in the khaki outfit of zookeepers, giving him the look of a late-night talk show visitor and an unearned power of celebrity. It was brilliant, though Dana had never before realized it: alpha male by appearance, which went a long way in this world.

The sheriff looked at each of them, then cleared his throat. "We'll see."

"Please don't panic," Dana said, finally finding enough equilibrium to speak. Sifongo's blow to her nose had swelled it from the inside, and her speech sounded stuffy, as though her voice box had moved higher into her head. She wanted to shake her voice loose. She needed better words, she thought, better arguments for a man who could not possibly understand why they needed Benji back unharmed. The sentence came to her then, something she would never have said otherwise but which she believed would reach beyond the keen stare of the sheriff. "That chimpanzee is a very *expensive* piece of property."

The sheriff nodded, his gaze softening with what Dana read as understanding.

After the sheriff left, Mary followed Dana into her office, stepping over the papers and books strewn by the escaped chimps. "You know, you won't ever live down saying that." She slid into the hard wooden chair opposite Dana's desk. "I can e-mail twenty primatologists with that story, and you'd be eaten alive at the next conference. *Property*? A monetary value on a chimpanzee? Maybe I'll get your job."

"Yeah, yeah. You can have it today." Dana tossed a soggy piece of pita bread into the waste can. With her foot, she swept aside the debris around her chair—USDA forms; textbooks; reams of loose paper; the brass clock her parents had given her, its face now cracked; a heavy-duty stapler; her calendar desk blotter, still turned to July; a slew of rubber bands and paper clips she never knew what to do with anyway. Oddly, Nyuki and the other chimps had left untouched the wall of photographs—portraits, really—of some of the chimpanzees who had come to live at the sanctuary. While Dana was tempted to believe the chimps had exhibited a sort of reverence for their own kind, she believed the intact display was no more than fortuitous; they had run out of time, perhaps, or discovered something more intriguing. She bent to pick up a handful of pens and pencils.

"At least Benji doesn't have HIV," Mary said. "That would destroy us." She slid a paper clip off Dana's desk and began to fiddle with it. Today, Dana was not even interested to see what Mary's fingers would do. "Who do you suppose released them?"

"I haven't had too much time to think about it. Someone who has keys, though. But I suppose keys wouldn't be too hard to get. We have ten sets checked out now. A roommate, a lover, even a valet could have access."

"A valet!" Mary laughed. She clapped both hands to her cheeks, her eyes suddenly bright, like polished obsidian. The paper clip, partly uncoiled, came close to poking her skin. "Like any of us is going to use a valet service. Do you even know of a place within fifty miles of here that *has* valets?"

"No," Dana admitted. She reached across and removed the paper clip from Mary's hand, to stop herself from cringing every time Mary gestured. "But we don't know how long the person, or people, planned this."

"An animal rights group," Mary said.

Dana shook her head. "I know Lindsay Brassett. Neither she nor her people would do anything like this. They support us."

"There *are* other groups. Extremists. People who equate animal rights with animal freedom, even if the animals are not capable of self-sufficiency. You can't bury your head on this one, Dana. Nobody but a fanatic would release those chimps."

"*We* are animal rights advocates," Dana said. "And we know better."

"The question is," Mary said with measured words as she picked up the paper clip again, "who *doesn't* know better?"

In any movement, social or political or even artistic, a fringe exists that takes the basic tenets to their extreme. Dana could see how an animal rights activist might extend his outrage at the conditions of laboratories to all forms of captivity, even to one, like the sanctuary, meant to alleviate the injustices already suffered. Still, this break-in did not follow the usual pattern of an animal liberation raid: property had not been destroyed (Dana was certain the chimps had done that by themselves), and no chimpanzees had been taken. Had the chimps proven too much for the liberators to handle? Had the activists planned to lead the chimps by the hand into waiting cars? Perhaps Benji had charged, scaring them off with his hair on end, his teeth bared, those massive arms raised in the air as weapons. Conceivably, someone could have been injured.

Until now, the sanctuary had been an invisible presence in Harris, buried deep in the woods. Long ago, Dana had stopped trying to explain where she worked and instead told people she was employed by the university, since mentioning the sanctuary evoked only glazed expressions. But what would happen if Benji exploded into someone's backyard? What would the average Harris resident do? Would he call the police or quickly reach for his shotgun? Would he hustle his children inside to safety, or would he approach the animal?

The weird thing was, Dana realized, that as angry and frightened as she was, she could not hate the people who had released the chimps. Their concerns, however misguided, were not far from her own. If something had prevented her from earning her degrees, she might have joined the ranks of the extremists. She wanted to take hold of the person who had done this and shake her, saying, *Don't presume to know what this sanctuary means. Don't make decisions you know nothing about.* The SCPP could not compare to a medical lab, and the thought that someone might equate the two brought burning tears to her eyes.

In the sixties, when Dana was a small girl and, unknown to her, the seeds of her own activism were being planted, it was considered radical to advocate adequate space, exercise, and anesthesia for laboratory animals. Then, animals were merely tools capable of unlocking the mysteries of humanity. As the scientific community moved from experimenting on other humans—usually disadvantaged or of color— to using animals, the public welcomed the change. No one thought to ask why chimpanzees intelligent enough to learn how to push buttons aboard space capsules could later be lent to medical laboratories. Why it was morally acceptable to infect them with incurable diseases that people would not wish on their own pets. Now, at the beginning of a new millennium, research was beginning to prove sentience in animals, a concept pet owners had long accepted in their own animals but were reluctant to generalize. Dana could never understand it: if you could look into your terrier's eyes and see him searching your face for signs of approval, if you could watch his legs twitch and imagine that he dreamed of chasing a Frisbee, if you could understand his loneliness as you left him each day for work, if you knew he had figured a way to open the screen door to get outside, how could you believe animals had no consciousness? How could you eat them, knowing your own fear of death?

Dana wished she could have every human look for one minute into the eyes of a chimpanzee and try to deny the thinking brain, the self, the soul that lay behind them. Whoever had broken into the sanctuary the night before must have known the soul without understanding what had irrevocably been stolen from it.

"The person is one of us," Dana said quietly.

Mary twisted a new paper clip into a tight tangle that caught the light from overhead. "Not one of *us*, but one of us."

Sometimes, it was uncanny the way Mary understood exactly what Dana meant.

Aided by two graduate students, Dana tussled with the nursery chimps, though her heart was not in it, not at first. The tumbling, raucous mass of arms and legs overwhelmed her. Soon, however, she could not resist their playfulness as they descended on her, tickling and poking and climbing over her. Dana tried to keep her laughs like a chimp's— wheezing as humans do when they exceed the barrier into silent, heaving laughter—but she could not help herself, the human laughter erupting from her spontaneously. Vicki, who was just learning chimp gestures, had even less control, but Inge, in her careful, studied way, rarely broke, not even into a human smile that to chimps looked more like fear. These motherless chimps had no one to teach them how to act around their own species. The adult chimps at the SCPP had proven to be poor teachers, perhaps because they themselves had arrived with few social skills. While adults could learn appropriate behavior the hard way—in the dynamic outdoor groups—it was too dangerous for the children. The job of the nursery staff was to teach the children hierarchy and submissive gestures, how to greet other chimps, how to recognize the signs of boundaries being crossed. Although Dana had serious doubts that a human—who could never completely understand the chimpanzee culture—could instruct a chimp in the ways of his species, she believed the effort counted for something, even if it did not mean as much as they all would have liked.

Bora, a youngster with particularly large and comical ears, jumped on Dana from behind. Dana lurched forward with the impact, then for fun threw herself into a sprawl, screaming like a chimpanzee. A band of three chimps drew near to see what had happened, their faces serious and worried. Then, with a play face stretched wide and long, Dana rolled over and over, bowling into them. Shrieking and laughing as they discovered her ruse, they took to the artificial trees, slapping each other before tumbling to the ground.

Dana sat back, suddenly out of breath, as though Benji had jumped on her chest. For a moment, she had forgotten about him, but now he leapt back into her, pounding her from the inside. She gave a small involuntary cry. At once, shy Fikira crept close to comfort her with a hug. Dana clung to the youngster, finding strength in her warmth, before letting her go.

The door to the indoor enclosure banged shut. Andy stood just inside in his khakis and boots, his expression conveying, in its very blankness, catastrophe. Andy moved toward the outdoor area where Dana sat. Inge tossed her blond braid to one side and silently shooed the chimps from Dana.

"What?" Dana asked.

Andy touched his temple with two defeated fingers. "A car hit Benji about half an hour ago. The police are bringing him in."

Dana stood. The slope of Andy's shoulders told the end of the story. "Oh, God."

"It happened so quickly. They said he didn't suffer."

He didn't suffer. The irony of those words strangled Dana. Without saying anything—she knew her voice would break—she left the nursery building, walked up the stone path, and stood at the edge of the parking lot, waiting. The fog had lifted long ago, leaving blue skies and a cruel sun that cut into her eyes. She stood there with no police car in sight, shielding her eyes against the sun, at a loss for what else to do. Benji was dead. Although this end now felt inevitable, she had not expected it, not really. She liked to believe, even now, that his life could have taken any course.

She tried to make sense of why the day had ended this way, but there was no sense to be made. Like any creature, human or otherwise, Benji had occupied a niche from which he had been plucked, leaving a brief emptiness in the structure of organisms. She could look at his death that way to console herself, but he deserved better than that. The problem was that Dana had never really known who he was, so she could not give him the proper tribute. She did not know Africa, and she did not know the real Benji. She knew only what had become of him.

Andy tapped her on the shoulder from behind. When she turned, he handed her a Coke. "I heard Nyuki ate your lunch. You need *something* in you."

"Thanks," she said, not knowing until then how thirsty she was. She drank the cola, letting the syrup coat the back of her throat. "The USDA will be swooping down on us."

"They should."

Dana looked back into the sun. "I know I locked the door last night when I left."

"Even if you hadn't, you certainly didn't leave the holding cage doors open. It's not your fault. Someone got a key."

Mary came out of the main building carrying the heavy blankets they used to warm the chimps while they recovered from the anesthesia of medical treatment or when they were ill enough for the infirmary. Dana never liked using the blankets because they were man-made, but the chimpanzees loved them. Sometimes, a chimp did not want to relinquish the prized cloth, finding novel ways to use it—to cover her head or to imitate human clothing or, Dana's favorite, to swat approaching humans like a poolside kid. Mary stood next to Dana, holding the blankets against her small chest. Dana could not bear to look at her; if she did, they would both start crying.

Dana heard the car before it rounded the grove of loblolly pines. Without lowering her gaze, she stooped to place the half-empty can of soda on the ground. The graduate students also must have been listening for the car because, two by two, they came out of the buildings and from the wooded paths: Peter and Holly, Barbara and Kaylee, Inge and Vicki, Darryl and Christopher, Liz and Merle. The students stood close to the main building, as though they doubted their right to step forward. Dana could not take her eyes off the patrol car as it inched over the gravel, blue lights flashing. Her hands were sweating and trembling so badly she had to press them against her shorts.

The county sheriff and one of his deputies got out of the car. Dana started walking toward them, afraid to look. The deputy walked around to the back and unlocked the trunk. For a moment, Dana wondered what the deputy would need from the trunk, then realized the men had transported Benji's body as though a tire found on the highway.

"Where do you want it?" the deputy asked.

Dana stepped forward quickly. "We can get him. There are enough of us."

"It's one heavy monkey."

"Ape, not monkey," Mary said, her voice taking on the edge that always made Dana cringe; it had the steely whistle of a scythe swung through the air. "You should've paid attention in second grade."

The sheriff quickly stepped between his deputy and Dana. "We'll help you."

"We can manage," Dana said. "May I?"

The sheriff nodded, gesturing for his deputy to step back, which he did. Dana gathered her courage for several seconds before she could look inside the trunk. There, Benji's head had rolled to one side, giving it a quizzical tilt, if not for the blood drying and clogging his nostrils and the purplish depth of a massive bruise darkening his face even further. His eyes were closed, as though he had blocked out the world in his final moment.

He didn't suffer.

Mary had spread the blankets on the ground. Struggling against the shifting weight, Dana and Andy lifted the one-hundred-forty-five-pound chimpanzee from the trunk to the blankets. Dana knelt next to Benji, stroking the head he had never allowed her to touch, playing with the limp fingers that had never been so gentle. He was at peace, she tried to tell herself; he had been released from his torment. But she could not believe her own platitudes. The tears in her eyes refracted the daylight into a kaleidoscope of meaningless colors. No one but Dana had truly *loved* Benji, who had been the dysfunctional part of their artificial family.

The sheriff said, "I'm sorry."

Dana tried to conjure up an image of Benji in motion, alive, but could remember only a still picture of the moment she met him, the venom in his eyes. It blinded her, this image; she could not find the blanket she thought she saw, for as she reached out, it vanished and her fingers clawed at air.

Mary caught her groping hand and placed it on the edge of the blanket. Mary's eyes said, *We can do this. Don't worry, I'm here.* Dana pulled the cloth tightly across Benji's body, as though he needed the warmth. They carried him inside, where Andy would note the injuries and take photographs and Dana would be forced to file paperwork, as though Benji had been a regulated substance instead of a living being.

A half-hour later, the university called to say a press conference had been scheduled late that afternoon at the campus thirty miles away, a location Dana had readily agreed to—anything to keep the media from this protected territory. She would have to drive. She would have to speak like a scientist to explain what had gone wrong at the sanctuary. She would have to appear impassive and logical, confident. Everything she was not right then.

Oh, Benji. Oh, Annie.

They did not have time to mourn. The living chimpanzees needed their care, and the studies in progress could not be stopped. Even on a normal day, the chores—cleaning cages, preparing food, taking inventory, ordering, caring for the children, doing paperwork—could barely be completed by evening.

As people passed the closed door of the examining room where Benji's body lay, they fell mute. The two empty cages at the far end of the building—Tekua's, now that he was in the smaller infirmary cage, and Benji's—echoed with their losses. Dana instructed the students not to clean out Benji's cage until the following day because it seemed disrespectful to remove so soon the signs of his life.

The fatigue in Dana felt as dense and gray as that morning's fog. Her thoughts swirled aimlessly, blind to each other, drifting away from her as she tried to grasp them.

Dana told Mary, "I'm going to the observation platform for a while."

"No, you're not. You don't have time. You have that press conference."

"I need air."

Mary took her firmly by the wrist and led her back into her office, kicking the door shut with her foot. "You need to change your clothes. To look more like a professor and less like a middle-aged kid. We should go over what you're going to say, so you can do it without breaking down. I'll drive you, and we'll go over everything in the car."

"Mary—"

"I know you don't want to do this. But you'll die, Dana, if you lose this job. And that's exactly what's at stake. You've got to come across as competent."

"I *am* competent."

"They don't know that. They have to see it. This sanctuary needs you. The chimps need you. Do you think the university spokesman is going to spin this the way you can? It's up to *you*." Mary's emotions danced across her face, fast and graceful twitches that could not conceal themselves: fear, protectiveness, determination, grief. The students often complained they never knew how Mary really felt, but every day Mary left a map on her face for Dana to read.

"You're right," Dana said finally.

"Come on. I'll drive you. First to your house, then to campus."

As they left the building, a man walked across the parking lot toward them. He had a slightly bowlegged walk, which struck Dana as oddly masculine, and a head of dark, tightly curled hair that receded just a little at the edges. He had a canvas backpack slung over his right shoulder and carried a piece of glossy paper in his left hand. The way he held himself reminded Dana of Chatu, one of the first juveniles to arrive at the SCPP.

"Hi," Dana said as she and Mary neared him. "May I help you?" She wondered if he was a tourist lost on his way to the Florida Panhandle.

"Are you Dr. Dana Armstrong?" he asked. Then, as if he could not trust her answer, he consulted the paper in his hand, which Dana recognized as a page torn from her latest article in *Journal of Primatology*. He moved his thumb to see the black-and-white photo of her at the bottom.

"I guess you have your answer," she said.

"I do." He stuck out his hand, and she shook it. "Samuel Wendt. I'm a freelance journalist. I wonder if you have time to answer some questions."

Mary slipped sideways between them. "The press conference is at the university. Dr. Armstrong will be answering questions then."

"Press conference?"

Dana nudged Mary aside. "Don't mind Mary. She's my pit bull. But she's right. I'll be answering questions at the university. You can follow us up, if you want."

His eyes focused sharply on her, marking his face with light crow's-feet. "What is the press conference about?"

Dana shot a look at Mary, who seemed as surprised as she. "I thought that's why you were here. The SCPP was broken into last night, and several of the chimps were released." *Oh, Benji. Benji.* The image of his head rolling to one side as they lifted him from the sheriff's trunk brought the bitter taste of blood to her own mouth. She could barely get the words past it. "Before we could capture the last one . . ." By the time Dana had left Benji in the examining room, he had already acquired the first smells of death, the stiffening of decay, the coolness of an inanimate object. "He was hit by a car." There. She made it. But Mary was right; she needed to practice getting the words out before she faced a room of local reporters.

"How about if I come back tomorrow?" he asked. "I'd like to interview you."

"If you didn't know about today, what are you writing about?"

"I'm writing an article following up on the families who participated in the chimpanzee language studies during the sixties and seventies."

For a moment, Dana could not react. She could not believe that this man, who seemed so unthreatening a moment before, had spoken the words he had. She saw in his eyes now a brutal spark, as though he knew exactly what effect his words would have on her. "Sorry," she said. She wanted him to hear the steel in her voice. "I really don't have time." She stepped briskly around him, striding toward the car.

"I've already talked to your brother."

Dana spun around, the gravel flying from her feet. "Liar!"

Mary, who was several steps behind, formed a gun with her fingers close to her chest. She pulled the trigger, giving her hand a little kickback, and said with her eyes, *You should have been more careful.*

THREE

Dana had struggled for years against the image of herself, flickering on white projection screens and later on closed-circuit televisions, as the blond girl playing and talking with a chimpanzee. Whenever she was introduced to primatologists and linguists, she caught the twitch of recognition in their faces. They always saw her first as a lab experiment, then as a colleague, a fate she feared she would never escape, not even as the director of one of the most forward-thinking primate sanctuaries in the United States.

Her father, Reginald Armstrong, had been a professor of psychology at the University of Oklahoma, where he and several colleagues were studying the linguistic abilities of primates. When he told the family about bringing Annie, then a baby, into the house as part of his cognitive psychology experiment, Dana had shouted and hugged him around the neck. Annie arrived (with all the camera equipment and data logs) dressed in real human diapers and a pink dress with white bows on the puffed sleeves. Dana's mother, Susan, resigned from her job as a kindergarten teacher to devote herself to her three children—two human, one not.

Dana's status among her friends soared, since she had the "neatest" pet anyone in the neighborhood had ever owned. "She's not a pet," Dana told them, just as her father had instructed. "She's like a sister. Chimps are almost human, you know." She had sounded so grown-up, so *professional* (a word her father often used with clear admiration), believing her place in her father's experiment was an honor.

Her brother, Zack, was only two when Annie came to live with them. As far as Dana knew, he never regarded Annie as part of a scientific experiment. To him, Annie really was a younger sister, someone who stole the attention he deserved, someone to tease and wrestle, someone to play with while Dana was at school. He must have loved not having to go to the babysitter's house every day, now that their mother was home full time.

Reginald had cameras installed in nearly every room, and the house filled with students and professors who came to witness Annie's interaction with the family. Dana's parents stopped talking as often and instead used American Sign Language. Zack did not seem to mind the hand signals, since he hardly talked anyway, but Dana, at seven, was used to spoken language. One day, she tried to tell her father how a girl had teased her at recess, only to have him insist that she sign the story. She had no words to sign the complicated hurt lodged inside her. Several times she started, but her hands felt inadequate and clumsy. Finally, with fury, she knocked her father's cocktail out of his hand. Although Dana remembered vividly the shocked expression on her father's face, the details of the exchange were less true memory than prompted, since her father had spliced the recorded scene with one of Annie, two years later, when she knocked a book out of his hand with similar frustration. As a college student, Dana had an amusing thought: perhaps the film said less about her and Annie than it did about her father.

Dana eventually grew used to their changed routine: American Sign Language lessons in the backyard tent every afternoon; students whose names she often forgot clambering with her and Annie over the new, elaborate play set; her mother now always there, the wisps of her brown hair tickling Dana's nose as she bent to kiss her. Dana forgot about the cameras and thought nothing of seeing strangers, notebooks in hand, following her through the house. The ASL she learned was modified to accommodate the slightly different anatomy of a chimp's hand; after the incident with her father, she was allowed to use the spoken word at the same time. Although she knew Annie was not a true sister and could never be, Dana loved her. Frequently, she pulled Annie in a red wagon over the rugged backyard, sometimes running so fast that Annie tumbled out onto the ground, laughing. Dana helped Annie dress when her mother was busy making bag lunches. They watched Saturday-morning cartoons together. Sometimes, Dana blamed her mistakes on Annie or Zack, whichever was more believable, and even entertained the notion from time to time that her parents loved Annie more than her. In the bare light of her parents' walk-in closet, where the cameras could not see, Dana taught Annie to say the sign equivalent of *shit—poop—*to express anger. Although Dana had never spoken that word aloud, she had heard boys use it. To sign it felt powerful and subversive. Annie liked it, too. To this day, as far as Dana knew, her father still believed, as did the rest of the scientific community, that Annie had come up with the curse word by herself. Although Dana never lost sight of the fact that Annie was an animal of a different species, she had a closer relationship with Annie than any child could with her cat or dog. After all, in the Armstrong household, they were equals—that is, until the grant money ran out.

Perhaps the scientific community had grown weary of signing chimps, since each experiment yielded only marginally different results from another. None of the chimps had been discovered to be brighter than a five-year-old child, though clear differences in intelligence among them were documented. Maybe the proposal reviewers for the National Science Foundation believed that it was funding too many similar studies. Or maybe teaching animals to be human was already falling out of favor. Whatever the reason, Reginald Armstrong lost the funding to continue his study of Annie.

"You can't just send her away," Dana, then ten, had argued. "You said she was our *sister.*"

"Send her where?" Zack wanted to know, his voice high-pitched with anxiety. He signed as he spoke, and his fingers had a spidery unsteadiness. "To an orphanage?"

"No, dummy. A zoo. You can't do this to her, Daddy. They won't let her watch TV. Or sleep with her doll. It'll be so *cruel.*"

Reginald Armstrong regarded his children with the level gaze that always made Dana's heart lurch with hope. He lifted his glasses off his nose. "Hmm," he said. "We'll see." Which was as good as a yes.

Her father's students removed the cameras—an immense relief, their mother said out loud, the first time Dana had ever heard her express reservations about the experiment. For the next few months, life in the Armstrong house continued more or less as before, but without the parade of scientists. It might have continued forever, Dana thought, if Annie had not gotten into her Halloween candy later that year. When Dana entered her room with her stack of schoolbooks, she saw brightly colored wrappers littering the floor. Annie was crouched on Dana's bed, clutching a fistful of candy bars. The bag containing Dana's Halloween candy had been ripped into long, ragged shreds.

"Annie!"

Annie leapt to the top of the bookcase, screeching, the candy still clutched in her long fingers.

"You jerk!" Dana screamed at her, calling her a shit in sign language. "I hate you! I wish you were dead!" She hurled her pillow at Annie, who dodged it by jumping back onto the bed. The impact of the pillow combined with Annie's leap knocked the top shelf of books to the floor. "I'm gonna kill you!"

Annie screamed back at her. She yanked Dana's piggy bank from the nightstand and smashed it against the wall in a shower of coins and porcelain. Wailing, Dana rushed out of her room and into Annie's, straight to the twin bed. With one swift, mean gesture, she yanked the head off Annie's doll. As soon as she did it, she knew she should not have. But the act was irreversible.

Barking, Annie rushed toward her in a blur of dark, angry fur. Dana, still stunned by what she had done, could not react as Annie grasped her hand and bit down on it all the way to the bone. Dana did not feel pain at first—only shock from both her act and Annie's. For a second, the immediate silence was breath held firm in her lungs. Then blood spurted from the wound, spattering their faces and clothes; the white bone underneath glistened. Both Dana and Annie shrieked, the terror of blood uniting them.

Susan Armstrong, probably already on her way after the books crashed, stepped into the room. "Oh, dear *God!*" she cried.

Susan applied a tourniquet and wrapped the wound tightly with a dishtowel, sent Zack off to a neighbor's house, and drove Dana to the hospital, leaving Annie alone at home.

Years later, as Dana learned more about chimpanzee behavior, she realized that leaving Annie unattended for those hours must have devastated her. A chimp's need to be accepted as part of the group outweighs almost all other needs. In one moment, which Dana had provoked, Annie was rejected by her family and left with no forgiving pat or hug. When the Armstrongs finally returned, Annie whimpered and sought out reassurance from Dana and her parents but received only glares. To make matters worse, Reginald Armstrong came into the house with a cage two days later while Dana and Zack were at school. Dana learned later from her mother that Annie had contritely climbed into the cage of her own accord.

The night after Annie was taken from them, while their parents slept, Zack woke Dana with his sobs as he stood next to her bed. In the moonlight, she could see he was wearing his favorite pajamas—shorts and a T-shirt decorated with multicolored flying saucers—which Dana always mocked, calling him "Mister Puny Space Cadet." His belly stuck out a little under the shirt, showing the baby fat he still harbored, and he smelled of soap and salt.

"I want Annie," Zack cried.

"Shh." Dana lifted the sheets for him to crawl in next to her. As Zack snuggled against her, she began to cry. She felt like a big, cruel baby. She had ruined their lives, and Zack, who should have had a protective older sister, had no one to save him. She stroked his head the way she had seen their mother do and found an odd comfort from the touch, the tousle, of his newly shampooed hair. She laid her bandaged hand on his back. "I'm here," she whispered. "We'll stick together. No matter what."

He struggled to turn, facing her with eyes she could not see. "Why aren't you scared?"

"I am. I just . . ." The unfinished sentence fell between them like batting, filling the space with something soft and inarticulate. Dana waited for Zack to accuse her of sending Annie away, but the high points of his face where the faint moonlight hit shone with trust and love, with the understanding they felt exactly alike, even if it did not seem that way.

Not once did Zack say he blamed her, not that night, not years later when he could fully comprehend what had happened. She often wished he *would* accuse her, so she could beg his forgiveness and he could look at her with the hatred she deserved.

When Dana was fourteen and they had moved to Rhode Island, she started demanding answers from her father. It was her age, and perhaps the proximity of the cold, wild ocean, the sea gulls that screeched as they came in from the bay, and the small, insular piece of land where they now lived that gave her tenacity, a feeling that she had the right to know. She and her new friends marched through their world with authority, empowered by what they perceived as their maturity, and she wanted admission to her father's secrets. She hounded him petulantly.

"Annie was never ours," her father said. "She belonged to the university. They decided what became of her."

"But *where* is she?"

"I don't know." He removed his reading glasses and looked at her solemnly. "I wish I did. It was out of my hands."

But it *had* been within his control. He had arranged for Annie to live with them after the grants disappeared. The university had allowed it *then*. As Dana argued with him, he merely shook his head sadly. He admitted nothing.

When Dana finally had the tools to search, she discovered Annie had been sold to a medical laboratory in Texas, which had then transferred her to another facility. Somehow, Annie and another chimp, having been accounted for upon leaving, never arrived at the intended destination. They had disappeared into the void of sketchy paperwork.

Dana still had nightmares of finding Annie in a tiny cage, gaunt, almost skeletal, sometimes one of her hands cut off, signing in the air, *You did this to me.*

I know where Annie is. I can take you to her.

The memory of Annie lived like a parasite inside Dana, a separate organism that was paradoxically a part of her, viciously attached, sometimes invisible, but surfacing from time to time with a painful spasm. The memory swirled and twisted, changed and grew, until, recalled, it surprised her with its new and unyielding life. Only recently had Dana realized that the memory of Annie would die with her and not before.

Her ex-husband, Charlie, had liked to tell people, and perhaps still did, that Dana related better to chimps than to people.

"Don't say that!" Dana had once shouted at him.

Charlie had grinned at her and shrugged, as though what he had said was good-natured and not apt to be taken seriously. However, he knew better than anyone the stereotype of the female primatologist, and that if he insulted her in this subtle manner, she would sputter with the kind of anger that would last well into the night. Although he never liked to admit he had a hand in any wrong, he sought out ways to enrage her.

"You smell like a beast," he said when the marriage hung together only by the threads of their short history.

She learned not to respond, to only walk upstairs with the steadiest, most stubborn clomp of her boots on the hardwood. The real failing between them, the weight that finally snapped those final strands of understanding, was that he could not comprehend why she dedicated her life, her waking hours, to chimpanzees. Charlie had envisioned a wife who was both ambitious and willing to cater to his needs, who could be published in scientific journals while keeping the bathrooms clean. Dana had made a similar mistake: she believed she could do no wrong in Charlie's eyes. She had married him thinking he would remain the same person who stood in front of the small chapel, straight-backed and slightly flushed in his tuxedo, a man who would always be amused by her failings.

She remembered the startling day when she looked into Charlie's eyes and realized he disliked chimpanzees. The bitterness of that knowledge swelled in her until she could do nothing more than turn and walk out of the room, too shocked to cry.

If the chimpanzees had been the final issue in their marriage, Zack had been the first. Zack crashed into their lives like a force of nature that you could not stop or entirely predict. You just had to wait it out to see if he wrought damage. As Charlie used to say, "Zack is his own kind of hell." Dana always crumpled inside at these words because her own husband could not understand the cords of love that bound her and Zack.

～\\～

Dana's hands were shaking from her encounter with the journalist. She had never expected the issue of Annie to follow her so indiscreetly to the sanctuary. There seemed to be a comfortable understanding among the staff and students—probably at Mary's insistence—that no one should bring up the subject, and this had allowed Dana to relax a little without those damn tapes crowding her small piece of world. Thank God Mary was driving to the university, since Dana was not sure she could keep a vehicle on the road right then. She pressed her burning forehead against the passenger window with the hope that it would lend some coolness. "I really don't want to do this press conference."

"I know. It sucks. But we have over an hour to prepare."

"A whole hour? Crap."

Mary laughed. How could she be so relaxed? But that was Mary, always merry when Dana was at her most glum.

"Let's practice. Dean Washington announces that someone broke into the sanctuary and released a number of chimps. While most were recovered immediately, one got as far as County Road 621 and was struck and killed by a car. Then he introduces you. What do you say?"

Dana sighed. For a few seconds, she struggled to find her professional voice. "First of all, I would like to emphasize what a tragic incident this is. The chimpanzee in question was rescued several years ago from a roadside zoo that kept him in deplorable conditions. We were in the process of trying to give him back a seminormal life. We are a facility dedicated to improving the lives of captive chimpanzees, animals incapable of surviving outside human care. We do not experiment on them, nor do we allow them to live in cramped quarters. We are not a zoo. Our sole reason for existing is to enrich stunted lives. For this reason, we are perplexed why someone would feel it necessary, or even desirable, to let them out of their protective habitat."

"How can you say you are enriching the chimps' lives if the chimp that died lived in isolation?"

"Benji was an unusual case. His traumatic past left him unable to socialize with other chimpanzees, and so we were forced to keep him apart from the others, although he had full access to an outdoor area and plenty of enrichment opportunities. He was given fresh fruits and vegetables daily—and loved both watermelon and spinach, not a combination I would recommend."

Mary glanced at her. "Do you think you need that last bit?"

Dana pulled her hair off her shoulders, then tossed it free again. "It shows he was alive, that he was an individual. I don't want them to believe he was expendable."

"Good point." Mary resumed her reporter's voice. "Was the chimpanzee dangerous, either to himself or others?"

Dana took a deep breath. "I won't whitewash it. Yes. He was dangerous. I was the only one he allowed inside his cage, and even then I was permitted precious few seconds. The person who released him unleashed a sociopath. It was an irresponsible and reprehensible act."

"How can you justify keeping such a dangerous animal in Harris? Don't you consider the safety of the public?"

"People visit zoos every day and let their children lean over railings to better see the animals. Many zoo animals are more dangerous than chimpanzees, even ones as volatile as Benji. We take the same kind of precautions as zoos to keep the animals contained."

"Why aren't these chimpanzees in Africa where they belong? Isn't Africa the best place for them?"

Dana looked sharply at her, but Mary was focused on the road ahead. "They cannot survive in Africa. Africa is a different world from what they know. They were born in captivity and can never be free. You can't teach another species what you yourself do not know."

Mary glanced at her, and Dana knew what she was thinking: Dana was speaking for herself instead of the chimps. Unlike Mary, who had studied the gestural language of wild chimpanzees, Dana had never been to Africa. She had never seen a wild chimpanzee and felt this hole in her knowledge to be a yawning cavern. The only thing Mary had that Dana wanted was Africa. That and maybe love—someone to come home to. Dana tapped on the window with her fingernails. "You aren't being Southern enough with your questions. You're being too direct, too pushy. If I'm going to face local reporters, their questions will sound gloriously civil, and I'll have to work hard to discover and answer to the anger. If I don't find it, they'll think I'm being evasive."

"I can't ask questions like that."

"I know. Neither can I. I'll just have to do the best I can and trust my instincts. You stand where I can see you. If you think I'm drifting dangerously close to the edge, tap your chin. And if I'm burying myself with every word, jump up and down frantically until I stop."

Mary grinned. "Like you'll pay attention."

The press conference went more smoothly than Dana expected. The questions were of the most basic kind, directed to understanding the situation more than to exposing underlying problems. Sitting in the back of the auditorium, Samuel Wendt never even raised his hand. His presence unnerved her anyway.

Dana returned home close to ten at night. The fog was back, shrouding her bungalow with the myths of werewolves and vampires— the sort of night that seemed either romantic or bone chilling, depending on the roil of the fog. She pulled into the driveway and edged up the dark, narrow path to the carport. Her headlights caught the back end of a beat-up Ford. She braked and turned off the engine. Zack. The house was as dark as always, although she knew better than to read anything into it. As she stepped out of the car, her skin felt sticky, and she could not wait to get into the shower.

Even before she flicked on the light, she saw him: long, lean legs outstretched, catching the porch light through the window, the fall of his hair, the concave curve of his body as he sat waiting in the chair. The figure startled her for only an instant because she knew it so well.

"Jesus, Zack," she said, flooding the room with light. "You could've turned on a lamp."

Her brother blinked in the sudden brightness. Unlike Dana, Zack had kept his baby blondness, and he wore his hair to his shoulders and often loose. Dana's cat, Humphrey, stretched lazily in Zack's lap, his back arched like a Halloween icon. "I wasn't sure you were coming home tonight," Zack said.

She went to him and hugged him hard, relieved as always to see him alive. "When did you get in town? You could've called the sanctuary."

His jeans were dirty at the knees. It tortured Dana to look at him too closely sometimes because all she saw was missed potential, a threadbare life, a gleeful insistence on going the wrong way. She never knew whether she had lost part of him or whether he had never been there to begin with.

He poked her in the ribs. "You know me. I never know where I'm going to be. After this, I might look for a job in Florida."

"Doing what?" Dana sat across from him, trying to make her voice as light and inconsequential as possible.

He shrugged. "Whatever."

"You have a car now."

"It works."

"Have you checked in with Mom recently?"

"What for? To get another lecture?"

She leaned forward. "She worries, you know. She never knows how to get in touch with you. *I* don't know how to get in touch with you." As soon as she said it, she knew she had gone too far. Zack's eyes narrowed. She stood. "Hey, I'm starved. I haven't eaten since breakfast. Want something?"

"You have any peanuts? I couldn't find any." The tone of his voice was almost accusatory.

"I'll pick some up tomorrow. I was thinking more about dinner."

He followed her into the kitchen and stood silently behind her as she opened a can of cat food, caught between her and the small table pushed against the window. After she fed Humphrey, she straightened, looking at Zack. "So, you want dinner?"

He shrugged, and she guessed he meant yes.

As Dana rummaged through the refrigerator, she saw he had already consumed most of her orange juice, as well as the rest of the hummus and a large hunk of Vermont cheddar Mary's husband had brought back for her from a conference in New England. She did not care, though, how much he ate, as long as he ate. Sometimes when he crashed in on her, he fasted, claiming he was in his "purification cycle."

Dana chopped vegetables for a stir-fry dinner, chattering about nothing of consequence as she tried to gauge the subtleties of her brother's mood. Zack could explode if she made demands on his attention at the wrong time, so she found it best to be inane. He grunted his responses until she spoke of the fog of the last few nights, and then he became animated. "I love fog," he said, stepping next to her. "It's creepy, like you're flying without a plane." He reached across the cutting board for a green pepper, and Dana almost sliced his finger.

"Stop that!" she said, swatting him away. "This day has been crap already. I don't need to spend the night in the emergency room."

"It would have been a hunting wound. Hunting for chopped peppers." He grinned at her in his goofy way, looking like a kid again. He flicked the back of her hair. "So why was your day so crappy?"

She hesitated—she should not have let that information slip. Of course he would want to know, and of course she would have to go through the story once more. She wanted to let it go, if only for a few hours. Zack was waiting, his eyes on her but his hand snaking back toward the cutting board. She sighed. "Some asshole set free a bunch of the chimps and . . ." She stopped and watched him snatch another piece of pepper. Their gazes met, and Dana thought she saw a flicker of amusement that vanished too soon for her to fully grasp. His face revealed nothing else, not even a twitch, but its blankness, which Dana knew was a carefully wrought expression for him, alarmed her. She wondered when he had arrived in South Carolina, today or the day before. "You don't have a key to the sanctuary, do you?"

"How would I get that?"

"You have the key to my house."

He snorted. "I've had that for years. You're accusing me of letting those chimps go."

"No." She formed her words carefully. "One of the escaped chimps was killed."

His face crumpled briefly before he righted it. "That would ruin anyone's day. Are you okay?"

Nodding, she returned to the vegetables, her cheeks burning, her eyes watering, struggling to set her jaw with resilience. *Benji*. Suspecting her brother, even for a second, of sabotaging the sanctuary made her ashamed of herself and her paranoia. But releasing the chimpanzees seemed exactly like something Zack would do. He felt a kinship to chimpanzees that even she did not. Dana had not known the true extent of Zack's identification with Annie until graduate school, when she had viewed some of the clips from the hidden cameras in their house: Zack letting Annie brush his teeth; Zack helping Annie hide from their father; Zack "secretly" squatting under the dining-room table, grooming Annie, allowing her a chimpanzee nature despite their father's insistence that she be raised as a human. Dana's relationship with Annie had been more sophisticated, spelled out with American Sign Language and English words. Dana had been the older sister, in charge, bossy, sure of her own place in the family.

"Tell me about this chimp," Zack said. "Tell me who he was."

As Dana began to tell Benji's story, the words caught and she cried freely, the salt from her eyes seasoning the vegetables on the cutting board. Zack threw his arm over her shoulders and held her, rocking her back and forth until all her tears were spent, the atmosphere laden with what had been lost that day.

Later, after they had eaten and Dana had showered, they sat side by side on the sofa, their feet propped on the coffee table Charlie had once protected with a set of wooden coasters and lemon oil. The late news was on, but it was all from Atlanta, nothing of interest. Dana could barely keep herself awake even though she worried about the sanctuary, whether the chimps were safe, whether the university had sent the campus police there as promised to keep out intruders. She felt herself drifting off into an uneasy sleep.

During a commercial, Zack said, "I have a plan to find Annie."

Dana struggled upright, saying Zack's words over and over in her head to understand them. A vile sweetness like ether burned in her nostrils as she remembered the words hoarsely whispered in her ear years ago, the breath alien and close: *I know where Annie is.* "Find Annie?"

"Yup."

"Oh, Zack. Don't do this. Please. I can't."

"I've got two people working on this. One of them is a writer. He's got the ins, Dana."

Dana groaned. "Oh, you *talked* to him, Zack? You shouldn't have." And she had called Samuel Wendt a liar. "What did you say? He'll make you—us—sound like . . . Well, he won't understand. That's all. He's not interested in finding Annie. He wants to rip us open and expose our guts to the world. Just like Dad did."

Zack kicked the table hard, so it shuddered across the floor a few feet. "Goddamnit, Dana. Nobody is more of a fucking butcher than Dad is. More of a fucking traitor." He clamped his hands over his nose, hyperventilating into them. When his breathing finally slowed, he looked at her with pleading eyes. "You have to trust me. I know what I'm doing."

The lines in her brother's face, laid bare by the overhead light, struck her as too mature for the way she thought of him. He was aging; they were aging. Somehow, it seemed impossible that their bodies had moved forward while their minds lingered, suspended, at a younger moment. "I trust you," Dana said. "I'm just afraid."

"You shouldn't be." Zack grinned with confidence, and Dana felt a subtle shift between them. "And when we find Annie, we'll celebrate."

Dana shivered with the pleasure of the idea, even though she knew it would never happen. Most likely, Annie had died in a medical laboratory years ago. *Oh, Annie.* "We should get to bed. I'll set up the guest room."

He nudged her off the sofa with his feet. "I'll sleep here on the couch. I like it in front of the television."

Dana turned off the lights and shuffled into her room, wondering about Zack's plan and what the writer would do with it. As intelligent as Zack was, he could be blinded by his own hope. She slipped between the covers, vowing that she would have to be vigilant about this. The last thing she wanted was for the entire country to make fun of Zack, who at six years old had not understood the artificial boundaries between humans and chimpanzees.

FOUR

Zack did not feel like sleeping. But it happened just the same, sometime after midnight when the evening news was rebroadcast and the commercials got less glitzy, more like videos that any jerk-off could tape. He hated the *early* late-night television of cackling laughs and celebrities tugging at their flashy clothes. Instead, he always hoped to stay awake until the good stuff came on: movies he had seen a few years back, horror flicks, infomercials that had a surreal feel to them that late at night, especially if they followed a sci-fi flick. This night at Dana's, he fell asleep before the good shows and awoke just before dawn with a dark spot of his drool on the sofa. The gap where his front teeth should have been tasted sour.

He could hear Dana clomping around in her bedroom as she dressed for work. The scent of shampoo and the damp mossiness of the local water hung in the air, so he knew she had already showered, probably already eaten. He smelled the coffee; he *loved* her coffee. It was not only the blend she bought (he would have to ask her what and where) but the way she brewed it: a particular brand of bottled water, extra beans but not too many, a fresh grinding every morning. The electric grinder usually woke him, but today it did not. He considered slipping off the couch to pour a cup but then decided to feign sleep. His sister, more than anyone, could easily extract a confession from him with the right look. She *knew* he had released the chimps, but she was not yet ready to believe it. Which was okay with Zack. He did not want to get her into trouble. He did not want her to hate him. Although he had never, ever intended for Benji to get killed, he had wanted to take away the anguish he saw in the chimp when he swept his flashlight over the cage. He wanted to shout out to Dana, "If you could've seen him! If you could've seen his eyes and all the pain there, you would've done the same thing!"

Well, he knew she would not have done the same thing, so there was no sense in letting her know he was awake.

He lay face down on the sofa so Dana could not see him smile if he started to lose his nerve. His arm hung over the side, and one leg stuck out over the end: nice touches, he thought. Dana was too good, too honest, to do something like what he had, and that nearly knocked him off the sofa with guilt. But he stayed, regulated his breathing so it was deep and heavy and childlike. Dana came into the room, picked up a few things not far from his ear, shuffled through the small house until she came back to the sofa, paused next to him. Then, swiftly, she bent and kissed him on the back of the head. In moments, she was gone. The door to her pickup slammed. The engine ground as she backed down the driveway.

Zack did not move for several minutes afterward. The spot where his sister had kissed him felt strangely bald and tight, the skin all prickly underneath. He liked that she had kissed him, as illicit as it felt. It was weird, having his sister kiss him like that, as though he were a sweet little boy instead of a screwed-up man entering middle age. She was like that— she did things without thinking because she meant them. Whenever *he* did something without thinking, disaster always resulted. Even when he thought through things. Like the chimp fiasco. He had looked into Benji's eyes and seen a kindred spirit, someone misunderstood and simply unlucky. He had meant to give the chimps the kind of freedom they deserved, but even in mercy, he had killed one. Zack rolled onto his back. Dana had no reason to love him, no reason to keep forgiving him and letting him crash at her house, but she did anyway. He didn't know what he would do if she started to hate him.

Releasing the chimpanzees was only a small part of what Dana could hate. He had snorted heroin, even shot up once or twice, and had found himself in an alley in Miami stripped of belongings and clothes. He had endured two dingy rehabs but this time had been clean for nearly six months. Still, sometimes a craving scratched inside his veins, and his organs felt shriveled, as though they needed to be filled with something other than blood. He had the will power to resist but did not know if he wanted to. Unlike some of the other guys he knew, he got stoned not because of boredom but because the world sucked and he knew it. He did not have an addictive personality or a low tolerance for pain. If he did, he never would have done some of the things he had.

He had fucked a woman with stringy hair he had met in a Chicago bar and who had turned up dead a week later. The police had brought him in for questioning. They had asked him, "Why did you want her dead?" Even though he had not killed her, he tried to think of reasons he *did* want her dead: the way she laughed at him when he tripped over her shoes on the floor, the stale nicotine-and-beer smell of her breath, the one ragged fingernail that had scratched his back and could have provided DNA evidence against him if she had not washed her hands properly. What would his father say if he knew his son had once been a murder suspect?

He had been arrested for driving under the influence but did not care that they took his license, since he could not afford the insurance anyway. No one had been hurt, no damage done, and now he could drive again. Still, it was a blemish worth hating. Another irresponsible act. Something he could never tell Dana because she often declined a second drink when she took him out to dinner, saying, "No more for me. I've got to drive."

Instead of being responsible, he always ended up being responsible *for* something.

He raised his head and saw that Humphrey was staring at him from the floor with his piercing yellow eyes.

"Don't judge me, you motherfucker," Zack said as he sat up, but he was not angry. He liked Humphrey and the logical way the cat seemed to perceive the world. If he had to be judged, let it be in the eyes of a cat.

In the kitchen, the coffee in his mug tasted okay, not great the way it usually did. A can of ground coffee next to the pot explained why. Even though he knew Dana had used canned coffee not to disturb him, it ticked him off. He poured the coffee from his mug back into the pot. Maybe when he got desperate he would drink it. Maybe he could convince that writer to buy him a decent cup of coffee.

⌒ᴧᴧ⌒

They sat in the town's diner, a small storefront squeezed between a bank and a flower shop. A huge sweet gum tree heaved the sidewalk in front and shielded the plate glass with the light yellow-green of autumn foliage. Sam Wendt had ordered only coffee, black, but had encouraged Zack to order a full breakfast, which he did: pancakes and syrup, fat rolls of sausage, grapefruit juice, and coffee dense with cream and sugar.

Zack eyed the small recorder placed between them. "Have we started?"

Sam reached across and pressed a button. "We can start now. If you can talk and eat at the same time."

Zack grinned. They had already been through this. Zack liked the combination of interview and meal; he felt more relaxed and chatty, less like a Subject and more like Some Guy. "Shoot."

"People aren't supposed to say that anymore," Sam told him.

"It doesn't mean anything. Not really." Zack knew from the moment he had met Sam that he was smarter than he appeared, his penetrating eyes seeing and remembering everything, even if his shoulders looked loose and nonchalant. Zack's advantage was that no one took him seriously, so he might get a few by Sam. Not that he intended to lie about his childhood. "I've been pretty nonviolent to a fault."

"What does that mean?"

Zack swallowed, then ran his tongue over his teeth to clear them of disgusting food particles before lifting his upper lip with one hand. "Two false teeth." He could not admit Dana had paid for them, that she had turned from his smile without them. "I screwed around with some guy's girlfriend, and he wanted to fight. He slugged me, and I stood there. You know how they say women like nonviolent guys? That's bullshit. He knocked me flat, and his girlfriend was swooning all over him. Like he'd just protected her from an ogre. I bet that night the two of them had the best sex they ever had."

"So you lost the girl and two teeth."

"Well, I lost the two teeth. The girl snuck over to my apartment two days later."

"Really? So the nonviolent guy *does* get the girl."

He shrugged. "I was better in bed. He was better in public." No sense in complicating the story by revealing that Becca had married the asshole and that he, Zack, still slept with her from time to time, whenever she could get away for a few hours. Zack shoved a huge piece of pancake into his mouth. He had forgotten anything he said might end up in print. Not that Becca would read it, but he did not want her getting beat up. Although she was tougher than she looked, bones could be broken. "You probably shouldn't print that. Not as is. Change names to protect the innocent, or whatever you guys do."

"You didn't tell me any names."

"Oh." The coffee had not done its work on his brain yet. He reached across and snapped the recorder off, his hand hovering over the button. "Dana isn't thrilled that I talked with you."

Sam took a sip from his coffee but kept his eyes on Zack's hand. Eyes like a cougar, Zack thought. Zack turned the recorder back on.

Sam placed his cup on the table. "What was it like, learning sign language and English at the same time?"

"I don't know. I don't really remember. None of it stayed with me. I'm kinda amazed I used to know it. Dana does, you know. Still know it."

"How do you know?"

"She took me a few years ago on a trip to Jamaica. Birthday present. Like I needed to be in the midst of Rasta and weed." He had already told Sam about rehab but had not admitted to the heroin part. He didn't want to seem like a junkie, just a guy who had experimented and then left it all behind. "Anyway, at the hotel, there was a couple with a deaf teenage daughter. Whenever they signed to each other, Dana couldn't take her eyes off them. Would you believe this? Sometimes, she even moved her lips. Like she was reading. I'm sure there was a lot she couldn't understand. You do know that American Sign Language has to be adapted for apes, right? Their hands aren't exactly the same as ours. She never learned pure ASL."

"Have you seen the movies of you and Annie?"

"Some." God, how he hated those. Every time, he wanted to cry, for all that they had, all that they missed. Annie always looked so happy in those films. He remembered very little of her, but the movies conjured up her particular smell and isolated images: the strength of her hands when she pushed him on the swing, the two of them sitting at the dinner table long after everyone else because they both refused to eat creamed spinach. Mostly, though, he remembered her loss. Nothing seemed complete and safe after she was gone.

"What are you remembering?" Sam asked.

Zack looked up, surprised at the generosity on the other man's face. In that moment, he saw that Sam could be a friend, that despite Dana's fears, Sam meant them—and the other families—no harm. "I'm trying to remember Annie," Zack said. "Most of what I remember is what it was like to have her suddenly gone." He lowered his eyes to the backs of his hands, taking care not to betray his intent. "I wish we could track her down and find out what happened to her."

"Have you tried?"

"Sort of. It's hard to know where to begin." He looked up with perfect timing—*Careful now*, he told himself, *this guy is no dummy*—and smiled. "That would be one helluva story, wouldn't it? A family reunion."

Sam's eyes squinted slightly, just enough to warn Zack to dig into his pancakes. He could not tell if Sam was onto him or simply thinking about the possibilities. Hell, even if Sam knew he was being manipulated, the reunion between the Armstrongs and Annie would make a fine story— compelling television, even a made-for-TV movie. If Sam was the man Zack thought he was, he wouldn't give a shit about being handed the idea. He would simply attack it.

Dana had once said, "She *died*, Zack. She couldn't possibly have survived. You haven't seen the inside of a lab. I have." Well, Zack would prove to her that she was wrong. He would prove a lot to her, about Annie, about chimpanzees, about him. And she would love him for it.

<hr/>

Zack sat in the perfect tree: an oak with thick, gnarled branches low enough to the ground so he could easily swing himself up and over, then climb almost as high as he wanted. He knew this tree as well as he knew the major routes across the United States, east and west, north and south. When he climbed it, he never made a mistake, never ended up on a branch that offered no easy exit, but instead reached his favorite vantage point with minimal movement. From his perch, he could see the back sections of the SCPP enclosures. The chimps sometimes gazed across the brush beyond the electric fence and then up to where he sat, but in two years, no human had detected him. Although from deep in the cool leaves he could see two of the observation platforms, the binoculars trained on the animals never found him. It was kind of funny, he thought now, how the wooden structures were called "observation platforms" when the people sitting on them, including his sister, were oblivious to everything outside their narrow focus. He snorted. These people were supposed to be *scientists*, for God's sake. Ph.D.'s: Puny-Headed Dolts.

Except for Dana, of course, who sometimes was so fucking brilliant he felt like he had a gene deficiency. It wasn't that he felt stupid as much as truncated. Always on the edge of something happening but never really there, like he had run into a glass wall and part of him kept going, forever lost.

When he reached into his baggy back pocket for the small brown bag of peanuts he had bought that morning, he almost tumbled out of the tree. He liked the way peanuts in the shell were so readily available in the Southeast, though he had to be careful to get the roasted, not the raw, ones. His mother had never liked to buy them because she hated the shells, the mess they made when one fell to the floor and someone stepped on it. He and Dana had begged for peanuts the way other kids begged for candy—at the circus when it came to town, when they visited their cousins in Cleveland and went to a baseball game, when the cheap carnivals took over school parking lots. It was one of the triumphs of Zack's adult life that he could buy as many peanuts as he wanted. Earlier, as he sat in his car, he had idly drawn smiley faces on the peanuts, making a whole bag of peanut people. He now crushed the shells perfectly between his thumb and the first joint of his index finger, letting the red-skinned nuts slide into his palm; he could do it with barely a sound. Of course, the chimps always heard him. The humans never did.

A group of eleven chimps (no, twelve—one was half-hidden by a bush) had gathered below him and were grooming each other. When he cracked his first peanut, they stiffened and glanced up at him, then resumed their activity. He loved that they knew who he was. The clearing had been made by the chimps themselves; last April, he had watched a couple of them tear a few saplings and wave them around, hooting and screeching at each other. Another day, a cluster of them had come to eat the leaves from a shrub, beginning the first stage of killing the bush. The location of this clearing was ingenious; Zack had determined by studying the sight lines of the platforms that the chimps had created a private area secluded from all but Zack's tree, from which he was absent for months at a time, depending on where he felt like being. He tried to toss a peanut into the enclosure, but the lightweight shell made the nut hang in the air and spin downward before it gained much momentum. After a few tries, he gave up.

Zack could tell the chimps apart, though he did not know their given names. Once, Dana had tried to introduce a few to him, to point out the individuals, but Zack preferred to identify them more intuitively, knowing that this one had a certain personality and that one chummed around with those two. Human names for chimpanzees struck him as not only unnecessary but ridiculous. Annie had been different because she was his sister, a not-wild not-chimp. His father had stripped Annie of her nature, just as he had stripped his children of theirs.

One chimp reclined against the trunk of a tree, picking at the moss beside him as a diligent female combed her fingers through his hair. Zack wondered if they got lice in the woods, or just ticks. What kind of bugs found their way through the wiry blanket of hair? Did mosquitoes raise welts on their skin the way they did on his, or were the chimps' immune systems unresponsive? The chimp being groomed—a large, muscular male—patted the female on the backside as she rose to attend to another. Zack smiled, thinking of Becca, of Laurie who lived in Memphis, of the women he had loved a little.

Chimps had the right idea. They had sex when they could and gladly accepted simple companionship when they could not. Instead of trying to fit chimpanzees into a human mold, humans should learn a thing or two from them.

Tarzan. Wasn't he a true heroic figure?

Zack would have given almost anything to drop softly among the chimps, to join them in their daily routine as they padded across the pine-straw carpet of their enclosure. No matter what Dana thought, the others in the indoor cages deserved the same kind of freedom. What could one chimp do to another? Intimidate one another, perhaps, scream a lot. He had never seen viciousness among chimps, despite what Dana claimed from her textbook knowledge. He had done right by the chimps, for if they could not have Dana's carefully constructed jungle, then they should have the rest of South Carolina. Even for only a few hours.

The distinctive creak of someone climbing the nearest platform startled Zack into alertness. The first few moments were always tense for him, even though no one ever glanced across the brush and around treetops to where he sat. Still, he sensed the danger.

Dana appeared at the top, not looking in his direction at all. He relaxed until he noticed that she moved more slowly than usual as she took her notebooks from her bag. She seemed tired, sad, not at all herself. It was the dead chimp, he knew, that weighed on her. He wanted to shout to her across the brush that the chimp had been free for his last hours, which was better than any of them could be.

FIVE

Dana sat on the observation platform, notebook open, binoculars to her eyes, trying to fight off the penetrating sadness. In a clearing not far from her, Neema offered her red bottom to the dominant male, Mwenzi, who crouched in the chimpanzee copulation position. A band of four eager males milled anxiously behind the couple. When Mwenzi finished his fifteen-second copulation, the next male, Uzanzi, mounted her. Neema, after only two days inside the enclosure, looked exhausted. By Dana's calculations, she still had at least another three or four days of estrus and would not be left alone until the swelling had shriveled.

As the males finished with Neema, Dana grinned, thinking that women should never complain about the duration of human intercourse. Neema had mated with five males in less than two minutes. Although Neema had established herself with the males of Group A, finding her place with the females would be essential to integration. The female social structure of Group A was unusually strong, since the high-ranking

Kimwando consolidated her power as though a male. Dana had written several articles about this rare female alliance, conjecturing that the strong personality of Kimwando coupled with the relative safety of the sanctuary, where male strength and aggression found little use, had allowed it. In Dana's eyes, Kimwando was a true feminist and leader. She had risen to power quickly and without noise, gaining respect and affection from males and females alike, adapting to the group and transforming it.

She could not help wondering whether Annie would have fit into this feminist group.

A twig cracked below, and Dana peered over the edge of the platform. Lindsay Brassett, the president of the local chapter of Animals Unite, appeared on the pathway.

"Morning," Lindsay said.

"Morning."

Lindsay climbed the ladder hand over hand. She was wearing a lime green business suit and pumps, which made the climb look awkward and foolish—everything Lindsay was not. "The police visited my office yesterday afternoon. They suspect we might have had something to do with your break-in."

"I wouldn't worry about it. The police are running in circles, that's all, sniffing at everything. You *know* they'll drop the case in a day or two." Dana was impressed, however, that the police had bothered to investigate beyond the SCPP itself. "These matters are usually quickly forgotten—except by the victims."

"Maybe. But I wanted to tell you personally that our organization was not responsible." Lindsay pulled herself upright on the platform. She was a tall, angular African-American who had once told Dana she could trace her history to a slave held on a plantation a hundred miles from where they stood. When she spoke, her voice resonated like a cello, and when she chose to remain silent, as she did now, she had a calming effect on Dana. With Lindsay, you never had the feeling she was unsteady or undecided but, rather, deliberate. Shielding her eyes with one hand, Lindsay scanned the wooded enclosure, going past, then returning to, the small group of chimps below. Most of the chimps were grooming each other. Neema abruptly got up and sauntered away from the others, perhaps to find a place to nap, or to find food, or simply to escape the amorous advances. As she disappeared into the underbrush, the males trailed after her like the entourage of a starlet, unrelenting and faithful.

"Oh, don't go," Lindsay said. The bushes shook from the movement below, then steadied. Only two chimps remained in sight. "Can you really gather reliable data this way?"

"We don't pretend to see everything. Up here, you can get a nonintrusive overview. When we go into the enclosures, the view becomes incredibly narrow and specific. Besides, I'd rather limit the number of people who go in. I have grad students who have *never* been inside, and probably never will go, because their research doesn't require it. This is supposed to be a sanctuary, not a research lab, though at times the university forgets." Dana pointed to a patch of ground near the entrance where the vegetation had been worn to earth. "See down there? We've made several artificial clearings ringed with fruit-bearing shrubs and trees to tempt the chimps into sight." Then, as though Dana had planned it, a single chimp crossed the area. From the gait, which had a little hitch in it, Dana recognized the female Tajiri. "See?"

Lindsay crouched next to Dana, her skirt bunched high on her thighs.

They looked over the woods, picking out figures who had not seemed there only a moment before and losing others. Every so often, Lindsay would gasp, and Dana would look over, alarmed, only to see an expression of rapture. Before long, Dana was taking notes again, comfortable with the other woman next to her and falling headlong into the artificial world of primates below.

After almost thirty minutes of near-silence, Lindsay said, "I can guarantee we had nothing to do with the break-in. We understand the animals here have already endured their cruelty and are now treated with respect and care." She turned her dark eyes on Dana. "We see you as our sister organization. You can't suspect us."

Dana sighed. "I don't. The police do. Or maybe they've already decided they don't. I don't know. But all people have to hear is 'activist' and they envision ecoterrorists."

"We can work together on this." Lindsay was now studying her more carefully, and Dana realized this was her primary reason for visiting: to preserve her organization. Although Lindsay undoubtedly cared about the welfare of the chimpanzees, she saw her life's work tottering, vulnerable to collapse under the weight of suspicion.

Dana touched Lindsay's knee with the edge of her notebook. "You had nothing to do with it, so relax."

Lindsay nodded. "The police said the culprit had keys. Someone you know, maybe?"

Dana's throat was too dry to answer right away. "Everyone who works here understands the implications of releasing captive chimps." She pulled the clipboard into the center of her lap. "We know nothing about how it was done. Or why."

Zack had not done it. He couldn't have. He loved the chimps, and he loved her. Such an act on his part would mean that he distrusted her motives and the means by which she sought to alleviate the suffering of captive chimpanzees.

The South Carolina Primate Project was originally conceived by Henry and Eileen Murray, wealthy philanthropists with a strong connection to the university. The Murrays had attended a lecture about the plight of captive chimpanzees, and both had been moved to tears. The next day, they called the university with an offer to "write a check, whatever it will take" to create a protective sanctuary for chimpanzees. They were not natural animal rights activists, but they had found their legacy.

The details of the sanctuary required more than a signed check— and more money than the Murrays had expected—and so movement toward the eventual goal was slow and knotted with negotiations. The trustees saw a primate sanctuary as a money hole—which it was, Dana had to admit—and demanded a more academic bent, a place that would benefit students as well as chimps. Both the director and the assistant director would have light teaching responsibilities, and the students would be allowed to observe chimpanzee behavior.

The anthropology and psychology departments began a battle for control. Neither Henry Murray nor Burton Washington, the dean of the graduate school and a mechanical engineer by education, understood the peculiar marriage of anthropology, biology, psychology, ethics, and politics tied to nonhuman primatology. The Murrays and Dean Washington liked Dana and her practical plan to create the SCPP, and so, by appointing her, they awarded the SCPP to the anthropologists.

Even now, the repercussions of that decision continued to surface. Dana expected to see the new shape of them emerge in her meeting with Dean Washington.

In the morning, Dana and Mary arrived at the main university campus within moments of each other. Despite their separate (and hierarchical, since Dana's was slightly larger) offices at the SCPP, they shared a single one, like graduate students, in the anthropology department. Neither Dana nor Mary cared, since they spent so little time on campus, Mary for her one course per semester and Dana for her one seminar a year, plus faculty meetings. Their space looked more like a locker room than an academic office. Their in-line skates, helmets, wrist guards, elbow pads, and kneepads hung on wooden pegs Dana had installed underneath the bookshelves. Although one shelf was crammed with books, the other harbored a jumble of running shoes, shorts, T-shirts, sweatshirts, rain gear, and wind pants, most folded but sliding off one pile into the next. Their old-fashioned wooden desks faced perpendicular walls, Dana's looking out over the paved access road to the back of the building and a garbage bin, Mary's facing a brainwashingly white wall.

Dana stepped into the room. Mary came in behind her, squeezing past, and tossed her briefcase across her empty desk. Despite the clutter, the room seemed empty of who they really were.

Mary said, "Don't worry. The meeting will go fine."

"Wanna skate after your class?"

"They're predicting thunderstorms this afternoon."

Dana squinted at the piece of blue sky between her window and the next building. "Maybe we'll get lucky."

Mary broke into a grin. "Yeah. Maybe we'll get lucky. Isn't it about time?"

As Dana walked along the path toward the dean of the graduate school's office, she realized that she might never be comfortable with the structure, the demands, the hierarchy of academics. Her life had always been tied to The University (always spoken with an emphatic *The* before it, as though no other of equal importance existed), if not hers, then her father's. But the lifestyle itself eluded her comprehension. Perhaps Zack, who had dropped out of college at nineteen, made more sense of it, having seen it from both inside and out. When she had called home to tell him she needed to cancel their lunch together because Dean Washington had asked to see her, Zack had said, "You didn't think he would ignore the problem, did you?" As though he had known all along she would be walking down this particular path with her palms moist from both Southern humidity and nerves.

She should not be anxious, she told herself. She liked Dean Washington, and he her, even if they did not completely understand each other.

As Dana walked across the campus, every student she encountered yielded to her, stepping off onto the grass or rotating shoulders sideways or simply stopping to allow her to dictate the paths they would take to avoid each other. If she looked younger, she thought, they might not cede to her, and she wanted one, just one, student to look at her face and not look away, to believe she might be an equal, a student. Of course, that was ridiculous. She had crow's-feet teasing her eyes and skin that was beginning to look vaguely mottled. Even if she looked five years younger than she was, they would not mistake her for a peer. By the time she reached the administration building, she felt the burden of age, of impotence and fatalism, even though those qualities were not usually a part of her psyche.

The dean's administrative assistant, Nancy Phillips, regarded Dana stonily, but Dana knew better than to read anything into it. Nancy greeted everyone that way—everyone who was not Dean Washington. "You may go right in." Nancy turned back to her computer screen even before Dana passed her desk.

As Dana entered the office, Dean Washington rose behind his desk. A large-boned black man with gray toying at his temples, he cut a distinctive appearance even seated, but standing, he was truly imposing, a giant unfolding himself to his full glory. The sanctuary was his baby, too, although in a wholly different way than it was for Dana; its integration into the graduate school had been Washington's first major project as dean. Dana had always felt this loyalty—until now, as she stepped toward him and shook the power in his hand.

He gestured for her to sit across from him. "Punctual as always."

Dana lowered herself into the leather chair across from him. "So, we're here to talk about the released chimps."

He smiled. "Exactly. The situation is more complicated than you might think."

"I'm listening."

"The people in Harris are concerned about their safety. You scared the heck out of the sheriff, and he made sure the Harris school kept the children in at recess. You know what that will do to parents. If you had let well enough alone, the chimp would have been hit by the car, and that would have been the end of that."

"And what would have happened if he had attacked a kid instead?"

"Last night, a few of us from the university met with a group of people from Harris."

Dana had a vision of fifty people crammed into a small living room somewhere in Harris, Burton Washington crushed from all sides. He would have handled himself well, not even breaking a sweat as he told them what they wanted to hear. Dana worried about something much graver, much more insidious: she had been kept from the meeting. This new secrecy could only signal the first erosion of confidence in her. Although she had tenure in the anthropology department, she did not as director of the SCPP. The undersides of her arms peeled painfully away from the leather armrests, and she realized she had been clutching the chair. She let her hands fall into a pile in her lap. "And?"

"You understand, we must keep the public in mind."

"As far as safety goes, yes. But I don't want them telling me what's best for the chimps."

"This isn't about the politics of animal rights, Dana. This is about the balancing act between science and public safety. Between the university and the rest of the world. We have a certain responsibility to the community."

"Of course." She was tempted to ask him why, then, he had disagreed with her calling the sheriff.

"I want to know—from you—how someone could have gotten a key."

Outside the window, to her left, students were flicking an orange Frisbee across the quad; their tosses were so expert that the disk never wobbled, never faltered in its incision through the air. It was always the skinny kids, she thought, the boys with stick arms and hard, thin legs, who played Frisbee on the quad. As though the speed and steadfastness of the Frisbee said things about them that their bodies never could. Oh, for a lazy afternoon like that. For the expertness of a toss. For making a statement without having to say anything. "I don't know," she said, looking back at him. "I let all the students have keys to get in and out of the buildings and cages all day. It's easier—well, it takes less time—if someone doesn't have to track down a key. We've never had a problem. Until now." Dana forced herself to continue looking at him and not to squirm in the chair. "I called a locksmith right away. The locks have already been changed."

"This has been very embarrassing for the university. The driver who hit the chimp is suing us for negligence. The group I met with wants to know how many chimps have HIV. How many with hepatitis. And they want reassurances these diseases won't be unleashed on their community. They want complete containment from you."

Dana leaned forward. "This is it, Burton: chimpanzees escape. I can't help that. My God, an orangutan escaped from the National Zoo in the middle of D.C. It's going to happen here. But what's *not* going to happen is another break-in that results in loose chimps. I can assure you of that. And I don't recommend that we divulge how many of the chimps have HIV."

"How many do?"

She hesitated before accepting she had no choice but to answer truthfully. "Six. One caged with a broken leg. The other five in Group B."

"Why do we even have HIV chimps?"

"Because someone in a medical laboratory injected them with it. And then had no use for them because they didn't develop AIDS. Exactly the type of chimp Henry Murray wanted to save."

The invocation of Henry Murray's name sobered Washington enough to throw his bulky frame back against his chair. "I want you to find the weak links in your security. And I want you to fix them. I am holding you personally responsible for every misstep that happens down there. I don't care if it's within your control or not."

"Yes, sir."

"These people want full access to the sanctuary. They want documents. They want proof that you're capable of containing the animals. Do you understand what's at stake here?"

"I understand exactly what's at stake." The sanctuary, like so many others in North America, could fall under siege by people who did not understand the debt owed these chimps. Group hysteria could lead to its demise. Dana wanted to fling open the large window to bring in a rush of fresh air, anything that might clear her head. She had become a small child in the dean's presence, and she hated herself for it. "But I won't allow them full access. It's not necessary, and it's wrong."

Washington began to drum the edge of the desk with his fingertips. "There's something else you should know." The tone of his voice—tired, conspiratorial, even afraid—caught her off-guard. He cleared his throat. "There have been rumors. Accusations. Not just in South Carolina, but nationally. There seem to be questions about the sanctuary and your competency."

She almost laughed. "Rumors? Accusations? About what?"

"I'd rather not say right now. Until I investigate further."

She knew her behavior was beyond reproach and so could not take this latest information seriously. However, Washington's tone alerted her that she should not dismiss the claims, whatever they were.

"Can you at least tell me how they came to your attention?"

"President Davenport passed them along." The moment when a man's compromised position is laid bare is not a pretty one. Washington lowered his gaze, and the skin on his face slackened so it looked achingly old and tired. Davenport had handed Washington *his* ultimatum. Maybe

Burton Washington had defended Dana. But with the president of the university asking questions, he had no choice but to take charge.

"What are the specifics?" Dana asked. "I should be able to defend myself."

"I told you. It's not necessary now. If things get dicey, I'll let you know." He rose, signaling the end of their meeting.

Dana stood as well and reached across to shake his hand. "You can tell President Davenport that everything is under control."

Washington spread his hands as if to say, *I doubt it will help.* "Just watch your step. And I mean it."

She nodded. As she left, she wondered where her enemies lay hidden, what they were scheming now. Although her ideas might have been considered radical by some, her approach was not. How could *anyone* fault her for what she did? With each step she took away from the dean's office, she become more and more angry. Davenport and Washington had believed the wafts of unfounded accusation over her solid word—and over what they had seen at the sanctuary. Were they trying to find an excuse to cut loose the expensive venture? Or did the release of the chimps and Benji's death really have grave repercussions beyond the SCPP itself?

Whatever their reasons, Dana sensed danger scuttling behind her.

They raced down the paved incline, breathless, fierce, the wind of their movement pulling the hair jaggedly from under their helmets. Their in-line skates, bearings well lubricated, whirred smoothly under their feet. Dana did not have to look over her shoulder to know that Mary, as always, was two strides behind. *One, two, three, four*, Dana counted. Her legs worked hard as she sped down the path. *Five, six, seven, eight.* Then the counting in her head stopped, and she became all breath and heart. Mary's gritty strides rasped in her ears. Three undergraduate women, their backpacks slung over muscular bare shoulders, dodged out of the way, shrieking playfully.

Dana waved as she went by. "Afternoon!"

And two beats later, she heard Mary say, "Sorry!"

As the path leveled, Dana leaned forward, her arms swinging, legs thrusting from side to side as she bore down on the oblivious Frank Maddox, a professor of English, who was walking his beloved Dalmatian on a red lead. With a rough *shuurr* of wheels, Dana zigzagged around Maddox and his dog. Both recoiled in fear until the dog regained his wits and, barking, lunged at her too late. She glanced over her shoulder to see Mary expertly dodge the dog.

"Sorry!" Mary called out.

"You're too old for that!" Maddox cried after them.

"Never!"

Dana wished she had the skating skills of some of the kids she had seen; then she would have soared right over the back of the pampered Dalmatian before he had a chance to react. She would like to turn in midair, skate down steps, ride along the tops of narrow walls. But all she had was speed and mean agility.

For the next forty-five minutes, they skated around the campus, terrorizing everyone in their way, not discriminating among students, faculty, and administrative staff. Dana imagined she was outracing Davenport and Washington, beating them to the end before they had walked even a few steps in their squeaky shoes. Whatever they had planned, she could beat. And if it meant waiting them out, she could do that, too. A few times, Mary uttered, "Fuckers!" and Dana knew Mary, too, was steeling herself for a battle, whether it came to pass or not. Finally, exhausted, they collapsed on the cool stone steps of the anthropology building. Dana relaxed against them, not moving, allowing the exhilaration of complete physical exhaustion to take over.

Mary unfastened her helmet. Her dark hair glistened with sunlight and sweat. "That always feels *so* good."

"You just like to scare the crap out of everyone," Dana told her. "Empowerment."

"*Dominance.* Hell, everything else in my life is shit, so why can't I have a little thrill when I nearly bowl over Maddox?"

"Your life is shit? Hardly." Dana thought of Mary's husband, Quentin, who now taught in the university's math department and who seemed to have none of the flaws of Dana's ex-husband, Charlie. But she knew Mary was talking about her failure to conceive a child—her growing obsession. Dana could see its toll in the fine lines around Mary's mouth and the way she had lately taken to staring into space. Although Dana did not understand why Mary seemed consumed by her inability to have children, she ached for her friend. "Not perfect. But not shit either."

Mary shrugged. "Kind of like work these days at the SCPP."

"No, that's *hell.*" Dana unlatched the plastic boots, yanking one off with a grunt. Her thighs quivered with fatigue.

Mary already had her skates off and was slipping into her sneakers, which she had tucked with Dana's under the shrubs next to the steps. But Dana struggled with her second skate, her weak and partially numb left hand, the remnants of Annie's bite, unable to fully help the right. She unstrapped her wrist guards to give herself a better grip. Finally, the boot came off, taking her sock with it. Mary stood in front of her with her skates already in hand and her guards—knee, wrist, and elbow—stuffed into the bowl of her helmet. Dana rubbed the scar on the back of her hand.

"Trying out for the roller derby?" a man asked.

Dana tipped her head so she could see around Mary. Sam Wendt stood with his legs slightly spread, as though expecting to have to take a punch. He did not look much like a journalist to her, although she could not honestly say what a journalist should look like. His stance was strong, purposeful, but when he spoke he seemed tentative, not at all like an investigator—though he *had* come back and found her here, at the university, instead of the more likely place, the sanctuary. She wanted to say something nasty, but she chose not to be that predictable. "I'm still not going to talk about the language studies," she said, focusing her attention, however maddeningly difficult, on getting her sweat-dampened sock back on. Finally, she gave up (why couldn't she get the darn thing on?) and pulled off the other sock as well.

"That's not why I'm here."

Dana looked up sharply.

He continued, "I have lots of info from the other families. I've interviewed your brother. I'll write, 'Dana Armstrong, currently a primatologist in South Carolina, declined to be interviewed for this story.' "

She stuffed her socks into one skate and slid her bare feet into her sneakers. "You may think that's a threat, but I kinda like the sound of it."

He laughed. "I thought you would."

The ease with which he laughed surprised her. She looked closely to see if he was making fun of her, but all she saw was an open, honest, expressive face; his amusement seemed more shared than at her expense. "So I get the loaded sentence in your article. Why are you here, then?"

"You hooked me. Gave me another story. I'm going to write an article for *The New Yorker* about the sanctuary. You know, one of those monster in-depth pieces they're so famous for."

She did not know. She was lucky to have the time to read the newspapers. She glanced at Mary to see if she knew, but Mary shrugged.

"Anyway," Sam said, "I plan to center it around the break-in because it's such a flash point."

"Flash point?"

"Yeah. Don't you see it? The break-in and its aftermath reflect all the issues. Public fears. The suspicions thrown on animal rights groups. The intimate relationship between the chimps and the sanctuary staff. The precarious position you occupy between your moral convictions and the demands of the university."

He had come up with all this after only four days? Mary, too, seemed taken aback; she stood slightly off to one side, her skates weighing so heavily in her arms that her shoulders looked uncharacteristically sloped and weak.

"This article might be able to help you in your fight against the university."

"How do you know about that?"

"Extrapolation. I was at the public meeting in Harris last night," he said. When his eyes rested on hers, she could barely breathe. "And I didn't like a word I heard."

SIX

Dana made room for Sam to sit next to her on the steps. As he accepted the spot, she became conscious of her bare ankles. She wore shorts, so her whole lower legs were uncovered; the knobs of her ankles, the rings of flesh that dipped nakedly into her sneakers, the tendons flexing there, seemed exceedingly exposed. "What did you hear?"

Mary, who stood above them on the steps, moved closer.

"Fear," Sam said. "Anger. Hysteria. Not only were they not seeing the big picture, they weren't even seeing the smaller one. I don't think anyone had a clue what a primate sanctuary is."

Dana covered her ankles with her hands. "Nothing new."

"But you'll talk with me? About the sanctuary?"

"Yeah." She glanced up at Mary. "Do you want to be a part of this?"

Mary shook her head. "Can't. I'm meeting Quentin for an early dinner."

"Give Quentin a smooch for me."

"He'll appreciate it. I'll take your skates in for you."

Dana stood and handed Mary her skates, which would have

overwhelmed anyone else, but somehow Mary held onto all four boots without looking awkward. Mary gave Sam a slight nod, then scampered up the steps and into the building.

"Let's walk," Dana said. Her muscles were already stiffening. "I assume your tape recorder will still pick up my voice if we're moving."

"Hey, I've even done it on the run. Literally. And I'd love to stretch my legs."

As the perspiration dried, it chilled her, and she wished Sam had come a little later, when she could have changed into fresh clothes. As they walked toward the historic area of the campus, Dana told him about the origins of the sanctuary and its philosophy. By the time they arrived at the wrought-iron gates, Dana was talking rapidly, and Sam was listening without interruption. He held the tape recorder toward her as they walked. She doubted he would be able to pick up their whole conversation, but she was so relieved her ankles felt normal once more that she did not care if he had to come back again and again to clarify her statements.

"So," he said, "Congress passed a bill allocating money to support primate sanctuaries. Isn't that enough funding to keep you going?"

Dana laughed. "Of course, it *helps*. But you would not believe how much it costs to run a sanctuary. We're still paying off the start-up expenses. The food alone is prohibitive. But then you add maintenance. For example, in the nursery, we have three-quarter-inch shatterproof glass walls so we can see in and the juveniles can see out. We have to have glass because they can slip between bars. Do you know what happens several times a year? A chimp leaps against the glass and bounces right off, hitting it just right—or wrong—and cracking it. Like in a windshield, the crack spreads. You can't stop the chimps from doing it. It's a common chimp play motion. So we have to replace the glass. We are actually budgeted for that expense, but if we estimate wrong and the glass cracks one extra time, we're screwed. And that's just one instance of how quickly we can get in the hole. And of course, we don't get all of the grant money. The university takes its cut, too."

"Its cut?"

"Yeah. Academic grants always have strings attached. The university takes a percentage, often up to sixty percent, for 'indirect expenses'—overhead. And part of Mary's and my salaries comes out of grant money as well. Then the research assistantships for the grad students working on the project. And *then* the leftovers are used to maintain the sanctuary. That's why I adore private donations. We can apply the whole amount to our work. Mary and I go on fundraising jaunts in September and March. The SCPP would collapse if any one of our three means of support vanished."

"Congress, grant money, donations," Sam muttered as he jotted them on his pad. "Hey," he said, stopping. She had already walked a few steps beyond him and had to return. "Give me an example of higher-level human behavior that has roots in basic primate behavior."

She laughed. "Really?"

"Why not?"

"If you promise not to freak out."

"Why would I do that?"

"Because most people don't like being compared to animals. And there's a certain sensitivity about similarities between people and chimps."

"I'm more open-minded than that. And more curious. Go ahead."

She squinted at him in the afternoon light, trying to decide whether she would mind if he disliked her. "Not long ago, some monkeys escaped in Virginia and threw bananas and crab apples at cars passing along the highway. Primates do that—they love to throw things, in a rage, which is often the case, or for fun. I haven't seen our adult chimps throw for fun, but the juveniles do. They toss handfuls of leaves at each other during a chase. One of my favorite youngsters, Chatu, used to throw a stick at his best friend, then look the other way, as though pretending he had done nothing. When his friend caught on, a wild chase erupted, the two racing around the nursery, screaming and laughing, leaping against the walls and pounding on them with their feet as they passed. Chimps are excellent throwers. They love to throw their feces at unwelcome visitors."

"I haven't seen humans do that, thank God."

"But you've seen them play baseball."

The realization of the connection was fun to watch as it swept across his face in twitches. "That's not the same."

"No, it's not. But think about it. Primates love to throw things. They play running games. They even touch the 'bases' of our walls, but outside it would be trees they romped against. Humans, with their high intelligence, have made rules for these games so a grumpy old male won't walk up and hit us on the side of the head for annoying him. We have found appropriate times and places for this behavior. And we love it. We love being able to toss a basketball into a hoop. We love to hurl a football twenty yards and have someone catch it. There's more. Watch how a baseball player who scores the game-winning run jumps down on home plate. It has the same resonance as a chimp hitting the trunk of a tree. We have taken the aggression of feces throwing and made it into entertainment."

Sam pressed his notepad to his midsection—which Dana saw was not quite as lean as she had first thought—and laughed. His amusement was contagious, and she started laughing as well. Dana wanted to throw her arms around him to thank him for lifting the dark spirits of the day. Before she knew what she was doing, she touched his arm with her knuckles. Embarrassed, she withdrew her hand. A roll of thunder made her look overhead at an approaching storm. "You want to get a cup of coffee? I have a long drive back to Harris."

"Sure. I could use a jolt myself."

As the thunderstorm broke, they sat knee to knee at a small, round table in a coffeehouse packed with students and professors. When Sam ordered his coffee black, Dana felt a small satisfaction, an affection for him, even, although she liked a splash of milk in hers.

When he caught her looking at his cup, he covered it with his hand. "It's an old newsroom habit," he said. "Black coffee. During college, I worked evenings at a local paper. The cream was always sour because no one wanted to replace it." He grimaced. "The powdered stuff stays with me for days."

"It's all chemicals, that nondairy stuff. It probably repeats because your body isn't equipped to digest it."

"Maybe." He slipped his hand off his cup so he could sip his coffee. "Do you eat meat?"

She shook her head. "I'm not vegan. Ovo-lacto, though I hate labeling myself with something so stupid sounding. But that's what I am. I figure if I'm intelligent enough to see the complexities within animals, I should respect them."

"And the rest of us aren't as smart?"

She laughed. "You can say that if you want. But I suspect it has more to do with conscience."

"And politics?"

"Maybe."

He smiled. "I want to do more research before I talk to you again. And I'm going to visit a friend in Savannah for a few days. Will you be around at the end of next week? To answer more questions?"

Dana straightened in her chair. She had allowed herself to forget that this was an interview. "Sure."

She wished she could have a normal conversation with someone who did not dream about chimpanzees the way other people dreamed of their families.

$$\sim\!\wedge\!\wedge\!\sim$$

When Dana returned to the sanctuary later that same night, darkness had fallen and everyone had gone home. The chimpanzees were asleep on their makeshift nests of straw and boughs, some in trees and some on the platforms Dana had installed throughout the enclosures. She turned on the lights in the main building, and a bittersweet longing embraced her. Instead of going into her office to do the work she had planned, she walked down the corridor to Benji's empty cage. She sat in front of it, her legs crossed at her ankles. She had cleaned out the holding cage herself, remembering facts about Benji's life with each sweep, but now the cage held nothing but memories, washed clean with disinfectant. It was strange when people died because you expected to turn the corner and see them again, and so it was with Benji. *Oh, Benji.* If only he had known how much she wanted to help him.

The front door opened, and Dana's heart quickened. But Mary, and not another disaster, stepped through the door. Mary, wearing pajamas and a pair of sandals, padded down the hall toward Dana.

In a low voice, so as not to disturb the chimps, Dana asked, "What are you doing here?"

Mary collapsed next to Dana, the hems of her cotton pajamas hiking up her calves. "Quentin and I had a fight. We had a great dinner, but when we got home, we had a fight." She started to cry. "I feel so weird lately, like I'm screwing up my life. Like I can't control who I am. I can't believe I picked an argument because he laughed at a sexist joke on TV."

Dana laughed. "You got mad at that? My God, Charlie used to make fun of me in public."

"That's pretty bad." Mary caressed the length of the bars. "I get scared sometimes. Like we're not going to make it. Like we'll turn out to be another statistic instead of a marriage. Quentin hates it here. What if he leaves me?"

Dana tapped Mary with her foot. "Don't worry, kiddo. Quentin loves you, and you love him. I can see it, feel it."

Mary covered her face with her hands. "I'm so embarrassed, I can't even tell him I was an idiot. On my way over here, I kept thinking that this is why God hasn't allowed us to have a baby."

"Believe me, idiots have babies."

Mary laughed, but it was a bitter sound that Dana realized reached much deeper than she could ever know. "Not *this* idiot." Her chest heaved with an enormous breath. "I'm so glad you're here. I *knew* you would be."

Dana wondered when she had become so predictable that Mary knew she would be sitting in front of Benji's cage as the hour drew close to midnight, when everyone else in Harris was home with their families, asleep.

⌁⌁⌁

The next morning, a small band of fifteen or so people arrived in the SCPP parking lot. They took hand-lettered signs from the trunks of their cars and began to picket in the corner closest to the main building. From the graduate students' office window, Dana read the placards through squinted eyes. Most were variations she had expected—"AIDS out of Harris," "Chimps Belong in Africa," "SCPP: Secret Chimps, Poor Protection"—but one made her burst into laughter—"Ban S.C. Primates from Harris!" She wondered whether the protester knew that she, too, was a primate.

"They're trespassing," Andy said as he came into the room. "We should call the police."

"No," she said. "That will only antagonize them."

"Maybe the people who broke in are out there."

"I doubt it."

Andy stood next to her with his arms crossed. He knew the people outside better than she did because he also worked at the local animal hospital. "I give their damn hunting dogs rabies shots, and they trust me then. I neuter their cats and even give droplets of antibiotics to their hamsters. What do they think? That when I spend the rest of my day here I turn into Satan?"

"I'll go talk to them."

"You're kidding, right?"

She made a face at him on the way out the door.

As Dana walked up the short path to where the protesters stood, she could feel them tense with the anticipation of confrontation. Some broke into nervous smiles. "Hi," she said.

A few answered. She wished Mary were not teaching that morning because Mary would know exactly what to say and do.

"I'm Dana Armstrong, the director of the South Carolina Primate Project," she said. She recognized one woman as the weekend pharmacist in town, a few others as members of Animals Unite. The rest she had seen around town. They had stopped moving, and their signs drooped in their fists. "I'd be happy to answer any questions you might have, either about the chimps or about what happened the other night."

"We want to keep our kids from getting AIDS," one woman said.

Dana regarded each face carefully before answering. "Your children have a much greater chance of getting AIDS by having unprotected sex than from a chimp. And I'm not being flip. The few chimps who have HIV can't transmit it except by bodily fluids. Unless you have sex with one, or treat his wound, or eat him, you're in no danger."

"What if one attacks me when he gets out?" the pharmacist asked.

Dana nodded. "You're right. That's a danger. A small one, though. Saliva is a weak carrier. You would have to share blood. But in the five years we've been here, Benji was the only chimp who came into contact with the public, and he did not have HIV. The reason this happened was because someone broke into the building and released him. I won't lie to you. It could happen again, and for other reasons. But you live with gators and snakes and rabid animals outside your door. Drunk drivers are on the road, and people own guns."

"You're taking our safety lightly!"

"No, I'm not."

"You don't *belong* here!" This cry unleashed a litany of others, and the small group suddenly seemed like a crowd closing in on Dana. They shouted at her that she had kept secrets from them, that she had jeopardized their safety, that she had no right to bring chimpanzees into their midst. Most complained of safety, but a few championed animal rights. She could not respond to any of them without shouting back, so she listened, trying to remain calm and upright despite the sting in her gut, until they expended all their words and fell silent.

"Would you like me to explain our safety features?" she asked.

The question caught them off-guard. Perhaps they had expected her to be defensive about their accusations. No one said a word.

Sensing that she had their wary attention, she sat in the dirt and drew a rough map of the sanctuary and the surrounding land, showing them the buffer zone and explaining why they had laid everything out the way they had. Dana could feel their distrust and their anger, but after a few minutes, she also had their interest.

~⋎⋏~

Tekua had begun his recovery from his broken leg. A week after the escape, he was still furious with the hard plaster cast Andy had wrapped around his injury. Andy kept him sedated, so he was too muddled to smash it off, but Dana worried what would happen when Andy decreased the medication. She worried whether Tekua understood that Andy had applied the cast not to torture him but to protect him.

Darryl, one of the students, said, "Tekua doesn't care if we have his best interest in mind or not. He doesn't have his *own* best interest in mind."

The four other once-liberated chimps, having stretched their limbs in freedom, pined for the outdoors in their distinctive ways.

Nyuki had come down with a cold, his buzzing now juicy and always followed by a nose-wiping swipe of his forearm, so he showed less interest than the other escapees in the outdoors. The skin around his nose had cracked; he allowed Dana to spread petroleum jelly around his nostrils to protect the skin. Dana could see the effort it took for him to breathe and to move about his enclosure. He often sat in the doorway leading outside, gazing longingly, snorting noisily for air.

Sifongo spent all his time in the outdoor area of his family's holding cage, hooting and hollering to the other chimps. Sometimes, he worked himself into a frenzy, rushing back and forth along the bars, hurling tires and branches, stomping up and down the series of platforms. Often, his fury ended with a plaintive whimper that stabbed Dana with her own inarticulate longing. The few times Neema answered her brother's call, he sat back, pouting.

Barafu walked outside and stared into the trees, not moving for hours except to occasionally inspect her chewed finger. Even when Dana called her inside for food, she ambled in reluctantly, often carrying the food back outside to stuff into her mouth.

Kitabu, too, had emerged changed. Having followed Sifongo through the woods for the hours they were free, she had developed a girlish crush on the older male. Her doll clutched to her chest, she leaned against the bars and stared into Sifongo's cage across the hall. Because Sifongo was rarely inside, she saw only flashes of him as he rushed by the doorway leading outside.

Dana held Kitabu in her arms, reading her nursery rhymes, but Kitabu wiggled around to catch a glimpse of Sifongo as he hooted madly outside. "Maybe you could be with him," Dana told the chimp, "if you did not need to use the toilet. Outside—no toilet."

Kitabu threw herself free of Dana's embrace and raced to the far corner of the cage, glaring.

Dana shrugged. "Soon, Sifongo will be outside with the other chimpanzees. They don't have a toilet. No toilet."

With that, Kitabu threw herself to the ground in a thrashing temper tantrum.

Although Dana would have liked to interact with Kitabu in chimp grunts and hoots, Kitabu considered such attempts an affront and always turned her back on Dana. Still, the young chimp's nature had not been entirely erased by her owners. She could not control her excited screams and bounces when she discovered a hidden treat in her cage and always looked around anxiously afterward, as though to see if anyone had witnessed her reaction. Dana had never wanted the young chimp to live alone in her holding cage—isolation went against the psyche of a chimpanzee—but so far the only comfort the staff had been able to use was human interaction: the twice-daily story times, the brushing of her silky hair, the games the graduate students played with her. They had tried before to introduce Kitabu to the nursery of children, but each time she had screamed for a full half-hour, never calming amid the scramble of curious chimps. Dana had been searching for the right moment to try again.

As Dana and Mary left Kitabu's cage after a storybook session, Dana said, "Kitabu's crush on Sifongo may be the opening we've been waiting for." She picked bits of straw out of Mary's hair and tossed them to the ground. "She seems to have finally connected with another chimp. Now that she's in love with Sifongo, she might be willing to give up her toilet and her doll."

Mary laughed in her high-pitched, schoolgirl way that made her seem years younger than she was. Her fight with Quentin must have been forgotten and forgiven. "There is always a catch for love, isn't there?"

Dana, who no longer trusted what passed for love, laughed with her. Of course, Kitabu longed for Sifongo not because she wanted sex—she was far too young for that—but because she wanted companionship, a friend, someone she could look up to and trust. Although Dana could try to integrate Kitabu into the nursery, she feared the effort would fail once again. After all, to Kitabu, her own kind might seem like savages, with their bared teeth and jubilantly powerful arms, the chaotic nursery nothing like the cool, composed rooms of an estate. Dana could only imagine what it must have been like for Annie, trapped in a fetid cage after once being treated like a human child.

"Are you okay?" Mary asked.

"Yeah." Dana loosened the fists she had made at her sides. "We'll try Kitabu in the nursery again." As she spoke, she felt as though she were falling headlong into a blindingly bright hole, and her eyes ached. She felt this same brutal rush of fear whenever she stepped into a lecture hall of colleagues, most of whom had seen her naked in a bathtub with Annie. If those movies had been taken recently, someone would have stopped their distribution by crying child pornography, but they had been introduced in a different time and in highbrow settings, so they became classics among linguists, psychologists, and even primatologists, who generally preferred viewing chimpanzees in their native habitat. The early viewers, especially, derived a kind of intellectual orgasm, a sublime realization that the line between *Pan troglodytes* and *Homo sapiens* had snapped and quivered like a wave set into excited motion.

"Did I say something wrong?" Mary asked.

"No. Just sorting through my personal baggage."

"Don't think you're the only one with that kind of stuff. We all have it. It just looks different as it comes around the carousel."

Mary's comment made Dana feel so ordinary, so much like everyone else, that her ruminations were exposed for their selfishness. "You're a good kick in the pants," she said.

SEVEN

*S*amuel Wendt sprawled on his motel bed in Orangeburg, fingering the books he had purchased in Columbia the day before. This part of the South, this Low Country, this swampy, tangled land, was not at all the South of his home in Arlington, Virginia, and nothing like the eastern Connecticut suburb where he had grown up. Towns here collected briefly at intersections, then dispersed into the woods, a trailer home rooted to a cement foundation here and there along the roadway, peanut farms wedged between stands of trees, logging tracts laying the earth bare. And then another hiccup of humanity. He wanted to go home to his Yankee South, but the draw of yet another article anchored him to this dingy motel room and its depressing surroundings. He hoped that when he visited his college roommate and his wife in Savannah it would be *civilized* there.

Maybe he was not being fair. Maybe he had not seen enough. But one thing was sure: South Carolina made him uneasy. The tourist locations—Charleston, Hilton Head, Myrtle Beach—were welcoming enough, but the *real* places, like Harris and Orangeburg and all the small towns speckling the map, made him feel lonely and odd. Everything seemed stuck in the past. Orangeburg's downtown had a bygone look, with flat, worn storefronts under ornate stone cornices. The commercial strip with its fast-food restaurants was no better. The entire area had a neglected air despite several nearby colleges. He just did not understand how anyone could thrive here.

He never would have expected someone like Dana Armstrong to willingly inhabit such a desolate place.

The books. He had to focus on them so he would not be so depressed. These were not his first primate books, since he had researched his article on the language study families, but they symbolized a new passage of his interest. He had bought books not only about wild primates but also about the famous women who studied them: Jane Goodall, Dian Fossey, and Birute Galdikas. He hoped to decipher the kind of woman who devoted her life to primates. Strange, he thought, as he leafed through some of the books, how women figured much more prominently in early primatology than they did in other scientific disciplines. Did these nonhuman primates—these near-humans—awaken something in women, or were Goodall, Fossey, and Galdikas only coincidentally women? He picked up first one book, then another, not able to decide where to begin. Finally, he closed his eyes and snatched up the first book his fingers touched, a volume on chimpanzee cultures.

He read for a while but then put down the book on the snagged bedspread. He could not get Dana Armstrong out of his head: the tilt of her head, the intensity of her dark blue eyes, the way her expression shifted from good humor to anger. He had yet to tell either Zack or Dana that he had spoken to their father over the phone; that information, he knew, might destroy the fragile relationship he had built with each. Reginald Armstrong had told Sam that the family article was "a brilliant stroke, a story that needs to be told," and had explained that his only mistake in the experiment was failing to recognize the possible lasting effect on his children. "I didn't see beyond the experiment," Reginald had said. "I should never have mixed my work with my family." Reginald had been the one to suggest that Sam would have to face both Dana and

Zack in person if he wanted any information from them. "The two of them are intractable," Reginald explained.

Sam did not need Dana to complete his original article. Or any of the Armstrongs, for that matter, since he had five other families already on the record. In the beginning, the Armstrongs were simply the first family on the list, an alphabetical starting point, nothing more. He might have ignored them after Susan Armstrong hung up on him, but when Reginald returned his call, saying he would be willing to cooperate, Sam started paying attention. If Reginald's surreptitious phone call had piqued Sam's interest, then his first interview with Zack, in Arlington, had hooked him. Zack had grown up into some kind of nut case—that had been apparent in the first few minutes of the interview. When Sam had asked his occupation, Zack said, "Drifter."

"Is that what you put on your income tax return?"

"Yeah, sometimes. Dana makes me fill them out every year."

When Sam tried to find out why Dana had so much influence over him, Zack said, "I like her to believe she does. She's my big sister. She needs to do stuff like that."

"And you let her?"

Zack shrugged, then grinned. It was a charming, goofy grin that caught Sam by surprise.

When Sam learned that Dana Armstrong had dedicated her life to teaching chimps *not* to be human, he expected to find an emotional mess. He knew she had a Ph.D., but he had once met a wacko who had earned two. When he first saw Dana, he could not believe it was she because *this* woman, even as stressed as he now knew she had been, seemed too competent and self-possessed. Yes, he had cracked her open with a single mention of Annie, but others in the language studies had reacted similarly. As soon as he had seen the conflict etched into her expression—the mixed desires to both shut up and talk, to block out any thoughts of Annie and the inability to do so—he knew he was going to be sucked into the realm she inhabited, that all his energies would go into understanding her. In Dana, he saw a thousand stories.

The phone rang. He rolled onto his back and stretched for it on the end table. "Hello?"

"It's Zack Armstrong. Did you find her at the university?"

Sam pulled himself upright. "Yes." Stretching the cord, he reached for his notebook and pen. "I talked to her."

"And?"

He hesitated. Reginald had said he should not lie to Zack, but he was tempted, just to wriggle his way into the family. "She wouldn't talk to me about Annie."

Zack laughed. "She blew you off."

"That's not true. I'm writing a second article. About the sanctuary."

There was a quick-breath pause before Zack said, "What about finding Annie?"

"I never said anything about finding Annie." He did not want to admit that the idea was smoldering in him, begging his attention, even though he was not sure he wanted to surrender to it. Surely, Dana had already attempted an exhaustive search. "I don't have time anyway."

"The sanctuary is a non-story, asshole. It's the break-in that got you, isn't it? Well, that's a non-story, too. Just some animal rights stuff that went wrong. The real gutsy story is what happened to the chimps who thought they were human."

Sam had to admit Zack had a point, but he felt compelled to make a small story big, instead of running the risk of making a big story trite. "I like your sister," Sam said. "I want to help her out."

"Jesus fucking Christ!" Zack yelled into the phone. "You want to *fuck* my sister! That's what this is about. I swear I'll kill you if you use those chimps to get her into bed."

"I think we're done talking." Without waiting for Zack to launch into another string of obscenities, Sam hung up the phone. Then, to ward Zack off completely, he took it off the hook and laid the receiver on the nightstand.

The Armstrongs, every last one, had burrowed inside him like chiggers, itching, waiting, festering. They each acted so secretive and weird about Annie that Sam had to wonder if they hid one painful secret, or if the memories, scattered differently among them, were too intimate to discuss with a stranger. They each trusted him only within a certain prescribed circle; if he stepped beyond it, they turned on him with vehemence. What was it about living with a chimpanzee that had so complicated them?

—∿∿—

The last person Dana wanted to think about was Sam Wendt. One interview, one shared laugh, one cup of coffee with him, and she could not get him out of her mind. It must be pheromones, she thought, something completely involuntary. He was not her type: too short, not charming enough, too much like Chatu, who, lovable as he was, was a chimpanzee. Still, Sam was with her wherever she went, not coming to mind all the time but occupying space, like a virus waiting to reach a critical threshold. The idea of him was gathering strength even as she told herself not to be so stupidly tempted. Her few post-divorce relationships had been brief and disastrous, and she expected no more of Sam.

She asked Mary, "What do you think of that journalist?"

Mary cocked her head. "As a reporter or as a man?"

Dana blushed as she had not in a long time. "A *person.*"

"He might not make a bad fling. Do you have *time* for anything more serious?"

Mary was throwing her own words back at her. Dana's marriage to Charlie had taught her the cruel lesson of limited energy: you could not be completely devoted to your career and still have a personal life. For two years after her divorce, she had deluded herself into believing she could entertain short-term relationships—*dalliances*, as her mother might call them—that would not infringe on her long work hours. But she soon discovered that men interested in her wanted commitment— Dana was no longer potential one-night-stand material. Her skin, though still supple, had acquired a mottled look; the thin lines of thirty had deepened into definite forty. Even her toned body no longer had the shape of youth: her breasts hung a little, the skin on her arms had more slackness, her buttocks creased where they joined the backs of her thighs. Any man interested in her would not be thinking exclusively of sex; he had to want more. Sam Wendt's attention was in many ways far more dangerous than his curiosity about her family.

Mary took Dana by the shoulders. "You weren't supposed to take me seriously, bozo. Go for it. What are you afraid of? That you'll fall in love?"

Dana had no illusions of that, nor did she want it. When she was in love with Charlie, she had thrown aside intellect for the traditional white wedding gown. All her feminist postmodern idealism disintegrated. She had loved the way Charlie could smile with one side of his mouth, the wild-eyed, crazy look he got when describing his work, the way he absently stroked the back of her neck when they sat next to each other. Those endearing qualities had pushed aside the imperfections.

On their first date, Charlie had brought her a plush gorilla and a single peach tulip. Although he gave her the wrong ape, it hardly mattered because Dana would forever see it as the most romantic moment of her life. She had looked at Charlie head on, taking in his wide smile that dimpled one cheek, his eyes as blue as early-summer sky, memorizing everything.

Hormones and bribery. You could not be held responsible for making mistakes when your body took over. The lusting body found a way to convince the brain, and if it succeeded, you called it love. She hated to think of it that way, but a scientific approach definitely made love, or even sex, easier to avoid. It prevented the aching sadness from taking over and tempered the realization that she had no one to hug at night. The fear she had of a life and death not unlike Benji's. Science could cut the emotion out of the world, and so make some things easier to bear. You could look at a stuffed gorilla and a tulip as a courtship strategy, not as the moment when you first fell in love.

⌒ᴧᴧ⌒

The protesters arrived in the parking lot the next morning around nine. Dana was scurrying around Group A with a bag of fruit over her shoulder, placing bananas and the first oranges of the season around the clearing she had selected for the day, while the students dumped and scattered the bulk of the chimps' breakfast in the center of the enclosure. She hid fruit in the crooks of trees, under bushes, on top of one of the platforms. When she saw the protesters, she waved to them. A few waved back, although as soon as they did, they looked to the others for reassurance, to make sure they had not betrayed the group. She noted that some people sipped from travel mugs, and that a collection of coffee cups had been placed at the base of the tree Barafu had once climbed.

After she finished feeding the chimps, Dana took a pot of fresh coffee to the lot. "Anyone want refills?"

The weekend pharmacist eagerly placed her mug under the spout, but the others hung back until Dana held the pot out to them and they had to either accept or refuse. Those who accepted picked up their cups from under the tree; a few shook out vegetative debris.

"Any questions I can answer today?" she asked as she filled the last cup.

"Yeah." Dana recognized the speaker as someone from Animals Unite. She wondered if Lindsay, who had maintained her support for the SCPP, was aware of this small division. "Why are the fences electrified? Why aren't these chimpanzees in a free habitat, as they were meant to be? Why do you continue to experiment on the chimps?"

Only the last question surprised Dana. "The fences keep the chimps contained, for both their safety and that of the public." She sought out the faces she knew were most concerned with this issue. "The shock doesn't harm them. I'll even touch it myself, to prove it." She strode over to the fence and touched it with her elbow. An unpleasant shock raced from the point of contact to her neck, spreading out its numbing force even after she dropped her arm from the current. "It feels as though I hit my funny bone. Not fun, I admit, but not dangerous either." They had followed her to the fence and now regarded her with different expressions, admiring her but also perhaps unsure of her mental stability. One woman stared at Dana's elbow as though she expected it to drop off. "They cannot live in Africa because they are not wild. And we do *not* experiment on them. Other people have in the past, but not us. We observe. That is all. We make sure they are never experimented on again. Believe me, some of these chimps have come from terrible places."

I know where Annie is.

Dana stayed with the group for over thirty minutes, explaining as best she could the aim of the sanctuary. When she finally excused herself, she was drained.

Mary met her inside the door of the main building. "You are *brilliant*," she said. "The perfect way to defuse the situation. And I'm supposed to be the political one."

Dana could not take credit for something she had done first on a whim. Besides, she was not naive enough to believe the town of Harris had accepted the sanctuary's presence.

～ᴧᴧ～

By early afternoon, the protesters had gone home for the day. Dana sat on the edge of the observation platform, her legs dangling over the side, and watched as Paka twirled a stick in the dirt, his eye on Neema across the clearing. Dana had never before seen this particular method of sexual invitation, but she recognized it at once for what it was: a pickup line, a swagger, a slow swirl of ice cubes in a mixed drink from the far end of the bar. Paka maintained eye contact with Neema, who looked over her shoulder to check the position of Mwenzi before scooting a few feet closer to her suitor.

Mwenzi took a few menacing steps toward Paka. Perhaps because Paka was still new to the group, Mwenzi took exception to his mating with Neema. As though pretending he had not noticed Mwenzi, Paka casually inspected the end of the twig and picked something off it while Neema leaned back to gaze into the treetops. Mwenzi studied first Paka, then Neema, before finally sitting between them, a wary chaperone. Because Mwenzi was the dominant male, his hair stood on end even at rest, giving him a huge, fierce, bristled look that Paka took in with sidelong glances. The other chimps stirred up the needles with their feet and hands and patted each other, as though to assure themselves they were not alone watching the silent confrontation. Mwenzi lazily scratched his cheek, then took a long look over his shoulder at Paka.

After a few tense minutes, Neema walked to Mwenzi and hugged him. Behind Mwenzi's back, Paka waved his twig at Neema, but she ignored him. Instead, she kissed Mwenzi and began a diligent inspection of his face, starting at his brow and moving with light fingertips down the length of his face and then folding his ear so she could see behind it. The edges of Mwenzi's mouth turned up into a quiet smile as he settled into the grooming. Paka tossed his stick to one side and disappeared into the brush. Moments later, he erupted into a noisy temper tantrum in the woods, out of sight but screeching loudly enough to be heard throughout the compound. Mwenzi gave a slight nod of acknowledgment.

Kimbunga, the leader of the neighboring group, would have chased Paka down to engage him in a fierce battle of authority, but Mwenzi knew his point had been made.

Dana wondered if Mwenzi could have tamed Benji. Safe within the enclosure but at the mercy of a chimpanzee hierarchy, could Benji have found a place? Perhaps she had been wrong to assume that his erratic and dangerous behavior would harm the other chimps, that his boxed-out space mimicking that of his previous cage precluded his release into the acres of brush and trees, that danger to humans translated into danger to other chimpanzees. Maybe she should have let the chimps battle it out.

Paka had quieted, though no doubt he was nearby, hoping Mwenzi would let down his guard.

Dana turned on her two-way radio and spoke with a hushed voice. "It's Dana. Is anyone scheduled to go into Group A today?" She waited while Inge, the graduate student in charge of manning the communications that day, scrambled to the radio desk.

Inge's voice sputtered out of the radio. "Barbara and Christopher were scheduled to enter in an hour, but Christopher is sick. Mary is taking his place."

"Have them look for any signs that Paka and Neema are together. Paka is smitten, and Neema looked like she was about to slip away with him until Mwenzi caught on. I'd like them to document Paka's pickup lines."

Inge's laugh cackled through the static. "Copy!"

Although Dana had fun imagining Paka's twig twirling as a pickup line, she knew it was different. Even so, by seeing the biological roots of primate behavior, she could more easily tolerate certain acts and gestures of her own species. She understood the culture of celebrity that had taken over American society since the advent of movies and television; the constant visual presence of performers and sports figures could be likened to the male chimpanzee displays that established dominance. Their size on Jumbotron screens effectively mimicked the piloerection of the male chimp that made him appear much larger than the other males. Of course, humans had a more complex society than did chimps, but the two species were closely related. Brothers and sisters.

Oh, Annie.

Annie never had the freedom Dana and Zack enjoyed. The human children could visit friends, go to the grocery store with their mother, and ride their bicycles up and down the street, while Annie had to keep her tricycle in the backyard with its concrete patio, elaborate playground, and tent, all hidden behind an eleven-foot-tall stockade fence. Once, while roller-skating with the Peaberry kids a few houses down, Dana fell and skidded in the street, the asphalt biting into her knees and the heels of her hands, her chin split as it hit. She ran home screaming, leaving her roller skates in the middle of the street. Annie must have heard her cries because by the time Dana reached the house, Annie was screeching in the backyard. Doug, one of the grad students, flung open the door by the driveway and ran to meet her as Annie scampered next to him. Doug picked Dana up, carrying her to the tent with Annie crying by his side. There, in the humid dankness, Doug and another student (Patricia, was it?) cleaned Dana's cuts while Annie stroked her arms and head, kissed her, pressed her doll against Dana's chest, and tried to fold Dana's arms around it.

Hurt, Annie signed. *Love Dana.*

Get better, Doug signed. *No worry.*

Worry. Love Dana. No want hurt.

Where had her parents been? Had they used the graduate students as babysitters? Or maybe, Dana thought, her mother had been getting bandages and antibiotic cream inside the house while the students and Annie calmed her down. Annie, with her astounding empathy for pain, refused to leave Dana's side even when Doug threatened to lock away her dress-up clothes.

Dana had been allowed to sleep with Annie that night, the smell of chimpanzee as secure as a thumb in her mouth used to be. They had slept with their arms around each other's necks, clinging with dreamy need, the warmth of another body leading them deeper into sleep. Why had it been so surprising to her friends and to graduate students across the country that they had loved each other as sisters?

"You're warped," Charlie had said once, smiling because they were still in love. "Your father doesn't have a clue how he messed you up. Look. You can't even sit still. Just like a chimp."

But Dana could never sit still, even before Annie came into her house. This was the problem of being a famous experiment: you couldn't escape it. Every trait, every choice was forced into a funnel of perception and came out in the same steady stream of clichés. She was who she was, nurture *and* nature.

⌒〜⋀〜⌒

Dana closed the door to her office to work on the budget and expenses of the sanctuary. She hated this part of her job more than anything, but the money saved by not hiring a business manager allowed the staff to feed the chimps an adequate supply of fresh fruits and vegetables instead of relying too heavily on Monkey Chow biscuits. Numbers and columns gave her shivers. They were demons, things she could not fight with ordinary powers. When she heard a knock on her office door, Dana said a silent thank-you for the interruption.

She expected Mary or one of the graduate students, maybe Andy stopping by to give her an update on Tekua, but to her surprise, she found Henry Murray standing there. His wife, Eileen, hung back a few steps.

"Henry! Eileen!" Dana grasped Henry's hand with both of hers, giving him a firm shake before she moved to kiss Eileen's cool, fragile cheek. Dana's affection for the Murrays went beyond their generous endowment to start up the SCPP. She loved the sight of Eileen's tiny neck, the way it held her simple necklaces in the thin-skinned depression above her trachea, and the levelness of her voice, which betrayed only a little her advanced years. Her spine was straight and long but not stiff, and she looked Dana in the eye when they spoke. Henry was more outspoken than his wife, though he generally tempered what he said with diplomacy. His facial structure was the type to look pinched and hard with old age, but he smiled so frequently Dana saw only glimpses of it. He wore brightly colored polo shirts under sports coats, as though he had no need for formalities now that he had made his millions.

"And how is our chimpanzee lady?" Henry asked.

"Fine, thank you."

Eileen cut in with her delicate voice, her purse swaying by the crook of her elbow. "Fine, even with dear old wild Benji gone?"

Oh, Benji. Her days were so busy that she was often able to make it through without thinking of his loss—until, that is, she slipped between her sheets and the creeping night carried new sadness. Zack's snoring presence in the next room sometimes chased it away, making her laugh into her fists at the roaring and snorting. Then she could accept Benji's death for what it was: a moving on, something that never should have happened but had, a moment to touch occasionally and stroke. "We miss him," Dana said. "But the others are keeping us busy."

"I see you have quite a fan club in the parking lot," Eileen said.

Dana shrugged. "They aren't in the way. I understand their concerns, and I think they're beginning to understand mine." She pulled out the only chair for Eileen.

Eileen waved at the chair as though it were a flying insect. "We would like a tour, if you could spare the time."

"We'd like to see how things are since the vandalism." Henry was looking at her in a way Dana had never seen before—a hard, scrutinizing appraisal—and her throat dried, just when she could have used her voice.

She reached for her bottled water and took a soothing sip. "Well, then. Let's go."

The Murrays often dropped by the sanctuary for a tour, but usually they called a day or so in advance. At first, Dana thought little of their surprise visit, but as they conversed about the status of the indoor chimps, Dana began to suspect they had intended to catch her off-guard and that they had already met with Davenport and Washington in Columbia. A tension started to build between Dana and the Murrays until it tasted like chalk in Dana's mouth.

As they stood in front of the nursery's glass wall watching Inge and Vicki romp with the juveniles, Dana said, "This break-in has been a shock for everyone. It's not just that one chimp died—that's bad enough—but that it could have been more."

Henry turned his back to the glass so that he stood squarely in front of Dana, his arms across his narrow chest. Eileen faced the glass, but Dana could see in her reflection that she was listening to them intently and not watching the games on the other side. "I'm concerned," Henry said, "because the culprit had a key."

"Everyone is. We've already had a locksmith change the locks. And we no longer allow the graduate students to take keys home."

"I would sincerely hope you aren't protecting someone. I don't like to be played for a fool."

He was not her boss, but he may as well have been. His money had been crucial to not only the founding of the sanctuary but also to its survival—and to the university as a whole. But the tremor in Dana's chest came from more than professional fear. The sternness in his voice felt like that of a father. In many ways, Henry was more of a father than her own. He liked to give her advice about small things in her life: the loose gutter she mentioned in passing, the kind of tires she should buy, the best restaurants in the state, how to tell the difference between the deadly coral snake and the nearly identical but harmless king snake. He complimented her on her problem solving and remembered trivia about her, such as her preference for Merlot. When he came to visit the sanctuary, he and his wife brought her gifts from their travels: T-shirts, silk change purses, tiny jade earrings, fine chocolates. At first, she had tried to refuse the gifts, but when she saw the need in his eyes to be generous, she could not. Henry and Eileen had been genuinely appreciative of Dana's work at the sanctuary and of who she was, so it wounded her deeply that Henry doubted her integrity. When she answered him, she could not keep the emotion out of her voice. "I would never play you for a fool. And I would hope that you know that."

Eileen turned to join them, and Dana saw the jewel of a tear in the outer corner of one eye. "We know that, dear. It's just . . ." She looked to her husband for help, but he would not meet her gaze. "We have heard some things at various functions. That perhaps . . . that the sanctuary is . . ." She lowered her head and did not go on.

"Is what?" Dana could feel her hurt blooming into anger.

Henry cleared his throat. "Some people have suggested that you haven't always had the welfare of the chimpanzees in mind."

"That's a bunch of b.s.!" She struggled to reign herself in. "No one, *no one*, can accuse me of not having the chimps' best interests in mind. Look at this place. It's a miracle. These chimps were once living in sterile cages, and now they're making their nests in the trees. You of all people should understand the goodness of this place. I've done everything within my power to give them larger lives. If it were up to me, I wouldn't allow *any* kind of research. I would leave them in peace."

Eileen touched Dana's wrist. "Dear, we had to ask. This is our mark in the world. Our legacy. And we want to make sure it is properly cared for."

Dana went to the glass wall and rested her forehead against it. Little Bora saw her and sauntered over, dragging a palm frond behind him. Dana laid her palm on the glass. "It's my legacy, too."

Bora slapped the window playfully, and Dana halfheartedly did the same.

Henry put his hands on both her shoulders. "I'm sorry, Dana. I'm sorry those things had to be said. But we've gotten them out. Addressed them. And now we can be united against whatever comes our way."

Dana turned so he had to drop his hands. "Do you know something I don't, Henry? What would be coming our way?"

He laughed lightly. "Nothing, hopefully. I have ways of ensuring President Davenport's loyalty to the SCPP. He's not a bad man, but he runs scared sometimes. Like most academics, he overthinks. And in his case, money and a snifter of good cognac usually loosen him up, let him see things aren't as dire as he imagines."

Dana clung to the image of President Davenport, a distinguished scholar, being manipulated by Henry Murray. "And how do you butter *me* up?"

"You, you're a little more expensive. For you, I have to bequeath millions of dollars and then some. I have to build you a private jungle. I have to promise you the world."

After the Murrays left, Dana could not bear to return to the SCPP finances, so instead she went into the woods to inspect the perimeter of the enclosures and to check the electric fence for damage and interrupted current. Armed with a voltmeter, wire cutters, insulated gloves, pruning shears, and a coil of sixteen-gauge wire for repairs, she set out. Already, autumn had softened the ground, and the sponginess under her feet felt dangerously unsteady, though it was not. Inside the enclosures, the chimps called to one another. Dana could not help dreaming of Africa, of the opportunity she had missed by concentrating so early in her studies on captive chimpanzees. She could have gone to the Gombe Stream Reserve and witnessed chimpanzees as they were meant to be. Maybe she would have been a better director for it.

She moved quickly through the brush, cutting low branches and bushes that had grown too close to the fencing, marking on a piece of paper those that would eventually have to be downed, testing the fence every twenty feet for electricity. As she paused to slip the pruning shears into her backpack, the hair on her arms stood. Normally, she would have attributed it to a breeze or a strange cry from within the enclosures, but now, with her emotions already heightened, she perceived it as danger. She froze, peered into the woods around her. Then she looked up into the leaves of an oak tree and saw Zack looking down at her. He waved. "Hey, big sister."

"Zack! What the *hell* are you doing up there?"

"Just watching the chimps."

"You can't do that. Where's your car? I didn't see it in the lot."

"I didn't feel like driving. I hitchhiked." He lowered himself from the tree, his sneakers shredding bark like confetti as he descended, and landed with a bounce on the ground. "I figured you'd be busy."

"I am. But you can't do this. Jesus. This is university property. No trespassing. If anybody saw you . . ." Then a sickening feeling came over her, tottering in her stomach. "How often do you come here?"

A thousand pictures and stories flashed across Zack's face—a movie in fast forward, too swift for the naked eye to take it all in. She saw all the times they had been caught doing something wrong—eating in their bedrooms, staying out past curfew, sneaking whiskey out of the liquor cabinet, stuffing dirty clothes under their beds. Dana saw the hole he had burned in the carpet in her and Charlie's house, and her discovery of it, round from the cigarette that had landed there. His face reflected not only the bad times but also the impish ones, when they short-sheeted their grandparents' bed and when they, at twenty-six and twenty-one, pretended to be Czechoslovakian in a Wisconsin diner. Dana could see history there until Zack's face acquired the eerie blankness she so despised. He shrugged. "Two, maybe three times."

And maybe more. Dana could almost hear the smirk behind his words.

EIGHT

Before Dana left for work in the morning, she knelt next to the sofa and tugged on Zack's limp arm.

"Zack?" At first, she had thought he was awake, but now she was not so sure. "Zack?"

"Mmm." He flopped onto his stomach.

The sun had not yet risen—daylight savings time had been revoked over the weekend to make mornings even drearier and longer—and an autumn night chill had squeezed in through the window cracks and the space under the door. She had barely slept, her feet and calves flexed with worry, her shoulders hunched with cold. "I need to talk to you. Before I leave for work."

He pulled the cushion out from under his head, slipping it over his face. "What?" His voice was muffled.

"I need to know something. You've got to tell me the truth."

He groaned, which she took as an encouragement to continue.

"Did you break into the sanctuary and release those chimps?"

"Why the hell would I do that?" He slid the cushion off his face to see her, his eyes only slits, before covering himself again. "Jesus. I would never kill a chimp."

"I didn't say you *killed* Benji. But I need to know whether you opened those cages."

"Drop it, Dana. Okay? Before you piss me off."

"Sam—the writer—is doing a story about the sanctuary, and I'm going to be meeting him again in a few days. I don't want him to uncover something I should've known. Besides that, my boss and other important people will have my head if they think I've protected you. I need to know. I need to hear the truth from you."

He tore off the cushion again and glared at her. "I didn't do it, okay? You don't give a shit about me. *You* don't want to get into trouble."

"I *do* give a shit. You know that." She stroked his arm, which was still hot from deep sleep. "I'm glad you weren't involved. I didn't really think . . . I just had to make sure. Pinkie truce?" She held her little finger a few inches from his face.

He broke into a grin at the mention of their childhood ritual. "Pinkie truce."

They hooked little fingers and gave a gentle tug before separating. She knocked his shoulder once before she stood, stretching. She was feeling girlish, like she should throw herself on the floor with a box of cereal and watch television in the semidarkness, like she should challenge Zack to something, like she should whack him over the head with a pillow to see what he would do.

"Gotta go," she said finally.

"See ya."

Dana slipped on her barn jacket, which hung loosely over her frame. She had already placed her briefcase by the door with her lunch inside, her keys on top of it, everything in order and ready to go. Humphrey wound his lithe body around her ankle, asking her to stay. As Dana bent to pick everything up and to toss Humphrey gently away from the door, Zack said, his voice the clearest it had been that day, like cold rainwater, "Hey, Dana, what would you have done if I said I *had* done it?"

She paused with one hand on the door. "I don't know," she said. "I was hoping you would say what you did." She slipped outside into the soft predawn air.

—⌒ᴧᴧ⌒—

When Dana arrived at the sanctuary, Lindsay Brassett awaited her, perched on the hood of her own truck. Lindsay wore uncharacteristically casual clothes: shorts and a hooded Chapel Hill sweatshirt, tennis shoes with socks that did not even reach her ankles. She tracked Dana's truck like a predator. It was too early for the protesters, and so they were alone in the lot, smiling at each other with recognition as Dana walked toward her.

Lindsay slipped off the hood and onto the ground. "Good morning."

"What are you doing here so early?"

"Waiting for you. I brought coffee." Lindsay swung open the cab door and reached across the front seat, emerging with two large cups wedged in a cardboard to-go beverage tray. "It's not Starbucks, but hey, it's caffeine."

"At this hour, I could take it intravenously." She took the coffee Lindsay offered. "Coming in?" She took a sip from the cup. The liquid scalded her lips, tongue, and throat as it went down. "Ow. You haven't been waiting long."

"Just got here, in fact."

Inside the main building, while Lindsay rolled one palm over her cup and watched, Dana checked on the chimpanzees and their cages before unlocking her office door and gesturing for Lindsay to follow. Once inside, Dana hesitated. It seemed wrong to sit behind the desk in such a formal, authoritative position, but she had only two chairs. Reluctantly, she took her own seat as Lindsay lowered herself into the other. Dana removed the lid from the coffee and blew on the surface. "Well?"

"Well?"

Dana laughed. She knew Lindsay hated to be hurried. She used to think Lindsay appreciated the slow unfolding of conversation but recently had decided Lindsay needed to structure, word for word, the politics of a difficult subject. "You have to admit it's unusual seeing you this time of day. It's unusual for me to see *anyone* before seven-thirty."

"The sanctuary has an eerie elegance this early, doesn't it?"

"Unless the chimpanzees are loose. Then you have an eerie chaos."

Lindsay smiled behind her paper cup, then took a small sip. "I can imagine."

"Are the police still bothering you? I was under the impression they had dropped the matter. Or at least pushed it to one side. They don't exactly have a wealth of evidence. Or do you know something I don't?"

"I heard a rumor you might be interested in."

"Oh?" Dana wanted to cut through the politeness with huge shears, but she restrained herself. Because her coffee had finally cooled a bit, she waited out the silence by drinking.

Finally, Lindsay had formed what she wanted to say. "You've heard of Dick Lamier?"

Even now, that name and the images it evoked made her insides cold and dead. "Yes," Dana said, fighting not to recall his smell of musk cologne and dog. "He taught at Brown for a while. My father's former colleague."

"I'll venture a guess and say he doesn't like you."

"Probably not." Dana swallowed, sorting through the words as though they were crumbling bricks, heavy and hard to grasp. At first, the logic was hard to follow. Then, as her mind, maddeningly slow, rebuilt the line of conversation, she began to see where Lindsay was headed. "You heard he had something to do with the break-in?"

"Well, not directly. And mind you, this is only a rumor. He has been making noise about your lack of qualifications to run a sanctuary. And he believes your congressional funding should be revoked because you allow research on the chimps."

"Research *on* the chimps?"

Lindsay smiled wryly. "That's what I heard."

"Who the hell would listen to Dick Lamier?" But Dana knew who: everyone. He had become a huge force in primatology, and she had spent part of her career trying to dodge him. Although he was aligned more with the psychologists—who saw chimps as models for human behavior—than the anthropologists—who studied them as a separate culture—their paths crossed occasionally at conferences. If Lindsay was right about Lamier, it explained why the break-in and subsequent liberation of the chimps had focused attention on Dana, instead of on the culprit. "How did you find out about this?"

"A friend called me last night. She wanted to know about the SCPP. What I knew."

"Lamier is an instigator," Dana said dryly. *I know where Annie is.* The words were as fresh in her mind as though they had just been spoken. *I know where Annie is.* "But I doubt he has the balls to do something as illegal as releasing chimps. Or even to organize it. He probably was hoping your friends would do it for him." As soon as she said the words, she could not let them go. She thought of the few members of Animals Unite who protested each day. "Your friends didn't, did they?"

"I don't think so. I don't know." Lindsay fidgeted with the cup still in her hands. Her eyes flitted up to the photographs on the wall, from chimp to chimp, then back to Dana. "I don't think so. Most of my friends aren't so radical. They can accept what you do. But there *are* others . . ."

It pained Dana, as always, to be reminded that some people viewed what she did as animal cruelty. She never minded being called a wacko or a tree hugger, or even being accused of loving animals more than people, because that kind of misunderstanding was common in America. What hurt most were the criticisms from people more closely aligned to her own thinking, groups she expected to be sympathetic. She did not *choose* to hold chimpanzees in captivity, but someone else had. All she could do was remedy what had already gone wrong.

Lindsay leaned across the desk and laid one hand over Dana's. Dana looked down, bewildered. "I'm worried about you," Lindsay said. "I wanted you to know you have an enemy."

"Thank you," Dana said. "Lamier has been my enemy since I was sixteen. He's appearing yet another time, like the serial killer in a horror movie."

She must have said this lightly because Lindsay laughed. "Well, now you know who's hiding behind the hockey mask."

Dana forced a smile despite the dread washing over her again, the tears threatening to break free any moment. *I know where Annie is.* As she walked Lindsay to the parking lot, she chatted about small topics—

about the weather, of course, but also about Lindsay's dogs and the new house someone was building in Harris—as though Lindsay's news meant nothing to her. But as soon as Dana turned to go back into the building, her vision blurred with pooling tears. *I know where Annie is. I can take you there.*

She was not sure she could make it back into her office without sobbing. When Lindsay's car popped and scraped over the gravel, Dana did not turn, did not wave, could barely hold her head up. No one in South Carolina could understand the breaking of her heart, the splintering of it into thousands of bitter shards. Only her parents knew, and then only her father fully understood the torture Lamier had exacted on her soul. But Dana could not bear to call her father. Too much had passed between them. Her footsteps sounded hollow; she had lost substance.

The chimps were quiet. The birds stopped singing all at once, and even the buzzing insects took a pause. Dana stopped on the threshold. *Goddamn Lamier.* She could not draw breath, and her heart shimmered in her chest. *Oh, God, Lamier, you asshole.* Her recollections threatened to crumple her to the ground, but she forced herself to keep walking. She hated Lamier more than ever for doing this to her, for sucking all the resolve out of her, for making her weak here, at work, the place where she usually felt the strongest. Nature jump-started its noise with a chimpanzee shriek, followed by the distant knocking of a woodpecker, a serenade of wrens and finches, the angry click of a squirrel. She fingered the ring of keys in her pocket. Instead of continuing into the building, she veered toward the enclosures.

~\\\~

Dana had been sixteen years old and a junior in high school the year Dick Lamier was granted tenure at Brown, but he had been a fixture in their house before that, ever since his arrival in Providence. He regularly ate Sunday dinner with the Armstrong family. Reginald liked Lamier's wit, his work ethic, his uncanny ability to pull in grants. Lamier did not have a wife or family in the area, only a large English boxer called Bert. Reginald told his family that it was their job to make Lamier feel at home in Rhode Island, so he would not take his brilliance elsewhere and leave

Reginald without an ally in the psychology department.

Sometimes, Dana liked Lamier. Sometimes, she found him annoying. He knew what to say to her when she felt left out, when she started to pick a fight with her mother or father, when she felt suddenly awkward and exposed, the way teenage girls do. Sometimes, though, he laughed at her naiveté, which she hated more than anything. She craved Lamier's attention, then despised it when she got it. Her mother was always saying what an attractive man Lamier was—and he was, in a square-framed, dimpled-chin sort of way. Although he was not tall, he had an aura of maleness and strength, and hazel eyes that flashed yellow, like glitter. Dana never found him handsome, though—she thought the hair at the base of his neck was disgusting. Later, she would wonder why that had bothered her, since she had an early affinity for the fully hairy chimpanzees. Once, Lamier had drunk too many glasses of her parents' cheap white wine, and Dana had caught him staring at her, his mouth drunkenly slack. As he met her gaze, he flicked his tongue, once, over his lips. Dana turned away, embarrassed, feeling as though she had seen something she should not have.

To celebrate his tenure, Lamier bought himself a red Mustang that roared magnificently into the Armstrongs' driveway. The whole family came out to see the car. Zack, who loved cars so much that, at eleven, he was already saving up for his own, met it with a shout. Zack raced around to the passenger door and slipped inside, pleading, "Take me for a spin, Dick! Please!" The way Zack said it sounded so funny that everyone laughed.

Lamier said, "Go ahead, Reggie. Take your son for a spin." He tossed the keys to Dana's father with an ease Reginald would never have had. Dana's father always fumbled with his keys. She marveled then about the differences between the two men, one a boring, intellectual father and the other a boisterous, daring man. Dana must have looked at Lamier with a new, appreciative glint because he winked at her. Later, when they were alone in the dining room folding paper napkins into triangles, Lamier said quietly to her, "I have a surprise for you, Dana Doll."

Dana blinked. No one had called her Dana Doll since the days of Annie, when the graduate students had coined the nickname. It was a babyhood name, something she had left in Oklahoma. "What?" She kept her voice low because he had.

He leaned so close to her that his lips brushed her ear, sending goose bumps everywhere. She could smell his dog. "I know where Annie is," he whispered. "I can take you there. But you can't tell anyone."

At the sound of Susan's footsteps nearing, he moved a few feet away and slipped a napkin under a fork, centering the utensil so it lay perfectly between points. Dana was so shocked she could not move, even when her mother stood across from her with her hands on her hips.

"Are you in dreamland again?" her mother asked.

"Yeah," Dana said. She willed herself not to look at Lamier. She had not yet processed his words beyond the barest bones of them; they clanked in her head almost without meaning, even though she could feel their heft. Annie was alive. That was all she could understand.

That night, as she lay in bed staring at the patterns the moonlight made through the blinds, she considered what Lamier had said. *I know where Annie is. I can take you there.* Not only was Annie alive, but she was nearby. Lamier had the power to take her to Annie, to let them hug, to give Dana the opportunity to beg forgiveness. She imagined Annie living with another family, perhaps even another one in the psychology department whose members were willing to put up with a strong-willed chimpanzee. Annie would be an adult now, maybe even a mother. Dana could not sleep from the excitement. But how would Lamier whisk her away without her family knowing? Had Lamier perhaps interpreted her stupid muteness as disinterest? She vowed to find a moment when she could get him alone and say yes.

The next Sunday, Lamier slipped her a piece of paper rolled like a slender cigarette. The paper hidden in her palm, she excused herself and locked the bathroom door. Carefully, sitting on the toilet lid, she unrolled the paper on her thigh. *Cut school on Thursday. Meet me at the corner of Thayer and Waterman: 8 A.M.*

Dana's face burned; she hid it even from herself by not looking in the mirror. She had never cut school. And the corner of Thayer and Waterman was so visible—she would be seen for sure. It hardly mattered that her friends had been cutting classes since the fall and had told her impatiently that it was no big deal, that everyone did it. Sitting there on the toilet, holding her hot face with two hands, Dana started shaking. She feared that if she stood, she would faint and crack her head on the pink porcelain sink.

When she finally emerged from the bathroom, everyone was seated at the table, passing food and laughing. Dick Lamier's eyes settled on her, and she gave him a little nod, which he acknowledged with a smile before slicing open the baked potato on his plate.

"You okay, hon?" Susan asked, laying a hand on her daughter's forehead as Dana sat. "You're warm."

"Maybe I'm coming down with something." Then, finding a stronger voice, she added, "But maybe I'm just hungry."

On Thursday, Lamier picked her up on time, much to Dana's relief. He must have been circling the block so she would not have to stand there in full view of her father's students as they slunk to breakfast and classes. He reached across to unlock the door, and she slipped in, slouching in the vinyl bucket seat. The Mustang had a feral growl to it, and Lamier drove with the windows open. As they sped down the highway, Dana's hair whipped as it never had in a car; her father hated a breeze. Soon, she was laughing at Lamier's jokes and finding him not at all a pain in the ass but a man worthy of respect, maybe even as good looking as her mother claimed. As long as she did not look at the back of his collar, she felt comfortable with him flying down the highway.

"Where are we going?" she asked.

"Massachusetts. About two hours from here. To a medical facility."

She knew nothing then of medical laboratories, so she settled down into the seat, smiling, deep into her own thoughts. In the days leading up to the trip, she had prepared herself for the possibility that Annie might not remember her, but she planned to remind her with the bits of sign language she could recall. *Love. Annie. Home. Happy.*

The medical laboratory gleamed like white marble (though when she got closer, she would see it was merely concrete catching the glint of the sun) and sat low among the rolling hills. Lamier graciously opened the car door for Dana, who was too excited to do anything but fumble with the handle. The air there seemed cooler, almost cold. Lamier placed one hand on her shoulder as they walked toward the front entrance. The hush of pine boughs lent a stateliness to the setting, and Dana thought what a magnificent place it was for Annie to inhabit, if she could not be home with her family.

The security guard at the front desk had their names on his clipboard. "All set," the guard said as Lamier clipped Dana's visitor badge to her shirt just over her breast.

Before they entered a doorway, Lamier took Dana by the shoulders. "It's going to be noisy, okay? The chimps don't know you. Are you ready?"

They walked down corridors, turned, entered doors, and finally met with a technician Lamier called Theresa, who handed them surgical masks and opened the door for them.

Dana stepped into a chaos that reeked of urine, feces, vomit, sweat, and cloying antiseptic. Rows and rows of chimps started screaming and pounding their cages. Handfuls of feces rocketed out from between the metal tubular bars. Long, scrawny arms, some bald as though human, clawed at the air beyond their reach. She backed into Lamier's solid body.

His hand lingered at the back of her neck as he slipped around her. "Here. Follow me."

Covering her ears, she walked the narrow corridor behind him, trying to focus on his broad back so she would not see anything else. The numbered cages were stacked two high, and every one held a chimpanzee. Metal trays filled with waste sat underneath each, and the chimps could easily reach down to their store of fecal ammunition. Dana's stomach cramped, and a thin, watery sweat broke out at the back of her neck. A fresh clump of feces hit her leg below the knee. *Don't pass out, don't pass out,* she told herself. Some of the chimps lay sprawled on the bottoms of their cages, their teeth bared but their bodies unable to threaten more. Six cages in the middle of the corridor held chimps whose heads had been split open and sewed up like baseballs, the skin raw and rimmed with blackened blood.

How had she done this to Annie? Her heart was desperate with prayers begging for forgiveness.

"Here we are," Lamier said. With his hands, he turned her to face a cage that held a raging female who gripped the bars with both hands and feet and rattled the small cage by swinging and swaying, slamming it with her body. Her mouth was drawn into a toothless grimace—either her front teeth had been pulled or she had lost them. Her complexion was mottled, and her dark eyes bulged with hatred.

Dana saw two horrifying things: the chimp was not Annie, and an angry, blood-red scar split the chimp's torso in half. Dana backed up into Lamier again, only this time he held her, spinning her around so she could hide in his shirt as he clutched her tightly. As her masked face pressed against Lamier, his musky, human scent mercifully overrode all others.

"It's not her!" Dana sobbed into his chest. "She's not Annie!"

"Are you certain?"

"Get me out of here!"

The shrieking, the feces, the puckered, bloody scars, the derangement in the eyes of the chimps, the desperation and rage tangible in the close air, the imprisonment of these individuals: could this really have been Annie's punishment for stealing Halloween candy? As Lamier guided her out of the housing area, Dana knew it not only could have been but was. Although the chimp she had seen was not Annie, Annie was somewhere, living the same life—if she was alive at all. The grief weakened her knees and throbbed in her chest. She prayed that Annie had died rather than having to experience what she had just seen.

Dana did not know how they emerged into the glaring sunshine of the parking lot. The fresh air rushed into her lungs, but her nostrils still burned with the lab, imprinting everything where she would never forget. They threaded their way through the cars in the lot, zigzagging toward Lamier's, and still Dana could not reign in her tears. The anarchy she had witnessed was too complete. When they reached Lamier's car, he let her fall back against the door for support.

"Oh, I'm so sorry, Dana," he murmured. "They told me it was Annie. Are you sure it wasn't? Chimps' faces darken when they mature. They change. Like humans."

She shook her head.

He traced the tears on her cheek with his finger. "I'll find her. I promise. I'll keep looking. Oh, Dana Doll." The last words barely out of his mouth, he bent down and kissed her eyelid. She could barely feel him, was not even sure it happened, until he kissed her cheek, her neck, her lips, gently at first, then with an urgency that frightened her. She tried to push him away, but he kept kissing her, stroking her, his hand finding the outer contour of her breast.

"No . . . no."

"It's okay," he whispered. "I'll take care of you."

He pressed his body against hers. The hard ridge of his erection startled her. She could not think, could not act. The chimps, the grief, *this*. And the harsh light of the sun blinding her. Could anyone see them? The rows of cars partially obscured them, and even then, would anyone care? This place where chimpanzees were split open and sewn back together like stuffed animals had no hope. She could not expect rescue in such a hell. It was the edge of the earth, where people, animals, things fell off without a trace into an unforgiving abyss. You could not crawl back from such a place. Her tears no longer meant anything, even as they rushed out of her eyes and etched her face with their hot salt.

No, no, no, she repeated to herself, but his lips so hard against hers prevented the words from reaching the air. She could not move against his bulk.

Then she glimpsed, as he forced her head slightly to one side, the hair at his collar. Later, she would not understand why this affected her, especially after what she had witnessed only minutes before. Maybe it was the last disgust, however small, she could hold. Her stomach turned instantly sour, the bile rising in her throat. Lamier must have smelled its approach because he allowed her head to go free just as she needed to turn it. She vomited onto the asphalt, and it splattered onto Lamier's lower leg. Cursing, he leapt backwards.

At first, she was mortified she had almost vomited into his mouth, but when Lamier made no other move to kiss her, she realized he kept his distance because of the rankness emanating from her.

She was clinging to the edge she believed she had fallen off.

"I'll get you home," he told her, not unkindly. He did not seem to take her throwing up personally.

Nodding, she wiped her mouth with the back of her hand and got into the car.

Dana no longer remembered much of what was said on the return trip, except that Lamier did most of the talking while she tried to smile and seem agreeable, anything to get her safely home. Lamier periodically reached over to tap her knee, saying, "Don't give up hope, okay? I'll find her." Perhaps she sniffled like a child, just a little, to make him interrupt his train of thought to reassure her. She hoped he had not kidnapped her, that he would not kill her. No one knew where she had gone. She imagined her body found mangled at the base of a ravine. As frightening as that image was, she considered it a just punishment.

As they neared the row of historical houses on Benefit Street where Lamier said he would drop her off, he gave her leg another pat, this time higher up. "We have to keep this our secret. Your father will try to stop us from finding Annie. You know that, don't you? The only way we can do this is as a team. Just the two of us."

Her freedom from Lamier was tantalizingly close. The car had slowed enough so she could imagine only bruises and small cuts if she were to leap out the door. But she was afraid to jump, so she forced a smile and said, "Okay." Then, fearing that it sounded as though she never expected to see him again, she added, "I'll see you Sunday."

The broad smile that deepened the cleft in his chin betrayed his relief. He *knew* he had wronged her. He had waited to see if he could get away with it. "See you Sunday."

When she walked into the house, she smelled him on her skin, in her hair; she tasted him in her mouth with the bile. She ran into the bathroom, where, behind the locked door, she brushed her teeth until her gums bled, spitting the foam like cherry pits into the sink, and then scrubbed her face with scalding water and biting soap that burned her eyes. She wanted to tear her hair out in clumps to get to her brain, where the disturbing images resided.

Her mother knocked on the door. "Dana? Why aren't you in school?"

Dana had forgotten about the timing. She had been so anxious to wash Lamier off her that she had come home a half-hour before school let out. This final humiliation was too much. If only she *could* disappear. With her hands twisted in her hair, she climbed into the bathtub, curled up there, and rocked back and forth. The tub was smooth and cool and let her slip into a ball at the bottom. If she had the energy, she would have reached up to turn on the faucet to cover herself with scalding water, but the effort seemed too great. Instead, she lay there, willing herself into a cold, rocking trance, her head banging on the porcelain, though she felt no pain, falling deeper and deeper into herself so she would not have to hear her own cries for Annie, for what was lost, for what she had done.

Her mother must have picked the lock because she burst in as Dana mumbled and cried at the bottom of the bathtub. Dana was already larger than her mother, so as strong as Susan was from hauling boxes of books for the bookmobile, she could not lift her daughter. "I'm calling your father," Susan said.

By the time Reginald arrived home, Susan had swabbed Dana's face with a cool washcloth and combed her long hair into a silky ribbon that lay across one shoulder and fell comfortingly along her jawbone and neck. As her father strode in, Dana had enough strength to struggle upright. She informed her parents that Lamier had told her to cut school so he could take her to see Annie.

"That place was horrible. The chimps were crazy and screaming, and they stank. Annie wasn't even there!" She looked into her father's eyes and saw that he knew exactly what she had seen because he had been somewhere like that before. She could read some of her own pain in his face, her disgust mirrored back, her horror. "I was crying, and then . . ." She had to tell, though she could not find her voice. So she buried her face in her hands and said into their magnifying cup, "And then he kissed me."

The tension was immediate and furiously restrained, the kind of atmosphere where everything wanted to break loose but could not because people were trying hard not to let it. When Dana found the courage to look up, her parents had identical faces—ashen and old. They could not look at each other; they could barely look at Dana. Finally, Susan, speaking in her gentle sickbed voice, said, "Honey, did he do more than that? Did he . . . ?"

Dana shook her head. "He couldn't," she said. "Because I threw up on him."

The startled pause toppled the room's tension. Susan broke into a laughter that had an uneasy edge but still sounded wonderfully relieved, even joyous. As she stroked Dana's hair, tears squeezed from Susan's eyes and smeared her cheekbones. "Oh, Dana, thank you!"

Even Reginald managed a thin smile, but behind it, his teeth were clenched. Dana imagined she would never break through that false smile, not even on her father's dying day. Seeing how impenetrable he was at that moment nearly made her cry again, but she looked away just as his expression became unbearable. Susan asked if she was ready to leave the bathtub, and Dana nodded. She ventured another glance at her father, who had started to leave.

At the doorway, one hand on the frame, Reginald paused. "He knew Annie wasn't there. He knew damn well."

Lamier never again appeared in his Mustang driving up to the Armstrongs' house, never ate dinner with them again, left Brown soon after, was not seen again by Dana until many years later. Zack demanded to know what had happened to him, but Susan set her jaw in her no-nonsense way and said, "He's busy. Professors get busy."

Although Dana did not like to think about that day, certain things occurred to her later that disturbed her almost as much as the events themselves. That Lamier was allowed to walk into the medical facility and go unattended into the chimpanzee room, that he knew his way through the polished white hallways, that he knew the lab technician by her first name—all of this meant he had not only been there before but *belonged* there. Most likely, he consulted for the lab to supplement his academic salary. And if he worked there, then he knew the chimpanzee he had brought Dana to see was not Annie, just as her father had said. Lamier had calculated and orchestrated. *I know where Annie is. I can take you there.* He fully expected the shock of what she had seen to propel her into his arms.

NINE

*D*ana unlocked the first door leading to the two enclosures and, once she had secured it again behind her, opened the next door, this one leading into the Group B enclosure. She shivered in the early-morning air. She always imagined that entering one of the enclosures was like going back in time, or to another world, or to a place that disallowed all the gritty, life-sapping realities that hounded her. She could cry there if she wanted, and no one would know. She went deep into the enclosure, following the path leading to what the staff called "the Rock."

The Rock was a large slab mysteriously deposited on the land; it stood about four feet high and had a small ledge like a seat on the side facing away from the compound of buildings. The Group B chimps used its flat top as a pounding stone to crack the pecans they plucked from a nearby tree; Dana and Mary used it whenever they believed the walls of their offices too thin for privacy. Its location put it far enough from the platforms and deep enough into the brush to make an ideal hiding place. Nothing on the South Carolina land belonging to the sanctuary resembled the Rock; it was an anomaly, something that just *was*. If it weren't for the Rock and its privacy, Dana doubted she would visit Group

B as much as she did. Like a bad teacher, Dana had favorites, and Group B was not hers. The two outdoor groups had distinct personalities, perhaps because of the tone set by the dominant members, perhaps because of human selection, however unintended. Group A was more gregarious, its squabbles brief and soothed by forgiving embraces. The females had established an unmistakable alliance that Dana had seen used against some of the weaker males. Mwenzi, the dominant male, was loving and generous despite his displays. Group B, on the other hand, seemed to have less cohesion. Dana rarely saw more than three chimps together at any one moment; the friendships in that group seemed less steady and more fluid. The dominant male, Kimbunga, ruled solely by intimidation and force.

Dana was deeply ashamed of her preference and had never mentioned it to anyone, not even Mary, though it must have been obvious. She *should* have loved all the chimps equally; she was in essence their protector, the person responsible for the richness, or lack of it, in their lives.

Today, three Group B females lounged on top of the Rock: old, overweight Tumbo; the quietly deceptive Mazigazi; and a chimp Dana suspected of being Mazigazi's sister, Sala. They looked at Dana, their eyes brightening. Mazigazi sauntered to the edge of the rock and offered her hand. With her scarred hand, Dana took Mazigazi's and panted on it, keeping her strong hand against her pocket holding the keys, in case Mazigazi tried anything. Sure enough, Mazigazi attempted to slip her hand undetected to Dana's shorts. When the two touched, Mazigazi screamed as she realized she had been caught. "You sneaky devil, you," Dana said, playfully slapping Mazigazi chimp-style. Mazigazi shrieked in return. Both Sala and Tumbo then came over to greet Dana with pant-grunts and bows. Once the formalities were over, Dana sat down on the ledge below the chimps, her back against the cold, damp rock, and the chimps resumed their stretched-out, lazy positions. The newly lit morning sky revealed nothing of what lay beyond the gray fog blocking out what was above: sunny sky or gloomy clouds. If only there were intense light, Dana thought; she needed light. Digging the heels of her boots into the spongy ground, she closed her eyes, shivering.

Lamier could do far more damage to her career and the sanctuary than her brother could, so if he was involved, she was in for a sickening ride. Lamier had written three books, reviewed journal papers and grants, sat on national committees, testified before Congress. His network of comrades stretched into every corner of primatology. How could she possibly defend herself? By now, the rumor he started could have a life of its own, with embellishments and modifications that even Lamier at his most nefarious could not have dreamed up.

Goddamn Lamier.

Branches cracked near the path, and Dana, opening her eyes, straightened. She sensed the same alertness in the three chimps on top of the Rock. Mary appeared, stepping into the small clearing.

"Oh, you're here," Mary said. "I wondered where you were."

"You heard Mazigazi and knew exactly where I was."

"Maybe." Mary sat next to her. "You look terrible. Did something happen?"

Dana peered into the familiarity of Mary's face: the polished skin, the hooded Asian eyes, the firm but forgiving mouth, the beauty of the bone structure, how it looked carved out of soft stone. She saw in Mary's searching expression someone who could understand her torment then, her anxiety now. Mary knew her complexities.

"We have a problem," Dana began. "An enemy."

Mary sat on the seat of the Rock and listened to Dana's story about what had happened with Lamier when she was sixteen. Dana was surprised at the relief she felt finally telling someone, especially someone who knew Lamier's reputation and who had read his articles, perhaps even at times believed him infallible—and yet who could still believe Dana.

"Oh, Dana," Mary said. "I really don't know what to say."

Dana took a long, deep breath, but it could not erase the frown that creased her chin.

Old Tumbo had been watching them. Grunting, she clambered over the edge of the Rock, slipped into Dana's lap, and wrapped her arms around Dana, kissing her. Sala and Mazigazi scampered close behind Tumbo, and as Tumbo moved toward Mary to give her a hug, too, they descended upon Dana with eager fingers to pick at her clothes and hair, to stroke her.

"They know you're sad," Mary said.

Dana reached out to touch Mazigazi's muscular arm.

Mary shook her head. "He exploited your weakness. I can't believe he took advantage of you like that."

"I talked to Lindsay today. It seems that maybe he's gearing up for another assault. He's been stirring up rights activists with stories about how we've exploited the chimps. He seems bent on discrediting me, and by extension the SCPP."

"You're kidding, right?" When Dana did nothing more than meet her eyes, Mary's whole demeanor changed. Her face folded into hard, stubborn lines, and she kicked the ground hard with the heel of her boot. "Don't you *dare* let him get away with this. You don't win battles by being nice. And you're sometimes too nice, Dana, too compassionate and empathetic."

Mary had never seen the way she fought with Charlie for personal territory, word by mean word. "Trust me. I know how to fight."

"You have to be *brash*. Hey, I studied to be brash, and I'm proud of it. My grandparents wanted my parents to bring me up as a good Japanese girl—demure, obedient, studious. Except I was American. We were all American, the hell with our ethnicity. Yeah, I wanted good grades, but no way was I going to end up like Hannah Hiyami, who stood at the edge of the playground with her only friend when everyone else played kickball. If you want to be a leader, you can't be demure. You've got to get in the game and get your knees skinned."

"I'm not going to give up. You know me well enough to know that."

Mary nodded. "I always regarded Lamier as a primatology god. And *you* never said anything. You even sat in the back of my class when I was teaching his comprehensive studies on chimpanzee behavior. How they sought to explain the seeds of human violence and politics, the origins of language, the way the human mind might develop. You could have come up to me afterward and said, 'Hey, this guy isn't all what he seems.'"

"That wouldn't have been fair."

"I thought I was your friend. Not just a colleague." Tumbo had moved over to groom Mary, and she returned the favor. "You could've trusted me."

"I do trust you. Why else would I tell you now? Other than you and my parents, no one knows about my history with Lamier. Not even my brother. I want to keep it that way."

Mazigazi, who was always fascinated with human hands and feet, began a diligent inspection of Dana's wrist. The mood had grown more tranquil with the mutual grooming. Dana felt the first stirrings of strength. She had worked too long and too hard to allow Lamier to destroy the sanctuary. She did not know how she could live without private moments like this, sitting among the chimpanzees, touching them and being touched, when once they had been confined to cages. What kind of a primatologist was Lamier anyway, for wanting to take this from the chimps?

Hooting broke out, and the trees around them shook with chimpanzees. The three females on the Rock lifted themselves upright on two legs, their eyes and ears searching, then finally concentrating on a heavy rustling in the bushes. Chimps, some of whom had been resting invisibly in the trees and others who arrived screeching and shaking branches, filled the brush and trees around them just as alpha Kimbunga pushed his way through the bushes. Sala and Mazigazi rushed to greet him, though others stayed back, justifiably uneasy in his presence. Kimbunga accepted the few greetings before pushing roughly to where Mary and Dana were. The humans pant-grunted their acknowledgment of him and his dominance, and he seemed to accept their rudimentary gestures. Tumbo bounced up and down, bowing to him, but her obesity slowed her, making her look awkwardly foolish in front of this male chimp, who merely glanced at her, dismissing her presence.

Dana pointed to Kimbunga, who had started to rock. "He's gearing up for a display. We'd better get out of here."

Kimbunga's hair stood on end, bristling, enlarging him even further, giving his small face a ferocity that always stopped Dana's heart for a beat. The chimps nearest to him, including Tumbo, scurried away and climbed high into the trees, whimpering, their faces stretched in anticipatory fear. Dana and Mary backed away slowly, so as not to provoke him. As he raised his arms high over his head, flailing, and leapt with such alacrity that he went from the top of the Rock to the forest floor in a blink, they ran full speed out of the clearing, stopping only when they could hear him drumming against tree trunks and cracking branches without getting any closer.

Out of breath, they started to laugh, but that only made them more breathless, and they wheezed, ludicrously synchronized, as Dana unlocked the door leading out.

"What a monster he is," Dana said as they slipped into the holding area between the two exits.

Mary had her own keys out and was unlocking the second door. "Who? Kimbunga or Lamier?"

Dana smiled. "Don't insult Kimbunga."

They stood for a few moments outside, getting their emotional bearings and catching their breath. Inge and Barbara trudged down the trail toward them with a crate of vegetables that must have arrived while Dana and Mary were inside.

"May we go in yet?" Inge asked, flipping her blond braid out of the lettuce.

"Sure," Dana said. "Kimbunga is winding down a display, so go into Group A first. I'll go up and get another crate."

As Dana trekked up the path, she wanted to spit out Lamier's name, to rid herself of him. Her vision had a clarity she had lacked for several weeks, the leaves sharply defined into curved and serrated edges, the gravel a thousand shades of gray, the lines of perspective focusing into a single, hard point on the horizon—the edge of anger.

In the following days, Dana did not have time to dwell on the idea of Lamier. If she had, she might have sat down among the cypress knees rising like hard ghosts out of the ground and not gotten up again. First, she dealt with the USDA inspectors who descended upon the SCPP, and then with the preparations to introduce several chimps to larger social groups. Kitabu was already proving to be the most difficult. When Dana took the young chimp, naked and without her human toys, into the nursery, Kitabu screamed and clung to her. Other than a brief interaction with extroverted Marika, Kitabu refused to join her own kind. Dana emerged exhausted and unsure of her ability to succeed, despite the preliminary USDA report exonerating the SCPP of any wrongdoing.

The protesters dwindled to a rotating crew of five or six that always harbored at least one truly hostile face. Dana had learned their names: Sue Ellen the pharmacist, Jack the unemployed paper-mill employee, Betsy the mother of three, Juniper the recent college graduate. They were the hardy protesters, the ones who did not care that they waved signs at the same ten people every day, that their protest site had been ill thought out, since they had no sympathetic witnesses, no public. Dana had to admire them for hanging on.

"I figured you'd run out of questions by now," Dana told them. "Or are you coming just for the coffee?"

All but one—Harold, the SCPP's nearest neighbor to the west— laughed. Harold's expression had never softened toward her, and he never accepted coffee. "We want you out of Harris," he said. "Completely."

"Well, that doesn't leave much room for compromise."

"The university is hiding what's going on here. I don't like it, and I don't trust you. You aren't telling us the whole story."

Dana regarded him carefully. Although the issue of safety had galvanized the citizens of Harris, what kept them coming varied from individual to individual: some were concerned about the well-being of the chimps, some continued to be uneasy about public safety, some did not like the idea of semiwild animals in their midst. Harold had just identified himself as part of the conspiracy theory faction. He was not a crackpot, just someone who did not trust electric fences and unmarked entrances. "Why don't you volunteer to work here for a couple of hours a week?" Dana asked. Before Benji's release, she never would have suggested pulling in volunteer workers from the community. "You could see for yourself what goes on."

Harold narrowed his eyes, and Dana guessed he was trying to calculate her motives.

"We're here protesting, not looking for something to do," middle-aged Betsy said. "Who do you think we are?"

"I don't know," Dana said. "I don't know you any better than you know me. But because you're here, I can only assume we have the same goals in mind: to keep the community safe and to protect the chimpanzees."

They stared at her, their signs tipping in their hands at awkward angles.

Dana knew they were so shocked by the apparent convergence of interests that they could not find the hole in her logic, though it was there, gaping and yawning. The question was not *what* they all wanted but *how* they believed they should get there, not the end but the means, the *way* to arrive at the same goal. Eventually, they would see this, but perhaps by then they would understand her position enough to accept it.

—⁓⁓—

A spider had bitten Zack on the thigh, though he could only guess it was a spider, having discovered the hive long after the culprit had vanished or been squashed by his rolling over it in the middle of the night. The bite raised a red, hard welt that itched not only on the surface but deep within the flesh where he could not reach. He clawed at it through his jeans. Sometimes, he slapped it so hard his whole thigh stung. The itch was constant and contagious, putting him on edge and giving him a hunger for everything: food, sex, drugs, the rough texture of sandpaper as well as the cool smoothness of silk.

"I have some cortisone cream," Dana said as she took the vacuum cleaner out of the small closet off the living room. "Or put an ice cube on it."

"Dammit!" He slapped his leg with such force that he could feel he might have bruised himself. And still, the itching lingered.

"You aren't having any trouble breathing, are you?"

"Do I fucking look like I'm having trouble breathing?"

"Then stop fucking whining." Dana bent her head over the vacuum cleaner, unwrapping the cord. She had come home from work pissed, and now she had to clean everything in the house, even though nothing needed it. She always acted like she was the only responsible one when, really, she was hardly perfect. He found a chink now and then. Take the sanctuary. She had created this place for chimpanzees and presented it to the public with a holier-than-thou attitude, as though she and only she knew what was best, and it turned out she had made mistakes. The whole world knew she had screwed up parts of it, but she refused to see this truth. Tough love. Dana needed that more than he did.

"Damn this itch!"

"Would you do something about it then?" She whipped the last of the cord free, and the plug hit the machine with a clack. "I can't stand to listen to you."

The phone rang. Dana's eyes were still spitting venom at him when she yanked the portable phone off the coffee table. As she answered, her demeanor softened. "Hello?" Although Zack could still hear the metallic edge of anger in her voice, she calibrated it to fall within casual limits. "Hi, Mom." She raised her eyebrows at him.

He could tell she was asking if he wanted to speak to their mother, which he did not. There lurked a danger that their father would pick up the extension, and they would be there, voice to voice, falling silent at the sound of each other's breathing. For a few minutes, Zack listened to Dana's end of the conversation. She had abandoned the vacuum cleaner in favor of the silent dustcloth. He watched her sweep through the room, her shoulder cocked to cradle the phone, and saw his own mother in her, never satisfied with doing one task at a time. The mundane information he heard, the questions asked, the expressions Dana adopted as she reacted to what their mother was saying: all of these paled in significance next to Dana's awkward ballet of work and pleasure, as though she could not enjoy a simple conversation.

He slipped out the door carrying his sweatshirt in the crook of his arm. The night was damp and cold but still smelled of vegetation, however dormant. A few days before, he had met a woman with skin so black it swallowed sunlight as it fell, and he wanted desperately to be with her. Carlee. He wanted her to consume him as she did light. He wanted to disappear, to escape the ordinary details of his life, to lose himself in a single moment without having to worry about all the other complications buzzing around him.

~\/\~

Dana decided that Sifongo and Barafu were ready to be introduced into the outdoor groups. Nyuki would remain housed in the main building for the time being because his cold had turned into a sinus infection that was being treated with antibiotics. She chose Group A for Barafu because of the strong female support group and Group B for Sifongo because of the shortage of males due to Kimbunga's ferocious attempts to foil their introduction. Sifongo's plight worried Dana because a male had not been successfully introduced into Group B in over a year. She feared that Sifongo's carefree, playful curiosity would be trampled by the ruthless Kimbunga. But perhaps the adolescent Sifongo would not threaten Kimbunga as much as if he had been an adult.

The entrance to the outdoor enclosures was a long, narrow building, not much more than a concrete and cinder-block hallway with a large holding cage at each end and two interior steel doors, each leading to one of the outdoor groups. The cages had skylights, barred fronts to let in a steady stream of fresh air, and slide-down metal doors that could be secured over the bars to keep out cold and hurricane-force winds. Usually, the outdoor chimps could wander in for shelter or assistance, which they did particularly in the winter, when night temperatures could induce light frost, but for the past two days the two cages had been closed to disinfect them and prepare them for their new occupants.

Poor Nyuki sat in the corner of his cage making frustrated buzzing noises with his lips as Dana and Andy carried first the sedated Sifongo and then Barafu to their temporary homes. Once there, the chimps regarded their surroundings with bleary, cross-eyed gazes.

Dana sat with Barafu, running her hand along the chimp's back, grunting reassurances as Barafu regained consciousness. Dana took one of the palm fronds the grad students had gathered for her and pooled water in it from the fountain in the corner. As she tipped the water into Barafu's dry mouth tiny sip by tiny sip, Barafu raised her clay-brown eyes in seeming gratitude. The drugs had exaggerated the droop to Barafu's mouth, and so the water spilled helplessly onto her chest.

Dana murmured the sounds of one chimp calming another.

Kimwondo, the highest-ranking female in Group A, and her adopted daughter, Alama, approached the exterior of the cage. Kimwondo stood calmly on her feet and knuckles regarding Barafu with an unwavering gaze, while five-year-old Alama hid behind her mother with one hand on Kimwondo's rump. At first, Barafu did not see the duo, but she was alert enough to follow Dana's sight line. As soon as Barafu spotted the chimps, her lips pulled back in fear, exposing her yellowed canine teeth.

Kimwondo sauntered closer and placed both hands on the bars, grunting before moving on. Little Alama screamed as she dashed far ahead of her mother.

"Friends," Dana told Barafu.

The cage at the other end of the hall opened and closed. Andy stood in the hall, his legs splayed. "Sifongo is doing great. I'm heading back to the main building. How's Barafu?"

"Fine. I'm going to stay with her a bit longer."

Uttering soft, soothing grunts, Dana delicately parted what there was of Barafu's hair and worked her fingers against the exposed skin. This contact between the two reminded Dana of the peaceful moments they had shared in the parking lot. In Barafu's hair, time was lost.

Mary entered the building, startling Dana back to reality. "That journalist is here. Should I tell him you're busy?"

"No. Show him in here."

"Are you crazy? In the cage? Barafu has never met him."

Dana laughed. "I meant out there. Get him a chair. We can talk through the bars."

"No flirting, though. You don't have time for that."

"Yes, Mom."

A few minutes later, Mary returned with Sam trailing behind her. She had made Sam carry his own folding chair, which he juggled with his backpack and a baseball cap he had tucked under one armpit.

"I'll be outside if you need me," Mary said.

Both Dana and Sam were imprisoned, but in separate cages, as he settled with a frown onto the chair he opened on the concrete floor. He continued to look annoyed until he saw Barafu lying across Dana's lap, and then his expression softened.

"Holy shit," he said. "Look at him."

"Her. Barafu. It means 'Ice' in Swahili."

"You know Swahili?"

"No. But I have a dictionary we use to name the chimps. I have no idea whether I'm pronouncing it right or not, but it's the most of Africa I can give them."

"Have you been to Africa?"

Dana traced the largest scar on Barafu's back. "No," she said. "It's one of my failings." Barafu shifted in her lap, trying to sit up. Dana groaned as she helped her get her balance. "My work is here, though. I can't leave now."

She looked carefully at him to see if he understood or if he, like others, thought less of her for it. His expression was unreadable, however, like dark water.

TEN

Sam could not believe Dana's courage, to sit with an animal he now knew capable of ripping off the arm of a man. He had seen the scar on the back of Dana's hand, and the way she protected that hand, curled against her hip.

Dana's light brown hair looked even lighter against the dark hair of the ape, her skin pale against the black skin she touched. Although Dana was taller—longer—than Barafu, she looked almost frail sitting next to the muscular animal. Stroking and murmuring from time to time to the chimp, Dana had a plain, stark beauty, the kind the branches of a winter tree have as they stretch over a fast-running creek.

Of course, here in South Carolina, they did not know winter the way he did.

He wanted to know what chimps answered to in her but could not ask, not just yet, because it probably all went back to Annie, a subject he had promised not to broach. Besides, if he did mention Annie, he might inadvertently reveal that he had begun research on her fate; he did not want to get Dana's hopes up.

He scooted forward, grasping the chair underneath him with both hands. "I've been poking around. There are a few rumors about the break-in, but nothing solid. The sheriff told me they don't have any evidence, nothing at all to go on. They don't seem to be trying very hard."

"And that surprises you? They see the chimps as property, which they are *legally*. Because the chimps have been recovered, the case has a low priority. But it shouldn't. Whoever did this wanted to discredit the sanctuary." A flicker crossed her expression, the emotions it held vanishing too quickly to identify.

"Do you know something I don't?"

"Not really."

Barafu rolled from her sitting position to an unsteady stance with four limbs on the ground. Slowly, stiffly, she made her way to the small running fountain. Dana followed the chimp but stopped a few feet away like a mother who wanted independence for her child but still felt compelled to protect her. As Dana ran her fingers through her hair, Sam imagined her scalp smelling strongly of earth and animal.

She was squinting at him. "Do you know what's more important than the break-in? Even more important than Benji's death?"

"What?"

"Giving chimps like Barafu a chance. *That's* what you have to write about. You probably can't see from there, but Barafu has scars all over her body because of the research done on her. Andy, our vet, thinks she also had a stroke. Her face droops on one side even when she's not sedated." She left Barafu, walked straight to him, and wrapped her hands around the bars so he had to tilt his head back to see her properly. The quick ferocity in her eyes mesmerized him. "Some people want us shut down because they don't understand what we do here. They don't understand how these conditions, however imperfect, are leaps and bounds—light-years, really—from what these chimps have known. I can't give them Africa, can I? They'd die. If nothing else, the poachers would be eating them for dinner."

"I've heard of the bushmeat trade."

Dana dropped her hands, turning from him. He wished he could see her expression; he suspected she hid some telltale emotion that was sweeping across her face. When she spoke again, still not facing him, she sounded exhausted. "What do you want to know about the sanctuary?"

He felt that she had given up on him, that he had not said the right words at the right time and now she was simply tolerating him. He wanted to come up with a question that would make her smile or that would stop her with its insight, but he had only the list he had composed before he arrived. He finally asked, "Why didn't many people in Harris know about the SCPP until the car hit the chimpanzee?"

She shrugged, now crossing back to Barafu, who struggled to cup her hand in the flow of water. "It wasn't a secret. People just didn't care, I guess. They didn't pay attention."

"And now they are."

"The only time we wish they weren't!" She gave Barafu a friendly pat. "Actually, we've had a good exchange of information—both ways—since the break-in."

"I was worried at first that you'd be lynched. And now I hear you have some of them sitting down with you for coffee. What are you, a . . . sorceress?"

"You were going to call me a *witch*!" She was grinning now, her eyes bright and teasing and nearly irresistible. "You're damn lucky you thought better of it."

He fumbled with his words until he found his next question, finally settling back into the interview format. They talked about the background of the sanctuary, how and why it was founded, the individuality of the chimps. Dana had a hold on him he could not explain; he wanted to sleep with her, and yet the idea, once there, seemed distasteful. He had never before felt this torn by a woman. Was it the chimps? he wondered. Did they make her seem too feral? He had read that many people found the similarity between humans and chimps disturbing, so much so that they thought chimpanzees disgusting, and he wondered if he was subconsciously guilty.

Barafu now moved with greater steadiness from Dana to the water supply and then to the view of the outdoor enclosure. Her gaze no longer lagged behind the movement of her head, and her gestures seemed more exact. He worried that perhaps Dana should leave the cage for her safety. Was his interview keeping her there, in harm's way? But Dana showed no signs of uneasiness. Finally, he asked, "Will she hurt you?"

"Barafu? No. Not intentionally, anyway. She's a quiet girl, not at all sure about her situation. But she's used to me. I wouldn't want you to come in here because you'd probably scare the shit out of her. For the most part, chimps aren't dangerous—not the way, say, tigers are. I mean, you want to avoid a male display at all costs. And you don't want to corner them or try to take their children away. Standard stuff when dealing with wild animals."

"But these chimps aren't wild."

She laughed. "You're right. But even though they've never seen it, they have the jungle in their blood."

"Do you believe, then, in the genetic personality of a species?" he asked. "Genetic predestination?"

Dana walked up to the bars. "You mean, that our behavior and thus our fate are decided by our DNA?"

"I guess. Do you?"

Her face was scrunched in concentration, hiding the small, winged strip of freckles across her nose. "No. Not really. We have minds, don't we? Choices." And then she broke into another wide, mischievous grin. He half-expected her to start climbing the vertical bars or to dart her hand through and poke him in the ribs. "But we *are* more ruled by genes than most people think. I see chimps do things that humans do. Gestures with obviously similar, if not identical, meanings. They have wars, infanticide, mental illness. They have political systems that keep order and sometimes slip into temporary anarchy. These things are written in our genetic code, perhaps. We *are* apes. And our brains, with their abstract ability, must constantly struggle against what our biological programming wants us to do. Usually, we don't act on these base instincts."

He could see it now, the quality Zack Armstrong called "fanatical" in his sister that gave her an aura of power. It was not a noisy, thumping, *demanding* kind of fanaticism, but it was nevertheless impassioned, her eyes glittering and her gestures emphatic. Sam had an urge to leap from his chair and ask to be let into the cage with her.

Dana said, "We try to do the right thing, the thing that is expected of us as members of society. To not violate our moral code *despite* our biological urges."

"Do chimps have morals?" he asked, teasing her.

She crouched in front of him. "That's just it. *Maybe.*"

"Maybe?" He became instantly wary; the shift in the atmosphere between them was swift and jarring. How could anyone believe that an animal would act from an internalized set of rules? This was the huge difference between humans and animals. How could Dana Armstrong, a seemingly rational scientist, actually believe in animal morals? His interest in Dana as a person vanished, and she became instead a subject, someone distant and odd, a person living on the fringe who people would want to read about, clucking their tongues and shaking their heads. He had expected someone the opposite of Zachary Armstrong, not someone with a different manifestation of the same problems. He wanted to prove her wrong, decisively. "If chimpanzees are so moral, then why did Annie nearly bite off your hand?"

She stared at him from her crouch. Her hand twitched at her side, the scar dancing against her skin, and Sam thought she was going to try to hit him through the bars. Barafu settled one black hand on Dana's back.

"We're finished," Dana said.

Beyond Dana's left shoulder, beyond Barafu, with barely a cracked twig, a group of chimpanzees broke out of the brush and into the clearing outside the cage, their nostrils flared. One hooted, loud and sudden, and Sam jerked back into his chair. Startled, Barafu screamed and charged toward the back of the cage, but Dana's body blocked her way. Barafu bowled into Dana, sending her sprawling across the worn concrete floor. Sam leapt to his feet. Barafu shrieked again and hopped up the tiered platforms, jumping up and down and making a racket matched by the chimps outside, who ran excitedly back and forth. Dana lifted herself a few inches off the floor, wincing before struggling into a hunched sitting position.

"Are you okay?" Sam asked. "Should I call for someone?"

Dana massaged her shoulder. "Fuck you," she spat. "Just . . . fuck you."

He went to the outer metal door and banged on it with his fists, shouting for help. Dana Armstrong was a fool, a complete fool, to be in a cage alone with a deranged chimpanzee. He pounded until his fists ached. Finally, just as he thought he could yell and bang no more, Mary Nakagawa opened the door.

"Quick!" he said. "I think she's hurt."

Mary pushed him aside with both hands. "Dana?"

"I'm okay," Dana said. She was seated flat on the floor, rubbing her shoulder. Barafu paced in front of the assembled chimps, swift and silent, as though her limbs were not touching the ground. "Will you please show *Mister* Wendt to the parking lot?"

"Yeah. Sure." Mary looked him up and down, as though he had done something criminal.

"Listen, I'm sorry—"

Dana turned from him. "Go fuck around with Dick Lamier for your information. You deserve each other."

"Who?"

Dana moved closer to Barafu, making soothing noises, not looking at anyone but the chimp, not answering.

Mary took Sam's arm and pushed him toward the exit. Sam had been escorted off property before, had been pushed out doors and had objects like pots and chairs thrown at him, but this felt more humiliating. He led the way outside, Mary close behind. He could feel her venom without turning to look at her. No doubt, Mary thought him responsible for Dana's injury. Mary pushed her way past him and strode ahead up the gravel path, glancing over her shoulder from time to time with contempt. The small group of protesters in the parking lot moved aside for them. Even they had not been banned from the property.

He pulled his baseball cap firmly on his head. He was used to making people angry, but not before he had milked a satisfactory amount of information. "Who is Dick Lamier?"

Mary did not slow in her trek across the parking lot toward his car. At first, he thought she was going to remain silent—she seemed to be Dana's warrior, the one who guarded her and tasted her food for poison, who knew everything but told nothing. He tucked his notepad into his backpack.

When they reached his car, she said, "He's a psychologist and primatologist."

"What—"

"That's all I'm saying."

Sam repeated Lamier's name over and over to himself so he would not forget it before he had a chance to jot it down, to guess the spelling. He opened the door to the rented sedan, his lips forming the shape of the name without the sound. The inside of the car buzzed with flies that scattered when he tossed the backpack onto the passenger seat. He leaned over to shoo them out the windows he had left open and to extricate the notepad and pen. Mary leaned through the open window. If he had decided to sit up right then instead of eyeing her as he stretched across the seat, he would have hit her in the chin.

"Do me a favor," Mary said. "If you find out Lamier had anything to do with the break-in, string him up for me, will you?"

"Sure," he said, just to get her out of his car.

As he drove away, leaving Mary standing in the parking lot with her hands on her hips, he wondered why he had thrown himself into the dank pit of this story and why he could not climb out. For every bit of progress, he fell backward to an even deeper, more obscure part, and now seemed no closer to understanding Dana and the SCPP than he had in the beginning. And Dana—she infuriated him. He found himself attracted to her one moment and despising her the next, although neither emotion lasted long enough for him to find his footing. With one phone call to his editor, he could escape this article by saying he had no story after all. Then he could move away from it quickly, finish the language study article without having to know another thing about the issues and people involved with the SCPP. He would not mind leaving South Carolina.

The name of Dick Lamier rang in his head.

When Dana arrived home, a car with Virginia plates blocked the access to the carport. She braked the truck, the gravel flying up angrily inside the wheel wells. Zack had brought another of his friends into her house. Could this possibly be worse than last time, when Zack had invited a gaunt man named Walt to withdraw from heroin in her guest room? Zack had pleaded with her to let Walt stay, cajoled, promised things from his heart.

"He has a baby daughter," Zack had told her. "You can't deny her a father. As long as he's on drugs, shooting up will be more important than his kid. And he hates himself for it. This may be the only window when he feels strong enough to do this. You can't kick him out now."

Of course she could not. The man had nowhere else to turn, and she could not refuse him this slippery moment of hope. Walt lay curled on her guest bed, soaking her sheets and her mattress with sweat and urine (she threw out the linens and mattress once he left, and bought new ones instead of tires for her truck), moaning and crying for three days. Even when she was at work, she heard his voice in her head. Zack had cared for him with a tenderness that surprised her; she could not remember seeing her brother touch anyone outside the family, not even a girlfriend. When she passed the half-open door to the guest room, Zack would be swabbing Walt's skin with a washcloth. She wondered how he knew what to do. Was it instinct, or had he seen withdrawal before? Unlike her, Zack did not seem afraid of each new minute of Walt's separation from heroin. He walked around the house with a calm that astounded her and even kept her from panicking. He cleaned, cooked, did things he had never done in her house before. Dana found herself waking up in the morning thankful for Walt because he had inexplicably drawn out the strength in her brother. A sense of responsibility. And that was worth the sleepless nights and the constant moaning she carried inside her head, all her worries and disgust and fear about what was transpiring in her guest room.

But when she returned home from work on the fifth day, Walt was gone, as were her television and stereo. The loss itself was not as great as the message: the past few days had been suffered in vain. Soon enough, if not already, the electronics would be converted into drugs.

"How the hell could you let him do this?" she asked Zack. "I *trusted* you."

He shrugged. "I knew this was going to happen."

"You . . . you *knew*?" She was so furious that her words sputtered and choked inside her. She felt exploited and, more than that, *stupid*. Her own brother had seen the futility of the withdrawal, but she had embraced a thin hope both for Walt and Zack. She took Zack's duffel bag, its rumpled clothes and tattered books spilling out, and hurled it into the driveway. "Don't you ever do this to me again!" she shouted. "Now get the *fuck* out of my life."

All this time, he stood on the porch, laughing at her fury. She slammed the front door and bolted it so he could not get back in. From the darkness of her bedroom, through the sheer curtain, she watched as he stuffed everything back inside his bag and then casually, as though nothing bothered him, walked down the driveway and disappeared onto the road.

Of course, he had come back several times since then. The first time, he asked why she had not yet bought a new television and then looked visibly startled when she said, "I can't afford it." She did not feel like explaining how she had to buy a new mattress and box springs, how then she needed new tires, how she hardly missed the electric drone of the television because she arrived home too tired to watch it anyway. A few days later, Zack came home with a television for her. She did not ask where it came from because she was afraid he would tell her he had stolen it, so instead she received it thankfully, not because she needed a television but because Zack had shown he was not as selfish as she sometimes believed.

Walt had been the last and most traumatic guest into her house, but he had not been the first. Now, as Dana walked around the car in her driveway, she wondered what new hard-luck case Zack had invited into her life. She was tired and still stung, hours later, from Sam's unthinking comment and his unwillingness to listen to what she had to say. It had been humiliating to be knocked to the floor by Barafu minutes after saying how safe she was.

And now Zack had brought home one of his buddies.

Humphrey ran out of the shadowy bushes to greet her. His tail sprang up like a rod when Dana stopped to wait for him.

"What are you doing out?" In the Low Country, with a lagoon not far away, cats lived in danger of being snapped up by alligators. Zack *knew*

Humphrey was not allowed outside without her. Oh, she was going to rip into her brother for this, the hell with a houseguest.

As Dana reached the front door, she realized she was grinding her teeth. Humphrey squeezed through the door as soon as it was wide enough and headed straight for the kitchen.

Inside, in the dimly lit living room, Zack was sprawled on the floor in front of the television. A thin, hunched woman sat next to him with her back against the sofa. Dana realized that all Zack's friends looked malnourished or deprived, as though he could never be drawn to good health. Dana dropped her keys on the table next to the door and turned on the lights.

"You *know* you can't let the cat out," Dana said, then was overcome with shock. The woman's face was twisted and pulled with swollen bruises, shining like oiled skin—purple, black, green, yellow.

"Hi," Zack said from the floor. "We already ate."

Dana waited for him to introduce the woman, but he made no move to do so. *God, I hope she's not a junkie*, she thought as she moved to the sofa. Then, *Oh, my God, she's so small and so beat up*. "I'm Dana. Zack's sister."

"Becca." The woman's voice was throatier than Dana had expected, the voice of a smoker or someone who had sung too much. Or someone whose throat had been crushed.

"She's married," Zack said, as though that explained her presence. Dana supposed that, in Zack's convoluted logic, perhaps it did. "I told her she could hang out here for a while with us."

With Zack, "for a while" could mean hours or weeks, but Dana pressed her lips together with no intention of pushing him in front of this stranger, who, now that Dana thought about it, was probably running from her husband. Perhaps Zack *had* done some good this time. "You can stay in the guest room. If you'd like."

Becca nodded. Dana could not tell how old Becca was, but she chose to think of her as young and vulnerable. Without the injuries, Becca was probably cute in a scared, mousy sort of way. Her one unswollen eye was large and brown; her hair was short and fashionable; her face was shaped like an inverted teardrop. Becca seemed the type of woman everyone would want to hug and protect, and even now Dana had to fight the urge to sit next to her on the floor and ask in a gentle voice if she was all right.

In the kitchen, Dana added more food to Humphrey's bowl and then stroked the length of his back while he ate. After she stood, she reached for a brown paper bag left on the counter and, peering inside, discovered it was filled with unshelled peanuts. Zack had drawn a little face on each in pen, the way they used to do as children. Dana smiled as she pulled one from the bag. *Peanut head, you're dead*, she thought automatically as she crushed the shell, then extracted the nuts.

"Are you eating my peanuts?" Zack asked from the other room.

"Yeah."

"Knock it off."

Dana tossed the papery shell in the garbage. As she opened the refrigerator door, she shook her head at the irony. Zack and Becca had eaten the last pieces of the homemade pizza she had made the night before. She really did not feel like cooking, so instead she settled for the last orange and a container of vanilla yogurt that expired that day. Tired, she sat on the stool by the counter, peeling the skin that sent citrus oils into the air, where she imagined they hung like miniature ornaments, dangling and banging against her nose. If only she could live by smell and taste, if only she could forget all the niggling problems that pestered her (and maybe one or two of the larger ones), she would find it easier to come home at night. She had thought it would be fun for a few days to have Zack waiting for her in the evenings, but he was never there when she expected. Now, he had his own company, this woman Becca, who probably had a six-foot-three, two-hundred-twenty-pound man on her trail. Zack always had a way of complicating an already complicated situation. As she bit into an orange section, Dana considered the idea that her brother was as unruly as an adolescent chimpanzee. He did not belong inside a house.

Zack padded into the kitchen. He wore no socks or shoes, and his feet looked extraordinarily thin and white under the frayed hem of his jeans. "You going to join us?"

"For what?"

"I don't know. For company." He lowered his voice. "You always know what to say. And I, well, could use some help."

Knowing Zack, he had something to do with Becca's beating—not as perpetrator, but as instigator—and she felt sorry for Becca, who had driven from Virginia to South Carolina in search of Zack, only to find him as he always was—awkward, confused, a little distracted. Dana sighed as she swept orange peels into her palm. "Okay. For a few minutes."

When Dana stepped out of the kitchen, Becca looked up from the floor, her cheeks slick with tears. Dana lifted the cotton throw blanket off the back of the recliner, opened it, and spread it like wings across Becca's scant shoulders, letting the fabric drop into place as it found the bones and flesh of her frame. Dana sat on her shins in front of Becca. "Do you need anything?"

"I'm okay," Becca said in a broken voice. "Zack . . ." Zack had come into the room behind Dana, and Becca looked at him now, silent, unable to speak the words she had intended. Zack could not meet her gaze, making Dana wonder what promises he had made, what promises he would break.

"Did Zack bring your bags in?"

"I don't have any."

Dana touched her on the arm through the blanket and felt a twitch in the muscles far beneath. "In the bathroom closet, there's a pack of new toothbrushes. Take your pick. And help yourself to whatever towels, soap, and shampoo you need."

Becca tugged on the blanket to keep it tightly wrapped around her shoulders. She was no longer searching for Zack, having settled her attention on Dana.

Dana continued as though she had not felt the burden. "You're too small to fit into my clothes, but you can borrow a T-shirt and shorts to sleep in. There's a Wal-Mart about ten miles from here. Zack can take you tomorrow to pick up a few things. Sorry about the lack of fashion around here." Dana reached for the remote control. "Let's find something light on TV."

As they settled on a sitcom from the eighties, Dana felt extraordinarily tired. She was not sure she could lift herself from the floor when the time came to go to bed. Every once in a while, she glanced at Becca but saw only blankness. Looking at her, Dana felt more depleted than sad; she did not know how to take away Becca's grief and fear any more than she knew how to erase her own.

ELEVEN

Zack sped around the curves of the country roads well beyond the speed limit; Becca's car drifted dangerously to the edge of the shoulder when he turned to the left and over the centerline when he turned to the right. Becca clutched the sides of her seat. He felt (perversely, he knew) pleased that he could frighten her. He wanted to be mean this morning, and daring—he wanted Becca to go somewhere else. He had given her Dana's address only because she had promised to collect his final paycheck from the Richmond paver who had hired him for the summer. He had never expected her to deliver the check in person. Becca had tethered herself to him while he was not looking, and that pissed him off.

"Slow the hell down!" she yelled.

She did not cower around him the way she did with her husband. She did not hesitate to tell him to shut up, or to criticize his taste in clothes, or to tell him why she had not called when promised. He guessed this was what extramarital affairs did to a woman: they made her bold and unpredictable, then suddenly needy. He had never gotten to this stage before, when his lover crossed over from dalliance to dependence. It pissed him off, frankly, that she had not even called to ask if he would put her up for a few days. She showed up with a car still registered in Mike's name, all beaten up and sad and homeless, expecting him to provide for her.

"Please, Zack, slow down." Becca's voice had softened to pleading now, a sort of desperation that made him feel vaguely powerful. He slowed down, feeling that he could snatch her relief in his fist and hold it there.

He *did* feel sorry for Becca. It was her unexpected arrival that angered him. She had been standing in Dana's driveway like a guilty conscience when Carlee dropped him off. "Who's *she*?" Becca had asked, the hardness there for a moment.

"A friend." Carlee was one of the sweetest fucks he'd had in a long time, but he was not going to confess that to Becca, who probably fancied herself in that role. "My sister's friend." A lie seemed like a good thing then. He had not yet seen Becca's face because the darkness shielded it, but as he got closer, he could feel it. She seemed bigger somehow, swollen in a dangerous, life-threatening way, and he knew then she had left Mike, something he had dreamed of happening in Richmond but not in South Carolina. Didn't she have any friends in Richmond who could take her in?

Zack had done some despicable things in his life but had never, not once, struck a woman. He had never even felt the temptation to slap a woman's mouth shut, the way some of the guys said they wished they could. When a woman got too yappy, he walked away. Simple. You didn't have to smash her face against a dresser. Walking away usually made them run after you, apologizing, asking you back, pleading with you to forgive them. Or it cooled them off by leaving them alone for a while. You did not have to break a nose.

"Mike found out about us," Becca had said.

He had tried to sound casual, like he didn't care. "Oh. You want to come in?"

That was that, and now, the following day, they were driving to the Orangeburg Wal-Mart, of all godforsaken places. Becca kept tucking the thin points of hair behind her ears, like she was nervous with him. He had really hoped Dana would blow up and make Becca leave. Instead, his sister had sent them to Wal-Mart.

"What do you want to buy?" Zack asked Becca.

"Underwear."

"That's all?"

"Maybe another shirt."

He had wanted to take her to see the chimpanzees but decided she would betray his hiding place with a sneeze or a squeak as a spider crawled across her arm. If not that, then she would have been bored after fifteen minutes. He had no idea what he was going to do with her. When he had tried to kiss her that morning, she had pushed him away, so sex was obviously out. Unless he could somehow sneak away to see Carlee. What was he supposed to *do* with Becca?

"I want to see an alligator," Becca said as she stared out the window.

"An alligator?"

"I hear they have them here. I've never seen a wild alligator."

He was about to tell her that all alligators were wild, more or less, because they did not bond with human captors, but then he thought better of it. It seemed too argumentative. Instead, he said, "When it gets warmer this afternoon, they'll come out to sun. Maybe we can find one."

In Wal-Mart, Becca dropped several packages of string-bikini underwear into the cart. The packages crinkled and rattled there, and Becca stopped in the middle of the aisle to stare at them.

"That it, then?" Zack asked. "Ready to bolt?"

"They look so tiny," she said.

He tugged on the shopping cart to get her moving, but her grasp on the handles was surprisingly strong and unyielding.

"I need something else," she said in a stronger voice. She plunged into the juniors department and emerged with three shirts, a pair of jeans, and black Lycra bike shorts. By the time they hit the cosmetics department to find makeup and a hairbrush, both of them had lighter steps and were quicker to smile, and Zack could even feel a new warmth rising off Becca's skin.

In the toy section, Zack found a plastic alligator, which he dangled in front of her face. "Wild or tame?" he asked.

"Definitely wild, but dead." She took it from him, tossing it into the cart.

They spent a long time sorting through CDs, picking out new ones they wanted—Becca liked R&B, while Zack preferred alternative rock—but in the end bought none of them. They stood in line to pay for the items. The cashier, a young black woman with towering hair, looked at Becca's disfigured face, then averted her gaze.

"Car accident," Becca said. "Always wear your seat belt."

"Oh, you poor thing!"

As the cashier swiped Becca's credit card, Zack felt Becca tense. When the green, glowing "Approved" flashed on the machine, she relaxed with a short laugh. For the first time, he realized she was a fugitive and had given up things to escape Richmond. Whenever *he* moved on, few people looked for him or cared where he went. He never left behind debts (he mooched a lot, but people did not expect to be repaid for that) or arrest warrants or anything valuable. Becca, though, had not simply drifted away from her home. She had *escaped*. The thought awed Zack, that she had mustered courage to do something like this. Even though her entire family lived in Virginia, she had driven south on the interstate to find him, to start anew. He, too, liked fresh starts. Maybe they had been attracted to each other because they were not all that different. By the time they stepped back into the Wal-Mart parking lot, he had recovered his previous warmth for her and no longer felt the irritable incongruity of her being there. He began to remember what her face looked like behind the bruises, and how much he loved to stare at it when she slept. He had never thought he would feel about her here in South Carolina the way he did in Richmond.

"You should get cash," he said. "Before Mike cancels everything."

The surprise on her face, as though she had underestimated him, gave him a surge of pride. "You're right," she said. "Let's find an ATM."

As they exited the bank, flush with Becca's two hundred, Samuel Wendt stood in their path. For a moment, Zack believed Mike had sent him to stop Becca's flight, but then he realized it was coincidence, the worst kind of luck.

"Zack!" Sam said, already eyeing Becca and her mangled face with suspicion. "You said you would call."

"Things came up."

Becca touched her fingers lightly to her face. "Car accident. Always wear your seat belt."

"Both of you? Was anyone seriously hurt?"

"I was wearing my seat belt," Zack said. "The tree was seriously hurt, though."

Becca giggled like she used to when they planned ridiculously elaborate excuses to distract Mike. "It was an alligator in the road. And I tried not to hit it. A wild alligator. Can you believe it?"

Sam seemed wary of the tale, his eyes returning to the bruises on Becca's face. Zack did not want him to ask more questions, in case they started cracking up with each new absurd detail, so he said, "Did you get a date with my sister?"

Sam extended his hand toward Becca, and it infuriated Zack that he was being ignored. "Samuel Wendt. I've interviewed Zack for a story I'm writing."

"Zack?"

"She doesn't know about that shit," Zack told Sam.

"Are you famous or something? Or a criminal?"

Zack draped his arm over her shoulder, finding comfort in the familiar boniness there. "He's trying to locate the chimpanzee my family once owned."

"A chimpanzee?" she said in her throaty way, as though she believed this as big a hoax as the car accident story.

"I told you," Sam said. "I'm not looking for her."

Zack grinned. "Yes, you are."

"Have you heard of Dick Lamier?"

Zack felt as though a chasm had opened underneath him and he was falling through a bottomless darkness, the smell of childhood in his nostrils. No matter how old Zack got, he could not escape the visceral response Dick Lamier always evoked. Zack used to fantasize that Dick was his real, secret father and so memorized every detail: the musk cologne that was so popular in the seventies, the way he cracked his knuckles joint by joint, the ease with which he slipped behind the steering wheel of a sports car. Zack's mother had flirted with Dick, he knew now, but the banter had seemed to him as fun as gift wrap, the way it crackled and stuck at the corners, revealing something new every time a piece of it was torn away. He knew the reason Dick Lamier had never come back in his red Mustang was because his father had been jealous of Dick's competence and his family's love for him.

Zack, sensing the danger of revealing too much, decided to stick to the basics. "He's just a family friend."

"A family *friend*?"

Sam's incredulity scared Zack. He wished he knew why Sam was asking. "Look. I've got to get Becca to her doctor's appointment. I'll call you later. Promise." He prodded Becca toward the car. Becca did not protest or even ask him to explain, once they were alone in the car. Sometimes, Becca was outright cool.

As they drove back toward Harris, Zack considered taking a detour to find her a lagoon and an alligator, but now that they had invented an alligator in the road and had a plastic one in a shopping bag, it seemed too mundane to spot a real one on a sunburnt bank. Becca poked around in her bags, her purchases making crinkly noises as she sorted through them. It seemed tragic that all her belongings fit in a translucent blue plastic bag, that all she wanted to do was see an alligator, that she had lived in a run-down house in Richmond with an asshole like Mike.

"How many credit cards do you have?" Zack asked.

"Two."

"What kind of cash advance can you get on them?"

"I don't know. A thousand apiece, I guess. I've maxed out the ATM card until tomorrow, then I can get another two hundred." She stopped rummaging in the bag. "Why?"

Zack slipped one hand to her thigh, stroking it, and held the steering wheel steady with the other. "You wanna go to Florida? Just take our stuff and go?"

"Just like that?"

"Just like that."

Becca looked out the side window so he could not see her face.

He wondered what she was seeing, if anything, beyond the pine trees that jerked past the window like a strobe light, one after the other—trunk, space, trunk, space. It was a stupid idea, thinking she would do something that spontaneous with him when she already felt unsteady. She probably figured she could not count on anything, not even him. She did not know him well enough to love or even trust him. After a while, she wordlessly let her head fall back against the headrest. He glanced over to see if she was crying, but she was smiling in a content, post-sex way.

"What the fuck," she said. "Let's go."

—∿∿—

Sifongo looked immense, his hair fanned outward with piloerection. Dana felt her own hair—light and downy on her arms, stubbly on her legs, heavy close to her scalp—prickle upright as Kimbunga tore through the area in front of Sifongo's cage, dragging logs and hurling rocks and pine needles at Sifongo as the younger male screamed back, leaping up the platforms and swinging himself against the bars with a rattling of both metal and animal. The only way Sifongo could gain admission into Kimbunga's kingdom was through submission, and so far he had demonstrated none, even though he was not even fully adult. Dana guessed Sifongo had been the spoiled child of Maggie's family, his place in the hierarchy of his small group fixed when his father had died of dehydration just before the family came to the sanctuary. Sifongo needed to bow to a stranger, and he could not.

Mary stood at the far end of the holding corridor in front of Barafu's cage, which was at the moment much quieter. "Tell them to knock it off!" Mary shouted.

Dana laughed. "I wish I could."

Although the other chimps in Group B were curious about Sifongo, most appeared only briefly, and intelligently so, for any chimp getting in Kimbunga's way as he displayed risked being injured or being used as a prop to fling about. Thank God most chimps did not establish their territories with fights to the death, as did some species, Dana thought. She did not believe she could take that, every day fearing death and dismemberment for the chimps.

Of the two, Sifongo calmed first and sat in the straw of his cage, his barrel chest heaving; as a ten-year-old male formerly in the company of women, he probably was not used to carrying on for so long. Kimbunga ended his display a few moments later, also spent, but instead of catching his breath, he knuckle-walked right up to the cage. Kimbunga looked directly at Sifongo. From where she sat, Dana could see his close-set eyes searching Sifongo's face, perhaps for an understanding of why he was there, perhaps to gauge his level of threat. His lips were pressed together in a tight line. Sifongo grimaced. Dana could tell he wanted to race to the back of the cage but chose to stand firm. With a grunt, Kimbunga sat in the dust. The two male chimpanzees regarded each other for several minutes, Sifongo breaking into grimace after nervous grimace. Then Kimbunga raised himself on two legs, his arms held out from his body for balance. Sifongo squatted so his head was much lower than Kimbunga's. He then slunk into the corner to the fountain, where he scooped large handfuls of water, glancing every now and then at Kimbunga. Satisfied, Kimbunga left.

Dana squeezed her knees to her chest, grinning, wanting to shout down the hall to Mary but afraid of startling Sifongo out of the new quiet. The gestures had been small—a simple crouch, a nonchalant departure—but they sent euphoria coursing through her. *Good boy, Sifongo*, she wanted to tell him, and her fingers twitched with the sign language even after all these years of disuse.

Slowly, Dana rose to stretch her legs, deciding to go down the concrete hall to relay the news to Mary, who sat cross-legged in front of Barafu's cage. Barafu had come close to the bars, facing Mary, her jutting brow furrowed, her lips twisted into an expression unreadable because of her partial facial paralysis. The chimp lifted her arms to her belly, one resting on the other. She then moved her arms gently from side to side. Dana stopped, an icy splash of disbelief leaving her gasping for breath.

Baby.

"Oh, my God," Dana whispered.

The thin thread of what Dana had seen pulled her step by step toward the chimp and her cage. Barafu let her arms drop and then put her full weight on her knuckles. Leaning forward so her face was almost against the bars, she grunted. Mary grunted back. Perfect chimp talk, except that Barafu then sat back again and formed the American Sign Language symbol for baby. Mary did not seem to notice.

Dana crept closer until she was right behind Mary, but her eyes rested solely on Barafu.

"Oh," Mary squeaked when she saw Dana. "You scared the hell out of me!"

Dana slowly formed her fingers into shapes they had not known in years. *You want baby?*

Barafu signed, *Yes.*

Dana's knees weakened underneath her and lowered her to the floor.

"Dana? What's going on?"

"Barafu knows sign language."

"Jesus. Oh, shit. She must have been one of the chimps in the sign language studies. Just like . . ." Mary sucked her lower lip into her mouth and held it there, silent.

"Just like Annie." Dana's thoughts swirled and collided and seemed to go nowhere, even as they multiplied.

Always lurking inside her was the possibility that a chimpanzee who knew sign language might arrive at the sanctuary. Dana scanned the files for any indication of this kind of history before she sat down and delved into the specifics of each chimp. Barafu's file had suggested nothing of the possibility, but there she was, signing. Dana shook with the knowledge that she had to confront not only the atrocities that had been committed against the chimp but also the possible communication of them. Although no chimp (or gorilla or bonobo) acquired a large enough vocabulary to convey complicated details, many attained the conversational level of a toddler and the comprehension of a five-year-old. How heartbreaking would it be to learn the story of those rows of cages in the words of a three-year-old? Dana did not want to face those words, and yet she would be unable to ignore them.

Among signing chimps, Annie was not the only one sold to a medical laboratory, nor was she the only one to vanish from the records. But

Barafu? Although according to the spare documentation she was too young for the flurry of experiments in the sixties, she had obviously been exposed to sign language, either before or during her stay at the laboratory. Dana tried to remember whether she had seen any previous gestures that hinted at the chimp's knowledge, but Barafu had kept to herself, chewing her fingers and devouring food, her detached stare more unforgettable than any gestures. So why now?

"Which chimps have come by the cage while you've been here?" Dana asked. "Any of the juveniles?"

"About fifteen minutes ago, Alama and Zabibu came with Kimwondo." Kimwondo, the highest-ranking female in Group A, had surprised them all by adopting the two juveniles within a year of each other, driving off the other females with persistent swats. Alama, the younger of the two and a female, still depended heavily on Kimwondo, while Zabibu often explored on his own. "Why?" Mary asked.

"I think Barafu just told me she wants a baby."

"What did you tell her?"

"Nothing." Dana rubbed the scar on the back of her hand, opening and closing her weak fist against her hip. Barafu was studying her with alert, hopeful eyes.

Barafu rocked the imaginary baby in her arms once again, and Dana allowed herself the illusion of coincidence, that Barafu had accidentally made the sign for baby. Then Barafu did the unthinkable. She signed again: *Love baby.*

Mary grasped Dana's wrist. "She's talking to you, isn't she? What else did she say?"

"She . . ." The words choked inside her. How could she answer Barafu's wish? Morally, Dana could not allow Barafu to have her own baby, even if her damaged, scarred body were capable of carrying a fetus to term. Dana could not be responsible for yet another chimp born into captivity. Although she allowed the females to "adopt" the juveniles, the youngsters available for adoption would require extensive care once introduced into the colonies, something Dana was not confident Barafu could do. Besides, most of the adult females treated the new children like prizes—perhaps the reason Kimwondo had fought for two. Barafu would never successfully compete against the female hierarchy. "She said . . ."

"She said what?"

"She said she loves babies."

Mary released Dana's wrist.

"I don't know what to say," Dana said. "What to do. I can't just walk away from her and pretend I didn't understand."

Mary ran her slender hands through her hair, and Dana watched the black sheets fall back perfectly into place. Dana's head ached, but if she concentrated on Mary's hands, it throbbed less, as though she could pass some of the pain to her friend.

"She wants to be a mother," Mary said, her voice breaking. "How can we say no?"

"You know why."

They said nothing for several minutes as they studied Barafu, who, chewing on one finger, searched each face for an answer. The bars between humans and chimp suddenly struck Dana as thick and impenetrable, impossible to unlock even with the correct key. She wanted desperately to grant Barafu this basic wish. The drive to procreate raged in every living organism, and there Dana was, denying it to the species closest to her heart. And what if this female had been Annie making a similar request? What would she have done then?

It did not seem fair to bestow special privileges on Barafu simply because she could "speak." This formed the painful core of the dilemma. Barafu's intelligence did not exceed that of the other females at the sanctuary; Dana judged her to be average, neither exceedingly dull nor bright, and certainly more psychologically traumatized than many. Without her signing, Barafu would never have been considered a solid choice for an adoptive mother. Yet once the desire had been stated, how could Dana refuse? Barafu's simple signs opened a door within Dana that she had tried to keep locked. *Oh, Annie.*

She had to let Barafu adopt.

Dana considered the seven juveniles in the nursery, two of whom— the female Fikira and the male Bora—were almost completely socialized. Would it be negligent of her to allow Barafu to adopt one of them? With

Lamier at her back, she could afford few mistakes. Another disaster could place the status of the SCPP in jeopardy. It might lose funding and public support, bringing about the death of everything the staff had worked for.

"What are we going to do?" Mary asked.

Dana tried not to let her emotions override her judgment, but the two were so tangled now she could not tell the difference. "We might be able to teach her to be a mother here in the holding cage."

Mary rearranged her legs underneath her. "That way, she would already have her child before she went out into the group. No one would challenge her."

"Teaching Barafu to be a mother could take weeks. This cage isn't designed for long-term holding. There isn't enough enrichment, especially for a juvenile. And what if it doesn't work? What if the juvenile is harmed and we have to remove her?"

"Her? You're thinking of Fikira, aren't you? She would be *perfect* for Barafu. She's a sturdy little girl, but quiet. Thoughtful, like Barafu."

Barafu watched them intently. Each time they spoke her name, she rolled forward as though to get up, but then relaxed back into her sitting position. The dullness had vanished from her expression, and when she scratched her neck with the finger she had just had in her mouth, Dana swore her droop lifted, if only a little, into a smile.

Four-year-old Fikira was one of Inge's charges. She was sweet-faced, with a broad brow, small ears, and eyes that seemed to take in everything without revealing their secrets. When Fikira first arrived at the SCPP, Inge had immediately looked up the Swahili word for contemplation—*fikira*. The young chimp had come from a medical laboratory funded by the National Institutes of Health, and although she had never been experimented on, she had been bred for use in AIDS research. When the research proved unpromising, the laboratory had found itself with too many chimpanzees for its small number of studies.

Dana was not sure if Fikira spent her minutes deep in thought or if she was emotionally muted. Like Barafu, she tended toward solitude and intent study, often gazing out over the room as though she saw nothing in it. "Fikira *would* be better than little Bora—he can be a handful.

Temperamentally, they're mother and daughter."

"Can you tell Barafu what we're planning?" Mary asked.

Dana shook her head. "I won't communicate with her in sign language. I shouldn't have done it in the first place. It's just . . . well, she took me by surprise. Sign language will just lead Barafu farther from who she's supposed to be."

As Dana regarded the passive chimp, she suspected Barafu's quiet gaze betrayed an understanding of the conversation. Barafu did not need ASL to understand, only to communicate. That done, she knuckle-walked toward the exterior bars to examine the enclosed forest that awaited her.

———∿∿———

Dana agonized over whether she had done the right thing by not communicating more with Barafu. Philosophically, the choice was clear, but what was she denying the chimp? And what was she denying herself? Because of the limited verbal intelligence of nonhuman apes, their complex interior lives would always remain in doubt, but sign language offered a sliver of how chimps viewed their lives—what they liked and disliked, what they observed, their priorities, *who they were at their core*. Washoe the chimpanzee and Koko the gorilla had already given humans a window into their minds, but Barafu was an entirely different individual who might offer something her famous counterparts could not.

Oh, Annie!

Either Barafu had learned ASL from humans long after the most famous language studies had ended, or she had picked it up from an older chimp, one who had been part of them, maybe even Annie herself. Dana had the paperwork; she went over all the details of Barafu's life but found nothing that suggested an opportunity to learn sign language.

At work the rest of that day, Mary seemed to avoid Dana. When they did talk, Mary regarded her stonily. Finally, Dana caught her by the shoulder and spun her around. "What's wrong, Mare? I said I was going to let Barafu adopt."

"You have an extraordinary gift and refuse to use it. You can *talk* with Barafu. You can connect with her. What harm could there be in that?

Barafu already is not who she was supposed to be. Refusing to speak to her in sign language can't possibly undo what she already knows. Who she already is. All you're doing is closing a big, heavy door on her." Mary was blinking away slivers of tears.

In Dana's view, Mary knew little about the dangers of drawing a chimp into a human world. "I can't," Dana said quietly. "I just can't." She could feel Mary pulling away from her, but Dana had nothing more to say.

"I've got work to do," Mary said.

Everything had changed the moment Dana saw Barafu sign. She did not understand how that could be, why such a simple gesture could unlock so much. Before, Barafu had been an equal with her peers, but now she had force. Dana did not want to succumb to this power, for to do so would be to deny the other chimps their due for no reason other than their failure to reach into her past. Dana shivered. The world as she knew it had disappeared into uncertainty.

⌣ᴧᴧ⌣

Zack's car was parked in the driveway off to one side, but Becca's was gone. Dana was thrilled with this development. She had Zack all to herself on this day when she had discovered a thread, however thin, to Annie: another signing chimp. She ran from her truck to the front door, flinging it open and yelling, "Zack! Guess what happened today."

She stopped two steps inside. No one had answered. Zack's belongings, scattered about her house for days now, had vanished. The worn and stained duffel bag he kept under the end table was gone, as was the portable CD player that had sat tangled and upside down on the coffee table no matter how many times Dana had righted it. The house was filled with a humming loneliness, the entwined whirs of the refrigerator and heat pump, the grinding of an electric clock, muted signs of life.

Her heart gave a start. Where was Humphrey? Had Zack let him out again? She finally found the cat curled up on her pillow with no inclination to rouse himself. He blinked at her, then covered his face with one paw.

Even Humphrey would not keep her company.

Dejected, she pried off her work boots and sat with her bare feet propped on the coffee table—as Zack would, she thought with a twinge of mean satisfaction. Right then, she wanted the twin qualities of irresponsibility and laziness. She wanted to be as careless as a piece of milkweed fluff. As she was settling into her rogue persona, the phone rang.

"Hi, it's Sam Wendt."

She hardly cared that she had been furious with him a few days before. She held a voice in her hands, something she needed desperately right then. "Hi. What's up?"

"Well . . . ," he said. "I'm heading back to Virginia, and I didn't want to leave without saying I'm sorry. For the other day. I don't know what got into me."

"Apology accepted."

"I appreciate it."

Desperate that the conversation was ending, she formed quick words. "Will you be coming back? To South Carolina?" She could not explain even to herself her sudden need for him, and she did not care that the tone of her words conveyed her emotions. "Don't you have more research to do here?"

"I don't know. I . . . If I need to, I'll be back. But I may have enough information for the article. And I can always call you. Can't I?"

"Sure." She really wanted to say, *No, you can't. You have to extract facts from me in person.* She acutely felt, this night more than most, how few friends she had here in South Carolina. Year had blended into year, and she had not poked her head out of the sanctuary long enough to make simple human contact. She had allowed her work to isolate her.

"I'll let you know when the article will be coming out," he was saying. "And thanks for everything."

She could do nothing more than mumble a good-bye before she was once again plunged into silence. Taking the remote control in her callused hands, she turned the television on and pressed the volume button until the voices were almost too loud to bear.

TWELVE

When Sam returned home to Arlington, he picked up his mail and sorted through it in the front seat of his car, feeling bereft. He had stayed in South Carolina longer than necessary, to get a feel for the people and the sanctuary and the land, but had come away with a hollowness, a sense that he had understood nothing. The rhythms of Arlington, once so familiar and comforting, now had a dissonance that jarred him. How could that be? He understood and loved Arlington, hated Orangeburg. But in Virginia, he felt off-balance and unable to think, depressed, desperate for a salve for his aching insides. He could not stop thinking of Dana. The tangle of her hair, her quick smile, the intensity of her eyes, the smattering of freckles. The scar that graced and cursed her hand. He could not get the unsettling sound of her voice out of his head.

He had dreams of her near dawn, moments before he awoke. Sometimes, she screamed incomprehensible words at him; other times, she took him by the damp hand to show him a mystery the dream never reached. He wished for something more erotic, but his subconscious never complied. Instead, he awoke with a longing he could not define. He had never felt this confused by a subject, nor been this obsessed. In her offhand, fanatical way, Dana had charmed him, and now he risked not seeing all sides, risked becoming a biased observer instead of an impassive one. He almost hated her for it.

His answering machine blinked with messages. In Orangeburg, he had made several phone calls in the dingy light of his motel room to people who might have known Annie. Now, the word had spread, and people left messages, wanting to talk about animal rights, laboratory conditions, donating money to animal rights organizations—but not about Annie. It had all taken place too long ago for most people to care about or remember. Part of Sam believed that trying to discover what had happened to Annie was a waste of time, something that could consume him and prevent him from finishing the articles he had already begun. He needed those paychecks. But another part of him, the true journalist, could not let the idea go. He wanted to find out Annie's fate and to learn what every person who handled her had thought. Had they known she could communicate? Had they understood she had been raised as a human? Had they stopped to look into the young chimp's eyes? Had they cared what they might find there?

When he was not thinking of Dana, he thought of the patchwork of hardwood groves, the ground that gave underfoot, the trilling of wrens and the hooting of chimpanzees. The article about the language study families stared back at him from the computer screen, immobile, peopled with characters who no longer interested him—with the strong exception of the Armstrongs.

When the phone rang on his third day home, he reached for it absently, glad for the diversion without considering exactly what the diversion might be. "Hello?"

"Hi. This is Dick Lamier. Is this Samuel Wendt?"

Sam, who had been leaning back so far it tested his balance, smacked his chair forward. "Yes."

"I understand you are researching the disappearance of university chimpanzees, particularly the one that belonged to the Armstrongs. I might have some information for you."

"I'm listening."

Lamier laughed heartily. "Not that easy, son. I want to meet with you. I'm visiting the National Institutes of Health for a few days and thought we could get together for dinner tonight or the next."

"Tonight is perfect."

Once the arrangements had been made, Sam paced the length of his apartment, trying to figure out how the two stories—the language study families and the break-in—had converged on Dick Lamier. Despite the commonalities of chimpanzees and Dana, the two articles had seemed completely separate until now. Energy surged through him at the prospect of talking to Lamier face to face. Tasting salt on his lips, he licked them as if in anticipation of a feast, a feeding of his craving.

Sam already knew a few things about Dick Lamier. Before leaving South Carolina, in his motel room, he had searched for Lamier on the Internet and been astounded by the number of hits: page after page either referencing or presenting Lamier's work on primates. It seemed inconceivable that such a renowned psychobiologist would first obtain keys to the facility and then unleash the animals, when he well understood the dangers to all concerned. Still, Sam trusted that Dana had spat out Lamier's name for a reason. She did not strike him as the type of person to mislead, even in anger.

As a journalist, however, he understood the law of multiple truths.

—∿∿—

It took Sam forty-five minutes of navigating traffic to reach the Bethesda hotel where Lamier was staying, and even then he was early. Ever since the call, Sam had felt like Lamier's prey, so he wanted time to order his thoughts before meeting him. However, Lamier lay in wait, already seated in the hotel restaurant where Sam had made reservations.

"Glad to meet you, Mr. Wendt," Lamier said, reaching across the table to shake Sam's hand without standing. Lamier was a stout man with a square face with a hint of jowls. His silver hair, thin but not balding, gave him the air of an elder statesman, but Sam also glimpsed something pathetic in his eyes, something worn and desperate, a man who had worked hard but whose dreams had never been completely fulfilled. He had already ordered a pale amber drink—Scotch, perhaps—on the rocks. Lamier did not seem inclined to begin speaking right away about chimpanzees, so Sam perused the menu, exchanging pleasantries while keeping a wary watch on him.

Lamier adjusted his silverware on the white tablecloth. "Now that we've ordered, you can ask me all the questions you want. But everything is off the record. I'm your Deep Throat."

They were hardly meeting in a darkened parking garage, but Sam decided to play along to see what Lamier had to say. He had expected a development like this, a jockeying for a power position by Lamier, and it did not faze him. "You called because you know something about Annie. Why don't we start there?"

"Actually, my information about Annie is really information about Reginald Armstrong. We were professors together at Brown. He confessed to me that he could have stopped the university from sending Annie to a medical lab but wanted to give it a chance to recoup some of its money. He was the one who signed the sales agreement."

"So?"

"He knew that the sales agreement was a falsehood of sorts. Annie appeared to be headed for a study of antibiotics. But a double trade was already in place. Another lab was in the wings waiting to acquire her. It wouldn't have looked right to send a signing chimp to a place that was performing brain damage studies. You see, Annie had more or less *measured* intelligence. She had rudimentary language capabilities. They could test damage to certain areas of her brain in ways they couldn't in other animals. She was in demand, an animal the researchers were willing to pay more for."

"Reginald Armstrong knew of the double trade?"

"Yes. He didn't want to appear directly responsible, but he knew it was going to happen. Even if Annie survived the experiment, she couldn't possibly have remained whole."

Sam's chest constricted. He could think only of Dana and Zack, nurturing their small hope that Annie was still alive and could be found. He tugged on the hem of his napkin in his lap. He had seen the old tapes of the Armstrongs as they interacted with Annie, so he had in his mind an image of the chimp as a young child. It did not seem possible that anyone would take such an animal and knowingly send her to have her brain removed bit by bit. Sam searched for a kernel of doubt that he could steal away with him. "But Annie never arrived at the second lab. Maybe she ended up somewhere else."

Their waiter had brought Lamier a glass of Sauvignon Blanc, and he now sipped it thoughtfully. "She never arrived at the second lab listed on the papers. The lab they *said* she was going to was not the lab she was sent to. The paperwork had her headed to a hepatitis study. Instead, she was sent to New York for brain surgery. She never disappeared. She was hidden."

"Can you prove this?"

"No. That's for you to do. And why this is off the record. Reginald was racked with guilt back then. Maybe he'd like to finally get it off his chest."

Although Lamier regarded him steadily, his voice had the sound of a sneer, and Sam wanted to reach across the table and grab him by his thick throat. Few people evoked this kind of response in him. He felt like an undeveloped teenager again, being pushed against the side of his house by his four older brothers and their friends, their hormones making them feel stronger, better, smarter, *superior*. Lamier saw him as someone puny and easy to trick. Not that Sam believed he was being made a fool. It just felt that way. "There was a break-in, you know, at the South Carolina Primate Project."

Lamier smiled as he ran his finger along the base of his wineglass. "The first step in Dana Armstrong's demise."

"What does that mean?"

"She was always a weak choice for the position. Not enough experience with primates. Too much rabid idealism and not enough scientific thought. For five years, she has managed to appear in control, but trust me, something is going to break. It *appears* she has the chimps' best interests in mind. But take a good look next time you're there. She keeps the chimps contained within electrical fences, not moats, as most outdoor facilities do. Chimps can't swim, so they stay away naturally from the moats. Chimps *can* climb, and so every one of them has been cruelly shocked by that fence. And if that isn't enough evidence for you, think about this. The chimps are outdoors twenty-four hours a day. She can't access them easily for medical care. The winters have been mild in South Carolina for the past few years, but wait until they get their first prolonged cold snap. The chimpanzees will die without shelter."

"They have holding cages, which are normally left open. And a few shelters scattered through the woods."

"The chimps I've known won't seek shelter from the rain. Do you think these will know how to avoid frostbite?"

Sam could not answer, and Lamier surely knew it.

"The worst crime she has committed, the very worst, most unforgivable crime, is her caging of several animals by themselves. Every primatologist worth his salt knows the emotional damage isolation can inflict upon primates."

"Aren't those cases temporary? As I understand it, the chimps are first acclimated to their surroundings and then introduced into a larger group."

"The one that died had been there since the sanctuary opened, and he never lived with another chimp. And you can put my objections to the way Dana Armstrong treats her charges on the record." The waiter arrived again, this time with their appetizers. Lamier leaned back as the waiter placed a plate of smoked salmon in front of him.

Sam nodded toward Lamier's plate. "I notice you aren't a vegetarian."

Lamier groaned and rolled his eyes in exaggeration. "You've been talking to too many rabbits." He leaned forward, his fork poised in his hand. "One look at human teeth and you can tell we're omnivores. Canines and molars. Meat ripping and plant grinding. Some primatologists—and I bet Dana Armstrong is one—have gotten it into their minds they should eat nuts and berries like other primates. The trouble is, chimps eat meat. They hunt other primates—baby baboons and red colobus monkeys. They eat bushpigs. So the idea of bushmeat—

eating chimpanzees and other primates—while deplorable from an environmental standpoint, has precedence not only in the human population but in the chimpanzee population as well. Now, don't get me wrong. I'm not endorsing the bushmeat trade. And I find the sport of hunting barbaric. But I'm saying that people need meat and fish protein. We will get it however we can. I'm not going to stop eating meat just because someone tells me I shouldn't. And since you ordered swordfish for your entrée, I'm sure you can understand."

"Let's get back to the SCPP. What do you know about the break-in?"

Lamier had used the brief pause to eat some of his smoked salmon, and now he talked with his mouth full, chewing between words. "Other than it's the beginning of the end? Not much, really. I heard about it, obviously. I have two theories, everything still off the record." He swallowed his food and took a long sip of ice water. "One: animal rights group. They know the chimps are in danger. And they don't like the fact research is being done."

"The chimps are *observed*. What harm could there be in that?"

Lamier shrugged. "I don't know what goes on behind closed doors. I *do* know one of their graduate students coauthored a paper with Dana Armstrong on chimpanzee reaction to wounded individuals. Tell me, how did they get injured chimps?" Lamier waited, chewing, as though he expected a response from Sam.

Sam could no longer think straight. "What's your second theory?"

"Dana Armstrong has allowed someone access to the keys, and she shouldn't have. She knows exactly who is responsible. She's covering both her butt and his."

"Who?" Then he knew. "Her brother?"

Lamier carefully wiped his mouth. "Could be."

Could be. Zack was wild, untamable, a pinball machine defying the laws of physics, shooting out at impossible angles, appearing where he should not. Although Sam believed Zack capable of releasing the chimps, he could not imagine Dana would risk her reputation to protect her brother. If Zack was guilty, most likely Dana did not know. Still, Lamier had voiced a possibility that needed exploration. Sam now had his excuse to return to South Carolina.

"Tell me," Sam said evenly, "what role you have in all this."

"Me?" Lamier crushed a caper with the tines of his fork. "I don't need to do something stupid to get my point across. I have access to the official channels, and that's enough for me."

"What does that mean?"

Lamier pushed his plate away from him, and this time he did sneer. "That, Mr. Wendt, is none of your fucking business."

⁓⋏⋏⋎⁓

Sifongo had been reacting to Kimbunga's presence outside his cage with appropriate submission, so Dana decided it was time to release him into the group. She waited until after the outdoor group had breakfast, until Sifongo had feasted on a favorite meal of spinach and watermelon, and then she flipped the switch that slid the bars open. Sifongo screeched in alarm, hopping up to the highest platform in his cage. He rocked back and forth for a few minutes, hooting and hollering, until finally, nostrils flared, he came down to investigate. Dana could see he was planning, calculating, aware that his skills were about to be tested.

The video cameras mounted to the ceiling within metal cages were recording every nuance, as were the ones on the roof above. Mary and all the graduate students perched on the observation platforms. Dean Washington had been invited to watch but as far as Dana knew had not arrived. Andy stayed in the hall outside the holding cage with Dana, ready with the tranquilizing gun in case Kimbunga decided to attack Sifongo. They expected Sifongo to endure some physical battering because that was what chimps did, but they were poised to decide when the line had been crossed.

Sifongo swatted the ground outside the cage, then pulled his arm back. He retreated a few feet.

Crouched in the hallway, Dana grunted reassurances to Sifongo, who stared at the open door while leaning on his knuckles. He stood perfectly still, without a twitch in his limbs, but his eyes were bright and alert. A series of thoughts—whether simple or complex, Dana would never know—rippled across his dark face as he took everything in. Sifongo knew Kimbunga ruled that space. Was he thinking of survival tactics? Or was he merely taking in the colors and the scents of the air? Perhaps he was remembering his last release, believing this one to offer the same freedom, the same game to find him and bring him back.

Dana grunted again. Sifongo turned to look at her, then swung his head back to the opening. Then, without warning, he charged through, across the leaf-lined clearing, and into the brush, vanishing in an instant.

"What the hell?" Andy laughed. "Where did he go?"

Dana stepped into the holding cage, turning on her two-way radio as she did. "Mary? Did you see where he went?"

Mary's laugh cackled back. "Not yet. I think he's entered the witness protection program."

"Where's Kimbunga?"

"I don't see him. He doesn't appear to be on the move."

They had to wait a full hour before they spotted Sifongo climbing a pine tree a hundred yards from the holding cage. Through the binoculars, Dana watched his purposeful climb to the top, where the branches swayed under his weight. Their captive chimps had fallen from trees before, as Tekua had when he broke his leg, and Dana had no idea how adept Sifongo was at gauging danger. He certainly had the balance needed to perch on a thin branch and look out over his new home.

Annie had loved attaining heights. She used to leap to the top of the kitchen cabinets and look down on the less-adroit primates in the house, flicking dust bunnies and dead insects at them while they tried to coax her down. Up high, Annie had twisted the cameras around on their mountings. Reginald had once tried to climb a chair to get to her, but Annie, laughing, moved to the far end, out of his reach. He slid the chair over, and she waited until he took the step up before scooting back to her original position, signing, *Annie good spider* and *You're it*. Susan Armstrong finally declared the top of the cabinets to be an Annie zone; they were to ignore her presence. Annie often sat there while Susan prepared dinner, and they all prayed she did not find something to throw into the food.

Annie also liked to perch on top of the jungle gym in the backyard. Dana had tried once to balance herself on the beam next to Annie but had almost fallen over backward as Annie gave her a playful slap. When Annie crossed the beam, she walked erect, her hands up for balance and her toes gripping the four-by-four from which the swings hung.

Dana had once asked Annie to teach her to climb the swinging cargo net so she could win a prize at the carnival that was coming to town, but Annie had signed, *You no good net. Annie good.*

Annie was right. Dana never was as good as Annie at climbing. It was a failing of her species. Even so, Dana had tried to climb the tree in the backyard faster than Annie could, and higher. She tried to jump farther and to rattle the swing set more vehemently. She tried to do running somersaults and to grab branches as she flew through the air. Her mother finally said to her, "I know we're treating Annie like a human, but the fact is, she's a chimp. There's a line there, Dana, and I don't want you injuring yourself over it."

The black-and-white movies had recorded everything. Those reels were not shown as often, but their existence made Dana cringe. People had probably laughed at her efforts, mistakenly believing she was confusing herself with a chimp, when really she was just trying to be better.

As Dana remembered this, a large, dark shape appeared at the base of the pine tree and slowly started to make its way up to where Sifongo sat.

Mary's voice startled Dana. "Do you see?"

"I see," Dana radioed back. She glanced at Andy, who was using his binoculars to look elsewhere. "Kimbunga's on his way up the tree."

"Oh, shit!"

Dana could only hope that Kimbunga understood Sifongo was an adolescent and not worthy of a full-blown battle. She and Andy watched in tense silence as Kimbunga made his stealthy way toward an unsuspecting Sifongo; the tranquilizer gun would not help them now. Several more seconds passed before the newly freed chimp saw the dominant male a few feet below him. With a screech, his mouth wide with fear, Sifongo leapt from his branch to another, but his escape route was blocked. The racket was deafening as Kimbunga threatened Sifongo. The branches snapped and shook as the two confronted each other, Kimbunga in pursuit, driving Sifongo higher into the unstable branches. Sifongo grasped a large pine cone in his hand as he scrambled to avoid the larger male. When Kimbunga came close enough, Sifongo hurled his weapon at Kimbunga, who hesitated to look after the falling object. Sifongo used the precious second of Kimbunga's inattention to slip below the adult. Once past, Sifongo swung and slid down the tree with Kimbunga in pursuit. By the time Kimbunga reached the ground, he was panting, and so sat at the base picking pine sap off his palms as Sifongo ran shrieking for cover. Dana squinted through her binoculars as she scanned the underbrush.

A few minutes later, a bush not far from Kimbunga rustled. Kimbunga glanced up, alert. Sifongo scooted out, panting in submission, and groveled before Kimbunga until the adult finally reached out to him with a pat. Kimbunga then allowed the teenager to groom him.

"Would you look at that?" Andy said. "Sifongo knows a thing or two about politics."

Dana grinned. "He learns quickly."

Mary shouted, "We did it! He did it!" Her voice was loud enough to carry over the distance between the platform and the holding cage without the radio.

The two chimpanzees raised their heads, listening themselves.

Andy stayed to watch the two chimps for signs of aggression while Dana left to share the moment with Mary. When Dana emerged onto the path, Mary was already running toward her, arms flailing over her head in celebration. Dana broke into a wide grin. As they met, they gave each other a smacking high-five. Dana brushed her hand against the smudge of dirt decorating Mary's cheek.

"Sifongo is *so* smart," Mary said as she found the smudge herself, rubbing hard. "He knew *exactly* what to do to escape!"

"And did you see the way he sucked up to Kimbunga afterward? It was awesome."

"And gutsy!"

"I'll bet you Sifongo ends up being dominant," Dana said. "Three or four years from now, Kimbunga will be cowering in *his* presence."

Their Sifongo. He was smart, well loved by his mother and his sister

Neema, looked up to by little Mbu. Perhaps those facts had given him the confidence and the quick wit to escape without a scratch from Kimbunga. Although it was tempting to imagine that all would go smoothly in Group B for Sifongo, Dana knew it would not be so. He was a maturing male and a threat to Kimbunga's power; he would be put in his place repeatedly. Right now, though, all Sifongo had to do was adapt and learn the social structure of his new group. He had already taken the first bold steps to that end.

When Dana finally released Mary from her embrace, she could not help putting her hands back on her friend. "I'm ready to let Barafu adopt," she told Mary. "Now that this is over with, I can concentrate on teaching Barafu motherhood skills."

Mary smiled, but her face had a drawn, tired look that alarmed Dana.

"Are you okay?" Dana asked, peering into Mary's eyes.

"I'm coming down with something, I think," Mary said. She looked away. "And Quentin . . . well, it's not worth discussing now. I'm all right. Really."

"Of course it's worth discussing."

Mary shook her head. "Not right now."

Dana would have pursued it further, would have made Mary confess what was bothering her, if Dean Washington had not right then appeared at the top of the path. He trudged toward them, the gravel slipping under his weight, his arms close to his sides as though he never feared falling, not even on this unsteady path. "I expected protesters to greet me," he said.

"They've left, for now," Dana said.

"I had a phone call. That's why I'm late."

Dana knew right away that the phone call concerned the SCPP—she could tell it from the worried look in his dark eyes. Mary had become as still as the tree she stood next to.

"We have problems," he said.

Dana took a deep breath. "Should we go inside?" she asked.

"I think so."

The three of them walked toward the main building in silence. Dana's feet felt leaden as the triumph of Sifongo vanished and apprehension took its place. She had expected a somber visit from Washington sooner or later—rumors never disappeared completely—and as she held the door of her office open for him and Mary, she was already bracing herself.

After Dana closed the door and they settled into the cramped space, Washington explained that the Sperry-Ashcrofts, who donated twenty thousand dollars a year to the SCPP, were withholding their contribution unless the sanctuary tore down the electric fence and found some other means, such as a moat, to enclose the chimpanzees. They had a list of demands, most more minor than the first. As the dean recited them, Dana regarded the photographs on her walls of the chimpanzees who had come to live there: the female Kimwondo gazing down with a smile at her first adopted son, Zabibu; little Chatu brandishing a stick over his head in a mock threat; Mwenzi puffed up and fierce, his expressive mouth drawn into a stern line across his face; Kitabu wearing an open book like a hat; the females of Group A gathered around Kimwondo during a grooming session; huge Uzanzi lolling on a log, his head tipped back and looking at the camera.

Washington coughed into his fist. "I don't know what to say."

"Twenty thousand wouldn't cover the cost of tearing down the fence and creating a moat, so it's a no-win situation," Dana said. "I'll call them and explain why we have the fence."

"It won't do any good. Mrs. Sperry-Ashcroft was exceedingly firm."

Mary, who was standing with her back supported by the door, pushed herself upright. "Our budget is tight. We can't survive without the money. Will the university help us out?"

"I doubt it. President Davenport . . . well, he isn't exactly sympathetic right now."

If Dana concentrated, her voice would sound controlled and exact, like a metronome instead of the screech it wanted to be. Everything inside her threatened to break loose in a panic, but she vowed not to let it. "Okay, Burton, out with it. Tell us what is going on."

He flinched. Although he clearly had hoped he wouldn't be asked such a straightforward question, he was also unwilling to dodge it completely. "What do you know about Dick Lamier?"

This time, Lamier's name felt sharper and more lethal than when it had come out of Lindsay Brassett's mouth. Dana glanced at Mary with a look that told her friend not to utter a syllable about what Dana had confessed to her.

"He was once a friend of my father's," Dana said. "He's a psychobiologist with a specialty in primates."

"And influential?"

Dana nodded. "In some corners."

"He has been speaking to animal rights groups about the illusion of those rights, and how some facilities purport to treat animals humanely when in fact they exploit them. The SCPP is on that list. Lamier has informed President Davenport that he has a petition with hundreds and hundreds of names. He seems to have Davenport's ear."

"I've heard he has been trying to stir things up against me. But believe me, this battle isn't professional. It's personal."

"Enlighten me."

"I can't." Dana could not reveal to Burton Washington the intimate details she had shared with Mary. She believed the price of her silence bought something of equal value—never having to look Lamier in the eye. An accuser always had to face the accused, and she could not bear much more than sidling away from him in a crowded conference hall. "He can't reach everyone," she said finally.

"That's what frightens me, Dana," he said. "Somehow, he seems to have a list of our biggest donors. He has contacted them personally."

"What?" Dana leapt to her feet and almost climbed atop the desk in her sudden outrage. "The break-in. All the papers were strewn about, and we assumed the chimps had done it." She knew she sounded crazy, but this had to be the answer. "Someone stole those records for Lamier." She dodged the desk and began to pace the small area between Mary and Washington. "This is incredibly unprofessional. How could Lamier have done this?" Despite what he had done to her, she had believed in his discretion and his commitment to his own professionalism. Either one of them—Dana or Lamier—could have sought revenge when the wounds were still fresh. But neither had. It had remained a sinkhole between them that each had skirted.

Her nostrils burned with the acrid smell of hate, and her ears rang. She could barely see distinct edges in the room around her: Washington was an immobile form, Mary transparent like a ghost. Everything felt thin and slippery, as in a fever dream, and she believed right then she was incapable of holding onto anything.

"We'll address this head on," Dana managed to say. "We won't ignore it. I will personally call everyone on our major donation list and explain Lamier's misunderstanding of the sanctuary. I can be as persuasive as he." The room solidified in a rush. Yes, Dana thought, they could cut off Lamier's tactics with honesty. She looked at Mary, whose face had no more color but whose eyes raged now with determination from behind tight lids. *They* could do it.

Burton Washington nodded, his chin cupped in his fist. "All right. I'll work on Davenport. You give me the information I need to tell him. If we don't have the president's support, the sanctuary might as well be closed."

Dana had regained her wits, and her mind raced with the issues they had to address. She began talking rapidly about the electrified fence, the type of noninvasive research at the sanctuary, the demands the university had made and how the staff had implemented them. She pulled journals and conference proceedings off the shelf to pile on Washington's lap so he could see for himself what they had published. The business of this consumed her, so she barely noticed when Mary slipped out of the room, her footsteps not as light as usual, her lips sucked inside her mouth.

THIRTEEN

$\mathcal{H}$arris closed down at six o'clock every night, sometimes earlier if shop owners determined business was not worth it. Now that daylight savings had ended, Dana had to speed down densely dark country roads, the branches of trees scraping her car as she passed, to reach town before the pharmacy closed. Earlier, yet another headache had begun to form its fist behind one eye, and when she had reached into her desk drawer for a pain reliever, she had found only one pill, not enough to carry her through the night.

As she rounded a bend, Dana almost rammed the back end of a sedan parked with its driver's half still on the road. She swerved in time to avoid it, swinging wide across the road. Her headlights caught the open hood and a figure peering inside with a small, dim flashlight. Her worst fear was breaking down on a country road, so without hesitation, she switched on her emergency flashers and backed the truck until her window lined up with the motorist. She saw then that she had stopped to help Sam.

"Need help?" she asked.

"Looks like it."

She parked in front of his car.

"I thought you went home," she said as she walked toward him.

"I did. But I'm back."

She massaged the side of her head with her knuckles. "So, what happened to the car?"

"It's a rental," he said, as though that explained everything. "The lights faded, and then the damn thing conked out. I bet the alternator is dying. I knew I should have driven down and used my own car. You wouldn't have jumper cables, would you?"

"Yeah." As she retrieved the cables from the back of her truck, she said, "I'll follow you into town because if it's the alternator, the charge won't take you far. We'll keep jumping it until we get to Parnell's gas station." She attached the cables and then leaned against her truck as they waited for the battery to charge.

"I won't be a reporter tonight," Sam said after a few minutes of silence, punctuated only by the whispery night sounds of the woods and the hum of the engines. "You don't have to be afraid of me. Or my questions."

"Afraid?" She laughed. In the night, with her face cloaked, it seemed easier to be honest, to confess. "I just can't talk about Annie." She had spoken Annie's name more times in the past few weeks than she had in the previous decade, and her statement now sounded like a lie. "I should've warned you."

"Don't worry about it. Let's just see if we can get the car started. And then I'll buy you dinner."

"You can't get anything to eat in Harris now." She glanced at her watch and saw it was almost six. "Damn. I won't make it in time. I need ibuprofen."

"I have some, but the bottle is all the way up in Orangeburg."

"Is that where you're staying?"

"Yeah." He was pointing his flashlight in and out of the recesses under the hood as though looking for something else. His head shot up. "Oh, shit."

She removed the jumper cables. "I'll drive you. I'll trade a ride for some painkillers."

"Are you sure? It's dark and pretty far."

She slammed her hood shut. She *wanted* to like Sam; she understood the curious mix of reserve and friendliness, his headlong tumble into obsession despite the cautious way he regarded his surroundings. "I rarely leave work this early. I feel like I have the whole evening ahead of me. Just get in your car and start driving toward town. Before that thing dies again."

They had to stop once more to charge Sam's battery before they rolled into Parnell's closed gas station in the middle of town. At six-thirty, under the moonless late-autumn sky, Harris resembled the ghost towns of Westerns. Dana dug a piece of paper out of her briefcase and scribbled a note on it, then snapped it against the windshield with the wiper blade.

"He fixes my truck all the time," she said. "He'll call me before he does anything. In case the rental agency wants to have it towed somewhere else."

With Sam in the passenger seat, Dana drove out of the gas station. She feared they would not have anything to talk about, that they would sit there with their faces illuminated by the dashboard into green alien masks so bizarre they could not even glance at each other. But when Sam started talking about the first time he pulled into Orangeburg, his voice settled on her like a purring cat, and she stroked it in her mind, listening to its inconsequential details with strange pleasure. She had thought him uptight, but now she saw that had been his reporter's stance. Now that he was a stranded motorist, he seemed both more commonplace and more gentle.

"It took me a long time to get used to this part of the country," Dana said. "Now, I'm used to the sanctuary. I guess that's a step forward."

"I'm too . . . I was going to say East Coast, but this is the East Coast, too, isn't it?"

"Too Northeastern?"

"Yeah. I'm too Northeastern. Too impatient, in a hurry. Not genteel enough."

"Trust me. Not everyone here is genteel." She was thinking of Judith at the diner in town, where she bought her coffee to go every Wednesday morning. Judith never said more than a word or two to Dana; though she was never impolite, she was not friendly either, even after five years of listening to Dana order a large coffee with a splash of milk, no sugar, and one blueberry muffin.

"You don't seem Oklahoman. I hear a bit of twang, but not much. Zack has more of an accent than you do. Twang mixed with Rhode Island." When she did not answer right away, he said, "I'm not being a reporter, I swear. It was only a comment."

She laughed. "My mother grew up in Pennsylvania and my father in Michigan. I talk like them. Besides, if you live in a university environment, you end up not being from any place at all."

"My father was the town doctor. Three generations of Wendts lived in my Connecticut hometown. We are so rooted there that it seems impossible to everyone that I live in Virginia."

They talked about nothing important, talked about themselves so factually that it was almost like discussing the weather. The dispassionate nature of their conversation allowed Dana to imagine that her troubles were not as bad as she thought. Every word felt lighter than the last. However, when she stopped the car in front of Sam's motel, the space between them became clumsy and viscous. The sullen remnants of their last argument suddenly lay there in the space between them. "I'll get your ibuprofen," Sam said.

When he came back, he thrust the bottle into her hand. "Keep the whole thing."

"You sure?"

"It's the least I can do."

"Okay. Thanks." She looked longingly at the medicine bottle but had nothing to drink. She tossed the bottle onto the passenger seat. Sam was leaning against the door, his arms along the window ridge. The garish light from the overhead lamps lit up the dark hair on its arms, and she noticed the strength in his forearms. She guessed he must lift weights. She wanted to look closer at them, to touch them, or at least to keep them pressed against her truck. "Are you finished with your article yet?"

"No. Yes. I sent the one in, as well as a small write-up on the break-in. Now, I'm writing the longer article. The complementary one."

"Complimentary?"

"Complementary. To go with the short one."

"Oh." The silence between them was getting more dense and impenetrable. She could no longer justify lingering there. "Well, I'd better get back."

"You don't want to get dinner? My offer still stands."

"Um, sure. Yes. I have time."

Sam must have remembered that she was a vegetarian because he suggested an "ethnically confused" Indian and Caribbean restaurant that he said served a decent vegetable curry. When they arrived, the restaurant was nearly empty, though most of the tables were still littered with coffee cups and dessert plates, as though everyone had only moments before stood in unison and left. Dana had been a waitress while an undergraduate, and she knew the exhaustion at the end of each shift. She guessed most of the staff was in the back eating, massaging their limbs, wishing they were done with their work for the night, groaning as they heard that another couple had walked in.

Sam ordered the vegetable curry, which made him seem predictable and staid. Normally, this would have turned Dana off because she thrived on exploration, but on a night like this, it seemed a relief. She wanted to be with someone who knew what he liked. Several times during dinner, Sam started to say something, then cut himself off. At first, she tried to ignore him, since she knew the reporter was struggling to escape and she did not want to talk about the sanctuary. Still, she needed to know what it was that periodically jerked his eyes away from hers and made them focus on the backs of his hands. Finally, Dana could stand it no longer. "Okay. You promised not to be a reporter, but *something* is eating at you. Out with it."

He grimaced and, oddly, blushed along his cheekbones. "I talked to Dick Lamier a few days ago."

"Oh, fuck." She lowered her voice. "Did he tell you that people should stop giving the SCPP donations?"

"Not in as many words." He looked directly at her, his expression calm but inquisitive, gauging. "He wanted me to take a look at the sanctuary. To see where it's unsafe."

She sighed. "It's not unsafe. It's revolutionary, and that scares a lot of people."

"What about the electric fence?"

"Well, at least Lamier is consistent. Why electric fencing? Because if we built a moat around the perimeter, we'd have alligators and cottonmouths swimming in it and on the banks sunning themselves. So tell me, which is safer? A moat or an unpleasant—but not damaging— fence? We had a donor today withdraw her support because she listened to Lamier's speech on electric fences."

"And what about the chimps housed in isolation?"

She stared at him long and hard before answering. Of all Lamier's criticisms, this was the most dangerous and the most persuasive, especially when it came to animal rights. "Those few can't get along with the others. It's not as though we *want* them to live alone. We give them as much as we can. But we have a responsibility to protect the other chimps."

"He also said the chimps might suffer frostbite during cold winters because they can't seek shelter."

"All I know is *our* chimps—most of them, anyway—understand they can get help from us if they enter the enclosure holding cages. Once, a viral infection swept through Group B, and the cage there looked like a doctor's waiting room. Four dehydrated chimps sat by the door while a couple of companions calmed them with grooming. Many places do bring their chimps in every night, just to make sure they're monitored carefully. We've made a calculated decision to sacrifice close medical attention for large areas of freedom. Believe me, Andy searches the enclosures daily for signs of sick or injured chimps."

"I said I wasn't going to be a reporter."

"Go ahead. I'm feeling generous, now that my headache is waning."

"I need to know something, Dana. I need to know why Lamier is out to get you. Zack told me Lamier was a family friend, but he's hardly acting the part. What is it, Dana? Should I know something about your relationship with him?"

Why did everything always have to come back to the past? It was as though Dana was not allowed a future. No matter how much she strove to escape the past, it returned to chip away at her like a chisel against imperfect marble, until nothing remained. "Dick Lamier *was* a friend of the family. When I was sixteen, he took me to a medical lab where he said Annie was being held. But it wasn't Annie. If you've never been inside a medical lab, you can't possibly understand how traumatic it was. . . . I think my father pressured him to leave Brown after that."

"But Lamier knew Annie wasn't there."

Dana felt as though an icy hand had been placed at the base of her neck. "That's exactly what my father said. How would Lamier know that Annie wasn't there?"

"I can't say. Not yet."

"Did you find Annie?" Her voice was rising to a shrill pitch, but she could not control it. "Did you find out what happened to her?"

He shook his head. His eyes expressed regret, maybe even a little pity, and she knew then that the shaking of his head was a lie, a substitute for words he did not want to say. Sam knew what had happened to Annie. She had known in her heart for decades that no good had come from Annie's sale, that only the slimmest of chances would find her alive after all those years, and now she saw in Sam's eyes that she had been right. She was thankful for the lie, however. Worse than knowing death was knowing the details of a horrible one.

"I've ruined dinner," he said.

"If you look at it metaphysically, it was ruined before it began." She gave a short laugh. "Your car broke down, and I've lost a huge benefactor—how could we possibly be completely cheerful? At least the food is good."

He grinned. "I like that. A fatalist who's also a hedonist."

"Something like that."

After dinner, they went out into the half-deserted street to Dana's truck, which in the strange illumination of the streetlights appeared black and colorless, cold even. Dana wished she did not have to drive all the way back to Harris. She entertained, briefly, the idea of asking Sam if she could sleep in his motel room—surely, he had twin beds—but then was mortified she had even thought of it. She rounded the truck and hopped behind the wheel.

As Sam opened the passenger door, he hesitated. "I've never owned an animal." Acting as though his admission had relieved a burden, he pulled himself all the way into the cab and shut the door.

"Never? Not even a dog or a cat? Or an iguana? Fish?"

"Nope." He pulled his seat belt across his chest and lap. "My older brothers begged my parents to get us a puppy, but it never worked. I wasn't especially heartbroken. The idea of a puppy sounded cool—every boy I knew had a dog—but I would've rather had a new bike."

She turned the key in the ignition. "Some people just aren't animal people."

"But maybe I am. I've never had a pet, so how would I know what I'm missing?"

"I don't know." She backed into the street and headed toward the motel.

"So, what is it like? To love an animal. To have one living with you."

Dana glanced at him, seeing in the quick flash of vision that he was serious and not making fun of her. "Like this," she said, striking the dashboard with her open palm. "Simple, direct, obvious. You don't skirt your love. You don't hedge it, and you don't live in fear the love won't be returned. You give her a big hug whenever you walk into the house, and you pet and coo, spoil her, whenever you feel like it. It doesn't matter whether she's a chimp or a cat—you love her openly. In return, she looks at you with eyes that accept who you are, whatever you are. You *know* each other in a way no two humans ever will."

"You think it's better than human love?"

She heard the same hardness in his voice as the day he asked her about chimp morality, but she was not going to tailor her answer to make him docile. "Not better. Different. Simpler. Your cat isn't going to divorce you."

He laughed loudly and suddenly. "I take it, then, you're divorced?"

She had not meant it to sound personal. "Yeah. I guess I should've married my cat."

"I think the law prohibits the kind of life you're advocating."

She laughed. "Well, if I've learned anything in this profession, it's that laws are not perfect."

As Dana pulled into the motel lot, she slowed the truck to a crawl. The harsh lighting gave the low-lying structure a look of desolation, and she felt sorry for Sam, having to live the kind of life that made this his temporary home. She pulled into a parking space. The same stubborn silence that had rattled them earlier settled inside the cab. Sam laid a warm hand on her elbow. She could not take her eyes off it.

"You have every right to hate me," he said, "but I'd like to invite you in."

She could not misunderstand his intentions. Maybe she *was* one-night-stand material to a middle-aged man who knew no one else in town. Her skin felt hot underneath his hand. Sam knew things about her even Charlie did not, and that frightened her; he had already peeled away the layers to the naked her beneath. In his free hand, his room key glinted dully in the light. They were suspended, she thought, held aloft by her decision.

When she lifted her eyes from her elbow, she found his face. The expression there stirred something odd within her. She could not call this feeling lust or distaste, but something disturbingly in between. Had it been so long since she slept with a man that it was now impossible? Her stomach fluttered at the idea of being alone in a depressing motel room with him. She was all mixed up, she thought, going crazy.

"I should get home," she stammered. "But thanks."

He straightened and took back his hand. "Oh. Okay." Then, as he recovered, he said, "I have a long day tomorrow, too."

She felt the stirrings of regret for having refused him. Maybe Charlie had been right when he suggested she see a therapist to correct her distorted view of what it meant to be human.

⌒⋎⋏⌒

Zack's dented car sat untouched against the bushes for days, until

Dana awoke to heavy rain and, remembering that her brother had left his windows open, scrambled through the downpour and inside the car. She half-expected to find the seats full of stray cats and lizards, all delirious from the drugs they had discovered in the crevices, but only winged insects inhabited the car, fluttering weakly against the roof. She sat behind the steering wheel listening to the drumming of water against the tinny roof. Through the windshield, the world resembled an abstract painting, color without form, blended by the density of water into a single integrated but incomprehensible object. She shivered under the weight of wet clothes.

As she did each time Zack vanished, she said a prayer that he would return again, safe and sane. He had never left something as valuable as a car before, and Dana, although not generally superstitious, considered it might be a bad sign. This rusted, mangled, coughing piece of machinery was all Zack owned—at least all she *knew* he owned. The Ford defined who Zack was as much as the sanctuary defined her.

Her fingers twitched. Should she? Once the thought came to her, she could not resist. She pressed the chrome button to the glove box and let the door fall open with a clunk. She did not know what she expected—a gun seemed too belligerent, drugs too obvious—but she wilted with relief when she saw only a few ragged maps, a crushed brown paper bag, candy wrappers, and a pair of broken sunglasses. Tossing her head back against the headrest, she breathed deeply for a moment before leaning forward again to pick the debris out of the box. She could not believe Zack, the way he stuffed garbage in the wrong places. Who knew where he had stashed trash in her house? She would have to check under the sofa cushions, in drawers, behind the roll-out trash can under the kitchen sink. With two fingers pinched in disgust, she removed the candy wrappers one by one and dropped them on the seat. As she pulled out the brown bag, which rattled with the recognizable papery shifting of a few peanuts, she saw the dull glint of metal that its removal had exposed: a single key. The key had the generic look of a hardware copy, but she recognized the shape at once as the type used at the sanctuary. She covered it with four fingers, hesitating for several pounds of her heart before she slid it out and caught it between her thumb and palm.

At first, she convinced herself it was the key to one of Zack's apartments, something he had never returned, or maybe something that let him into a permanent residence he had never confessed to her. But the fantasy could not sustain itself within her, not with what she knew about her brother. Against the metallic light of the day, she examined it. The pattern of the teeth was too familiar to dismiss.

Damn you, Zack.

She breathed hard with the evidence of her brother's betrayal in her palm. The world outside was obscured by sheets of water drawing wide, viscous lines through color and form, over the glass and metal that contained her, and she imagined everything outside had disappeared with her discovery.

Where are you, Zack? Tell me about this, clear your name, tell me I'm wrong.

Hurriedly, she crumpled the trash together into a ball with the key. She dashed through the rain toward the house, even then knowing how she would throw the whole mess into the garbage and knot the trash bag tightly to hide it. On Monday, when she made the trip to the dump, none of what she had discovered would be left behind.

FOURTEEN

$\mathcal{Z}$ack's untied shoelaces snapped against his bare ankles as he trudged across the beach toward Becca, who was sleeping on a magenta towel. The beach was almost deserted, so she stood out in shades of pink—skin, bikini, towel—against a field of beige. She should have been hung over, but her expression was serene.

"Hey," he said as he dropped to the sand next to her.

Her eyes were hidden behind large sunglasses. He could barely tell that she was still healing. "Hey," she said in a dreamy voice. Even in late fall, the Florida sun was restorative; she looked healthier and stronger after just a week of it. Each day, Zack remembered more and more of who she was.

"You're practically the only one out here," he told her.

"Chickens." The hint of a smile appeared at the corners of her mouth. "You're up early."

He shrugged. "I missed you. You hungry?"

"Not yet."

"You *hungry*?"

"Go away, Zack. I don't want that either."

He sat there for several minutes in silence, looking out over the whitecaps of the ocean. A line of pelicans skirted the shoreline overhead. He shouldn't have come out to the beach, he knew that now. Their daily routine had already been established, and his breaking it by being up before noon threatened the delicate equilibrium. She wanted nothing to do with him, yet he could not leave. He felt like he was going to turn inside out from the waiting and the knowing and the uselessness the day had suddenly shown him. He wanted to rake his fingernails along the length of his face and down his chest.

After a while, the rhythm of the waves calmed him. He snuck a peek at Becca, who despite the cool day already had tiny beads of perspiration, like diamond chips, vibrating on her chest. God, he was crazy for her. He couldn't figure out how it had happened, or when, but he felt sometimes like a dog begging for that one kind look, a touch on his shoulder, a smile of approval. Yeah, the sex was great, but the rest . . . He could not understand it. He hungered after her in ways he had never known with another woman. So he sat. And waited. The day warmed and dried the back of his throat, giving him a cloying, sandy thirst. A few people arrived with blankets they snapped into the wind before letting them settle to the ground. A couple even went into the water and swam crisp freestyle strokes beyond where the waves broke. But Zack said nothing. He shifted slightly in position, and then only to chase the small cramps of inactivity that nagged him.

Finally, Becca sat up with a lazy smile, removing her glasses like a movie star. The skin around one eye had a yellow-green tinge, and Zack winced. "I'm hungry now," she said. "What do you want to do?"

He reached out to brush the downy hair along her arm. "I want to make you happy."

"Happy?" She laughed, too loudly. "God, Zack, I'm running from my husband, and happiness is the last thing on my mind. I just want to survive. So what if we start with a couple of doughnuts and a cup of coffee?"

"Okay."

She softened her voice. "I *am* happy sometimes, Zack. Here and there. Don't ask for more right now." She slipped her sweatshirt over her head and wiggled her arms into the sleeves.

He wanted to tell her that he understood perfectly because that was how he had lived his life for years—scared, scrambling to get through that day and the next, finding only glimpses of contentment that vanished sometimes as quickly as they appeared—but he knew better. He stood and held out his hand to her. "Come on. Let's get breakfast."

With Becca's towel and beach bag on one arm, he could barely remember South Carolina. It seemed so long ago, so unimportant. They staggered through the sand, their ankles giving way to the shifting ground beneath and their legs working hard against it. Everything here—the ground, the light, the colors, the sounds—seemed to be an integral part of him. His muscles were kneaded free of tension, and his mind was less troubled.

Becca stumbled. Zack darted his hand out to catch her. When she smiled her gratitude, he touched the nape of her neck where the skin was soft and the hairs like whispers. He closed his eyes just briefly to try to remember this moment, so he could go to it whenever he screwed up, which was inevitable despite his newfound calm.

"I want to do something wild," she said so quietly he could barely hear her. "I want to do something I've never done before, something most people would shrink from. And then we can talk about happiness."

⌒⋏⋏⌒

Dana could tell that something preoccupied Mary. At first, she believed it might have been their argument about Barafu, but Mary waved her away with a smile when Dana tried to apologize. "That's over. You were right," Mary told her. "I let my emotions get in the way of my judgment."

"Are you concerned about the Lamier mess?"

"Of course. But I'm pretty confident we can handle that."

"Is anything else wrong?"

"Nope. Why? Do you think I'm pissed at you or something?"

"I don't know."

"Well, I'm *not*."

Dana finally concluded that Mary's distraction had nothing to do with the sanctuary. She reasoned that when Mary was ready to confide in her, she would. In the meantime, Dana had to concentrate on reversing the damage of rumor.

They set up a command post in Dana's office. The computer printout of donors, divided into groups of varying financial support, was stacked in the center of the newly cleared desk. Four phones had been arranged on top of the desk with chairs beside them; the wires linking them to their jacks snaked down the desk, across the floor, and out the door, crisscrossing on their way to the offices. Mary, Kaylee, and Christopher took their positions.

Although Dana had held these phone marathons before—the staff did it twice a year using the main campus facilities—her hands started shaking as soon as she picked up the receiver. She kept thinking of Zack and her own carelessness. How she always left her sanctuary keys on the table by her front door, even on weekends, even when she went out. How easy and tempting she had made it for him. She wished it had been Lamier who snuck onto the property, so she could exact her private revenge, but Lamier was simply attacking on another, more legitimate front, at a time when Dana could barely get her wits together to combat him.

Had Zack stolen the sanctuary's mailing list? Was he, and not Lamier, responsible for the withdrawal of support?

Dana dialed the first number. At first, she could not find her voice, but as it broke tremulously into words, she gathered strength and persuasion. This was her job—she had to do it, and she could do it well. And so she did. She listened to the others in the room as she spoke and gauged their level of success as she was measuring her own. Some contributors had no intention of withdrawing their support, while others had already pledged their money to other animal protection organizations. The wavering ones, though, were the people Dana needed to ferret out.

Between calls, Dana glanced across the small room at Mary. Mary's eyes were lowered, the receiver pressed to her ear. Dana stared. Mary looked different to her, not on the surface but deeper, more intangibly. What Dana saw, or felt, was less evidence than intuition. A subtle shifting of Mary's expression and coloring of her skin. As Dana continued to stare, trying to figure out what was different, Mary looked up and flashed her a smile.

Mary finished before Dana and slipped out of the office with a wave and a mouthed, "See you later." Dana doggedly finished her list of numbers to call. When she finally thought she was done for the day, the phone rang. She considered allowing the machine to pick up—she could hardly bear the thought of pressing the receiver to her ear for another second—but answered it anyway.

"Hello," she said as cheerfully as she could muster. "SCPP. Dana Armstrong."

"Hi, Dana. It's Sam. I'm home, in Arlington."

Arlington. It had been several days since she left him standing in the motel parking lot. "Hi."

"Listen. There's something I should have asked you but didn't. I guess I was a little afraid." He seemed in a rush, as though he had made up his mind to speak but could not pare his thoughts. "And I'm still chicken now, which is why, I guess, I'm calling you long distance instead of asking you in person. Someone—and I won't say who—implied that Zack may have been responsible for the break-in. What do you think?"

She tried to maintain her breathing in a steady rhythm, like that of deep sleep. Ever since finding the key in Zack's car, she had been able to dodge its implications. She had told herself she was too busy, that Zack had left Harris anyway, that she had already taken away his mode of entry by throwing the key out. She had believed she could ignore what she knew, and it would slip into the past. "I don't know what to think."

"Do you have any reason to suspect him?"

She could not lie, not to Sam, but she could not tell him the truth either. Zack was her brother and would still be in her life years from then. She chose her words carefully. "Why would Zack do something like that? It doesn't make sense, does it? But you should really talk to him. Unfortunately, I don't know where he is."

"He's not staying with you?"

"Zack is like a stray cat. He'll wander in when it's convenient for him, then he'll move on to someone else's bowl of milk. For all I know, he's in Mexico."

"Would there be a reason for you to suspect that he's gone out of the country?"

The laughter exploded out of her as unexpectedly and naturally as the detonation of a jack-in-the-pulpit seedpod. "I've *never* been able to figure out his migratory patterns. If you pin him down, let me know. My family would be appreciative."

"I can't pin *you* down either," he said.

Although she knew he did not mean it sexually, they both realized after the words how they could be interpreted, and that gangly awkwardness again came between them. This time, Dana was determined to be the one who broke it. "I'm exactly what you see," she told Sam. "I live and breathe chimps, and everything else I do in my life is filler. You may want to see me as a complicated, hard-to-decipher person, but I'm not. I don't have time for complexity."

He laughed. "I know enough about you to see the undercurrents. You haven't allowed them to surface, that's all."

Fine, believe what you want. She had been honest about herself, and he did not believe her. "Listen, I'd love to chat. But we're losing donations to Lamier's little speeches. I've been on the phone all day trying to rally support. I really can't stand another minute of holding this phone to my ear."

After she hung up, Dana sat for several seconds in her chair trying to rein in her fear that Sam would expose Zack, and therefore her. She had been stupid, that was for sure. Then she remembered Mary. Whatever was bugging Mary had to be more manageable than Zack.

Dana found Mary outside Barafu's cage. They had given Barafu a chimp doll, which they were teaching her to nurture. Fikira was old enough not to be carried, but she needed the protection and assistance of an adult. By using the stuffed chimp, they hoped to introduce Barafu to the concept of childcare. Mary had already spent hours with Barafu on this. Even though Dana had planned to do much of the work, Mary always beat her to it. Mary now sat outside the cage, her shoulders leaning against the bars. She did not seem to be watching Barafu, who, crouched in a corner with her "baby," inspected the doll under the arms, then flipped it over to examine the fur on its back.

"How's Barafu doing?" Dana asked.

Mary drew herself out of her reverie limb by limb until she appeared completely alert. She glanced at Barafu. "Okay. Of course, a toy is not the real thing."

"If she rips the head off, it's a good sign she may not be ready."

"What makes a good mother? Why aren't all women equally gifted when it comes to raising a child? Can you actually be *trained* to be a good mother?"

Dana sat across from her so that the toes of their boots touched. "I wish I knew. I wish it were simple."

"Do you think you'd make a good mother?"

"No. I'm too involved with my career. I don't want to give anything up. I'd resent the time a baby would take."

"So you think a woman can't do both well? Career and motherhood?"

"I said *I* couldn't. The best mothers *want* to be mothers." She stopped. "Wait. This isn't about Barafu, is it?"

Mary shook her head, then met Dana's gaze. "I'm pregnant, Dana. It happened."

"Oh, my God! Mary, that's *wonderful*. I can't believe it." Goose bumps prickled her from head to toe as she scooted over the cement floor. She threw her arms around her friend and held her close as Mary burst into tears. "Oh, Mare, I hope those are happy tears."

Mary shook her head in the embrace.

"Okay, what's wrong?" Dana grasped Mary by the shoulders and moved her away a little, so she could see her better. "You're supposed to be thrilled."

Mary wiped one finger under her eye. "There's so much . . . Maybe because I thought it was never going to happen, I could want it. But now that it *has* happened, I'm not sure. Not sure if I can do it."

"Of course you can."

"I'm so *tired* all the time. And I feel like I can never swallow. I'll throw up."

Dana laughed. "Sounds normal to me."

"What if I don't *like* normal?"

"Your body has decided to have a normal pregnancy, damn what your brain wants. If you had it your way, you'd be giving birth to a full-term baby with a genius IQ after a gestation period of an hour. Sorry. It ain't happening that way."

Mary looked away and into Barafu's cage. Barafu, seeing the shift of attention, ambled over to them, knuckle-walking with the doll clenched in one hand.

"Hey, girl," Dana said. Then she grunted a greeting.

Barafu grunted back. She sat facing them, her eyes brighter than Dana remembered ever seeing them, and signed, *She baby.* To make no mistake, the chimp gestured toward Mary.

"Did you tell her?" Dana asked. It seemed out of character for Mary to talk to the chimpanzees.

Mary shook her head. "It's been freaking me out. You know when we thought she was asking for a baby? I think she was telling me that I'm pregnant."

"But I asked her if *she* wanted a baby."

"Barafu may be an opportunist."

Dana sat back on her heels. At first, Barafu had signed only the word for baby. Dana had been the one to probe further, asking leading questions. The language between them had been so simple that Dana had allowed herself to make wrong assumptions. "If you're right, I've screwed myself," Dana said. The lesson of it weighed on her. "I was stupid. Letting Barafu have a child could be construed as negligence. What will that do to the sanctuary's funding?"

"You're still going to let her try to adopt Fikira, aren't you?"

"I promised. And Inge has been readying Fikira." They had Barafu's complete attention, even though the chimp could not possibly understand their conversation. Dana had to look away.

"It won't fail," Mary said. "I won't let it." Barafu shifted her position against the bars so her hair brushed against Mary. Mary began grooming the chimp, her head turned from Dana. "I can't have contact with the HIV and hepatitis chimps until after the baby is born."

"That's easy to arrange. We'll just keep you out of Group B. And no Tekua."

Mary lowered her head closer to Barafu's hair, intent upon the task. "There's one more possible complication."

"Whatever it is, we'll deal with it."

Mary's fingers hesitated on Barafu. "Quentin is looking for another job. Outside South Carolina. If he accepts something, I'll have to go with him. I can't have a baby without him. I can't do this alone."

This news felt like the last blow she could absorb. Dana almost said she would help Mary raise her child, that she would do anything to keep her there in Harris. "Does he have any offers?"

"No. It may be a moot point. But I wanted to warn you."

Mary is leaving. Dread grew like fast-spreading cancer inside Dana, and her skin burned with its poison. Mary was her only friend in South Carolina—what was Dana going to do without her? She felt the acute loneliness of the future even before it had become reality. With a short sob of desperation, Dana threw her arms around Mary and clung to her friend. Mary burst into tears again.

"I don't want you to go," Dana said into Mary's head. "I need you."

Barafu reached through the cage and patted their heads, trying to comfort them.

"Oh, Dana. I'm so scared. I don't know what to do."

Dana sniffled as they separated. "If you go, I won't hate you for following your heart. I *can't* hate you." She blinked back her watery vision and stroked Barafu's arm through the bars, the chimp regarding her with mournful eyes. Dana grunted reassurance. Barafu then looked past her to Mary, whom she reached out to, gently. Dana ached with the realization that Barafu had bonded with Mary. "Maybe you should come back inside with me."

"I'm fine. Barafu and I are almost finished with our baby work today. I feel better now that I've told you."

As Dana rose to leave, Mary and Barafu looked up at her, their expressions mirrors of each other's, and Dana was struck with the image of the two of them as sisters, one chimp, one human. Their mutual understanding of maternal desires excluded her. She looked away, down the corridor toward the exit.

Everything was slipping away.

Oh, Annie.

Near the end of her time with the Armstrongs, Annie had pointed to the fence gate in the backyard and signed, *Me go out.*

Dana's mother had signed back, *No. Annie stays home. Silly girl. We play here.*

Annie pouted. *Annie go out. Me.*

No. Annie belongs here.

Annie had hurled herself against the stockade fence, rattling and pounding it until Dana thought the whole section would collapse. Her mother tried to stop her by taking hold of her arm, but Annie was already too strong for all of them, and she easily shook herself free. Dana, at nine, had a sudden insight about what it meant to be Annie: the fence, the human clothes, the frustrating language, the rituals, the circumscribed life. Bellowing, Dana ran toward the fence and threw herself against it, one shoulder crashing into it like a weak battering ram. She jump-kicked the fence. She shrieked. She hammered on it with her fists alongside Annie.

"Dana Joyce Armstrong!" Susan yelled. "Stop it this minute or you're grounded."

Dana knew better than to fear being grounded, so she screeched and thumped with Annie while Susan, her hair corkscrewed by the humidity, the perspiration already soaking her armpits, shouted at them to behave. Everything about Dana ached—her shoulders, her knees, the tough bottoms of her feet—but she wouldn't stop, not until Annie did. Susan's eyes were wide, her mouth twisted and desperate. Dana knew they had pushed her mother too far, but she could not stop. She turned to Susan and gave the loudest, most belligerent chimpanzee screech she had ever uttered; it came from the depths of her diaphragm with the force of rage. Susan must have seen the jungle in her daughter and been shocked by it, must have realized the beast her husband's experiment had given birth to, because she burst into tears and ran into the house. Although Dana felt a tug in her chest, a small terror at having brought down her mother, she kept battering the fence until Annie, too tired to continue, fell into a crouch in the dusty yard, emitting a whimper. Dana wrapped her arms around Annie and snuggled into the familiar bulk of the chimp.

Good Annie. Dana love Annie.

Annie love Dana.

Dana felt sorry for her mother, but not wholly. Her mother had no understanding of Annie's demand. Annie did not want only to leave the yard but also freedom from her small plot of life and the family that contained it. She wanted to go to school, perhaps, to have her own friends, to explore what lay beyond the rectangle of beaten-up grass that held all she had ever known. Annie knew she was caged in the Armstrong house against her nature and desire, and she wanted something more for herself, even if she did not understand what awaited her. Susan, as much as she truly loved Annie, never saw past the animal exterior to understand the complexities that lay underneath.

Dana *had* known Annie. But she had never known Benji, nor would she ever know Barafu. In trying to enrich their lives, she had distanced herself—and all humans—from them. Was this really the best philosophy? Would it be better to share knowledge of one another, since the chimps could never be wild anyway? Dana wished she had the answer. She began to doubt her right to construct their world as she saw fit, to decide whether they should be allowed to reproduce, to dictate who would live in which group. She was playing God with the chimpanzees' lives and yet was only human.

And now Mary was leaving her. The only person capable of keeping her grounded.

As Dana exited the holding area, she banged her shoulder against the steel doorframe as though she had no sense of her own size. Cursing, she rubbed her throbbing joint with one hand and swung the door shut with the other. She took a few steps toward the main building and her office, but sheer exhaustion overcame her, so she stopped. Acorns were falling from an oak tree alongside the path like the patter of rain, and she watched one strike the gravel and ricochet off into the soft carpet of pine needles. Above, two squirrels chattered and bounced from limb to limb. Instead of continuing to the main building, she turned around in a decisive grind of gravel and headed toward the nursery outbuilding.

The nursery was in an early-afternoon uproar, the juveniles scrambling after one another up the fake trees and through the tire swing, skidding around the poles, slapping one another with glee. Even through the viewing walls, the noise was deafening. Dana stood next to Inge and Barbara with her palms against the glass. Kitabu, naked and without her doll, cowered in one corner while her peers dashed in their mad game of tag. As Marika scampered toward her, Kitabu, her mouth going from play face to fear to play face, held out her hand. Marika slapped it as she went by, and Kitabu shrieked and covered her head, squishing herself further into the corner, as though she hoped to disappear. When she finally dared to peer from behind her arms, her eyes at once met Dana's, and she lifted her arms, asking to be whisked away from the mayhem.

"I'm taking Kitabu out," Dana said. "This is too much for her."

"She's fine," Inge said. "Who wouldn't be overwhelmed when these guys get going? Before long, she'll be joining them."

Dana's arms twitched with longing. She wanted to rush into the enclosure to rescue Kitabu and hug her close; she imagined Kitabu felt as *she* would if she were stripped naked and locked in an unsupervised mental health ward. The fear, the misunderstanding, the chaos—they would be too much to bear. The juveniles chased each other with an eagerness foreign to Kitabu. She would have been punished for such behavior by her wealthy recluse. If Kitabu was capable of wondering (and Dana believed she was), she would likely be thinking, *Why are they getting away with this, and when will we all pay the price?*

Six-year-old Bora picked up a palmetto frond and walked toward Kitabu on two legs, waving the frond above his head in an awkward imitation of a male display. As he came toward Kitabu, his mouth opened wide in play, Kitabu grimaced and shrank from him. At once, Bora set his jaw as fiercely as a six-year-old could and charged, swatting Kitabu with the frond before leaping away with a delighted hoot. Kitabu screamed. She rushed for the door and pounded on it with flailing arms.

Dana could take it no longer. She hurried around the corner to the door. As she opened it, Kitabu, still screaming, exploded into Dana's arms, where she bounced and cried and clung to her.

"Shh. It's okay." Dana stroked Kitabu's warm head. "Shh." Then she said to Inge, "I'm taking Kitabu back to the main building for the day. We can try again tomorrow."

Without a word, Inge turned away, but Dana had seen the knot of disagreement between her eyes.

On the way up the path, Kitabu buried her head against Dana's chest. Her strong, hairy arms wrapped around Dana's torso, and Dana marveled how, when really frightened, Kitabu found her chimp grip as naturally as a child called out his mother's name. Poor Kitabu. Everything she had loved had been taken from her. Dana laid her cheek atop Kitabu's head.

As soon as Dana placed her on the floor of her cage, Kitabu raced to the child's potty in the corner. When she was done, she pulled on her shorts, snapping the waistband as though to assure herself they were really there. She then picked up her rag doll and clutched it to her chest.

"Want me to read a book?" Dana asked, sitting on the straw-strewn floor.

Kitabu selected several picture books from her pile and, holding them and her doll against her chest, made her way toward Dana, walking upright for a few staggering steps, then on one folded-under hand for a few more. Kitabu climbed into Dana's lap and leaned heavily on her, waiting. Dana imagined that if she were to close her eyes, she might believe she held a human child, her own, perhaps. As Dana took the first book, she glanced down at Kitabu, who was drawing a finger across the cover art. Dana was filled with love for her—for her delicately folded ear, for the way she held her doll, for her fascination with picture books, for everything that defined Kitabu. Dana opened the book to the first page, which depicted a pig in a sty. Kitabu tilted her head back to see Dana, her face radiant. Dana smiled at her.

Kitabu loved farm animals, so the first book was a pictorial inventory of a barnyard—one cow, two lambs, three sheepdogs, four pigs. . . . By the time Dana reached the eight horses, Kitabu had relaxed against her, no longer stroking the images with her blunt fingertips but content to see them from a distance. Before they finished, Kitabu's head lolled sleepily onto Dana's sore shoulder.

Dana sat there until her back could take it no longer. She scooted a path through the straw matting until her back met the relief of the wall. Kitabu's face was so sweet and helpless in sleep that Dana wondered why she had tried to take away her innocence by traumatizing her in the nursery. Just as quickly, she knew she had been wrong to remove her. Kitabu belonged with her own species.

Mary appeared outside the cage. "Dean Washington is on the phone."

"Tell him I'll call him back."

Mary looked hard at Dana, then at Kitabu. "I thought the plan was to let Kitabu spend six hours in the nursery today."

"You should have seen her, Mare. She was terrified. She doesn't know what to do when the babies get into their frenzy."

"And she's going to learn here, in solitary confinement?"

"I know my job. Okay? Now, are you going to tell the dean I'll call him back?"

"You can't blow him off."

Dana traced the pink brow ridge of Kitabu's face, and the chimp stirred under her touch, averting her face in sleep. "I'm not blowing anyone off," Dana said. "I'm doing my job."

"I hope this has nothing to do with what I told you," Mary said as she turned. " 'Cause I'd be really pissed at you if it did."

Dana could not bear to look at Mary for fear Mary would see straight into her heart. She could feel Mary's indecision—whether to go or stay. *Stay*, Dana mentally told her. *Don't let me be this mean to you.* But after a moment, Mary moved down the hall with the rapid clunk of work boots on linoleum. Dana let her head fall back against the bright blue cinderblock wall. When she closed her eyes, she could see Annie.

FIFTEEN

$\mathcal{Z}$ack had friends in Florida. He introduced Becca to some of them, and then told them under his breath, "Hands off." They understood that he was sleeping with her, and maybe that was all they understood. He tried not to spend much time with them, for fear Becca would discover their common bond of drug abuse. He did not want to give her a reason to leave him.

Becca told him that she liked Rocky, who had a goofy charm not unlike Zack's, and Pete, because he seemed like a gentle soul. Walt had unnerved her at first—he was an observer, and that made her edgy—but she had grown to admire the breadth of his knowledge, from how to keep the lines in the center of the road painted straight to how many teeth a nurse shark had. You just had to ask Walt, and he would tell you. Even if he was lying, he certainly made an authoritative case for his "facts."

Becca distrusted Nate (whom Zack did not like either, but he came with Walt, like a pair of Twinkies under cellophane) and hated Kurt because he was sleazy and unkempt. Kurt laughed through his nose (which Zack always found hilarious but Becca thought disgusting), and when he spoke to Becca, his eyes were always on her breasts. Zack figured Becca had the right to her own opinions, even if he disagreed with them. He would have trusted Kurt over Walt any day, but then again, he did not have breasts.

Besides making judgments about his friends, Becca continued to harp on the idea of doing something daring. She asked Zack if he would help her come up with a plan, but he was not imaginative enough for her. In desperation, he suggested they have sex in a restaurant, but when she demanded that he explain the logistics, he could not come up with a plan that would not land them in jail.

"Well, then, jail will be new," he argued. "And something that will shock people."

"I've been in jail," Becca said. "And it's no big deal."

He knew she had spent only one night in jail, after fighting in a bar, drunk, with her husband. She had thrown an oil lamp that exploded on impact, causing a small fire that the bartender had quickly extinguished. Jail for her *had* been no big deal because she was passed out for most of the time. Zack was not about to push the matter, however; he did not want to spend *any* time in jail, not after the nightmare of being interrogated in Chicago after the stringy-haired woman's murder.

"How about a party?" Zack asked her as they lay side by side on the bed in the motel room. He was beginning to sense she was disappointed in him. If he could not thrill her, he would lose her.

"How about drugs? Hard stuff."

He stiffened, then consciously relaxed his muscles so Becca would not guess. When he spoke, he used his most casual voice. "Drugs? Why?"

Becca rolled over on her side to face him. She propped her head on one hand, looking down at him. "Why? Because you know how."

"Me?"

She was laughing at him now. "Knock off the shit, Zack. You've been there, maybe you still are. Except I checked all the drawers and couldn't find anything. You think I don't know? Well, I'm not that stupid. In Richmond, you kept your stash in the breadbox."

He grasped her slender wrist. "I love you, Becca. And I don't want to see you go there."

"You think I haven't seen worse? I've been beaten, kicked, thrown down the stairs. What the hell is a one-time high? I need to, Zack. My life needs a kick in the ass. *One* time."

"You don't want that kind of god, Becca."

"*One* time." When he said nothing, she wrenched her hand free and leapt off the bed. "Jesus. All my fucking life, men have been telling me what I can and cannot do. I'm sick of it. Love me? Bullshit. You don't even know me. If you did, you'd know why I need to push myself to the edge, so I can come back again. It's a rebirth, stupid. Like the phoenix coming out of the ashes. It's *freedom*."

He wanted to ask, *Freedom from what?* but he feared the answer would be him. Becca did not know how the drugs would chew at her veins, how the craving would burn inside her. She could not know how wrenching withdrawal was. Worst of all, she could not know how the mere suggestion of an illicit high had dried his mouth with longing. How he suddenly needed the rush more than she did.

"Please," he said. "I have something dangerous. I know just the thing. And if you're not happy, then I'll take you to Walt."

"What is it?" Her voice was hard and level, as though she were setting each word in concrete.

His hands trembled against the polyester bedspread. "South Carolina. The sanctuary where my sister works. We can sneak inside, be in the woods with the chimpanzees. They're wild, and if you're not careful, they can rip your arm off. You know that scar my sister has? One almost bit off her hand." He tugged on her fingers. "Please, Becca. How many people have gone into a forest full of chimpanzees? I swear, it's much more dangerous than drugs." He had to get her to South Carolina because he did not know any dealers there. He could find the stuff, sure, but it would require effort. Here, all he had to do was pick up the phone or stroll the beach. The ground seemed to be shifting like sand, only he was lying on a mattress in a seedy motel. The perspiration gathered along his hairline and beneath his ponytail. God, he wanted that rush.

Becca twisted her wedding ring round and round her finger. Why she still wore it when she wanted a rebirth mystified Zack, but he was not going to ask. Becca had a reason for everything, an explanation that ultimately made him feel stupid. She was staring at the vinyl drapes, still rotating the ring, when she said, "All right."

He pushed himself off the bed and started to gather up the few things they had—dirty clothes, a box of granola bars, the plastic alligator, toothbrushes they had bought.

"Not now," she said. "We can leave in a few days. I want to savor the idea first." She slid her purse off the dresser. "I'm going shopping."

Zack started toward the door, but Becca stopped him with a withering glare.

"*Alone*," she hissed.

He sat in the artificial light of the motel room. Sunlight came through the plastic curtains in pinpricks and slices where it had cracked. When Zack and Becca had registered, the room had smelled of disinfectant and old fabric, but now he could smell only Becca. Delicious, angry, fierce Becca. So different from what she was before. He was going crazy for her. If only she would look at him with softer eyes, then he would know they were going to survive. She had awakened in him a craving for everything: food, drugs, sex, love, life, *her*. She was also crushing him, that much he knew.

⁓⌒⌒⌒

Reginald Armstrong stretched his legs in the struggling New England sun and unwrapped the prosciutto and provolone sandwich he had bought. It was an unusually warm day for November, in the low fifties, but even then, he was the only one sitting outside and enjoying the last of the fall warmth. As students walked by, he observed them, noted how those by themselves walked with heads down, how those in groups drifted across the grass. A male student walked his mountain bike (in the city!) as he talked to a young woman, who shrugged her backpack up on one shoulder every few strides. Reginald smiled. The young man appeared too eager, his expressions too hyperbolic, he thought, but the woman did not seem to notice that her friend, or acquaintance, was wooing her. Couldn't she see that he was *walking* his bike, when it would have been much more efficient for him to ride? Reginald took a bite from his sandwich to keep from laughing out loud. Most of the students at Brown seemed too young and oblivious. They walked with gaits that claimed immortality and worldliness, when they had neither. They had the laziness of privilege but when pushed could excel beyond Reginald's expectations. As he opened his Coke, he was thankful he had moved to Rhode Island, had left behind the immensity of a state university years before. Here, he could sit on a bench, eat lunch, and watch the unfolding lives of students he recognized. He would never retire, he thought, never give in to age unless a grave disease began to claim him. He did not want the title Professor Emeritus, which said, *Hey, buddy, you're finished, but you can pretend you aren't.* Right now, with a light course load, he still owned who he was. The department needed his name and his grant money.

"Making fun of the students again?" a voice behind him asked.

Reginald did not need to turn to know it was Hans Werner, another senior faculty member in the psychology department. "I *never* make fun of them. I just enjoy them."

Hans joined him on the bench. His gray curls always had a wild, lopsided look, as though he had just then awakened from a deep sleep. He stretched his legs out exactly as Reginald had. "I hear Dana is in deep trouble."

Reginald looked at him sharply. "How did you hear that?"

Hans shrugged. "Word gets around."

"Among psychologists who couldn't care less?"

"You really should be less cynical."

They sat in silence for a few minutes; Reginald was not going to give him the satisfaction of chiseling conversation out of him. Finally, Hans cleared his throat. "Dick Lamier seems to care a lot."

"Aha! Dick Lamier. The crystal ball is getting clearer. He taught here, you know, for seven years. His first job. We had a falling out, so to speak."

Hans nodded. "Does Dana know that?"

Reginald snorted, the bitterness of it still within him. Lamier had taken his little girl and raked his poison fingernails across her soul. Reginald would never—and could never—forget the sight of Dana curled in that bathtub, her innocence lost. "She knows."

"I heard through a mutual friend that he's out to get her job."

Reginald tipped his head back as he drank from his soda. He rested the can on his thigh. "He doesn't know squat about Dana's kind of work. He's a psychologist. Or psychobiologist, as I hear he now likes to be known. While I'd hate to be his enemy, I think Dana can weather it. She's tougher than I am. Besides, as far as I know, her job is not up for grabs. Why would Lamier want it anyway?"

"Chimps."

"Chimps? Hell, he *has* chimps."

Hans shook his head. "His university has decided to close down their primate lab. They had been talking about shutting it down for a couple of years now because Lamier's grants were the only money coming in. I guess it's no longer politically correct to study the psychology of chimpanzees. Here's where it gets interesting: not knowing the lab's future was already in doubt, a group of students protested its existence in September. Instead of defending the lab, Lamier announced his resignation as a gesture of support for the animal rights activists. He agreed that the federal requirements for housing primates were too minimal and that, while he took steps to enrich the lives of the chimps in his studies, he could do only so much, given the facilities. He vowed to see that all the chimps still housed at the university would be placed in accredited sanctuaries, to live out their lives in tranquility. Can you believe it? He gave his own lab the final chop of the ax. He screwed himself out of a job, and now he needs a new one."

"Jesus." At first, Reginald could not believe Lamier's stupidity, but then he realized Lamier had always calculated ways to escape. "That sly dog," he said. "He knew *exactly* what he was doing. He sniffed the ass of politics, that's what."

Hans laughed. "Meaning?"

"He knew the lab would be closed, if not this year, then next, or the next after that. It was a matter of time. So what does he do? He finds a field where it's still politically correct to have captive chimps. Americans have begun to frown upon colonies of nonhuman primates housed at universities and medical labs. They won't stand for it. They want chimps retired and living like human seniors in semitropical places where they can frolic. It takes the guilt away. Lamier knows it damn well. The South Carolina Primate Project is, as far as I know, the only sanctuary that is both associated with a university and amenable to observational research. Damn him, he's smart." Reginald was sure that Dana's association with the SCPP made Lamier's scheme only sweeter. "But Dana is no fool. And she's good at what she does. I can't imagine the university would jettison her just because Lamier wants in. He's not even an anthropologist."

"You've been out of primate research for decades, Reggie. Things have changed. My friend says the lines between anthropology and psychology have blurred. Lamier gives talks to animal rights groups. He has actively campaigned his contacts at the National Science Foundation. And my friend says he has even met with the president of Dana's university. Reggie, he sits on a lot of committees, referees quite a few grant proposals. He is one of the lords of primatology. So he's in an excellent position to carry through on this."

"As I understand it, the SCPP is on the government's list of approved sanctuaries."

"And you think that status can't be changed?"

Reginald knew all too well the politics of scientific funding. Everything was at the mercy of public opinion. In the early sixties, animals, even apes, were simply beasts. Oddly, as the civil-rights movement—and later women's liberation—gathered strength, people began to turn a more sympathetic eye toward not only members of their own species, but to others as well. If people had made mistakes in estimating the intelligence and value of black Americans and women, couldn't they also be guilty of far less obvious underestimation? Through language studies, scientists were given the opportunity to "elevate" other intelligent species to something close to—but not equal to—humanity. Dolphins and chimpanzees were considered to be bound only by their different vocal cords. The original movie *Planet of the Apes*, with its talking apes and their human slaves, was to many people an evolutionary possibility, reflecting the fear that intelligent species might one day avenge their mistreatment. The underlying thought was, *We should treat them more like humans.* Money flowed into experiments that sought to unlock intelligence. But now, with the rise of environmentalism and species protection acts, the emphasis had shifted to conservation and preservation, the right for animals to be what they were. The remake of *Planet of the Apes*, with its message of primate species living together in peace, revealed the subtle cultural changes that had occurred over nearly forty years—the movement from fear to empathy. Dana, whether she wanted to admit it or not, rode the crest of this new wave, just as he had ridden the earlier one. If Hans was right, Lamier could be the rock in her path. Reginald sighed. "And your friend thinks Lamier is capable of such a coup?"

"Unfortunately, yes."

Reginald had made too many mistakes during his lifetime, and his handling of Lamier's cruelty toward his daughter was only one of them. He realized now he should have brought the incident with Lamier and Dana into the open. He should have called the police and the head of the department, so everyone from that moment on would have known the truth. Lamier would have been properly disgraced, keeping him from the powerful position he now occupied. Back then, however, you hid any dishonor, especially if it involved your daughter. Reginald leaned forward from the weight of how important the sanctuary was for Dana. She lived for it; she breathed it. When she had come home for a visit last year, he had been jealous of the flash in her eyes when she spoke of her work. She had evoked memories of his own passion, of times when his intelligence and ability seemed unlimited, of the adrenaline that had coursed through him day after day. He struggled to refocus his attention on Hans, patting his kneecaps with a sigh. "Thanks, Hans. For telling me." It did not matter that his daughter was middle-aged, independent, and a scientist in her own right; his insides still churned at the idea of Lamier coming after her. This time, he felt as powerless as the last. He could only pray that Dana was as fierce as he believed, and as stubborn as he was.

After Hans left, Reginald opened his half-eaten sandwich. He really should eat healthier foods, he decided. A chill had worked its painful way into the bones in his hands. Sighing, he tossed the sandwich into the garbage can a few feet away and plunged his hands deep into his coat pockets. He walked toward his office.

He had never regretted bringing Annie into his family, only what had come of it. She had been a lively chimp, full of impish intelligence that had tried him as much as his own children had. Annie had given Dana and

Zack a bigger view of the world, a tolerance, an understanding of what it meant to be different. Yes, they did not have a normal upbringing, but what was wrong with that? Dana and Zack had stimulation other children never knew. They had firsthand evidence of the intelligence of another species. He had given them a gift. If he had not been so frightened when he saw the puckered black stitches stretched like awkward lace across Dana's purpled hand, he would have kept Annie. He did not expect Dana and Zack, who were both childless, to understand why he had given Annie back to the university. He had struggled to protect his children since their births, and he could not stop because Annie had become the threat. The agonies of imminent danger and love had torn at his gut for three days until he could take the pain no longer.

Susan had called him a coward for whisking Annie away while Dana and Zack were at school, for not preparing them, for trying to pretend everything at home was the same as it had been when they stepped onto the school bus that morning. But everything had changed. *He* had changed. He had not been a coward as much as a desperate man.

Dick Lamier must have known from the start how the entire Armstrong family was both bound and separated by Annie.

Reginald softly closed the door to his office and, exhausted, collapsed into his chair. Suddenly, retirement did not seem so far-fetched.

This time, he *was* a coward. He could not bring himself to warn his beloved daughter, for fear of all it would drag up.

———✦———

Sifongo spent his time methodically exploring his new, larger enclosure. Each day, he kept to a small section of the ten acres, climbing trees, peering under shrubs, patting fallen trunks with an open palm. He examined the three sheds, which were automatically heated when the temperature fell below forty degrees. He climbed on top of each, jumping and pounding on the roofs until he could no longer take either the excitement or the novelty—Dana could not guess which—and leapt to the reassurance of the ground. From time to time, he sat back to chew quietly on leaves and survey the area with his wide-set eyes. The other members of Group B were agitated, pacing or shaking branches, hooting with an edge that sliced through the woods, but some of the bolder chimps approached Sifongo. Nervously, Sifongo greeted each new acquaintance with pants and bows, submissive to even adult females. The chimps accepted his submission with obvious wariness. Although still an adolescent, Sifongo was large, boasting almost as much bulk as Kimbunga, and no one wanted to underestimate him.

Mazigazi and Kuiga monitored the newest member of their group like expert spies. Dana often saw them squatting behind shrubbery or thick-trunked trees, motionless, watching Sifongo's movements. Every so often, one of them, usually Mazigazi, lurched forward as though she were about to go to him, but then the other would lay a hand on her back to still her.

Kimbunga displayed several times a day now, even in the distant corners of the enclosure. Each time Sifongo heard the accelerating hoots from the dominant male, he froze and cocked his head, grimacing as though the ruckus hurt his ears. Mwoga, Chokaa, and Sufu, the lesser males in Group B, also vigorously displayed, but only when Kimbunga was absent. Sifongo regarded their theatrics with avid curiosity and fearlessness. He must have known that these three males were not true warriors. Dana duly noted each incident on her clipboard as the slow-moving late-autumn flies hummed around her ears.

The unspoken trouble with Zack buzzed around her like the flies.

Somehow, he always ended up being her burden, like a stone tied around her neck before she was thrown into the river. Sweet, goofy Zack—all trouble, and yet he never knew it. Once, when Dana had been married to Charlie for nearly a year, Zack showed up, unannounced as always, with the surprise of gifts: beeswax candles, Belgian chocolates, and a tub of granola he had made himself. Zack ate his granola every morning of the week he stayed with them, bragging about it, glowing whenever Dana or Charlie decided to eat some. He never put the top on properly, however, and Dana would sometimes find it in the pantry about to spill onto the shelves. A month after Zack left, moths hatched in the granola. Dana had not thought to check the lid, so the moths fluttered everywhere like gray ashes and left their eggs to hatch into worms that pressed their soft bodies into the creases between walls and ceiling, into boxes of cereal and pasta and flour, on top of shoes and books. The moths flew into Charlie's hair, beating their small wings and then lying still, so Dana had to carefully pick them off her husband, one by one. When she had collected several insects inside a clean salsa jar, she freed them in their small backyard and ran from them with her hands over her head.

"The gift that keeps on giving," Charlie said.

Eventually, Dana and Charlie threw out all their food, washed the pantry walls and shelves with diluted bleach, and began storing all opened foods in an ever-increasing inventory of plastic containers. Charlie wanted Dana to chastise Zack, but Dana refused, saying, "He didn't know moths were in there." Still, from that time on, Charlie referred to Zack as "Mothra," even to his bewildered face. Dana did not have the heart to explain the nickname.

"Maybe someday I'll make you guys some more granola," Zack said a few months after the disaster.

"Great source of protein, Mothra," Charlie said. Finally, something in Zack's face, a shifting around the mouth, betrayed a sudden but incomplete idea of what must have happened. Dana felt bad for her brother, who had tried to be generous for a change, and who must have felt then as though even his good intentions turned sour.

As Dana fell into a trance pondering her brother, she almost missed Sifongo's sighting of Mazigazi and Kuiga in the bushes. Sifongo's gaze hesitated on the shrubs as he swiveled to take in his surroundings, but then it continued past, as though he had not seen anything after all. He stuffed a leaf in his mouth. Dana might have been tempted to look away, or to climb down the ladder because she needed to stretch, if she had not noticed the puffing of Sifongo's hair and the increasingly rapid movements: the fierce chewing, the way he picked at himself, the darting of his eyes. He rolled forward on his knuckles and began to bounce faster and faster until he leapt straight up into the air. He threw his arms out to his sides, screaming, and charged toward the two hidden females. Shrieking, they fled, scampering crazily in different directions as Sifongo wildly displayed, grasping anything loose nearby to hurl into the bushes: rocks, sticks, fistfuls of pine needles. He tore into the brush and chased several more females out of their hiding places. Barking, they retreated while

Sifongo carried on. Chokaa, an adult male, charged into the clearing as though to punish young Sifongo for such intimidation, but he, too, began barking in fear, screaming, as though Sifongo were a dominant male and not just a blustering teenager. Chokaa finally sat at the base of a tree, squeaking.

Kimbunga tore through the woods in a blur of dark, patchy hair. His angry body crushed the vegetation around him as he broke into the clearing. Chokaa took to the trees. Sifongo, wrapped up in his display, did not see Kimbunga until the dominant male was on top of him, pounding Sifongo's back with his typical ferocity, knocking the young chimp to the ground in a cloud of dust and pine needles. They scrambled madly, so Dana could not tell one hairy arm from the next. Flashes of yellowed teeth, the blood-red of gums, fists coming down on muscular flesh, barking and screaming—a brutal tumble of images assailed Dana, who knew she was powerless to stop the chimps. The fight lasted far longer than Dana thought possible. Finally, Sifongo escaped with a chimpanzee shriek so piercing that Dana wanted to cover her ears. Kimbunga raced after the adolescent for a few yards but then pounded the trunk of a tree instead. He leapt and spun and thrashed for a few more minutes in triumph.

Once he had calmed, Kimbunga sat down to survey his territory, his lips set grimly. One by one, his group emerged to kiss the back of his hand or his thigh. The chimps sat around grooming each other, but every time Kimbunga moved, they grimaced or scooted back or rose to flee. Dana scanned the bushes, looking for a sign that Sifongo was not seriously hurt, that only his pride had been wounded, but she could not find him. Finally, the bushes rustled, and all but Kimbunga turned to see Sifongo emerge, squeaking in submission, so low to the ground it appeared as though he might kiss it. Sifongo took a few steps toward the large male, then retreated, then bravely crawled closer. Kimbunga glanced in his direction, and Sifongo bobbed nervously, asking forgiveness with his bows. Kimbunga turned his back. Anxiously, Sifongo crept closer. At last, Kimbunga reached out and patted him on the back of the head, then casually, as though nothing had happened, left.

Dana could feel the relief spread through the group after Kimbunga disappeared into the woods. Sifongo yawned widely with a flourish of his hand around his mouth, then sat back to pick at something between his toes. Chokaa walked toward him, but Sifongo made no move to ingratiate himself with this male. Instead, he glanced at Chokaa, then back at his toes. Chokaa sat and began to examine his own toes, his eyes glancing up at Sifongo now and then. Sifongo grunted. Chokaa scooted a little closer before reaching out an arm to the other male. The females, scattered around the clearing, sifted through one another's hair while anxiously watching the two males out of the corners of their eyes. Chokaa let his arm fall into the dust. This caught Sifongo's attention, and he looked directly at the older male, grunting softly. Chokaa, his head bowed, wiggled closer. This time, Sifongo gently touched him first on the head and then on the shoulder, gathering Chokaa closer so he could groom him. With his back to Sifongo, Chokaa shifted from a worried to a content expression. The females edged closer to the two males. As Chokaa returned the favor of grooming, Sifongo serenely watched the other chimps. Mazigazi and Kuiga, the two females he had chased into the woods, offered their rumps to Sifongo for a pat, which he did with the magnificence of a dominant male, although he was only a teenager and had not won his fight against Kimbunga.

Dana was aghast. Although she had predicted that Sifongo would one day dominate, she had not expected to see his influence for several years. Chokaa and the females had demonstrated respect to this new, upstart adolescent, something she had never before witnessed. Was Chokaa that weak, and was the power vacuum Kimbunga created around himself that pronounced? What had Sifongo done to elicit such immediate respect? Sifongo must have marked himself as a future leader, the one who would depose ruthless Kimbunga, and the chimps were already lining up to ally themselves with him. Sifongo had doled out more affection—pats, hugs, grooming—than Kimbunga did in a week, maybe two. When the time came for Sifongo to truly challenge Kimbunga, the chimps would be on his side. But why? Why this child king? Dana traced the line of her scar, thinking. Somehow, his fight with and subsequent submission to Kimbunga had earned him power.

"Knock, knock," Mary said from below.

Dana grinned. "Who's there?"

"Gloom and doom." Mary had more rosiness to her cheeks today, though Dana could not tell if it was a natural glow or an applied one. "Tekua smashed his cast off, and Andy needs your help."

"I'm coming down." Notebooks pressed under her arm, Dana descended the ladder, jumping off a few rungs from the bottom with a soft thud into peat. "I want you to do me a favor."

"What?" Mary started walking with her, three strides to Dana's two. "Whatever you want."

"I want you to take over—completely—Barafu's adoption of Fikira. Barafu likes you, maybe even identifies with you. I need to focus my energies on keeping this place afloat."

"Of course I'll do it. I'd *love* to do it. But—"

"No buts." She knew Mary's reservation: that Dana had overseen all the adoptions prior to this one. It had been selfish of her, Dana knew now, to exclude the staff from the most glorious of chores—giving a mother a baby and a baby a mother. She had already given several babies back to their own species, and now Mary deserved the thrill of seeing how their socialization methods succeeded.

Mary caught Dana's hand in hers. "You aren't mad at me, are you? For getting pregnant? For Quentin?"

Mary's expression was so grave that Dana laughed. "No, I'm not mad. How can I get mad at something you've wanted for as long as I've known you? The baby part, anyway. Not Quentin's job search. *That* I'm mad about." She could not help recalling her own marriage and what had happened when she announced she was taking the South Carolina job, and they had both run, free from each other as their cage split wide open. She did not want to see that happen to Mary and Quentin. They were more in love than she and Charlie ever had been. You could tangle your fingers in the affection and friendship that ran between them. She sighed. "Your marriage is what's most important, especially now."

Mary kicked a smattering of gravel ahead of them. "Hey, you want to go to a movie tonight? Quentin is away."

"Sure. You pick the flick. I'll catch you later."

Mary halted. "You know what? I'm going back to the platform. I need a break. I've been wrestling with the babies, and my body aches all over."

On the way to the main building, Dana tripped on a root that had always been there, bowing out of the ground, a pitfall she knew well to avoid. But this time, the first in five years, she hooked her foot in its arc and tumbled forward, breaking her fall with her outstretched hand. Her papers tumbled like birds with clipped wings set briefly free. She picked herself up, brushed pine needles from her shirt and pants, and then retrieved her notes. Dana could not remember feeling this off-balance since she had separated from Charlie. Back then, she had cut corners so close that her shoulders and hips were always bruised. She missed steps and one afternoon fell down half a flight at the university. And she had locked her fingers in the car door after closing it with them curled around the edge. Fortunately, none of the incidents seriously hurt her, though she had lived in a constant state of humiliation.

She flexed her wrist to make sure she had not broken any small bones. When she knew she was all right, she continued toward the main building.

Sixteen

$\mathcal{T}$he separate primate stories Sam was working on had been at first little puffs, then larger wafts, but now they twisted upward in a great plume of idealism. He could make a difference in the world, he thought, with what he had seen and now knew: he was going to find out what had happened to Annie; he was going to expose primate research for the horror it was; he was going to nail sneering Lamier for all his scheming and mock sincerity; he was going to save the sanctuary from the ignorant public. Dana was the flash point for it all. She started the smoke rising, and she fed it. The other parts of the story were mere kindling.

He knew things about Dana he was not even sure she knew.

The few people who disliked Dana did so because of her zealotry. They found her uncompromising and pigheaded, not only when it came to animal rights but also in more personal situations. Amy Watkins, one of Dana's classmates at Wisconsin, told him how Dana had never forgiven her for not remembering to buy balloons for a surprise party they threw. A former colleague in Arizona complained that Dana had banged on their shared wall every time he clipped his fingernails. "How the hell could she even hear?" he asked, his anger palpable over the phone. "And why did she care?"

Most people he interviewed were exceedingly protective, a fact he found perplexing, given the politics he had discovered in primatology. "I used to stop by her apartment every morning," Bruce Caras, a caretaker at the San Diego Zoo, told him, "and knock lightly, to make sure she would be up on time for class. I don't think she ever knew it was me, or that I'd even knocked, because she never came to the door. The knock must've been just loud enough to rouse her because I'd hear her stirring a few seconds later."

"Was she often late to class?" Sam asked.

Bruce laughed. "Until I took over. Her head was always elsewhere. Brilliantly elsewhere. I hated to see her get reamed out in class. She'd look so . . . meek. Which wasn't Dana at all. When she wasn't embarrassed, she'd be all fire. Some of the professors—I remember Dr. Plotz in particular—used to goad her into action just to wake the rest of us up."

Dr. Plotz agreed with Bruce Caras. "Oh, yes, I remember Dana well. And I mean the real Dana, not the one in her father's experiment. Dana had spunk that was fun to toss around the class. I'm sure she thought I was an asshole, but that's the price I paid for interesting classes."

More than these things, Sam knew what it was like to sit close to her, the heartiness of her laugh, the terrain of her face, the swell of emotion in her voice.

He had been baffled by her rejection—he completely misread her, and it had been a blow. Oddly, though, he found himself attracted to her even more, now that he knew she did not want to sleep with him. Her rejection had infected him with a longing to know everything about her. If he could not have her body, then he wanted who she was.

Sam studied the old films that had been transferred to DVDs. He kept them in a brown box on the back seat of his car, as though they were pirated movies he intended to sell to passersby. Whenever he was in a motel, he would take the cheap DVD player out of his trunk and plug it into the television set so he could run them as he started to fall asleep.

He did not know how many times he had watched the films when an observation startled him into sitting upright in bed (he was home then, in Arlington). The black-and-white graininess, the visual pops, the squiggly hairs, the undeveloped splotches—they had distracted him enough not to see the subtleties of what he was viewing. This time, however, he saw past the marks of aging to the truth: each time both Zack and Dana entered a room, Annie ran first to Zack and then to Dana, as if she preferred the cherubic toddler to the more reserved, deliberate girl. Annie studied Zack's face more closely, with eyes that swept slowly over details; she stroked him and clung to his hand, the two of them crouching under tables and behind furniture, lost in their own conspiracy. In the education tent, they spent hours learning signs as they stacked blocks and assembled simple wooden puzzles stamped with images of animals. Annie wrestled with him and played tricks on him; she laughed when he fell for them again and again. When Annie turned her eyes on Zack, they were adoring. With Dana, her gaze was more scrutinizing. As Dana arranged her play dishes or talked to her dolls or set the table, Annie glanced in her direction now and then, seemingly uninterested, but when Dana left the room, Annie eagerly re-created the same movements. In the education tent with Dana, Annie became more serious and intent upon learning. Her performance on tests, as the narrator noted, increased in Dana's presence, although the narrator attributed this to the influence of a more developed child, not to the relationship between Annie and Dana.

It was not that Annie did not love Dana—for she did, openly, with kisses and sign language—but that she was more cautious with her. Did Dana know this? Did she know a distance separated her from Annie? That her brother had been more intimate with their sibling chimpanzee?

Sam sank back into his pillow. He wanted Annie to have liked Dana more than Zack, wanted Dana to be the favorite, the most loved, the wisest. He did not trust Zack and did not like him, and so wanted the shiftiness he saw in the adult Zack to have emerged in his early childhood. Dana had been the one to make something out of the experiment when she grew into an adult. She brought new research to light about the complex social networks established even in captivity, the primal instincts and gestures that even a lifetime of human interaction could not erase, the triumphs as well as the tragedies of individual chimps. He wanted Dana to be the one Annie loved best. He wanted Annie to be able to see who Dana would become.

But Annie, of course, had not possessed any special powers. She just was. To think of Annie as both educated in humans' ways and at their mercy saddened him.

The paper trail to find her had led nowhere, but Lamier's information had directed him back to Reginald Armstrong. Although Sam had talked to Reginald over the phone for the language studies article, he suspected the facelessness of the interview had been a mistake. He needed to go to Rhode Island to confront him. Sometimes, a face-to-face encounter yielded greater truth.

Sam did not know what to expect in person. In the old films, Reginald had a serious, almost condescending presence in his black-framed glasses and short, impeccably groomed hair. He wore dark suits and white shirts with thin, simple ties. Sam found him an imposing figure not because of any physical attributes but because of the studious intensity, the way he emphasized certain words, the unyielding look he gave the cameras. Age, Sam knew, enhanced some personality traits and diminished others. He could not imagine facing even greater sternness.

The drive from Virginia up the Northeast coast was never one Sam enjoyed. Whenever he went home to Connecticut for visits, he arrived surly and exhausted, having navigated congestion at Baltimore, Wilmington, Philadelphia, the George Washington Bridge over the Hudson River, and the Bronx, where burned-out cars littered the shoulders as monuments to theft. After the Bronx, he had to contend with Bridgeport and New Haven. As he bore on past his childhood-home exit toward Rhode Island, he had the image of going to the edge of hell, all for an interview. By the time he arrived in Warwick, where his hotel was located, he could do no more than collapse into bed, still wearing his jeans.

The next morning, Sam arrived at the Armstrongs' Victorian house with sleep still itching in his eyes. Susan Armstrong opened the door. "Hi," she said, and he could hear Dana's voice in that single syllable.

Susan, who had seemed as studious and deliberate as her husband in the films, surprised Sam with her animation and her broad, strong stride as she led him into the living room. Both Dana and Zack resembled her strongly, though each child had taken something unique from her: Dana had inherited the musing set of her lips and Zack the watery blue of her eyes.

She gestured for him to sit on the sofa. "Reggie is on the phone with a student. He'll be right down. Meantime, would you like coffee or tea?"

"Coffee, please. Black." He could not believe this was the same woman who had hung up on him when he wanted to talk about the language studies.

In Susan's absence, Sam studied the living room and what he could see of the rest of the home. At first, he was disoriented because this was not the Oklahoma house of the old films, not even in decor, although he recognized, in the adjacent room, the dining-room table under which Zack and Annie had groomed each other, believing themselves hidden. He also recognized the oval gilt mirror hanging across from him; Annie had dragged chairs to it so she could explore her face and sign to herself, *Annie beautiful. I love Annie. Annie bad girl.* In the Oklahoma one-story house, the mirror had seemed too ornate and out of place, but here, it belonged with the pockmarked hardwood floors and the Oriental carpets. The house had a feel of wear, of good intentions grown thin, of stasis.

Susan returned with a hand-painted mug filled with coffee. "If you want a refill, just ask. I have a whole pot in the kitchen." She sat across from him, lowering her voice. "I understand you've talked to Zack. How is he?"

Understanding at once that she did not want her husband to overhear their conversation, Sam kept his voice low. "I haven't seen him in a couple of weeks. But he looked fine. And was in good spirits." He did not want to mention the car accident or the woman Zack had been with because he did not understand this family well enough to know its boundaries.

"He disappeared again," she said. "He was staying with Dana, and then he left without a word. At least he was eating."

Sam laughed. "I can swear to that as well. Doesn't he call you? Or visit?"

She shook her head. Her bobbed gray hair swung like a skirt. "We have a modern fractured family."

"Because of Annie?"

She glanced toward the stairs, but when Reginald's full laugh, muffled by a closed door, tumbled distantly, she seemed emboldened. "Reggie and I had a rocky point in our marriage fifteen or so years ago. Zack took it personally. He doesn't speak to his father. Barely speaks to me. He doesn't understand the bonds of history. How a relationship can be destroyed and then rise out of the ruin."

Sam wanted to say that Zack barely understood the concept of relationships, let alone the more practical matters pertaining to them, but he was there as a journalist, not an adviser. He needed to be on guard, looking for fissures to pry open. "You wouldn't speak to me before. Why are you being so frank now?"

She smiled broadly, and Sam could see the kindergarten teacher of long ago. "My children are my children, no matter how old they get. I don't want them paraded around in public like freaks. Reggie never understood this. They've endured enough. But the damage has been done, I'm sure. Or the healing has begun. If Dana and Zack can talk to you, then so can I."

"Zack wants me to find Annie."

Susan's blue eyes focused sharply on him. "What have you found out?"

"I'd like to talk to your husband before I say anything."

Susan stared at him, her mouth slightly slack, her eyes unblinking for what seemed like minutes, before she finally spoke. "It's better to dream of a happy ending."

Reginald Armstrong came down the stairs, looking frailer than Sam expected. Sam stood quickly, waiting, fighting the impulse to rush to the base of the stairs in case the older man fell. Once on the floor, however, Reginald moved with a fluid grace. As he advanced into the room, Susan retreated like a hermit crab backing into its shell. Sam could not help wondering what difficulties their marriage had survived.

What circumstances had sent Zack spinning from them like an off-kilter gyroscope. Why this couple so tangibly did not wish to share space.

"Hello, Mr. Wendt," Reginald said.

"Pleased to finally meet you."

"Likewise."

As the two men shook hands, Reginald's eyes sparked with a ferocity that startled Sam, though it should not have, since Dana had regarded him similarly. She had inherited her father's eyes, physically and spiritually. Sam and Reginald sat across from each other, Sam sinking into the cushions of the sofa while Reginald arranged himself across from him with a remarkably straight spine in a Windsor chair. They talked generally about chimpanzees and about Reginald's current work on human cognitive development before Sam asked, "How much do you know about your daughter's work at the SCPP?"

Reginald's expression became suddenly unguarded, his eyes more animated and his mouth turning up at the corners. "I'm not a primatologist, Mr. Wendt, but I'm darn proud of what Dana's doing there. Make no mistake about it, Annie was not mistreated, but we should never have acquired her from an animal trader. She was most likely stolen out of Africa, where she rightfully belonged. I stand by my work, and always will. But at the time, there was only one place for Annie to go once the experiment ended. Now, with the SCPP and other sanctuaries, there's a little hope."

"Where *did* Annie go?"

"The university didn't want to keep such an unruly animal, particularly one they viewed as dangerous. We had no studies for her, and I could no longer keep her in my house. The university sold her to a medical lab. As you know, she was soon lost track of."

"I spoke with Dick Lamier in Maryland a few weeks ago."

"I suspected as much."

"You did?"

"You're a watched man, Mr. Wendt."

"That sounds ominous."

Reginald smiled thinly. "Scientists like the world to believe they're objective, but they have agendas. Especially in disciplines that border on the political. You will find enemies of the most seemingly innocuous proposal. That's the way it is. I can't say opposition is purely intellectual. As a psychologist, I know all too well how personalities and perceived snubs, under the guise of professional differences, come into play in the academic arena. I've done some digging of late. And I've found certain people are wary of your intentions."

"And Lamier is one of them?"

"Lamier is but one of them. I'm a little puzzled, though, because from all accounts his wariness is tempered by delight. There are rumors that he hopes you'll discredit my daughter."

"I don't see how I would." Still, Sam felt slightly sick that he was being used—by Lamier, by Reginald, by Zack, maybe even by Dana. He cleared his throat. "What Lamier told me might have some impact on *you*."

"Oh?"

"He said you knowingly sold Annie to an intermediary research firm that intended to send her to a brain damage study."

Reginald sagged in his chair and then, as though a thickly coiled spring inside him had been released, abruptly stood, his fingers flying to his temples. He turned toward the gilt mirror; the instant before he turned away, Sam saw a mixture of fear and agony reflected in the creases of his expression. "So this is how he's going to weaken her. Have you told my children this?"

"No. Not yet."

When Reginald turned to face Sam again, his face had hardened into a stone mask. "Lamier is a bastard. He took a partial truth and twisted it into a lie."

"So tell me your side."

"My side? There's no *side*. There's the truth, and then there's Lamier." He leaned toward the hall outside the living room. "Susan! Come here." When Susan Armstrong did not respond, Reginald waited, his brow furrowed. Sam expected him to call to her again, but he did not, even when the house fell silent except for the running of water in the kitchen, the clatter of dishes, the squeak of the floorboards. Sam was about to tell Reginald that he thought Susan had not heard when she came into the room, wiping the last residue of soapsuds on her pants.

"What?" Her voice had the edge of impatience.

"I'm going to tell this young man everything I know about Annie. Dana and Zack are going to learn the truth as a result, so you'd better prepare yourself, since they wouldn't come to me in a million years."

Sam watched Susan's face, then Reginald's, as they lapsed into silence. As the communication between them flashed like electrical impulses, too quick for his own interpretation.

"Annie is dead, isn't she?" Sam asked.

Reginald hesitated, then broke eye contact with his wife, who sat in the chair he had occupied only a minute before. "Probably. I would say most likely. Despite what Lamier may have told you—"

Susan sprang from her chair. "Dick Lamier! What the hell does he have to do with this?"

Reginald silenced her by holding up a flattened hand and said, "The university owned Annie. The only reason they allowed us to keep her for the two years we did was because they had no other place for her. I couldn't afford to buy her—she was valued at several thousand dollars—but I never told the children she could be snatched from us the moment another Oklahoma researcher needed a chimp."

"It was actually nice to have her in the house without the cameras," Susan said. "She was a boisterous girl, but we loved her. And the stress level dropped the second we didn't have to be on our best behavior."

"But Dana and Zack came first. They had to. When Annie bit Dana, I gave Annie back to the university. I had to protect my children. I had no choice."

Susan nodded. "I was behind the move one hundred percent. Annie was getting bigger and stronger—and more aggressive. She didn't belong cooped up in a tiny house."

Reginald sat on the edge of the coffee table, so close that Sam could smell his cologne. "What happened next was a crime. Annie could not be integrated into a zoo exhibit because she no longer had the necessary chimp behavior. The university didn't have the space or the money to keep her for long, so they arranged to sell her to a pharmaceutical lab in Texas. We all thought she would be used to test the viability of a new line of antibiotics. That seemed reasonable to me, given the few options, so when I was asked to sign the paperwork selling her, I did. About two weeks later, I received an anonymous phone call at home as we were eating dinner. The caller said that Annie had never been intended for the antibiotic trials, that she was en route to New York for a brain damage experiment."

"When Reggie told me about the caller that night," Susan said, "I cried. I had been the one to insist that Annie be taken out of the house after Dana's accident. I screamed and pounded on Reggie to get him to take her away."

"I was already thinking it," her husband said. "It wasn't your fault." Reginald cleared his throat. "After the phone call, we decided to buy Annie back. We would do whatever it took to rescue her before they did anything to her. We planned to use the small college funds we had already saved for the kids. If we had only thought things through, we would have done that from the start." He pressed his fingertips against his eyes, then looked at Sam with an expression akin to surprise, as though he had forgotten he was relating his story to a stranger. "The next morning, I called the lab in New York, but they claimed they had no plans to receive a new chimp. I began to believe, rather hopefully, that the call had been a hoax, so I called the lab where we had sent Annie. You see, Susan and I had made some emotional and financial decisions the night before, so even if Annie was not on her way to brain surgery, I was determined to get her back. My children were going through the motions of life like zombies. Susan couldn't do anything as simple as boiling water without crying. And I . . ." He glanced at his wife. "Even I could not get through the day without running into a wall or stubbing my toe or finding some other reason to swear up and down. Annie may not have belonged in our house, but I was not going to be responsible for her torture. She was our girl."

"She *was*."

"I thought I could fix this mess. But when I called the Texas lab, they said they had sent her to a Georgia lab. And the Georgia lab said that while Annie was listed on the inventory sheet, she had never arrived at their facility. I spent every waking minute for the next month trying to track her down. I even drove to Texas to search their cages in case she was still there. I found only the most miserable conditions one can imagine. I couldn't believe I had sent her to a place like that. And to think she probably ended up in a worse place . . . It was too much to consider. Of course, we told Dana and Zack none of this. We didn't want to cause them any more pain."

Sam tapped his pen against his knee. "So why would Lamier accuse you of complicity?"

"Because he tried to rape our daughter, that's why," Susan spat.

Sam tried not to show how stunned he was by this revelation. But he was speechless. Dana had not even hinted at this past. He had failed to see the chink, to open it up like the gaping wound it was and reach inside to feel its pulse. At the same time, he felt he should not have been told this truth. "Did you report Lamier?" he finally asked.

"Dana was only sixteen." Susan's hands were trembling in her lap, and Sam tried not to stare at them. "And she was not physically hurt. So we took care of it ourselves."

The puzzle was assembling itself faster than Sam could think. "Lamier left Brown because you threatened to file charges if he didn't."

"More or less." Reginald eased off the coffee table and began to walk around the living room, pausing to straighten the frame of a New England watercolor and to shift a glass elephant several inches on the cherry-wood sideboard. "One of my colleagues has informed me that he's now on a campaign to destroy her reputation."

"It seems that way."

"Well, then, damn him to hell," Susan said, rising. She cast a long look at her husband before she strode out of the room. After a few moments, a door closed loudly upstairs.

"She hasn't gotten over it," Reginald said.

Sam nodded. "Dana told me about Lamier taking her to the Massachusetts lab. But she left out the sexual-assault details. How did you know that Annie wasn't there? Maybe she survived the brain damage study. Or maybe that was a false lead to begin with."

"Lamier worked at that lab as a consultant and used the facilities for some of his work. He knew Annie's story and would have told someone long before then. Besides, that facility in Massachusetts was only a few years old at the time. Every chimp there had to have paperwork, having recently arrived, and Annie would have surfaced. Even years later, Annie was still famous. If Lamier hadn't come forward, someone else would have." Reginald's fingers hovered above a picture frame of the family taken years ago, when Dana was a teenager. "If Dana told you about Dick Lamier, then she knows what Lamier is up to. Someone already warned her." Reginald's relief was visible as he brought one hand to his forehead. "That Massachusetts facility was shut down years ago, thank God. When the government cracked down on experimental primate use." He sighed. "My children think I'm the bad guy, for raising Annie in a human environment and then ripping her from it. But if you put my actions in the context of the times, I was on the cusp of forward thinking. Not many of us thought chimps could acquire language skills. People believed, as some still do, that language separated humans from the rest of the animal kingdom. I helped prove the distance to be an illusory one. My work helped form the groundwork that acknowledges the grave need for sanctuaries like the SCPP. Dana is my legacy, and not only genetically. Yes, I was naive in believing Annie could have a life away from us. But Dana, too, is naive in her own way. In her own time."

"How is that?"

Reginald grimaced. "Unfortunately, I don't know. Not yet. Only the future will tell."

SEVENTEEN

Dana felt the tug as she always did in the twenty-four hours prior to an adoption. Her body heated like the first stirrings of a fever, keeping her from the deep sleep she needed and parching her mouth. As she stared at the luminous numbers on her bedside clock, a superstition worked its way into her mind: if Barafu bonded with Fikira, the SCPP would survive. And then she felt sick to her stomach.

When Dana arrived at the SCPP, the day already felt restless despite the cool temperature and the complete clarity of the air. The sky's gray light teased at the edges, threatening to turn pink with fiery day. Already, the chimps were stirring with the soft grunts of morning dreams. Instead of going to her office to catch up on paperwork, Dana went directly to the narrow building leading to the outdoor enclosures, carrying a box of food for Barafu.

Barafu was still asleep high on a platform. She had fashioned a nest out of the fresh straw and branches that had been placed there the day before. Dana had turned the lights on so she could find her way down the hallway, and now Barafu flopped away from the brightness. Dana sat cross-legged on the concrete floor to wait.

Mwenzi screeched his morning wake-up call for his group. Barafu tossed one arm over her head.

Dana grunted a greeting. Startled, Barafu sat up quickly, her eyes not yet focusing, her movements stiff from arthritis and sleep. Her face brightened when she saw the box next to Dana. She ambled over, wincing in morning pain, but a smile toyed at the strong corner of her mouth.

Dana imitated the high-pitched shriek of a chimp who had found food. She hopped up and down excitedly. Barafu joined her, screeching, gesturing frantically for Dana to hand over breakfast. The two of them carried on for several seconds before Dana finally passed an apple between the bars. The ruckus attracted three members of Group A, who stood outside hooting and whimpering and begging to be let into the cage they could normally access. They eyed Barafu and her apple.

Dana handed Barafu another apple. Without thinking, she signed, *Share apple.*

Dana tensed as she realized her lapse. Barafu held the apple against her chest. Did she understand? Dana could not tell, but an exhilaration—a trapped part of her suddenly set free—made her realize how much she had wanted to sign to Barafu. Could there really be harm in communication? Soon, Barafu would join Group A and be forever changed, her knowledge no longer accessible. Cautiously, Dana signed again. *Share.*

The chimp's eyes brushed over Dana's hands as though she had seen nothing, but Dana could not tell if Barafu, in her greediness, chose not to see.

You will get a baby today.

This caught Barafu's eye, although she did not respond. She was too busy eating the second apple. Patiently, Dana waited for her to finish. With one finger, Barafu pushed up the drooping side of her face before letting it fall again. She steadily regarded the box by Dana's side. Dana feigned ignorance. The other chimps had already moved away to find their own breakfasts, so nothing was left to distract Barafu.

You will be a mother. The girl's name is Fikira.

Barafu glanced at Dana's face, then away. Although she started to get up, she sat back down as her eyes rested on the box.

Dana decided to attempt a more simple approach. *I love you.*

Barafu signed, *I love baby.*

The baby's name is Fikira.

Baby.

Do you understand?

Me.

Yes, you. You will get a baby. What is her name?

Baby loves me.

Are you hungry?

Baby.

Dana closed her eyes and took a deep breath. When she opened them again, Barafu had moved away a few feet, her back to Dana. She lifted one foot in the air to inspect between the toes.

"Barafu! Look what I have." Dana opened the box noisily to get Barafu's attention, and removed a carrot. "Carrot."

Barafu spun around on her backside and propelled herself toward Dana.

"Questions first. Then you get the carrot." Dana decided to speak as she signed, in case Barafu understood only bits of ASL. Or could not remember it well enough. Barafu concentrated on the carrot that Dana laid on her lap. To get the chimp's attention back to her hands, she clapped them loudly. "Barafu. Who taught you to love babies?"

I love baby.

"Yes, I know you love babies. Who taught you how to say that?"

Me.

"You taught yourself?" Dana laughed. "I don't think so."

Barafu pouted.

"I'll give you the carrot in a minute. Did another chimp teach you?"

Barafu pointed at the carrot. *You. Me.*

"Say 'carrot' then. And I'll give it to you."

Her shoulders heaving with frustration, Barafu slapped the ground.

Dana knew she had only moments before Barafu would hurl herself into a temper tantrum. Still, Dana had one question left to ask, one that frightened her so thoroughly she had not even let herself consider it before then. But if she did not ask it, she knew she would never be able to see Barafu without pain and wondering. "Barafu. Did Annie teach you how to sign?"

Barafu's face went still, and Dana could not breathe. It was a possibility that Barafu had learned sign language from another chimp—why not from Annie? Washoe, the well-known signing chimp, had taught sign language to her adopted family, so it would not be surprising if Annie had done the same. But Barafu's stillness deepened to a blankness of expression, a giving up, a resignation that she was not going to get the carrot or anything else. Dana pressed her hand to her chest. This kind of blackmail might have been exactly the sort of treatment that had led to the chimp's obsession with food.

"Here you go, Barafu," she said as she slipped the carrot toward the chimpanzee. "I didn't mean to upset you. I only wanted . . ." What *did* she want? Words seemed as useless then as they had a few minutes before. She did not know whether she felt anguish or relief knowing that Barafu's past, and her few signs, would remain a mystery forever. That Barafu had no special link to Annie.

One by one, Dana pushed another three carrots toward Barafu. Delighted, Barafu clapped her hands once before gathering the roots into a bouquet that she held under her nose. She sniffed the length of them before sticking them all in her mouth, where they sprouted like flowers in a narrow vase.

Dana laughed, and Barafu paused, looking down at the carrots through slightly crossed eyes. She lifted her chin high and shook her head, her mouth breaking into a play face that sent the carrots tumbling to the floor. Dana took the last remaining carrot from the box and stuck it in her own mouth, clowning around the way Barafu had. Barafu smiled as she held the carrots on top of her head like horns. Dana stuck hers out of one ear. Barafu countered by dividing the carrots and holding them pointing outward from her nipples. Dana placed hers in the middle of her forehead. The two joked around like that for a few more seconds, both laughing at the other's inventiveness. Barafu finally settled down to crunch loudly on the carrots, smacking her lips in satisfaction. Only then did Dana realize what a huge step Barafu had just taken: she had delayed sating her hunger for a moment of social interaction. But it was the silliness of the exchange that lingered with Dana. She felt lighter in spirit than she had when she arrived. It did not bother her that this kind of play was the most she would ever communicate with Barafu, or that the past would always remain murky, never completely within reach. She cared only about how Barafu had put aside her deeply rooted gluttony for the pleasure of a good laugh, and how she, Dana, had fallen under the spell of Barafu's awkward charm.

The door down the hallway opened and closed. Mary appeared at the entrance, her face ashen and stark.

"Morning sickness sucks," Mary said as she joined Dana. "I should've done a Barafu and adopted."

"You'll live." They sat in silence for a few minutes as they watched Barafu finish off the carrots. Mary's arrival made Dana feel unexpectedly guilty, as though she had been caught in the middle of a crime. "I tried to talk to Barafu in sign language this morning."

Mary glanced at her sharply. "Really?"

"I know I shouldn't have. I know I said I wouldn't. But it just happened. And then I couldn't stop."

"I'm sure they have a circle in hell for sinners like you."

Dana jostled Mary with her elbow. "Stop it. I'm serious."

"I know you are. And you're also insane. You're too hard on yourself. So you signed to Barafu. Big deal. I rolled through a stop sign this morning."

Dana stared past Barafu to the open area of Group A, into the trees and shrubbery that betrayed only small signs of the chimpanzees who resided there: a few broken branches, a limb stripped clean of leaves, dusty depressions in the ground where the chimps might have paused for a grooming session. It was funny, Dana thought, how the very beings who defined the space for her could disappear and yet still shape what she saw. "You're right. It wasn't a big deal. I don't think she knows more than a few signs anyway."

"What if she did?"

"Well, I can't very well say, can I? Because she doesn't. I don't know how things would've changed if she had started to rattle off her life story."

Mary threw her arm around Dana. "My advice to you is to work on things you *can* change. The things that count. Like the survival of the SCPP. Enriching the chimps' lives. *Living.*"

Dana smiled down at Mary. "For a queasy, loudmouthed shrimp, you're pretty wise."

"Yeah, yeah. And *when* do I get your job?"

Dana would never give up her job, not willingly, and she saw for the first time that Mary had nowhere to go, no room to expand except under her. Maybe if Mary did move with Quentin, she would find other opportunities available to her.

"You're the best," Dana told her. "Now go get Fikira ready."

⌒〜ʌʌ〜⌒

Becca told Zack she was ready to go back to South Carolina, but first she wanted to say good-bye to his friends, who, she heard, were on the beach. She did not say how she knew where they were, or which friends she meant (because certainly they would not all be together). Zack understood he was not allowed to be part of the farewell, even though they were *his* friends. If he truly cared about her, she said more than once, he would understand her need for separation. Jealousy reminded her of Mike.

After Becca took off for the beach in her yellow flip-flops and oversized sunglasses, Zack counted to sixty, in case she had forgotten something and would come back. Ticking off seconds like that calmed him somewhat, but his blood felt too thin and runny—hot, charged. He picked up the phone and dialed a number he had memorized months ago. The phone rang and rang and rang until finally the answering machine picked up. *Damn.* As Dick Lamier's voice intoned a carefully spoken, frustratingly long message, Zack tried to think of what he could say. He was not even sure he should identify himself or leave a message at all, because what more could be said? The machine beeped.

Zack swallowed. "Forgive me, Dick, for what I'm about to do." He slammed the phone down so forcefully that he knocked it off the night table and onto the floor.

Neither Dana nor Dick would understand why he promised Becca what he had. They might even hate him for it—and they were two of the most important people in his life. Still, he knew no other way to save himself and Becca from the downward spiral she wanted to enter.

He could not bring himself to ask Dana's forgiveness. She always had such unrealistic expectations for him, unlike Dick, who accepted him for who he was, flaws and all. Ever since Zack had looked him up six years before, Dick had proven himself to be a true friend, a father, really, someone who knew Zack inside out and could still love him. Dick had gotten him out of that murder mess in Chicago—well, Dick's lawyer and Zack's innocence had—and Dick had given him the money to buy the Ford. Zack would do anything to repay Dick's kindness—except abort the trip to South Carolina.

Zack decided to pack what few items he and Becca had. He stuffed his clothes into the duffel bag, pressing them down hard to squeeze out the spaces so he could close it. He then carefully placed Becca's clothes in the plastic mesh beach bag she had bought. He had noticed she took greater care with her things than he did with his, folding and smoothing and adjusting them, so he did the same. He took her cosmetics out of the bathroom and, curious, inspected her lipstick, eyeliner, mascara, foundation, and blush. It was really weird how women applied makeup— like war paint, which explained a lot. He could not imagine layering his face with this stuff. After packing Becca's belongings, he checked under the bed and in all the drawers for items he might have missed and then stopped, stunned, in the middle of the room. What was it about Becca that made him so careful? He had never in his life checked so thoroughly a space before leaving it.

The worst part, the *true* part, was that as he fell in love with Becca, she came to hate him. She had transformed him needlessly, for what good was a man who would check under the bed if you didn't want to be with him? There he was, hopeless, packing for her and about to take her on an adventure that, should they be caught, would jeopardize his relationship with the people who loved him. He sank miserably on the bed. *Fuck this.* His insides had already been shredded into little bits of tissue. He could not sit around waiting to bleed to death. God, he was such a wuss.

Checking his pockets for the quarters he had been hoarding, he left the room and walked barefoot toward the soda machine. He figured they would need drinks—and caffeine—as they started out, so he bought two twenty-ounce bottles of Coke. As he retraced his steps, the plastic bottles sweated in his hands, dripping in rivulets of condensation. They were going to have a hot day, he decided, more like sticky summer than November.

When Zack stepped inside the room, Becca was standing next to the packed bags, her mouth slightly agape. *Oh, God, I've done something wrong again.* He handed her a bottle of soda. "Here. I bought you something to drink."

She twisted her sunglasses in her hands and began to cry.

He wanted to walk out the door and start over. He wanted to take back the last days and weeks. He wanted to go back to Dana's house on the day Carlee had dropped him off and Becca stood in the driveway, waiting. "I'm sorry, I'm so sorry," he told Becca. "I'll drink it myself."

Sobbing, she held it out of his reach. "I *want* it! I do."

Zack shifted his weight from one leg to the other. "I . . . I don't know what you want, Becca. Tell me. Just stop crying, and I'll do whatever you want."

She flopped face down on the bed, pounding the pillows in her puzzling grief.

Zack did not know whether to leave or go to her, so he ended up standing in the same spot. "You hate me," he finally said. "I know that."

She flipped over, her tears suddenly stopped. "*No!*"

"Then what is it, Bec? I don't get it. I can't do anything right."

Becca held her tiny hands out to him, so he took them and let her guide him onto the bed next to her. He perched there, waiting, believing he would have to leap away from her in a second because she would change her mind about wanting him close.

She sniffled. "I've been so mean to you, and you've done nothing but try to make me happy. What's wrong with me? I've become Mike. Treating you like he treated me."

"Don't say that. Don't compare yourself to him."

She was shaking her head. "I've been treating you like shit. And look! You packed all my things. You bought me a Coke. You were thinking of what I wanted and needed. I didn't think of you, Zack. I can't believe that I was so mean. It's not like me, you know that, don't you?"

"I've known you for years," he said carefully, sure that the smallest misplaced word would make her hands fly about his head, "and nothing you've said or done has made me like you any less."

She smiled through her red-streaked face, then threw her arms around his neck. "You are a real gift. How could I be so blind? I swear I'll never underestimate you again. Give me another chance, will you?"

He kissed her, feeling the stirrings of relief and lust but also sensing, because he knew enough about women, that trying for sex would backfire. The warmth inside him, the mending of his guts, and the lightheadedness were enough right then. "You know how I feel about you. Are we still going to South Carolina, or is that no longer in the plans?"

"South Carolina," she said. "I have to get this out of my blood. Okay? So I can move on and get out of this Mike phase."

He would do anything to get her out of her Mike phase. As he threw their belongings in Becca's trunk, he began to whistle, feeling the promise of the day and the change of fortune it had brought. He felt strong again, and capable. When Becca came out of the motel office, still wearing her yellow flip-flops, he could not take his eyes off her feet. They seemed to have minds of their own, their tendons and bones flexing under the skin like individual workers, carrying Becca to him despite all his fears.

⁓⋎⋏⁓

Late in the afternoon, as Dana stepped into the hallway leading to the outdoor enclosures, something nervous fluttered like hummingbird wings in the back of her mind. She hesitated, absently tracing the numbness on the back of her hand. What was it? She felt as though she should be elsewhere. Checking on something. At the end of the hall, in

Barafu's cage, the leaping form of Fikira stilled the uneasiness inside her and propelled her forward.

Mary squatted in a corner of the cage, her forearms resting on her thighs, her expression intent on the interaction between the two chimps. Barafu sat in the middle of the cage, sucking on her finger, and Fikira, her play face on, bobbed on one of the platforms.

Yesterday, Fikira had been terrified of Barafu; although she had been housed for several years with her mother in the laboratory, her exposure to adults had been minimal. Today, though, Dana could see that a breakthrough had occurred. Fikira hopped off the platform to the ground, then crept quietly behind Barafu. When Fikira was close enough, she batted Barafu's back, then scampered up the platform as Barafu turned. Barafu, like an adult human, pretended surprise that no one stood behind her, a smile toying at the corner of her mouth. Fikira laughed. Dana could tell this game had been going on for a while.

Dana gave Mary the thumbs-up sign. Mary nodded.

The play soon ended inside the cage. Fikira embraced Barafu as the adult chimp held her arms away from her body, as though she did not know what to make of the gesture. Then Barafu pushed Fikira away. Fikira rubbed her eye with a fist, whimpering. Mary went to them and lifted Barafu's hand to Fikira, trying to encourage the adult to groom the child. For a few seconds, Barafu held Fikira's face in her hands and picked at her brow and under her chin before moving her own body into position for Mary to groom her. Mary gave Dana a look that said, *She has to do better than this*. Once again, Mary tried to reintroduce Barafu's hands to Fikira, but Barafu walked away, miffed. Dana sighed. During meals, Barafu still ate with the same piggishness, leaving nothing for Fikira. How would Fikira survive in the more competitive environment of an outdoor group without an adult to consider her interests?

Again, something nagged Dana, snarling in her thoughts like a small trapped insect. She thought, *I should check the electric fence today, maybe now*. The idea did not make sense because she had patrolled the perimeter a few days before. Still, it buzzed annoyingly inside her. She did not believe in prophetic powers, but she believed in instinct and the enigmatic workings of the senses. Sometimes, she reasoned, the brain received cues unconsciously, unsettling the neurons, imparting knowledge below the surface of cognitive awareness. Humans were after all primates, and thus born of the jungle, albeit long ago. Certain vestiges of survival skills had to linger in the genetic material. You could say, "I had a premonition," when really you had read the map of information your brain had been gathering while you attended to other, more conscious chores. Dana listened, head cocked, but heard nothing, not even a chimpanzee bark or the crackling of branches. She peered through the bars and past the chimps into the outer area and still saw nothing out of place. But what harm would it do to walk the perimeter?

Before she went out to inspect the fencing, Dana poked her head in the graduate students' office. Kaylee, Vicki, and Darryl were huddled around the small television screen watching a replay of Sifongo's introduction. "I'm checking the perimeter," Dana told them. "And maybe the woods. You can reach me by two-way." She patted the walkie-talkie clipped to her belt.

Darryl let his weight fall back into his chair. "Do you need someone to go with you?"

She smiled. "Thanks anyway." She could not get it out of her mind that Darryl—or any of the other students—never offered to go with her. Something was in the air, she thought, something uneasy.

As Dana stepped onto the path on the far side of the parking lot, she could see already how nature was bracing itself for winter. Autumn was the loneliest of seasons, she thought, when the colors drained out of the woods and left nothing of comfort. In the summer, the sun struck Dana's skin with full force, but now it caressed and pooled slowly, sprinkling itself drop by drop, cooling almost as soon as she felt it. The shrubs had stopped producing new leaves at the tips of their branches, and the oak trees had dropped a hard carpet of acorns. The few deciduous trees in the woods had begun to thin their branches, shedding burnished leaves. Here, in this part of the South, winter was only part withdrawal, the rest patient waiting, a kind of breathless pause until the days lengthened. Live oaks grayed like sick old men but never surrendered all their leaves, and when the Spanish moss dripping from their gnarled branches frosted, they resembled demented Christmas trees, glittering with knotted tinsel. To Dana, this odd sight only reinforced how winter did not belong here, how it crept upon the land like an infiltrator bent on sabotage, how its very brevity implied an inappropriate lurking.

Dana paused by the tree where she had once spied Zack. She looked up into the branches, expecting to see her brother smiling down like the Cheshire cat, but the tree held nothing more than a cardinal that flew off soundlessly as soon as she spotted it. She missed Zack. He never allowed her the sisterly pleasure of a good-bye kiss, or even a meager moment of well-wishing. He just left. *Damn him.*

At the base of the oak, she saw a flattened patch of ground. With a start, she realized she was looking at the spot where her brother had landed repeatedly upon jumping down from the tree. *Two, maybe three times?* As she began to walk away, a scattering of tan near the base of the electrified fence caught her eye. She bent down to inspect it and found a littering of peanuts, some bleached by the sun and washed by the rain, their pen faces almost gone. But some had crisp ink, as precise as a pen could make on the dimpled surfaces of the shells. It had rained since Zack left. The dews had been heavy. The presence of the new shells could mean only that he had returned. Dana craned her neck to listen and to see around shrubs for bits of unnatural color or movement. Zack had come back. Her heart raced as she scanned the treetops before moving on.

She did not come across any additional signs of Zack, and after a while, she stopped looking. This walking of the grounds was always so peaceful that she felt herself slipping into a trance in which all was forgotten and nothing but the terrain remained. The chimps inside the enclosures were quiet—napping, perhaps. Right then, it actually sounded like South Carolina, the birds twittering with the last of their summer voices, an insistent breeze like a hissed whisper ruffling the drying leaves. Dana reached the last stretch of fence and slowed her pace, not wanting to relinquish the tranquility. On the other side of the wire but out of sight, Group B erupted into a squabble; the voices of Kimbunga, Chokaa, and Sifongo barked and screamed over the lesser noises of the others. Dana flinched at the sounds of aggression. She had been listening and watching these territorial fights for years, and each time she worried.

She did not know which she noticed first—the insulated wire

cutters lying on a patch of moss, the fence bent back into a flimsy door, or the thick gloves poking out from under a pile of pine needles—but for a few disorienting seconds, none of it made sense. She stood dumbly before the scattered clues until they registered. *No.* She wondered if she could—or even if she wanted to—cover for Zack yet again. She grabbed the gloves and wire cutters. *Damn him.* Her breathing quickening, she ducked through the opening in the fence and stood up too quickly, too furiously. A live wire touched her back and shot its current down her spine. *Damn him again.* With the gloves on her hands, she squatted to repair the fence from the inside. Then something else hit her: the screams she was hearing were not only chimpanzee but also human.

EIGHTEEN

*A*s Dana dashed across the line of crushed vegetation into the heart of the enclosure, she whipped off the gloves and reached for her radio. "Group B! Group B! Group B!" she shouted into the transmitter. She could not think of other words or commands, or anything coherent at all; communication was trapped by the fear inside her. She heard the shouts of her brother up ahead and the shrieks of a woman. Breaking into the clearing, she saw with horror Kimbunga leaping toward Zack and kicking him squarely in the chest, knocking him to the ground. Teeth bared, hair bristled enormously, Kimbunga charged and grasped Zack's ankle as he passed, dragging him for several feet. The male chimps hopped about excitedly, barking, while the females shrieked from the trees. Becca, whom Dana had not noticed before, stood in Kimbunga's path. As the chimp released Zack's ankle, he continued his charge straight toward Becca, a blur of dark and ferocious fur. Becca's mouth opened in a soundless scream.

"Run!" Dana shouted. "Move!" Then she yelled a loud, aggressive *WRAAAA.*

Kimbunga turned to see his challenger, giving Becca enough time to crash through the shrubs. He came at Dana with bowed arms and teeth glittering with saliva. She chimp-shrieked and made frightened submissive sounds, running behind a stout pine trunk, then another, but Kimbunga found a fallen branch that he raised above his head, showing all the chimps around him how strong he was, how intimidating, how *in charge.*

The chimps were shaking branches in the trees and deafening her with their shrieks. Mary and Darryl ran into the clearing across from Dana. Mary's cheekbones were slashed pink with exertion, and she stopped, wiping her forehead with the back of her hand. Her other hand held the tranquilizer gun. Dana's heart skipped a beat when she saw Mary, who was supposed to stay out of Group B to avoid contact with the HIV and hepatitis chimps.

Zack rolled over in the dust. Slowly, he raised himself on all fours.

"Stay down!" Dana cried. She could see Mary's eyes assessing the situation, understanding it, as her adept, slender fingers loaded a tranquilizer into the gun chamber. Darryl held the pack of medical supplies against his chest like a shield.

Kimbunga, still agitated, hurled the branch at Zack, but it fell short between them. Out of breath, Kimbunga lumbered toward Zack on two legs, his chest puffed, his arms high, and Dana realized with a start that Mwenzi would have calmed much sooner than this. Mwenzi would have seen the motionless human form long ago and begun to wind down, so this newest incarnation of Zack would have seemed less threatening, already defeated. But Kimbunga continued his display of dominance, even as his lungs labored from the effort, making Dana wonder what the difference was between Kimbunga and Benji, who had been kept from other apes. Zack, his hair snarled with leaves and pine needles and dirt, rose to his knees. His face had the bewildered rumple of childhood, of waking from a nap and not understanding the time, day or night, or where he was.

"Get down!" Dana told him. She wanted to run to Zack, to pull him to his senses, to cover him with her body, but Mary was already aiming the tranquilizer at Kimbunga.

Kimbunga fell to his knuckles and charged full force, his broad shoulders braced like a battering ram. Zack made his hands into fists, and Dana realized with shock that he meant to fight the chimp. But instead of leaping on Zack, Kimbunga ran past, clipping Zack's shoulder with his own, and Zack was knocked backward. The soft pop of the tranquilizer gun cut through the air. Dana ran toward her brother, not caring about the danger but about rescuing Zack, getting him to lie still, to submit.

Kimbunga, the blue dart embedded in his backside, screeched and carried on, batting the ground with his fists and feet, furious. His eyes glaring, he turned to see what had caused him pain and yanked the dart out of his flesh. But by then, the tranquilizer had entered his bloodstream, already glazing his eyes and slowing his movements just a little, enough for him to sit down to catch his breath. His brow furrowed in a frown. He had not meant to hurt anyone, only to establish his dominance.

"Got him," Mary said, coming all the way into the clearing. The chimps were still yelling in the trees. Mary stood tentatively between Zack and Kimbunga, who had not yet submitted to the medication.

Zack was lying on his back in the dust, his blue eyes gazing upward at the matching sky, his breath shallow and pained. Dana knelt and leaned over him. "Zack? Are you okay?"

"I think he broke my ribs." And then, improbably, he grinned. His false teeth had been knocked out and his lip had swelled, so he looked demented. "I showed him, didn't I?"

Dana sprang to her feet. She could not look at him, could not look away. She kicked a clump of pine needles and sticks on top of him, the tip of her boot just missing his rib cage. "You idiot! Don't you realize how *stupid* you are? Mary saved your ass." She kicked at the ground again.

"Cut it out!"

"Fuck you." She started walking away, then paced back. "You could've been killed."

"You're in here all the time. What's the big deal?"

Mary held Dana's gaze for a long two seconds before breaking it. A few feet away, Kimbunga fell over with a sigh. Mary hurried to attend to him. Dana caught the crook of Darryl's elbow. "There's a woman somewhere in here," Dana told him. "Her name is Becca. Find her and get her out of here." She tossed her radio to him. "Ask for help if you need it."

Darryl nodded. Handing the medical pack to Mary, he set out to find Becca. Mary radioed the main building, asking Inge to call Andy to the sanctuary.

"Oh, God, this hurts." Zack groaned and sat up.

"Of course it does," Dana spat. "You're an idiot."

"You could've been seriously hurt," Mary said. "Or worse."

"Give it a break." He struggled to his feet, both hands holding his left rib cage tightly. "I grew up with a chimp. I know chimps. And I also know Dana. No way would she be in here if she could get killed."

Dana tried to control her rage. "You *don't* know chimps. You didn't even really know Annie. You can barely remember back that far. Jesus, Zack, don't you think that I *trained* for this job? That we take precautions and still run the risk of injury? We don't just unload chimps into these enclosures. We get to know them, and let them get to know us. We build trust. You can't just barge in here and expect the chimps to act like Curious George and you're the Man in the Yellow Hat. It doesn't work that way, not in real life. Why do you think Annie almost bit my hand off? She didn't do it because she was bad, but because she was a chimp. You just entered an adult male chimp's territory and didn't think anything of it. Another day, you might have gotten away with it, but today he felt threatened. He needed to show his group who's boss. Did you ever consider this might happen? Did you know this about chimps? Do you know how to show submission? Do you fucking know *anything* about chimps?"

He stared at her open-mouthed for several seconds, so long that she believed she had finally gotten through to him, but then he said, "I don't feel so well. I'd better get to a doctor." His face had paled, and a glitter of perspiration broke out on his forehead. He wobbled at the knees.

"Throw your arm over my shoulder," Mary said.

Zack cried out as he lifted his left arm, but he did as he was told. Dana ducked her head under his right arm to hold him up, but as his flesh touched hers, she almost wept as the reality of what had happened pieced itself together, jagged bit by bit. She had been wrong to assume that one day Zack would grow up. Somewhere, she had read that a person's maturity and personality became fixed around age twenty-five, so why should she expect her brother to be anything more than he always had been? It was like hoping for a normal life for Benji. You could pray and strive and hope, but you should not expect results.

"You're lucky I didn't shoot you with the dart," Mary told Zack as she struggled with him on one side and the tranquilizer gun slipped off her shoulder on the other. "And that I hit Kimbunga on the first try. You could've gotten it in the ass."

"Well, thank you." Zack tried to laugh but cut it short with a howl.

"Where did you learn to shoot like that?" Dana asked Mary.

"Summer camp. We shot bull's-eyes with twenty-twos. I just imagined Kimbunga with a target painted on his flank. *Pfft.*"

Although Dana could imagine Mary in a summer camp with other dirt-streaked kids, she could not see her learning how to shoot. "Did you like it? The target practice?"

Mary shrugged. "I was good at it. I never thought about what a gun meant. Now, of course, I'd be mortified if someday my child learned how to shoot." She patted her stomach.

"You're having a baby?" Zack asked.

"Yup."

"If it's a boy, name it after me," he said, grinning toothlessly.

As though considering the request, Mary raised her dark eyebrows, but Dana could see underneath to the spark, the amusement, that was meant not for Zack but for her. The idea of saddling a newborn with Zack's name and what it implied was ridiculous. You named a child after someone you trusted or admired, or after the pleasing sounds the letters made, the heft of it in your mouth. Names evoked images and baggage, and Zack did not have a prayer that Mary would name her child after him.

Dana slipped her free hand around Zack's wrist and gave it a gentle squeeze. He looked at her first with surprise and then with a small grimacing smile.

The evening air shivered with damp cold, the kind of chill that drives you under the blankets even though the windows are shut tight. Dana had not turned the heat on yet; every year, she resisted for as long as possible, not so much to save energy but because she hated to admit that winter was drawing near. Cold made her ornery; the frayed ends of her self-control threatened to touch and ignite her into nastiness. It did not help that Zack now lay sprawled on her sofa with his head in Becca's bony lap, a gangly reminder of everything that had gone wrong with the day. Dana had been inclined to forgive him, or at least to be gentle with him, but his cavalier attitude peeved her. He had not even tried to apologize. As they watched television, Dana picked up the items Zack and Becca had already scattered around her house: sweatshirts, magazines, empty beer bottles, socks, shoes, that stupid plastic alligator.

Zack yelped as he shifted position, reminding them all, as he did every few minutes, of his two broken ribs. Becca cooed and stroked his loose hair that spread in her lap like blond kelp. "Poor baby," Becca said.

Dana wanted to shout, *It's his own damn fault!* Instead, she dropped everything in her arms into a hard, sudden pile by Becca's feet. Becca started, her eyes wild for a moment after the impact, but Zack just rolled his eyes.

"You can't scare a man who's been beaten to shit by an ape," he said. Becca laughed as she picked a stray hair off his forehead.

Zack and Becca had joked all evening about their escape, reveling in it, inspecting it with such good humor that Dana wished she had the backbone to throw both of them out. Neither had asked her what their foolishness would do to her job, even though they had overheard Dana's cell phone call to Dean Washington on the way to the emergency clinic. Certainly, they had heard her explanation and awkward apology, heard the tremor in her voice, could tell she was being reamed out for this new public-relations nightmare. And still Zack and Becca joked as though their intrusion had nothing to do with her.

Dana closed herself in her bedroom. No matter what risks Zack took, he always emerged with no serious injuries and the ability to move on. Even without being told, she knew Zack would not be charged with trespassing. He never was. Dana was sick of it, of *him*.

Her bedroom had a half-finished look that today depressed her, even as she sought refuge in it. She had left her marital bed in Arizona, where it belonged, and upon her arrival in South Carolina had bought a queen-sized mattress and box springs, fully intending to find a bed that suited her, something unlike the massively masculine sleigh bed she and Charlie had shared. She had thought brass, or maybe even the romance of a four-poster rice bed, something carved in maple or cherry, but she had never even looked for one, leaving the mattress sitting in its crude metal frame. She had painted the walls a light mossy green and the moldings a crisp white, had bought a comforter in blue and lavender with just a hint of the green, but had never bothered to purchase curtains, instead relying on the blinds left by the previous owner. Only one picture hung on the wall, an oil painting by her undergraduate roommate, Kelly, now a professional artist, who had given the canvas to Dana as a wedding present. The painting, a woodsy landscape, looked neglected amid the barren walls. Everything was neat—no newspapers or magazines, no dirty clothes, no knickknacks decorating the top of the dresser, not even a few coins scattered on the nightstand—but Dana realized for the first time that this bespoke not of care but of her inability to fashion a space that reflected her personality. She had started and then abandoned the effort. She wondered now, as she stood helplessly in the middle of the small room, if she simply did not trust herself enough to move in fully. It had been years, and her bungalow still looked as though she had boxes to unpack.

The doorbell rang. Dana sank to her bed, covering her eyes with both hands. What friend had Zack invited this time? What new crisis? She considered hauling the quilt her grandmother had given her for a wedding present out of the closet to stuff along the base of the door so she would not have to listen to whatever was going to happen outside her door, but that was more effort than she was willing to exert. She longed for a double row of pillows, a good book, and maybe a glass of Merlot. She rolled over onto her stomach and buried her face in her pillow until she could barely breathe.

There was a soft knock at the door, and the sound of Zack's breathing hissed into the crack. "Dana? Open up."

She sighed. Couldn't he figure out she wanted to be left alone? But like a ringing phone, Zack demanded to be answered, and Dana could not ignore him. She rolled off the bed and shuffled to the door, opening it.

Zack stood in the short hallway, and behind him was Sam Wendt. Dana felt a shock and an odd embarrassment at having Sam inside her house, peering into her bedroom. Sam ran his fingers through his curls as she stepped out quickly into the hallway. The awkwardness was palpable. She had turned Sam down and yet here he was, just outside her bedroom, chaperoned by her brother. The three of them stood in the dim hallway, shifting, licking their lips, trying to find something safe to look at.

"Hi," Sam said around Zack, who stood almost crushed between them. "Can we talk?"

Dana had the urge to escape the house and her brother, to take Sam out of the messiness that was her life. "Outside," she said, already striding toward the front door and pinning Zack against the wall. "Come on." She took her jacket out of the coat closet and stepped outside without putting it on.

On the porch, the chilled, damp air felt breathable, a relief. Dana could feel Sam at her back, though she had not once turned to see if he was following her. She inhaled deeply twice before trotting down the two steps to the ground. She wiggled into her jacket. "We can walk along the road. There's no shoulder, but hardly any cars drive by."

Sam leapt from the porch straight to the ground, bypassing the steps like a kid. "Your brother is back in town."

"You don't know, then?" She could not see his face in the dark, and did not want to.

"Know what?"

They were walking quickly now, down the driveway toward the road. Dana imagined that if she continued at this pace, she could outrun all the things that dogged her. It seemed years ago, when it was only weeks, that she had discovered the fast, dark shape of Barafu hurtling through the fog. She held back a sigh. "I figured you'd heard somehow. Zack and

Becca broke into one of the outdoor enclosures today. Before we could get a dart in him, the alpha male pounded Zack."

"He looked okay to me."

"He would have told you about his war wounds if you had stayed longer. If you had stayed another fifteen seconds."

"You think Zack broke into the sanctuary before? The first time?"

She stopped. They had traveled far enough from the house that it appeared as only yellow light through the trees. The rest of the countryside was invisible in the night; clouds had covered the moon so only the darkest sketch of tree limbs remained, though Dana knew they would begin to appear, one by one, as her eyes adjusted. She wished she could see Sam's expression. "I don't know for sure," she said. But as her words echoed inside her head, they disgusted her. She was sick of diplomacy, of being the director of the sanctuary and Zack's sister, of being so guarded that no one knew who she was. Hiding the truth hurt more than her own self-worth. It hurt the SCPP. "No, I *do* know for sure. I don't have proof, but I know it was him."

"Lamier was right, then. He was sure Zack released the chimps, and that you were covering for him."

"I was *not* covering for him!" Even as she said it, she felt the shame of a lie. She had thrown away the key, after all, and had not told anyone about finding him perched in a tree at the far end of Group A. Despite the facts, she had not until that moment fully understood the depth of her self-deception. She had wished for Zack's innocence so fervently that she allowed herself enough doubt to wriggle free of her responsibility. No wonder Zack always emerged unscathed—she always saw to it. "Dean Washington already knows what Zack did today. I called him right away. I'm sure he, too, has made the connection between the two incidents."

They walked in silence along the side of the road. Dana's feet kept meeting the crumbling edge of the asphalt, and several times she slipped off onto the soft ground. Sam took the inner part of the road, a few steps toward the center. Dana could feel him thinking. The tension in his body, the way he set his gaze on the dark ground in front of him, and the shift in the atmosphere made her aware he was mulling something.

He finally said, "I found out what happened to Annie."

Oh, God. Annie.

"I didn't want to tell you until I could confirm it with several sources. Do you want to know?"

A sickly sweet fear pushed its way into her nostrils and head, into her gut. "Is it going to be in your article?"

"Yes."

She sucked in the cold air, hoping it would steady her, but instead it felt like a blow to her chest. Zack had done this. He had pushed Sam to uncover the truth about Annie, and he had tricked Sam into believing that she, too, shared this desire. Now, she had no choice but to learn what had happened. She could not bear ignorance when everyone else knew the truth. "Tell me, then. We can keep walking." She needed to be in motion.

"Your father knowingly sold Annie for medical research. He signed the papers himself. He and the university expected Annie to be used to study the effectiveness of antibiotics. He didn't know, however, that the contracted laboratory intended to immediately sell Annie to another facility that wanted her for a study your father never would have allowed. In fact, although your father didn't admit it, this other facility had come to him directly a few months before she bit your hand. He turned them down."

Her heart was beating so furiously she thought she would keel over into the dense shag of ferns alongside the road. "What was the study?"

"The cognitive effects of brain damage."

She saw an image of Annie—unconscious, incisions oozing blood and pus, eyes rimmed red—as vividly as though it were before her eyes. It blinded her to all else. Sam and the South Carolina road no longer existed. *Annie.* As the picture shifted in her shaky field of vision, it evoked the acrid smells of urine and laboratory disinfectant. And then Dana realized she was not seeing Annie at all but the female chimp in the Massachusetts lab. She could not picture Annie. The entire night world began to tip slowly and irrevocably to the left. She had no choice but to follow the tilt. As straight as a tree blown over by a hurricane gust, she fell sideways onto the pavement, where she lay stunned, her weak hand curled under her ribs.

"Are you okay?" Sam asked.

"I'm . . . I'm sorry," she said, not knowing how she had lost her balance.

"I shouldn't have been so blunt." He helped her regain her footing, so she stood upright again. He held her hand.

Dana's eyes had adjusted to the dark, and she could see parts of his face, and how much her fall pained him. "I'm okay," she said. "How did they do it? How did they hide what was going on?"

"The paperwork said she was sold to another lab, but she never arrived there. That's why you couldn't find her. The paperwork was false. Your father found out about the switch almost at once, and he tried to save Annie, but it was already too late. He took all the family savings and tried to buy her back, but no one would admit to having her."

Dana feared she would tumble again. The memories of those first days without Annie came back to her: her mother staring through the kitchen window over the empty backyard with soapsuds clinging to her motionless elbows; her father refusing to look at them, his eyes darkened by bruised circles, as he ate late dinners by himself; the smell of Annie lingering in closets and on the sofa; the silence that none of them had the power to break. They said little to each other during daylight hours. At night, Dana could hear her mother drone on in the next room as she read bedtime stories to Zack, and she knew Zack would soon appear in her doorway, his pajama bottoms drooping at the butt, his fists rubbing his eyes, looking like the baby he wanted to be right then. "We'll find her," Dana had always told him, until the words no longer had meaning and they dropped the pretense. Dana remembered how Annie used to collect piles of pennies—she called them *Pretty hards*—and stashed them in unexpected places. Several weeks after Annie had left and it was clear she was never returning, Dana had pulled a stuffed rabbit out of her closet, exposing a small pile of shiny pennies. Dana could almost see Annie's blunt, peach-colored fingers pushing them into place, the care and secrecy with which she hid them. Dana had gathered the coins into her fist, clutching them, crying silently because she did not want anyone to interrupt her grief. This many years later, Dana still had the pennies, which she had placed in a small musical jewelry box decorated with a ballerina. It had been years since she wound the mechanism, but she occasionally peered inside to look at the pennies, now tarnished and marked with her fingerprints. She had never guessed that her parents— her father—had tried to reverse what had happened. Only now, as the South Carolina woods rustled with night creatures preparing for winter, did she realize how young she had been when Annie was taken away, how by necessity, by her age, by everything, she had not been privy to all that had gone on. She had known almost nothing.

Sam squeezed her fingers.

"How long did she live?" she asked.

"She died during the surgical procedure, about a month after she arrived. She was under anesthesia, so she never felt a thing. She never lived with the damage they intended to study."

Oh, Annie.

How was she going to tell Zack? All these years, he had harbored the hope that Annie was still alive and that they would find her. Zack had believed Sam would be Annie's savior, the one who finally found her alive and well and living under an assumed name, the one who would bring goods news and a family reunion. Though Zack could barely remember Annie, she had become his mythology.

Oh, Zack. Oh, Annie.

"You would have liked Annie," she said.

"I know I would have."

Dana's tears came fast and sudden. She had suspected this fate for Annie and had accepted it years ago, mourning in increments, but it still shocked her. With the surprising unleashing of tears came a guttural despair. Sam pulled her into a clumsy embrace that, as their bodies got used to each other, began to mold into something more natural. Dana wished Barafu *did* understand sign language so she could sit with her and tell her, *I know what you survived. I know how lucky and unlucky you are.* Barafu had lived the life Annie might have led, and Dana did not know which was worse, to die or to live through it. She clenched her teeth. Annie had given her the SCPP; she had given Dana the passion to protect other chimps. Dammit, she was not going to let her brother and his girlfriend and Lamier, and whoever else wanted to thwart her, keep her from Annie's legacy. Dana disengaged herself from Sam and stepped back, wiping her wet face on the back of her sleeve. "Sorry."

He pulled a stray lock of hair away from her face. "I would've thought you inhuman if you'd shrugged all this off."

Even in the darkness, she could see the affection in his expression. She was thankful she had learned about Annie's fate from Sam and not someone else. He understood more than anyone her double lives—the past and the present—and how they intertwined. "I need to get out of here. I can't face Zack right now."

"Do you want me to drive you somewhere?"

Dana felt so pathetic right then that she laughed through her sniffles. "I can *drive*. But I have nowhere to go. My only friend is married, with stuff of her own to deal with. My brother and his girlfriend have taken over my house."

Sam shifted his weight from foot to foot. At any moment, she expected him to turn from her, but instead he lowered himself to the edge of the road. "You're so right. All work and no play. Very dull and very alone. You might as well be describing me."

Dana sat next to him. He smelled mildly of sweat and of a cologne she could not identify but that had an intrinsic maleness to it, like loam and metal and hardwood shavings. "Then I don't have a corner on the market?"

"God, no." He vigorously rubbed his hands over his face, as though trying to wake himself. "What do you do for fun?"

"Fun?" She laughed. "*Fun*?" Wiggling from side to side, she settled her legs so that her ankles crossed and she could rest her head on her knees. "Actually, I'm not all work. I roller-blade and go to a few movies with Mary. Eat out. But that's not the same as . . ." She could not say it, not the exact words. "Being married wasn't any better. In fact, it sucked."

"That's because you didn't marry the right guy."

"No argument there. Were you ever married?"

He shook his head. "I thought I was going to be a couple of times, but things broke down. The first relationship fell apart because I was immature, the second because she was. Well, the second because she cheated on me." He paused. "I've never told anyone else that. It's taken me years to get over it. It's completely emasculating to have the woman living with you choose someone else. The betrayal goes deeper than love."

"I'm an incredibly loyal person." She said it without thinking because it was true, but her words now sat between them awkwardly. To the south, the brush of headlights illuminated a stand of trees. "Car," she said, standing.

They quickly moved off the road a few feet into the ditch. Sam kept his eyes on the headlights, following them until they grew too bright. He averted his face and then looked directly into Dana's.

"Let's do something fun," he said. "Tonight."

The tone of his voice resonated inside her; she had forgotten how seductive the male voice could be. She had to ground herself, steady her voice and thoughts, before she spoke. "I'm game. But these parts aren't exactly hopping." The night was cold, and despite having buttoned her coat up to her chin, Dana shivered. And then she remembered what Sam had told her about Annie. Funny how she was able to push that aside for a few minutes, she thought, and how powerfully it came back. "I'm not sure I can do fun. But I don't want to be alone right now."

"Well, then, we can drive to Hilton Head to watch the sprinklers come on at the golf courses."

She laughed. "I'll pass. Are you still staying in Orangeburg?"

"Yeah."

"Even Orangeburg is more exciting than watching sprinklers. We could go out for a drink." She looked directly at him, although she knew he could not see her eyes through the darkness. "Or get a bottle of wine to take back to your room."

He did not miss a beat. "I already have a bottle of wine in my room. And a DVD player. We could pick up some cheese and crackers. Watch a movie." He hesitated, and that scared her until she heard his voice again. "I'm supposed to interview Dean Washington tomorrow morning."

She knew what he was thinking: that he had promised to drive her. He was envisioning driving back and forth between Harris and Orangeburg all night, then back up to the university. "I could follow you up in my car."

"No. Really. I promised. You did the same for me once. When my car broke down." She could hear him swallow and imagined his Adam's apple sliding up and down as he navigated his way through the possibilities. "You aren't the only one who could use some company."

"Well, let's go, then. Give me a minute. I need to grab my keys and stuff."

They walked in silence to the house. The porch steps were lit by a bare incandescent bulb, and this embarrassed Dana. Why hadn't she bought a light fixture when she first moved in, when she'd seen the moths battering themselves directly against the bulb, singeing their wings and dotting the glass with specks of baked insect blood? With Sam there, she saw that perhaps her life was as threadbare as Zack's, layered only with the thinnest gauze of respect. She stopped at the door. "You sure this is okay?"

In the light, she could see his broad grin. If his voice had a shape, it would have been full of curves and dipping slopes, sanded smooth. "Of course it's okay." He sobered. "I'm the one who ruined your night."

Annie, oh Annie. The pain in her heart felt as deep and as wide and as savage as a jungle. "Once again, it was ruined before."

Zack opened the door and stepped out. "Hey, I wondered where you guys had gone. Becca fell asleep, and it's too quiet in there. Oh, my ribs are killing me."

Dana sucked in her lower lip to keep herself from destroying the gentle mood she and Sam had fallen into. She wanted to say something cruel about Zack's missing her only when it suited him. Just seeing him rekindled her rage. And there also lurked the secret she was keeping from him: Annie was dead. Still, she maintained an exterior calm; Sam's physical presence helped her hold onto it. "We're going to take off in a second." Then she slipped inside the house, leaving her brother with Sam, knowing that Sam could handle anything Zack threw his way.

A few minutes later, Dana emerged with her handbag, keys, and a heavier coat, under which was hidden the unopened bottle of red wine she had seen sticking out from under the sofa. Rent, she reasoned.

Sam stood against a porch support, his arms loosely crossed, while Zack muttered a few feet away, not at Sam but looking into the wild darkness beyond. Dana grinned. She knew Zack had tried something—a few words and gestures—that Sam had called him on. Zack should know better than to mess with someone like Sam.

"Ready?" she asked.

Sam pushed himself away from the post. "Yup."

Zack grunted as they tromped down the porch steps.

As Dana closed the passenger door to Sam's rental car, she removed the wine from her coat and held it up as a trophy. "Zack's," she said.

Sam laughed. "I bet people don't steal much from the guy."

"I've waited at least twenty years to find something worth taking."

Sam backed the car down the driveway, one arm hooked over the back of Dana's seat, his head and shoulder turned toward the rear. The casualness with which he held his arm there thrilled her, as though she could slip into a normal life after all and no one would notice. *This is the right decision.* She reached over to touch his bicep. "Thanks."

He smiled. "I'm not sure for what, exactly. But you're welcome."

In the silence that followed, Dana looked out the window so Sam could not see her, even if he glanced her way. The way he drove—aggressively, but never too fast to take the curves—made her feel slightly powerless in the passenger seat. At his mercy. "You know," she said, keeping her face from him, "I've gotten really out of practice with some things." She felt like a teenager again, full of angst, living in fear of pimples and bad breath, awkward and gangly and unsure. "Maybe you should just take me back home." She looked his way quickly and saw his eyes were on her, not the road.

Without saying anything, Sam pulled the car to the side and flicked on the emergency flashers.

"What are you doing?"

He leaned over and kissed her, catching her first on the cheek but then, as his hand guided her chin toward him, on the mouth. She stiffened for an instant but then relaxed into his embrace, seeking out his lips as he did hers. She had forgotten how surprising a first kiss was, how lips touched and felt, tongue, the dizzying rush of emotion and lust, the way she wanted to fuse herself with another's flesh, the desperate hunger—how primal and urgent everything became. When Sam finally drew away, leaving Dana's mouth feeling gently crushed and empty, she involuntarily sucked in a deep breath.

"There," he said, putting the car back into gear. "We got that out of the way."

All the way to Orangeburg, Dana was dying for another kiss, for him to touch her and for her to touch him. As they entered the town limits, she reached over to his coarse cheek, and she felt weak when he leaned into her touch.

In his motel room, they did not bother with the wine or a movie. They made love with an urgency that still allowed for gentleness, for stopping to look at each other's eyes, for Sam's fingers to linger on her skin. But it was the force of their need that took over.

Afterward, Dana laid her head on Sam's bare chest, the two of them sighing and laughing at themselves.

Sam cupped her head with his palm. "Do you realize that this is the first time I've met a woman's entire family *before* I slept with her?"

"I think it's amazing that you would sleep with me, having met them."

"Or you with me, considering what I dredged up."

Dana considered that perhaps she had slept with him precisely because of what he had exposed in her. Annie and her fate now hovered between them, unspoken but there, like a ghost. The weird thing was, Dana realized, that because Annie *was* there, she felt unhindered and open. Sam had performed an exorcism of sorts. "Are you going to get in trouble because of tonight? Conflict of interest or something?"

He kissed her head. "That's for me to worry about. You have to worry about saving the sanctuary and disarming Lamier. And minimizing the damage Zack did today."

She nodded, then watched as Sam's eyelids fluttered shut. He drifted into sleep, a small smile still on his lips but fading to the slackness of unconsciousness. This intimacy between them could not last, she knew, even if they both wanted it to. They had careers and lives in different states, had crossed paths only temporarily, had reached out to each other in passing, holding on for as long as they were able. For this brief contact, Dana was grateful. She felt as though she had escaped from a claustrophobic routine and entered a more expansive place. She kissed the dimple in Sam's sleeping chin, and it startled him awake, his brown eyes quickly wide and confused, then, as they focused, content before they shut again. Dana wanted to burrow her head into the soft hairs of Sam's armpit and stay there, but instead she rolled over on her side and fell asleep.

NINETEEN

Oh, Annie.

Those were the words she woke up with. Dana leapt out of bed, her heart and mind racing.

"Whoa!" Sam stood across the room buttoning his shirt. His legs, naked in the light of the morning, were slightly bowed but strong, with sparse, dark hair. Dana let herself fall backward onto the bed. "Bad dream?" he asked.

"Yeah. I guess." She combed her hair with her fingers and winced as they caught a few knots. "Do I have time for a quick shower?"

"Sure. As long as we leave in twenty minutes or so."

On her way to the bathroom, Dana peeked between the drapes and saw that the morning had an early dampness to it. The small parking lot outside was full of cars with dewy windshields, and they all harbored looks of abandonment in the gray light. Dana shivered, but not from true cold or even discontent, only gratefulness that she was inside. "I'll be quick," she said.

Dana stepped into the shower and turned the water as hot as she could bear. Little bottles of motel shampoo and conditioner were tottering inside the soap dish, along with a small bar of soap. She found it odd imagining Sam breaking the seal of each bottle to portion out amounts into his open palm, using them to lather his hair. She picked up the shampoo by the thimble neck and for a moment could not bring herself to unscrew the cap. Somehow, it seemed more intimate to share shampoo than to sleep together. Their bodies would have similar scents for the day, as though something basic had changed within them. She opened the bottle and tapped thick shampoo into her palm.

She emerged from the bathroom in a cloud of swirling steam. The towel was scant and scratchy, too thin to absorb the moisture clinging to her skin, but still she felt luxuriously relaxed, catlike even. As Sam saw her, his face furrowed. She stopped.

"What?" She checked behind her to make sure she had not dragged anything embarrassing out of the bathroom. "Is something wrong?"

"No." He shook his head and then sat on the edge of the bed, shoe in hand.

Dana swayed in place. The water droplets gathered on her thighs and ran down her legs in frantic tickles that she resisted scratching. Sometimes she was such a coward, but today she felt as though she could no longer afford to be. What did she have to lose? What if Sam told her he had made a mistake about her, that in the daylight Dana no longer attracted him? The better to know, she told herself. "You can be honest."

"Honest?" He paused, then laughed. "It has nothing to do with you. No, no. Trust me—not at *all*. It's . . ." He laughed again. "I'm not used to having a seminaked woman walk out of my bathroom. It struck me as weird. And a little surprising."

She grinned, and her legs felt free again, so she walked over to the bed and lowered herself next to him. "So it's been a long time for you, too."

"I've gotten used to being alone." He pulled on his shoe and let his foot drop to the carpet. The movement was so casual, so free of angst, that Dana hugged his arm. He kissed her bare shoulder. "Too many nights alone in motel rooms, too many nights alone in a quiet apartment, so now everything else is shocking." He leaned over and brushed against her lips. One of his hands came to rest on her damp thigh, and even as she kissed him, she concentrated on his palm, to remember what his touch was like in case she never felt it again. She could let him disappear, she decided, as long as she could recall what it felt like to be treated gently. As Sam drew away, he brought a strand of her wet hair to his nose. "You smell great."

Dana threw back her head and laughed.

"What's so funny?"

She did not want to tell him about the shampoo and the intimacy she had imagined in its perfume, so instead she said, "My ex-husband used to say I smelled like a beast."

"Then bring on the jungle."

"I'd better get dressed. We don't have much time, and I'd hate for you to have to explain to Dean Washington why you're late."

As Dana gathered her clothes in one hand, she noticed the hand-labeled DVDs next to the television. The night before, she had been so focused on what was happening between her and Sam that she had failed to see what the small room contained, but now she knew. The DVDs were her childhood, her life, Annie alive. She could pick them up and leave the motel room with them without Sam's having the courage to stop her. She looked over her shoulder to meet his steady gaze; he knew she had seen. Then, with a quick inhalation, she stepped away from the television. The films were done, part of the past, and nothing more could be gleaned or lost from them.

$$\sim\!\!\wedge\!\!\sim$$

After Sam dropped her off at the house, Dana let herself in quietly. No one was awake yet, and it felt eerily like any other morning. The door to the guest room was shut, and Dana tried not to make the floor creak on the way to her bedroom. She changed her clothes, ran a brush through her almost-dry hair, brushed her teeth. The beginning of the day really did feel like any other, except for the warm flutter, like beating wings, under her breastbone. Her mind kept drifting back to what it had felt like to fall asleep on Sam's shoulder, the smell of him, the curve of his muscles.

In the kitchen, Dana started to remove coffee beans from the freezer but then remembered that it was Wednesday, her day to stop by the diner for takeout coffee. Zack could make his own damn pot. She squatted in front of the refrigerator, searching for something to take with her for lunch. Fortunately, Zack and Becca had not been in the house for long, so she had leftover bean chili in a plastic container and two apples. She slipped her lunch into a brown paper bag and creased it shut.

Zack shuffled into the kitchen wearing boxer shorts and no shirt. She jumped. She had not heard him stirring. "Morning," he said. "I heard you come in."

She closed the refrigerator with her hip. "I'm leaving for work."

He slid onto a stool. "So early?"

"I always leave this early." She tried to get around him, but he had stretched out his legs. She needed to step between them and over, something she was not quite sure she could navigate with so little sleep. She pushed on his knees. He did not move.

"Don't be pissed about yesterday," he said. "What Becca and I did is over."

"It's over as far as you're concerned. *I* have to deal with the fallout." She did not want to argue with him this morning. She hesitated; she had to tell him about Annie but was not sure this was the right moment. Then again, no time would be right. "Sam told me some bad news last night."

"What?"

"He found out that Annie is dead. She died a long time ago. Soon after she left our house." Last night, the news had been so new and brutal that she would have told him the exact details of Annie's death, the how and why, but now she saw no benefit in doing so. Zack did not need yet another graphic image added to his mental archives. Besides, at least one of them should be spared the painful knowledge, and it was too late for her. "That's why no one could find her." She braced herself for Zack's reaction, expecting him to either lash out in violent anger or crumple, completely helpless in the face of the news.

Instead, Zack looked at her blankly. "Annie isn't dead."

She sighed. "But she is, Zack. I know you don't want to believe it. I don't want to either. But it's true. Sam wouldn't tell me that unless he had proof."

"Or unless he wanted to sleep with you."

"Oh, yeah, like that kind of information is going to seduce me."

"It worked, didn't it?"

Did he really believe that she had been helpless against Sam's charms? That she had not made a choice? That she could not tell the difference between honesty and manipulation? Maybe Zack couldn't, but she could. He was trying to turn everything back on her, to deny the truth so he could defend his own version of it. She was so furious with him that she could not speak.

Zack was grinning. "*This* is your problem, Dana. You are so fucking arrogant. You think you know everything. The truth is, you don't. You don't know shit. You don't know *shit* about chimps, and you don't know shit about Annie. She's alive."

"Yeah? And how do you know this?"

"Dick Lamier told me."

The sneering syllables of Lamier's name chilled Dana. Zack was not supposed to know Lamier anymore; he should have been a childhood memory. "Lamier knows Annie is dead."

Zack shook his head. "He thinks he knows where she is. He's promised to help me find her."

Dana collapsed onto the stool next to her brother, who regarded her with triumphant, certain eyes. Zack's blind faith in Lamier evoked the past in excruciating detail. The smell of dog hung in the air, as though Lamier himself stood next to her. *I know where Annie is. I can take you there.* "That's exactly what he told me before he tried to have sex with me. At sixteen."

"What?"

"Yes, Zack. That's why he stopped coming to Sunday dinner. It wasn't because he was too busy or was looking for another job. He was exiled. And he was damn lucky that's all that happened to him."

"But—"

"Sam Wendt uncovered the truth. Annie is dead. She ended up in a brain damage study and died on the operating table. Lamier has known the truth, or most of it, anyway, since we were kids."

"Dick wouldn't lie!"

She took Zack's face in her hands, squeezing. "You broke into the sanctuary twice. I know you let the chimps go. Did Lamier have anything to do with that?"

He knocked her arms away. "All he wanted was the donor list. It was my idea to let the chimps go. I never meant any harm. You know that." Although his face had the first lines of age, his eyes, blue and insistent, were the same ones that had looked to her for guidance when they were little. "I swear I didn't mean any harm."

"It doesn't matter what you intended. It's what you *did*." She narrowed her eyes. "You screwed me over, Zack. I may lose my job because of you. If I do, I'll *never* forgive you."

"You can't lose your job because of something I did."

"Like hell I can't! Lamier has been using your actions against me. He's convinced donors to withdraw their support, and animal rights activists of my negligence. *Who* made all this possible?"

"Dick isn't after you. He's looking out for the chimps. That's all. He knows a lot more than you do, Dana."

Dana leaned into him with her hands on his knees, her face inches from his. "If you choose to believe him over me, then that's just one more example of your crappy judgment."

His feet slipped off the bottom rung under her weight, and he started to cry. Dana felt the mechanism of his hold over her—the urge to comfort him, to make him promises, to absorb his sorrows. His vulnerability was so raw and quivering that it awoke in her the nights following Annie's departure, the marriage between guilt and pain, fear and lies, the power she promised she had (but never did) to make things right. She brushed her right hand over the back of her left, reading her scar like Braille. The pull of his need was like a beautiful song, irresistibly melodious, but she shook it off. "You and Becca have twenty-four hours to get out of here," she said as she straightened. She strode out of the kitchen, out of the house, to the safe confines of her truck and the road beyond.

Zack made a pot of coffee using canned grounds, and the brew that came through was as black as river sludge. He did not care how it tasted or what it looked like. He drank cup after cup until his hands jerked as though pulled by strings. Becca had not yet awakened, so she did not care how he screwed up the coffee. He wished he could overdose on it. He had been so gullible and so joyous, like a stupid puppy piddling on the carpet, when Dick had asked him to obtain the SCPP donor list. Still, everything Dick had said made perfect sense, even now. And Dick was so damned brilliant.

Releasing the chimps had never been part of the plan, and Dick had been furious with him for it. But Dick had not been there. He had not seen the dark eyes reflecting the hall light with venom and sorrow, with hopefulness and hopelessness. Zack had intended to do nothing more than print out the list, then slip out undetected, but the chimps had heard him. When they awakened, they called out to him. How could he have resisted? You could not look into those eyes without wanting them to be free. You just couldn't. The chimps had hooted with delight as they charged toward freedom. They had somersaulted and jumped between walls. They had spun as though dancing in celebration of the possibilities of their lives. The only one who had not left at first was the one who died, the one Dana called Benji but whom Zack thought of as the Shaman. The Shaman saw images in his head that no ordinary man or chimp could see, perhaps knew the shady boundaries between life and death, perhaps visited with the spirits that haunted him. The Shaman had been in a trance until Zack stood before his open cage and waved his arms. Only then had the chimp come to life, hurtling through the opening and narrowly missing Zack, ramming into the cage opposite, into the doors along the hall, and finally charging out into the night. Some of the chimps had stayed behind to explore the building, and Zack had no problem with that. Wasn't that part of freedom, to know the secrets of that which had once held you back?

His fingernails jittered along the counter with accusatory *tap, tap, taps*. He wished he had the guts to take a knife and slit himself from throat to naval.

Annie was dead, had been for years, despite the dreams he had of her still alive. How cruel those dreams had been, because they had felt like prophecies. He wanted memories of Annie like Dana had, instead of the yawning hole where Annie should have been. Of course, he had never expected to recapture the moments he could not remember on his own, but he yearned for something more than black-and-white films. Now what? There was still hope that Dick had been right. He had no reason to lie.

Becca's soft steps in the bedroom—her tiptoeing, really, something so delicate as almost not to be heard—startled him and bled the tension out of him. The sound of her, though it was no more than a breath on his eardrums, evoked the entire woman: her broad forehead and large eyes tapering to the pointed chin he liked to hold in his hand; her hair cut short to allow her entire face to be exactly what it was and no less; the thin wrists and ankles that seemed both easily snapped and durable; the curve of her as she lay on her side, from her shoulder over her rib cage to her tiny waist to the flare of her hips. *I have Becca.* The grin across his face was sudden and unstoppable. The hell with all these worries. He could lose himself in Becca, always, could find the core of peace there that would harbor him, and the rest of the world would disappear. He had never known this about love.

Stealthily, filled with the mischievousness of a lover, he crept toward the bedroom. He wanted to burst in on her and playfully sweep her up to toss her back into bed; he didn't care how much it would hurt his ribs. Lately, Becca had been sleeping to noon, their roles reversed, and the surprise of her up so early thrilled him. At the door, he had to bite his lip to keep from laughing. Then, with a hoot, he turned the knob and opened the door, a split second of pure surprise.

Becca stood by the nightstand dressed only in a T-shirt. She yelped, and Zack skidded to a stop as he saw in her hand the bag of white powder. She looked down at it, then back at him, attempting too late to hide it.

"Where the fuck did you get that?" Zack asked.

"Walt. Before we left."

He strode to her and grasped her wrist, pressing hard until she let go. He could tell by the color it was pure heroin—refined stuff, the kind you could snort. You could go back to bed, ride the high until you felt like standing again, smile at your lover through the delicious haze, as though you were drugged by love, not heroin. "How long have you being doing this shit?"

"Only a week. It's not like I'm an addict or anything. God. I don't use a needle. Just in the morning, you know. Once a day. And hardly any. Look, even *you* didn't notice."

He knew the siren call of heroin. He had been hooked after his second hit, though he had not admitted it until months later. The drug had given him a respite from the crazy, jumbled mess in his head. The rushes had been like snorting the whole of life, then settling into peace. His first time had been a gift, his second a sanctuary. But his third had been out of need, his innocence gone; he had wanted to retreat into the drug's downy realm. He saw no need for the pain of everyday life. As the bag in his grasp itched with the familiar song, he knew how Becca retreated into it without yet understanding that it had hooked her completely, that her body and mind would scream out for it.

"I'm *not* addicted," Becca repeated.

"Then I can flush this?" But it wasn't really a question. He could not keep the desolation from his voice.

"Listen," she said. "I've been through hell for years, Zack. All it does is take the edge off. Nothing more."

He nodded. Was it worth telling her she was already a junkie? He held the bag out in one hand, weighing it, remembering. Although Zack knew the reasons to keep her from it, he also understood from the depths of his heart how much she needed it. How much *he* needed it. He could not bear to look at the tears flooding her eyes. He loved her, and she was afraid of him and what he would do with her beloved heroin. That wounded him far more deeply than anything else that morning.

The coffee was eating away at his stomach. His belly felt seared, his head hot as though with fever. The cool skin of the bag promised tranquility and apathy, a swallowing of the betrayals—his and Dick's and Becca's. Unlike Becca, he was not innocent; he knew full well the seduction of heroin was a rape. To submit was the purest violation of the soul.

He touched Becca's face and felt the small muscles under her skin quiver. She was gone from him right then, in another place, with another lover. He had lost her.

"I want to be with you forever," he said.

"Me, too." Her face flashed with the animation of happiness, but her eyes flicked from his to the bag.

He followed her gaze and found he, too, was mesmerized by the proximity of the drug. The lull of it. The scratch of it that now clawed inside his veins, begging for release. The happiness that lay there, if only brief and illusory. The duality of freedom and enslavement. This he could share with Becca; they could fall down the abyss together and enjoy the free fall like kids on a roller coaster who did not know the track would end suddenly, midair.

Yes, he thought. *Yes.*

<hr>

When Dana entered the diner, she waved to Sue Ellen, who was having a before-school breakfast with her three children, and to Mike Bennett. Jack Niles and other paper-mill workers, both laid off and employed, lined the counter and gave her various nods of acknowledgment. A man she did not immediately recognize smiled at her from the nearest booth. Then she realized: Dick Lamier.

"You wouldn't avoid terrorists very easily," he said when he saw she had recognized him. "Everyone says you're here Wednesday at exactly this time, and sure enough, here you are."

She counted each step toward him so she would not lose control. Lamier was older than she had made him in her mind, though his features were unmistakable. He still had that slickness she remembered—the smoothness of voice and gesture, the impeccable hair, the bronze skin, the way he held himself with ease—but he also had a frayed aura, as though he had used his charm so often over the years that it had abraded in spots. As she reached the table, she could barely breathe; his proximity evoked the past more vividly than she had expected. "What are you doing here?"

He smiled. "Meet your probable successor. I thought you could give me a tour of the SCPP today."

"Dream on." Dana directed her attention to Judith behind the counter. "Coffee with a splash. And a blueberry muffin to go."

"Doing it right now," Judith said, the first time in five years she had admitted she knew Dana's routine.

"Sit down?" Lamier asked.

"No."

He wagged a finger that had the beginning gnarl of arthritis. "The psychology department backs me, you know. They've been negotiating with Davenport and Washington for weeks. It's only a matter of time." He held a menu to his head as though performing a magic trick. "Hmm. In fact, I predict the decision will be made . . . tomorrow. You *do* have a meeting with Washington and Davenport tomorrow, you know."

Dana did not know, but she finally saw the situation with clarity. Lamier could not have orchestrated such pressure on his own; he was not after her but her position. The psychology department had never given up its bid to control the SCPP, and in Lamier, it had found a champion. How ridiculous to have believed that Lamier had such power by himself. She laughed. "If they think you're the card up their sleeve, then they're fools." She was not going to make the same mistake he just had by laying out her hand too early. "I think your psychic abilities are bogus. Like the rest of you."

His expression darkened just a little, enough to give her the taste of a single droplet of blood. "Don't tell me you still hold a grudge."

"A grudge? Is that what you imagine I must feel?" She shook her head. "You're a bastard, plain and simple. The SCPP doesn't need someone like you."

"Dana." He said her name with such conviction that she felt compelled to listen. "Believe me, I didn't mean to do what I did back then. It just happened. I hope I can be forgiven for my youthful indiscretions."

She wanted to mock his choice of words but could not. "I might be able to forgive what you did then, but I can't forgive you for what you're doing now."

"Fair enough." He splayed his stocky hands on the table. She saw he had ordered tea, and that surprised her. "I don't need your forgiveness.

To tell you the truth, I'm glad I made that mistake back then. Your father had my career under his thumb, and our falling out liberated me." The disdain worked its way back into his voice. "Just as the SCPP should be liberated from you. I have the clout and the ability to raise enormous amounts of money. You don't have those skills. That makes me the better choice."

He was right in a way, but the SCPP was not simply a fundraising institution. She had developed a rapport with the chimps that could not be duplicated; they were as sensitive to loss as humans. And what about the anthropology graduate students? Could they be tossed aside and replaced with psychology students? She thought not. "Maybe if we were to argue primatology issues, we'd find we aren't all that far apart. But when it comes to the SCPP, it's my realm, not yours. You're deluded if you think otherwise."

"Time will tell."

Judith had come over and now held out Dana's coffee and muffin. As Dana fumbled for the money, she kept an eye on Lamier. She wanted to catch every nuance between him and the citizens of Harris. Everyone there had overheard the conversation, and they burned with the news not yet passed on, though Dana could not guess the spin, for or against her. People concentrated on their plates of eggs and grits, too polite to reveal what they were thinking.

As Dana climbed into her truck, she began her own scheme. Now that Lamier had revealed he wanted her job, she had a chance.

Dana arrived at the sanctuary before anyone else, as usual. She brushed the muffin crumbs from her lap and surveyed the quiet parking lot. It was odd, she thought, how they all adjusted to the time change because there she was, an hour earlier than the month before, and yet the light looked exactly the same. Mary would probably show up in a half-hour, the graduate students when the light was pure and new. The chimps, too, woke earlier, at the first signs of dawn.

After checking the security of the buildings, Dana went to Kitabu's cage. Kitabu hooted an excited greeting when she saw Dana. She somersaulted toward the entrance.

"Big day today," Dana told her as she unlocked the cage and stepped inside, putting her hand out to discourage Kitabu from charging through the opening before she could close it. "Shorts off."

Kitabu understood the words well, and she crossed her arms defiantly, chin raised.

"I'm serious. Shorts *off.*"

Dana's voice must have sounded commanding enough, since Kitabu, grimacing, removed her shorts. The chimp whimpered.

"Don't cry, Kitabu. You're a *good* girl. Come on. We're going to have some *fun!*" Dana held out her arms.

Kitabu's apprehension vanished as she leapt onto Dana, hugging her and giving her an open-mouthed kiss. Where had she learned *that*? Dana wondered. Kitabu had always kissed like a human, not a chimp. "There is hope for you, after all," Dana told her. As she stroked Kitabu's head, the young chimp leaned into her with what felt like a sigh.

Most of the youngsters in the nursery were still asleep, worn out from the day before, but a few stirred. Bora lay on his back with his feet in the air, tugging on his toes one by one. Marika calmly pushed a piece of straw against the wall. When Marika saw Dana and Kitabu, she scampered to the door.

"Good morning, Marika. I have a friend for you. You take good care of her."

Marika hopped up and down so her face appeared and disappeared in the window. Kitabu squeaked and scrambled out of Dana's arms despite the attempt to hold her tight.

"Kitabu!" Dana set her lips in chimp disapproval, an expression that sent Kitabu into hysterical groveling. "I'm not giving in to you anymore." Her face as stern as that of a dominant male, she took Kitabu's hand and led her firmly into the nursery.

The nursery smelled familiarly of chimp and hay and the rubber of the tire swing, though its silence seemed alien. Dana realized what an opportune time she had chosen to take Kitabu inside, since the chimps had not fully awakened and were not their usual boisterous tumble of arms and legs. Still, Kitabu cowered against Dana when Marika, curious, approached with an outstretched finger.

"Hello, Marika. You remember Kitabu. Give her a hug, Kitabu."

Kitabu looked up at Dana as though Dana were crazy.

"Marika is a good girl. A friend."

Still, Kitabu huddled against Dana. Dana recalled how Annie had protested that day in their backyard, pounding on the stockade fence, and how she, Dana, had joined her, not expecting to make a difference but as a gesture of solidarity. Gestures were not enough, Dana knew now. Kitabu's retreat into what remained of her human life only fenced her in more. With her weak hand, its scar white against her perspiring skin, Dana stroked Kitabu's head. *Please forgive me,* she thought.

When Kitabu ventured a few steps from Dana to explore, Dana stood and rushed out of the nursery, closing the door behind her so quickly that Kitabu froze until Dana was outside, looking in. The realization of her predicament unfolded muscle by muscle on Kitabu's face. Shrieking, the young chimp flung herself against the door, battering it with her fists and feet. The commotion woke the remaining chimps, who hooted and took to the ropes and platforms, screaming in fright. Dana turned away. She saw an image of Annie doing the same, locked in her laboratory cage.

Kitabu's cries pierced the glass and concrete walls. She found the side of the nursery that had glass almost all the way to the floor and pounded on it with open palms, crying, her eyes seeking out Dana's with their desperate fear. Kitabu believed Dana had rejected her, had abandoned her in a strange and chaotic place, and she was as frightened as a child lost in a crowd. Dana averted her face; she did not want Kitabu to see the emotions ripping at her heart, to see how much she wanted to rush back inside and rescue her. Tears streaming down her face, Dana hurried out of the nursery building, running when she reached the gravel path.

It was for Kitabu's own good.

She did not want Kitabu to end up like Annie, a chimp who was more of a scientific sideshow than an individual. Given the times, Annie had been doomed the moment Reginald's university had bought her, but Kitabu, while still legally viewed as property, had the opportunity for a larger future. Kitabu had been fortunate to arrive at the SCPP instead of a medical laboratory, and now Dana saw that anything less than full introduction would be a disservice not only to Kitabu but to all the chimps under her care. If she could not give Kitabu a family, then Lamier would be right: he would be as good, if not better, than she. And Annie would have lived and died in vain.

———∿∿———

Dana's eyes were still itchy from crying when Mary arrived for work. Mary took two steps into Dana's office before her smile vanished. "Dana! What happened?"

"It's been a tumultuous last twenty-four hours."

"You mean because of your brother?"

"That was only the beginning." She told Mary what Sam had said regarding Annie, about her brother's reaction, about running into Lamier at the diner, about abandoning Kitabu in the nursery so the young chimp could learn to cope on her own.

"Whew." Mary sat on the edge of Dana's desk. "You okay?"

"Yeah." She grinned. "I also spent the night with Sam Wendt."

"You little vixen, you!" Mary laughed. "It's about time you had a romance."

"It's not a romance. More like a fling. It can't last."

"Why not?"

Dana rolled her eyes. "You know damn well. He lives in Virginia. And despite what Lamier thinks, I have no intention of leaving South Carolina. Absence does *not* make the heart grow fonder."

"So when I first started here and the closest job Quentin could find was in North Carolina, you fed me a load of crap?"

"Basically, yes."

Mary swatted at her. "Now you tell me!"

"Your case was different, and you know it. You were already married. And I've been divorced for six years, without a regret. Why would I want another commitment? I like not answering to someone else. One night with Sam was perfect. Sleeping with him reminded me that there's a world beyond Harris."

"Don't joke about such a serious matter!"

"You'd better hope that there's something beyond Harris if you and Quentin leave."

Mary sobered. "Harris itself will be easy to leave. We've tried hard to be Southerners. But Quentin is a New Yorker, and I'm a California girl. You know me, I've done everything possible to blend in, as much as an Asian non-native can, but Quentin just can't adjust to the pace, the accent, and the Southern perspective."

"What if Lamier is successful in ousting me but doesn't get the job himself? What if they look to you for my successor? Will you stay then?"

"I can't, Dana. I'm pregnant. Remember?"

"The university can't discriminate. Besides, they don't know yet."

"But that's not the point! You don't know how hard it is to get through each day without collapsing from exhaustion. And after the baby is born, I couldn't possibly do what you do. I'll have other responsibilities. I was hoping to cut my hours a little, take a short leave. You know I'd do almost anything for you. But not this."

"So then if Lamier wins even an inch, the SCPP as we know it is through."

"Can we deal with that if and when it happens? I won't let the SCPP collapse if it's within my control. But I'll be fumbling with motherhood. Look, I can't even teach Barafu to be a good mother. Why would you want me to take your place? No one can. But there are tons of primatologists who would be better at it than me."

Mary was already nesting, protecting, nurturing the life inside her, sacrificing. Dana felt at once saddened and relieved that she would never experience this. "You can't judge your mothering skills—or primatology skills—by Barafu. We're talking different species. You do what you can." Then something surprisingly obvious occurred to her, something she should have realized long ago, except that she had fallen into the habit of routine, thus blinding herself. "Do you realize how *stupid* we've been? We have Maggie and baby Mbu right now. They haven't been introduced into a group yet. Maggie can teach Barafu how to be a mother. By example."

Mary blinked several times, then broke into laughter. "We've never had a biological mother and child before. Maggie has raised three chimps. She's probably the best expert we've ever had." She pressed her fingers to her mouth. "Oh, shit. Morning sickness." She rushed out of Dana's office to the bathroom across the hall, slamming the door shut behind her with her foot.

"Serves you right!" Dana shouted through the door as she passed. "The baby sides with me."

As she headed to the nursery to check on Kitabu, Dana swore that Lamier was *not* going to win, not this time.

When she peeked in the nursery window, Dana's knees weakened. Kitabu was playing with Marika. The two chimps clung to a rope, Kitabu a couple of feet above Marika, and they swatted each other, their faces spread wide in play grins.

Kitabu spied Dana. With a hoot, she leapt off the rope and scampered toward the window, her face already in the grimace of distress. Dana backed down the hallway and out of sight. *What an actress*, Dana thought, *what an expert manipulator*. But she could not blame Kitabu for wanting to be pampered with individual attention and for craving the routines of her former life. Who would want to leap into something new and alien, if things could be kept the same? There was comfort in sameness, in inertia. You could feel like you were moving through life when really you were coasting.

As Dana left the nursery building, Mary was coming down the path toward her.

"There you are," Mary said. "President Davenport's office just called. He wants to meet with you and Dean Washington tomorrow morning."

"I know," Dana said. "Lamier told me. The psychology department is making a bid to gain control of the SCPP."

"That bastard."

"This is it, Mare. This is the meeting where we find out what is going to happen."

Mary scrunched her face into a hard knot. "So you were right. If they screw us, I'm not going to take it quietly. Every damn primatologist from here to Africa is going to know the scheming that went on."

Although Dana knew that Mary would fight with all her heart, she would fall short of doing what Dana wanted most from her: preserving the spirit of the sanctuary if Dana could not. That meant Dana could not afford to stumble. She had the whole day to compile her research and documents, to call in her favors and muster support, but the hours between then and her meeting with Davenport and Washington seemed impossibly scant.

TWENTY

*W*hen Dana arrived home that night, her head packed full with plans and possibilities, she expected Zack and Becca to have left. Zack usually fled at the first sign of confrontation. That she had given him a deadline would only hasten his departure. But as she pulled into the driveway, both Zack's and Becca's cars were still there, hulking pieces of metal, shackles, the things that would hold her down when she most needed agility. With a long sigh, she turned off the ignition and sat back in the darkness, gathering what remained of her wits.

She should not have to deal with this, not now.

Still, she had given Zack twenty-four hours to leave, and only twelve had passed. She told herself not to read anything into his continued presence, though she could not stand the idea of finding Zack lounging in his underwear and Becca huddled unseen in the bedcovers like a burrowed rabbit. An infestation of two.

As she got out of the truck, irritation crawled up her arms and into her head. She could feel the bitchiness rising, readying itself for another confrontation with Zack. She slammed the door shut. She was annoyed with Sam, too. He had not called that day—not even to tell her how his interview with Dean Washington had gone—and even though she fully believed her night with him would be her last, she could not help being angry with him for making the truth all too obvious.

Even before she reached the front door, she heard the whale music a graduate student had given her a few years ago, its plaintive wail unmistakable. Inside the house, the lights were ablaze, every one of them on, searing her vision as she stepped in from the night. The whales deafened her with their shrieks. "Jesus, Zack!" she yelled. "Are you *nuts*?"

Dana turned off the stereo. Zack was not in the living room, nor in the kitchen. Dana found him and Becca sitting facing each other in the narrow hallway, their knees drawn up to fit into the space. Becca had her eyes closed and head tipped back, but Zack slowly turned his head to look up at Dana.

"Heya, sis," he slurred. A bag of white powder rested on the floor next to him.

She did not need to see the bag to know Zack and Becca were high on something. She felt sick. Even when she looked at Zack through her most cynical eyes, she wanted to see his goodness, his possibilities, not this miserable waste of a man on the floor.

"Get the hell up!" Dana shouted. "Get the hell *out*."

Zack smiled lazily. "Chill."

Becca opened her eyes and regarded Dana as an alligator might, cold and distant, sizing her up and then dismissing her with a sigh. She slid back into her stupor.

"Get up, Zack!"

He shrugged.

If Charlie had walked in right then, he would have shaken his head and told her she should not be so shocked. He might even have laughed at her naiveté. Although Dana knew Zack took drugs, she had never seen more than the residual glassy eyes and smelled more than a waft of sweet marijuana lifting off his clothes, things she had been able to ignore or write off as experimentation. He would find his way, grow up, she always reasoned. Now, her brother, nearly middle-aged, homeless, was in her hallway high on hard drugs, and there was nothing she could do. She could not make this right. If she tried, he would only find a way to wrap his arms around her neck to drag her down with him.

Dana searched the guest room to find car keys. Coming across Becca's first, she carried their belongings outside to Becca's car, where she dumped them in the trunk. After she finished, she stood over Zack.

He looked up at her. "You're a piece of work." The sentence sounded like a single, drawn-out word.

"Get in Becca's car. I'm driving." She jingled the keys in front of him.

"We haven't run out of time yet. Twenty-four hours."

"Believe me, you've run out of time. Now get the hell up before I call the police." For good measure, she reached over and swiped the drugs from him. "I'll give this back when you get in."

"This should be interesting," he said as he struggled to his feet. "Very interesting. C'mon, Bec."

Becca seemed less inclined to leave. Once Zack plopped in the back seat, Dana went back inside and half-carried Becca, who would take a step or two and then sit down. Finally, when the two were in the car, Dana returned inside to flush the drugs, since she could not risk getting pulled over and being arrested for something she could not even identify. She did not want this drug to exist for one moment longer than necessary.

Once the pavement under the car hit a steady resonance, Zack and Becca fell asleep like toddlers, content to have their heads loll back and forth across the headrests in the back seat. Dana did not have a plan, not really, except to get the two of them out of Harris. She knew where she was headed but not what she would do when she arrived.

⌒ᴧᴧ⌒

Dana always found Orangeburg disorienting at night, as though she were on a plane spinning out of control with nothing more than a milky horizon in sight. Each road seemed different—darker or brighter or narrower or wider—by night, and she felt lost, though she was not. She drove up and down various streets looking for a good place to park, somewhere out of the way and yet visible. Finally, she pulled into a grocery store's parking lot and stopped the car in a darkened area.

Becca had fallen over Zack, the two of them lying in a heap across the back seat.

Looking at her brother, Dana could not stop the creep of nostalgia and sorrow. She could not understand where they had parted, when he had crumbled and she had pushed onward. It seemed inconceivable that the little boy in the flying saucer pajamas had wiped his tears and become this screwed-up man. Part of her yearned to gather him up and nurse him back to normal life, but another, tougher side knew she could not survive that. His gleeful disregard for boundaries would destroy her. They each had their addictions—she, the chimps, and he, his self-destruction—and she needed to protect hers. She could not stand up for both him and her right to direct the SCPP.

Before Dana got out of the car, she reached over with an open palm to make sure they were both breathing, asleep instead of dying. Her hand brushed Zack's nose by accident, and his eyes fluttered open for a few seconds before they rolled back into a dream.

Dana slipped out of the car and closed the door, taking her purse and leaving everything else, including the keys. Each step that carried her away from Zack was easier than the last. When she reached the edge of the parking lot, she broke into a run, her breathing shallow and tight, her head pounding with her pulse.

In this strange town, in the darkness, Dana had never felt so alone and stranded. Everything seemed to suck the energy out of her: the closed stores, the houses lit with their interior glows, the cars that passed her with their drivers only shadowy outlines, the scrubby grass in between cracks of cement. Although she knew intellectually she had done nothing to harm her brother, in her heart she felt a guilt as deep as her loneliness.

No longer running but jogging, Dana headed toward Sam's motel, though she knew he might not be there. He felt like her only chance for sanity right then, so she prayed that she would find him, that his not calling was not an outright rejection. Behind the building, four cars were parked, and miraculously Sam's was one of them. She leaned over her knees to catch her breath and wiped the sweat from her forehead. When she felt less panicked, she knocked on the door. She realized then, and only then, that she should have first called the cell phone number he had given her.

Sam must have peered through the eyehole because the door opened wide. "Hey!"

She had forgotten the exhilaration of being with someone new, how it effervesced in her bloodstream like too much oxygen, how it made everything seem unpredictable and undefined. For a moment, she could not remember why she was there, and when she did, it seemed almost trivial. "I hope I'm not being presumptuous, but . . ."

He laughed. "Presumptuous? *I* called you. Come in."

She could not move. Standing this close again, she remembered how comfortable she felt with him, and how scared. "You called me?"

"You didn't get my message? I didn't want to bother you at work, knowing how tense things are, so I called you at home. I wanted to see you. *Come in.* Instead of standing out there in the dark."

"You wanted to see me?" She walked into a tumble of books, DVDs, clothes, and empty soft-drink cans. The room had not looked like this last night. It did not bother her, not in the least, that he was a slob some days, some not. She found it almost endearing, like discovering that powerful Mwenzi fell into rapture when his ears were inspected. She needed this vulnerability in Sam, this imperfection, so her own would not be as glaring. He was scrambling to pick things up. The DVDs Dana had seen the night before were strewn across the bed. It unnerved her a little that he had instant access to the images of her childhood, that he could sort through them at his leisure, without her.

"I didn't get your message. But I came anyway." She sat on the edge of the bed, overcome with relief that he had called her after all, that the risk in showing up at his door had not been as big as she feared. She pushed the DVDs to the far side of the bed. "I ditched my brother in a parking lot about a mile from here. And now I'm stranded."

"What did Zack do this time?"

"He and his girlfriend are high on cocaine or something. He's screwing up his own life and taking me with him."

Sam eased next to her on the mattress. She was afraid that he would start kissing her, wanting sex again, when she was too distressed to consider it. But he brushed her arm with his knuckles, nothing more. "It was only a matter of time, you know. Before he bottomed out."

She nodded.

"How did you ditch him?"

"I didn't tie rocks around his feet and throw him in the Edisto River, if that's what you mean. I just left him and Becca passed out in the back of her car. I know it seems like nothing. But it was all I could think of."

"It's the message that counts. Zack will be pissed."

"Yes, he will."

"Smart move." He hesitated. "He'll be back, though. Even if you change the locks to your house, he'll be back."

"Oh, I know. It's like those horror movies when the monster only gets slowed by the bullets fired at him. He roars and flails about but still marches toward his victims. Maybe this buys me enough time to run for cover."

"Or to awaken another monster to fight him."

"You must have watched all those Japanese monster movies as a kid, too." She pursed her lips. "Speaking of monsters, I ran into Lamier today in Harris. I know what's afoot. Lamier is trying to get the directorship for himself. With the backing of the psychology department. I can't figure out why he'd want it, though. Someone as well known as he doesn't need the headaches of a sanctuary."

"Lamier lost his own lab. He needs another."

"Oh, my God." It made perfect sense. "He's *not* going to get the SCPP. I may lose the directorship myself, but he's not getting the sanctuary. I've done my homework. I have a meeting tomorrow morning with the powers that be."

"Well, I did my part. I asked enough pointed questions about Lamier to make Washington break into a sweat."

"And that's supposed to make me feel good?"

He twirled her hair with his index finger. "I have other methods to accomplish that."

"And very good ones, too. But they won't save my job."

"I know." He shook his head. "But my journalism might. I've dug into this issue deeply enough to expose all the behind-the-scenes stuff. It will be hard for Davenport and Washington to act when the public eye is on them."

Dana shook her head. "Universities are surprisingly immune to outside criticism. Back when Annie was living with us, you could have told my father all that you know today, and because you're a journalist, he would have dismissed your views. He thought he knew best. Davenport and Washington aren't going to do anything they don't believe in. They're intelligent men. And as much as I hate to admit it, so is Lamier. Lamier believes that he's just making sure his research can continue, for the benefit of humanity. He wants to deepen our understanding of ourselves through chimp studies. Does that sound so bad?"

"Not if you put it that way."

"But it *is* bad. Because he's not thinking of the chimps. That's where my father went wrong. You can say the same about my moronic brother. Oh, Sam, I don't know what I'm going to do about Zack."

"He's an adult. *He* has to do something."

"But he's my brother!"

He stroked her arm. "Listen, you've already done more than most sisters would. It's time to cut him loose."

"I feel responsible for him."

"Why?"

"Because . . ." She had already bared her body, why not her soul? Still, the confession came with difficulty. "Because Annie's death was my fault. Because Zack was completely screwed up by what I did."

"It wasn't your fault."

"Yes, it was. I tore the head off Annie's doll, and she bit me in anger. That's why my father sold her to a lab. Because of me. It was like she died, only no one would admit it. Zack was just a confused little boy. I was the only one who understood what he felt. And even then, I wasn't good enough. I couldn't keep him out of trouble. Away from drugs and deadbeat friends."

Sam held her chin in his fist and forced her to look at him. "Listen. You were just a kid, too. None of it was your fault. Annie did not belong in a human household any more than she belonged in a lab. *Something* would have happened, and you know it. Her fate was not your fault. And neither is Zack's. He chose his own path."

She saw in his eyes that he wanted her to view Zack the way he did, but she could not. "No one chooses that path." She covered her face with her hands. "I'm as messed up as he is."

He gathered her in his arms. "You are not messed up. You are passionate. Intelligent. Responsible. Everything you should be."

She leaned against him, feeling the weight of everything she had to fight. "I feel like my life is slipping away. I can't hang on."

"Yes, you can. As soon as you realize your own strength, you'll do it." He let her go with a kiss.

If only, she thought.

He smiled. "We should get moving. Before Zack beats us home."

———∧∧———

Dana left Sam asleep in her bed. She did not have the heart to wake him as the dawn edged in through the windows, since sleep had settled so comfortably into his expression. His face was creased by the bed linens, and his curls were pressed in odd, boyish depressions that Dana found irresistible; she touched them lightly with her palm, taking care not to disturb his sleep. The night before, she had found it astounding that he intuited her need to be held and kept warm, nothing more, and this morning, she was equally amazed by the calm that came over her when she touched him. She began to wonder at what cost she could preserve this barest glimmer of a relationship.

She crept into the kitchen. Without Zack, the house had a serenity that settled on her like fine down. She could stay here for another hour, she thought, and revel in the morning, share it with Sam. But she really wanted to check on the sanctuary before she drove up to campus. With slow, looping handwriting, she left Sam a note asking him to meet her for a late lunch in Columbia, if he could. It would be a long drive for him, but he would understand why she needed to see him afterward, good news or bad. She poured coffee into a travel mug and left.

Although the drive to the sanctuary was not long, this morning it seemed unusually short. Dana drove so automatically that she jolted to consciousness only when her tires hit the ruts at the beginning of the dirt driveway. The sun cast long shadows across the ground. Chimpanzees hooted their morning greetings to one another. If she closed her eyes, she could imagine she was in Africa at last.

To her surprise, Andy had already arrived. She found him working at the small metal desk in the corner of the infirmary. As always, he was dressed in his tan safari shirt and pants, but his face had the ragged look of a man who needed a shave.

"Hey," she said.

"Morning!" He pushed the paper away. "For once, I beat you to work."

"Yeah, I see. What are you doing here so early?"

"Inventory. If the USDA comes in for another inspection on the basis of yesterday, I want to have all the drugs accounted for."

The mental picture of Zack and Becca passed out in her hallway almost made her cry out in alarm. "Well? Are they? Accounted for?"

"So far." He hesitated. "I'm probably not supposed to tell you this. But I was asked to check the inventory when you weren't here."

"They don't trust me."

"They think you're using drugs?"

"No. But I have an enemy who knows that my brother does. Do me a favor and call them with the results as soon as you're done. I'm meeting with the bigwigs later this morning, and I'd like to erase that concern."

He nodded and went back to his work.

Dana walked down the hall toward the cages. The chimps heard her approach; they hooted their greetings, and she hooted back. As soon as she reached the first cage, Kitabu shrieked with delight and ripped her shorts off, flinging them into the corner. By the cage door, she hopped and bounced with her arms held out high.

Dana laughed. She wished Mary could see Kitabu's eagerness to dispense with clothes. By the end of the day yesterday, Kitabu had discovered chimpanzees could be fun after all. "You want to go into the nursery already, do you?"

Kitabu whimpered.

"Okay, okay!"

Dana took her master key out of her pocket and unlocked the new metal key box mounted inside the broom closet. She knew the other chimps expected breakfast, but she could not deny Kitabu. When Dana opened the cage door, Kitabu leapt into her arms, clinging with extraordinary force, and gave her a wide, open-mouthed kiss.

Hand in hand, they walked down the path to the nursery. Dana suspected that soon Kitabu would rarely walk on two legs, that like most chimps she would prefer the speed and physical ease of knuckle-walking. Once inside the building, Kitabu yanked her hand free and ran the length of the hall to the door leading to the already-tumbling mass of juveniles. Kitabu closed her hand over the knob, hooting at Dana when it would not turn.

As soon as Dana opened the door, Kitabu scampered inside, then drew up short, as though surprised she was there. She cast a long, almost frightened look at Dana. Bisi and Marika hurried to Kitabu and embraced her. Immediately, Kitabu's anxious expression melted. The trio of girls joined the others with playful slaps and arms thrown over shoulders.

The future was beginning to look like a mirage on a desert highway, rippled and uncertain and tricky. Dana had been kidding herself. Even if Mary had agreed to take over for her, the university trustees would never approve her for the permanent job. Mary did not have Dana's experience and prestige, and therefore could not be expected to bring in the needed donations and grant money. The university would be more likely to appoint someone like Dick Lamier, who had an established position in the minds of people who counted.

All or nothing, Dana realized. Like Kitabu thrown into the nursery. Like Sifongo's introduction to Group B.

With a huge sigh, Dana sat down to watch the exuberance of the juveniles, hoping to absorb some of their energy. In only a few minutes, she would have to leave for Columbia, but for now she wanted to ignore what lay ahead.

Twenty-one

Dana arrived on campus as classes were changing, so she had to shuffle her way toward the administration building, caught behind moving barricades of students walking three or four abreast. She tried to dodge them at first but found she would only get caught behind another group. Whether she liked it or not, her pace was regulated. She glanced at her watch. She had made good time by going exactly eight miles above the speed limit the entire route, and so could stop worrying. She might even arrive at the president's office a few minutes early to orient herself, to neaten her mind. *Don't worry, don't worry,* she told herself. Still, she walked too quickly, having to slow almost to a stop as she came close to stepping on heels.

The campus was worlds away from the sanctuary, and Dana had never felt it so keenly. The spaces were open and bright, populated by wholly different species of trees and plants because of the higher, drier nature of the land. The South Carolina Low Country, where the SCPP was located, had a primordial atmosphere, with its unkempt Spanish moss and thick layers of prehistoric ferns, but here the land was tamed and regimented, its old trees surviving not because of perseverance but because humans had decided they should. Dana wished she could escape back home to her American jungle, that these two separate worlds could be severed from each other, that she did not have to answer to the concerns of those who ruled here.

Dana was ushered into the president's office by his secretary. As she stepped inside, President Davenport rose, along with Burton Washington, both Murrays, and Peter Perrott, the chairman of the anthropology department. While in the past she would not have been comforted by Perrott's presence, this time she was relieved to see him, knowing the power had not yet shifted to the psychology department. Even so, she could not bear to look at him, or anyone but Davenport, for fear of what she would see there.

"Sit down, Dana," Davenport said as he gestured to the only unoccupied chair. He sat at his desk, donning a pair of wire-rimmed reading glasses to silently page through a stack of papers.

Dana liked Davenport, respected him, but since he had an entire and diverse university underneath him, he could not possibly know more than the superficial issues, the visible ones that threatened stability. He had deans and department heads to manage the rest. She wondered how much she could trust Washington, and whether Perrott, with whom she tried to minimize her dealings, was strong enough to keep the SCPP under his aegis. Whether Lamier, with his worn charisma, had persuaded Davenport. She could not stand the silence any longer. "I ran into Dick Lamier yesterday in Harris. I guess you've been talking extensively with him. He seems to believe he'll be the next director of the SCPP."

Davenport removed his glasses with a twist. "Does he?"

"That's what he said."

Henry Murray made a funny noise, something between a cough and a hiccup. Startled, Dana glanced up, but she could not read his expression. Eileen Murray had turned her eyes to Davenport, awaiting something with pursed lips, and Dana followed her example.

Davenport slipped his glasses back on. "I received an unusual number of faxes, e-mails, and FedEx letters this morning." He glanced over his rims. "It seems you've been doing a little public-relations work on the side."

"I couldn't let the accusations that I've neglected the chimps stand untested."

He nodded. "I have letters from animals rights groups, zoos, universities. And a fax from a United States senator."

"Really? A senator?" She wondered who had orchestrated that coup—in less than twenty-four hours, no less. She had made her pleas via e-mail and phone, and had allowed her plight to be broadcast from there.

"The phone has been ringing off the hook from people in Harris wanting to know what's going to become of the SCPP. Some people want to make sure you stay there, others want the whole place closed. It bothers me deeply that they're aware of this meeting."

Dana had underestimated Harris; its citizens were not as passive as she thought. "Obviously, I enlisted the aid of my colleagues to make my case, but I didn't make a public statement. Dick Lamier confronted me in the Harris diner, and several people were within earshot. At least two of those people once protested at the SCPP." She tried to smile. "I guess you could call them turncoats. They're now fascinated with what we do."

Davenport shook his head. "The SCPP has been a public-relations nightmare of late. What I can't figure out is why you still have the unfailing support of the Murrays. And good words from Burt, and Pete here throwing a tantrum about the very idea of changing the SCPP." He leaned forward with his hands clasped in front of him on the desk. "You see, I have a problem. *You* have a problem. A loose-cannon brother. Whether you like it or not, he is a liability."

"I can't control him. I've kicked him out of my house, but I can't do much more than that. You *do* know Dick Lamier had my brother steal the list of donors during the first break-in, don't you?"

A surprised pause froze everyone in the room. Dana fixed her eyes on Davenport, waiting, but it was Washington who spoke. "That's quite an accusation. Do you have proof?"

She studied the backs of her hands, understanding how weak her case was. "My brother confessed it to me yesterday. Unfortunately, that's all the evidence I have. But I do have evidence of something else about Lamier. At the beginning of his career, he consulted for a medical facility in Massachusetts." She zipped open her briefcase to remove the few documents she had been able to find at such short notice. Carefully, she slid them across the desk toward Davenport, who adjusted his glasses slightly as he skimmed the first page. "These are some newspaper articles about the lab when it closed. They tell how the chimps were emaciated and surgically deformed for the sake of science. I've also included a statement from a psychologist who worked there at the time, saying that Dick Lamier initiated many of those studies. Lamier was interested in the psychology of trauma. Talk about a public-relations nightmare. Installing a director at the SCPP who did this kind of work."

As Davenport silently read the statement, Eileen Murray, her hands folded like birds perched on her purse, caught Dana's eye with a quick wink. The gesture, albeit slight, gave Dana the courage to lift her chin.

"Yes, this would be a PR disaster," Davenport said. "But it does not erase your own."

Burton Washington spoke up. "It's not that we blame you for your brother's actions. We have to protect the sanctuary."

Perrott added, "I told them, of course, that you and I could work on security."

Davenport ignored Perrott. "What do *you* think we should do?"

Dana was thinking fast now, sensing room to wriggle free but not knowing how. They waited for her to say something, Henry with his head cocked, Davenport motionless, Washington with arms across his chest, Perrott with a finger pressing on a nostril, and tiny Eileen with her thin, brushed eyebrows arched like aqueducts. They expected something from her, though they would not articulate it. And then Dana knew: they wanted her to acknowledge her place below them, her dependence on their goodwill, her indebtedness. This was not about punishment; it was about power and loyalty, the fear of betrayal. She might have banished Lamier, but she had not erased the damage he had wrought. Perhaps something about her, something wild and independent, seemed a threat to them. It did not matter *why* they wanted her submission, only that they did. "As I said, I can't control my brother. No one can. You are the best people to decide what's right for the SCPP, so if you request changes to our current structure, I'd be happy to follow them." She nodded to Henry and Eileen, though it was difficult to move her neck under stress. "This is your dream, your baby. I wouldn't want to jeopardize it. Nor would I want to do anything that would embarrass the anthropology department, the dean's office, or the university at large." She took a deep breath because she was approaching the dangerous part of the groveling, the point that would finish her if she had misread any of the signs. "I understand the embarrassment I've caused. The difficulties. You've stood by me until you felt you could no longer." She licked the roof of her mouth so the words would not stick there. "If it would ensure the longevity and success of the SCPP, I will offer my resignation."

The air in the room fell suddenly mute and heavy, like a stage curtain dropped, end of act. Davenport stood slowly and walked to the window while Dana counted the seconds that passed. *One one thousand, two one thousand, three one thousand.* She tried to imagine he saw something lighthearted outside: Frisbee players, or a young couple holding hands under a beech tree, a scene that would make him realize that the recent events at the sanctuary were inconsequential. Davenport cleared his throat and turned back toward her. "I don't think that will be necessary. I agree, you can't be expected to control a grown adult. And you've been up front with us from the start. I believe that until recently, you were unaware of your brother's involvement."

Dana swallowed as she recalled the key she had discovered in Zack's glove box and how she had disposed of it.

"To repair some of the damage, I would like you to launch a serious campaign to educate the public about what you do there. And I don't mean only the people living in Harris. I want these animal rights groups that Professor Lamier got so worked up to understand that *you* direct an institution devoted to animal rights. I understand there's a journalist who is writing about us. I want you to cooperate fully with him."

Dana saw in his face several truths: that Davenport already knew she had spoken extensively to Sam, that she should have notified his office before she had, and that, despite her missteps, Sam had been instrumental in opening Davenport's mind to her case. But thank God Davenport had no way of knowing she had slept with Sam. "Yes, sir."

"I believe we're done, then." He stood, and everyone else followed. "I expect to receive a written plan of action from you in two weeks."

Dana stood and shook President Davenport's hand, then turned to Burton Washington, who, as he clasped her hand, nodded with approval. Washington lingered a moment with Davenport as the rest of them left, Dana between the Murrays and following Perrott.

Eileen grasped Dana's hand as they walked. Her cool, fragile skin felt reassuring and calm, and Dana smiled at her, squeezing back. When they had left the reception area, Perrott turned and, walking backward, said, "Stellar job, Dana. Of keeping your cool and all. I would have gone ballistic if they handed over the project to the psychology department. It would have been extremely . . . gratuitous."

"That's why we came, dear Dana," Eileen said.

"We wanted to keep it from you as long as possible that this was going on," Henry said. "We didn't want it to distract you from the host of other problems you had to deal with. John Davenport called us a week ago to ask what we thought. And I'll tell you, Eileen here gave him an earful. We insisted that we be present during all discussions. They wouldn't dare insult us, for fear of losing future donations."

Dana smiled as she realized a kernel of truth she had failed to see in the past. "President Davenport is too savvy to have taken the psychology department's bid seriously—unless he felt he had no other choice. Think about it. He was the one who granted the SCPP to anthropology. No, he just felt things were getting out of control, and he started feeling around. Shaking people up. Planning to sacrifice me if he had to. But it would have been a major pain in the ass to switch departments."

"Could have fooled me," Perrott said as they reached the exit. "When Davenport called to say the psychology department had recommended Dick Lamier for your position, I couldn't believe it. Chest pains for days afterward. He sounded deadly serious."

A threat works only if there's real danger, Dana thought. "What's done is done, and we're still standing."

While Perrott continued toward the anthropology building, Dana stopped to say good-bye to the Murrays, who both looked drained. Henry's hands trembled in hers as she clasped them, and their tremor reminded her that the Murrays would not always be there. She leaned to kiss him on the cheek. "Thank you," she whispered in his ear.

He smiled at her as they drew apart. "We're going to Peru next month. What would you like us to bring back for you?"

"A llama," she said. "Or a guanaco."

"Oh, they *spit*," Eileen said, as if the request had been serious.

Dana laughed, then kissed Eileen. "You two take care of yourselves. When you get back, all the chimps except for Tekua should be out of the holding cages."

Eileen shook her head. "All your babies will have left the nest!"

"Unfortunately, there will be more. We'll do what we always do."

As Dana walked alone back to her office, she saw Dick Lamier and the chairman of the psychology department heading shoulder to shoulder toward the administration building, their expressions eager, like hyenas sniffing a carcass. Lamier's gaze, wandering and finding Dana, sharpened into keen interest. His eyes narrowed, searching her face across the distance between them, but she turned away. She did not want him to see the smallest involuntary flicker of triumph. She wanted him to misinterpret her turning away as defeat, as humiliation, as desolation, so he would cover the small distance to the president's office expecting one thing but finding another, sick with horror as the meeting unfolded.

Dana felt irrepressible, like a kid with the whole world opening up before her, unable to decide which treasure to explore next. She tipped her head back to drink in the moment. The sky was an opal blue she did not recall ever seeing overhead; it had the depth of cold winter tempered by the gentleness of spring. It was the kind of sky she could disappear into, time passing without her. A bird flew by, its angular wings flexing gracefully, and Dana was struck by the ease with which it cut through the air. Everything around her seemed fresh and unexpectedly visible. She was tempted to do something corny, like spinning around with her arms open or dancing to the beat of her joy, allowing herself the freedom to be carefree for a minute, but she shook herself free from the impulse.

Since the meeting had been so brief, Dana reached her office an hour before she was to see Sam, but she could not bear to remain inside, trapped. After changing into shorts and a T-shirt, she gathered her in-line-skating paraphernalia and carried it outside to the front steps. She strapped everything on and stood, adjusting her helmet so it sat firmly atop her head. As she pushed off, she concentrated more on gliding than on pushing her body to its limits. She headed for the center of campus. Every once in a while, she increased her pace until she caught herself, then fell back into a more leisurely rhythm in which her thighs and calves did not strain and her lungs did not quicken with the effort.

When she finished skating, Zack was waiting for her outside her office door. His hair was stringy and unwashed, his face unshaven, his clothes the same as when she had seen him last. His hands twitched by his sides, and his feet danced under his weight.

"Get out of here," Dana said in a low voice.

"I can't *believe* you did that last night. Left us. We got picked up. We spent the night in jail."

"Well, then, you can be happy that I got rid of the drugs for you, or you'd be spending a lot more time there. Now, get out of here. You've already caused enough damage." She removed her keys from her shorts. "I mean it."

"I'm not going until you tell me why you did that."

Dana glanced up and down the hallway. She did not want anyone to overhear their conversation; she had just triumphed over one obstacle and did not need more gossip about her circulating in the department. She unlocked the door. "Come in. Just for a minute."

When Zack walked in, he seemed bewildered to be standing there amidst the books and skating equipment and bare walls.

Dana placed her skates on the shelf next to Mary's. She faced him with her hands on her hips. She no longer had any reservations about pushing him too far. "You want an explanation? This is your explanation: you screwed me. You betrayed me, and you betrayed the chimps, and you even betrayed your own intelligence. Everything is always about you and what you want, and I'm sick of it. You know, life isn't about *feeling* good, it's about *doing* good. And when I saw you and Becca there strung out on whatever drug that was, I finally saw the truth. You are never going to change. You're never going to think of anyone but yourself. I'm through trying to help you. I'm through with *you.*"

"But you're my sister."

"And you're my brother. Yet you still trusted Lamier's word over mine. I'm not supposed to feel upset about that?"

His eyelids fluttered closed for a moment, and when he opened them again, the blue shimmered. "I never wanted to hurt you, Dana. I didn't mean to."

"You never mean to," she said. "But you do. Listen, I've always tried to give you the benefit of the doubt. When you flunked out of college, I thought you'd find your feet with a year off, that you just needed a little maturity. And then the year turned into years. And when you kept getting fired from jobs, I kidded myself that they just didn't appreciate you. Even when it came to your refusal to speak with Dad, I thought you'd eventually be able to see him for what he is, and not for what he did. Even when all these beliefs turned out to be false, I consoled myself with the knowledge that, if all else failed, we'd have each other. But I was wrong, wasn't I? You act as though I owe you everything and you owe me nothing. Why is that? Is it because of Annie? Because you blame me?"

"Annie?" His eyes darted about the room as though they could find explanation somewhere on the walls. "What does Annie have to do with this?"

"If you won't say it, I will. You blame me for what happened to Annie. I ruined our lives."

"Is that what you think?" He gave a short, hard laugh. "I've never blamed you. Annie has nothing to do with this. I'm a screwup, Dana. Whenever things start going my way, I do something stupid to ruin everything. I can't stop myself. I don't know why, but I can't. The last person I want to drive away is you. I need you. You're all I have."

Dana met his gaze. "But you're not all I have."

Zack's expression flickered as he began to understand her meaning.

He cleared his throat. "Becca left me."

"I'm sorry."

"I'm in love with her. We were going to get married on the beach in Florida as soon as she divorced Mike. The only reason I snorted yesterday was because I didn't want to lose her. You've got to give me another chance."

"Listen to yourself, Zack, and tell me which part of what you just said makes sense." Dana shook her head. "I'm sorry things didn't work out for you, but it's not my problem anymore. You've worn me out. I can't feel sorry for you anymore. I don't even want to look at you."

"So that's it? You're just going to write me off? I'm not good enough for you, is that right?" He said this last with such distaste that Dana's heart skipped a beat.

She took a deep breath to settle her resolve. "I love you, and I always will. But quite frankly, right now I don't like you, or what you've become. When you stop using drugs, when you hold down a single job for a year, when you get a permanent address with a telephone and actually pay rent and utilities on time, then you can come visit me. Then I'll know you're serious. And *then* I will allow myself to care again. But I don't want to see you a second before. I swear I'll call the police if I do. And if that means we never see each other again, then so be it. The choice is yours."

"But—"

"I have nothing more to say to you."

"You have to—"

"*Nothing.*"

He stared at her slack-mouthed, but she refused to let the hardness in her eyes waver. She knew now what their mother had meant when she said, "Zack is a rolling stone that *does* gather moss. I pity the person standing at the bottom of the hill, taking all that crushing weight." At the time, Dana had been shocked that a mother could think that way of her son. She had called her mother cruel. But now she understood. It had taken decades, but she understood.

Zack shrugged. He shuffled backward, seeming to know where the door was without looking, his eyes rimmed red with both exhaustion and addiction, need. "Have a good life, sis."

"Yeah. I will."

And then he was gone. Dana sat in her chair, unable to hold herself up any longer. She wanted to wish him good riddance, but she could not celebrate Zack's departure. The truth was more bittersweet, a sorrowful relief, the feeling she had when a new chimpanzee arrived to fill the spot opened by a death. A gain at the expense of a loss. She would have to be strong in the years to come, for she had no doubt that someday Zack would show up at her house, hoping that time had tempered her resolve, and she would have to refuse him again unless he had truly changed.

She closed the door to her office and pulled the blinds.

Dana and Sam sat in a small vegetarian café not far from campus. The dampness at the nape of Dana's neck lingered as a reminder of her skating, which in turn recalled all that had gone right with the day, instead of what had gone wrong. When she leaned forward to tell Sam about what had transpired inside the president's office and how she had seen Lamier afterward, she could feel the ferocity in her eyes and the animation in her face.

"So, nothing happened?" he asked when she was done.

"Are you kidding? *Everything* happened."

He laughed. "I guess it depends on your perspective."

"I started out today thinking I was going to lose almost everything that's important to me. How can I possibly see it any other way?"

"You're right." He fingered the straw in his drink. "I was waiting to find out what happened today before I sent in my article. The decision to keep the SCPP intact has been made. I have nothing left to write. I'm done here."

"Congratulations." With her fork, she poked at the grilled vegetables she had been eating ravenously only moments before. "So you're going home, then."

He nodded. "I can't really justify staying any longer."

She knew this was coming. So then why did it hit her so hard? Had she allowed herself to dream that they had something lasting, even as she consciously thought otherwise? Maybe Mary had convinced her on some deep plane that such a relationship was possible, but in reality,

Dana and Sam had very little between them: one night of lovemaking and one more of exhausted sleep. She had been mean to him more than once, and he had prodded her psychic wounds. She looked down at her plate with the hope that Sam could not see her disappointment. "I'll miss you," she said.

"Can we try to work something out? To continue seeing each other?"

She looked up and almost told him he was delusional, but she saw in the serious creases between his eyebrows that such a statement, even said with affection, would wound him. "Like what?"

"We can e-mail and phone each other. I can drive down to visit you one month, and you can drive up to visit me the next. It's not ideal, but it *can* be done." He reached across the table and took her hand. "Look, I'm not going to pretend to know whether this is going to work out between us. But it's worth finding out, isn't it? If we don't try, we'll never know."

"What if it *does* work out? Then we're screwed. I've just secured my position here at the SCPP, and I'm not about to leave it. And you have your own career. Like it or not, that's who we are—our jobs."

He laughed and started eating again, taking a large bite of his focaccia sandwich. His cheeks filled out like a chipmunk's as he chewed, his eyes resting on Dana, his mouth and finally his throat working on his food. He was teasing her with this silence, she knew. When he had swallowed, he said, "Dana, I'm a *freelancer*. The only reason I live near D.C. is because my first job was at the Smithsonian. I love that area, and I'm not going to promise that I'll move down here. But I could if I wanted."

The possibility that they might be able to sustain a long-distance relationship soared inside her. A few minutes ago, the idea had seemed not only improbable but impossible, but now she could see the distance between South Carolina and Virginia as well as she could the territory surrounding the sanctuary: a cord the shape of Route 95, checkered by rest stops and gas stations that bound his urban world to her wilderness. "I'm willing to try it."

"Really?"

Dana had to laugh. She was not such a great prize. "Obviously, you have no idea what you're getting into."

He grinned. "Isn't that half the fun?"

"Yeah. And half the battle." She glanced at her watch. "Shoot. I have to get back to Harris. Mary and Andy were supposed to put Maggie and Mbu in with Barafu. I'm dying to see how they're doing."

"Go ahead. I'll take care of the bill."

She stood. "You understand?"

"Of course. I'm obsessive about my work, too. And I'm not good at saying good-bye."

She leaned over and kissed him, inhaling his scent so she would not forget it. "We're too much alike not to get along. Call me when you get home."

"Will do."

Dana smiled. They were two stunted adults, although no one would have guessed it from the outside. From the distance of a few feet, they had the lacquered finish of professionals, of two people interested in each other, of ordinary people, when really they had allowed their jobs to consume them. She wondered if she could die peacefully knowing this about herself, then decided she could. Charlie used to say to her, "No one has ever died wishing he spent more time at work," but she could see herself praying with her last breath for one more chimp, one more lost cause to bring back from the brink. One more hour at work. And now she finally had the promise of something to balance it all.

———— ·⋀⋀· ————

Dana found Mary sitting next to Barafu's holding cage with her chin resting on her knees. Mary looked like a child, small and frail, watching her stronger friends play outside. On the other side of the bars, Maggie and Barafu groomed each other while the juveniles slept, both belly up. Dana felt an overwhelming fondness for Mary and her vigilance, the way she never gave up, the familiar muscularity of her small figure. She could not picture Mary in a few months, rotund and wobbly.

"Hey," Dana said as she started down the hall.

Mary scrambled to her feet. "Well? What happened with Davenport? You didn't call."

"I came to deliver the good news myself. Lamier was turned out on his butt, and I still have a job. They didn't fire me. They didn't ask me to resign. In fact, I offered to step down, and they wouldn't let me."

"You did *what*? Were you trying to make my life a living hell?"

Dana grinned. "I don't have to *try*."

Mary gave her a powerful hug. "Oh, my God, you don't know how worried I was. I couldn't have taken over for you, Dana. I wasn't at all prepared."

"Looks like you did okay with Maggie and Mbu on your own." She nodded toward the cage. "Success?"

"Oh, they did that on their own. I'm only an observer. The weird thing is that Fikira seems to have taken a liking to Maggie, so much so that I think Fikira wants to adopt *her* as a mother. I wouldn't be surprised if Maggie, not Barafu, is the one who ends up looking out for her."

Dana felt the tug of Zack's absence, but she tried to push it aside. "What are you doing tonight?"

"I've already called Quentin. You're having dinner at our house. I thought it was going to be a cry fest, but now we can make it a celebration."

"Good, because I really don't feel like crying." Dana gave Mary a quick, strong hug. "You're the best."

Mary turned to her with droplets of tears clinging to her lashes. "*We're* the best. When we're old ladies, we'll still be cleaning cages and hooting like chimps and taking every hard-luck case that comes our way." They locked gazes with the unspoken admission that they might not be doing this together.

"I wish Mbu could be the last of the line. The last baby that needs us." The loneliness of that dream, of Mbu living out his days in the sanctuary by himself, the last captive, was offset by the one of chimpanzees thriving in Africa, where she had never been and where she had never been needed, a distant land bereft of what she guarded here in South Carolina. Dana brightened. "Come on. If Quentin is cooking, then I know it has to be good."

They walked shoulder to shoulder down the hall and out into the fading light of late afternoon. The chimps in both groups had fallen silent with their night preparations of gathering cut boughs for their nests on the interior platforms as well as, among the more accomplished, actually bending springy branches to support their weight in sleep. A cardinal chirped, and a group of graduate students laughed from the parking lot just as a final, halfhearted squabble broke out in Group A. As the ruckus died down as quickly as it had begun, Dana felt the sounds lodge deep within her, already a memory. She peered inside the enclosure, trying to see, but dusk had stolen the edges of things so they were faint and indistinguishable, vanishing into a sameness that Dana knew, in her heart, was not the truth.

ACKNOWLEDGMENTS

I would like to thank the New Jersey State Council on the Arts for its generous support of this project.

Several individuals within the primatology community were extremely patient with my questions: Roger and Deborah Fouts, Stewart Hudson, Anthony Smith, and Linda Koebner. I thank all of them heartily, and I hope they find this novel honest in its portrayal of issues central to the plight of captive chimpanzees.

I am also indebted to Mylène Dressler, Cris Mazza, and Paul Chung for their critical eyes during the writing of this book. I thank Carolyn Sakowski, Steve Kirk, and the rest of the staff at John F. Blair for loving this book as much as I do and for seeing it through to publication. As always, I thank my husband, Daniel Lopresti, for his frank appraisal of what I have written and his unfailing support of my work.

Non-profit Organizations
Dedicated to the Welfare of Chimpanzees

If you are interested in supporting the welfare of non-human primates, you may contact one of the following non-profit organizations:

The Jane Goodall Institute
4245 N. Fairfax Drive, Suite 600
Arlington, VA 22203 USA
Phone: 703-682-9220
Fax: 703-682-9312
www.janegoodall.org

Save the Chimps
PO Box 12220
Fort Pierce, FL 34979
Phone: 772-429-1678
www.savethechimps.org

The Fauna Foundation
17 Rue St Pierre
Chambly
Quebec
J3L 1L6
Canada
www.faunafoundation.org

Friends of Washoe
Chimpanzee & Human Communication Institute
400 E. University Way
Ellensburg, WA 98926-7573
Phone: 509-963-2363
Fax: 509-963-2234
www.friendsofwashoe.org